Remedial Magic

Remedial Magic

☽ ✦ ☾

Melissa Marr

BRAMBLE
TOR PUBLISHING GROUP | NEW YORK

REMEDIAL MAGIC

Copyright © 2024 by Melissa Marr

Designed by Jen Edwards

A Bramble Book
Published by Tom Doherty Associates / Tor Publishing Group
120 Broadway
New York, NY 10271

www.brambleromance.com

Bramble™ is a trademark of Macmillan Publishing Group, LLC.

The Library of Congress Cataloging-in-Publication Data is available upon request.

ISBN 978-1-250-88413-8 (trade paperback)
ISBN 978-1-250-88414-5 (ebook)

Our books may be purchased in bulk for promotional, educational, or business use. Please contact your local bookseller or the Macmillan Corporate and Premium Sales Department at 1-800-221-7945, extension 5442, or by email at MacmillanSpecialMarkets@macmillan.com.

First Edition: 2024

Printed in the United States of America

0 9 8 7 6 5 4 3 2

To Amber, my wife, my heart, my sanity.
I found words again because you walked
into my sword class that fateful day.

Remedial Magic

Prologue

The witch stood in the forest, staring at the earthen rift. People would die; such a thing was inevitable now. The furrows in the earth were deep enough that a noxious goop not unlike congealing blood began to burble to the surface.

Several hobs popped into the small clearing nearest the furrow.

"What have you done?"

"That's wretched." One of the hobs gagged loudly.

"It had to be done," the witch said mildly.

One hob, a tiny woman no more than a half meter tall, put her hands on her hips and glared at the witch. "Witches will *die* from this."

The goop oozed across the loamy soil, leaving plants withering with rot and disease. Despite the severity of the crime, the hobs were limited in what they could and could not do. Hobs, of course, were made by magic. They were the physical embodiment of the very thing that caused witches to come to Crenshaw. In essence, if magic were made sentient, it would be a hob—diminutive, omnipresent, and occasionally terrifying.

Not that most witches realized that! They had once, the first witches here in Crenshaw. The hobs painstakingly explained magic, built a castle to teach them lessons, showed them the rules, explained the whys and what-fors and if-thens, but witches started out as regular folk. Humans. And humans were remarkably obstinate. Over time, they'd decided they knew better, taken over the castle, and generally gone about mucking things up.

And this witch, this beastly selfish witch, had ripped a hole in the ground so poison spilled out into the haven that magic—that *hobs*—had made for their progeny. For really, that was what witches were, difficult foolish children of magic. No matter that magic healed their bodies and made their lives last for centuries. No matter that they had everything they had needed in this small safe hamlet.

The witch walked away, singing cheerily, as if poisoning the very earth that sustained witches was something jovial.

"Do we fix it?" one of the hobs mused.

The general muttering that rose up continued for some time, until one hob—Clancy by name—said, "No. We do not. They need to face consequences for their dimwitted actions."

"It was *one* witch!" a sweeter hob pointed out.

"Was it, though?" Clancy looked around at his fellow hobs. "Quite a lot of them talking about going back to whence they came."

Hobs exchanged looks. Going back, of course, would be dangerous. That was why Crenshaw existed in the first place, to prevent magical folk from going about in the unmagical world.

And that, as they say, was that. The fate of Crenshaw was in the hands of the witches now. They'd figure it out or die.

1

Ellie

"Ellie!" Aunt Hestia's voice cracked through the old farmhouse like a whip.

Elleanor Brandeau exhaled in relief. Every day, that insistent voice was like a pressure valve opening, easing the panic that Hestia would vanish. *Again.* As a younger woman, Hestia had disappeared without a trace for several years. The grumbling archaeologist upstairs rarely mentioned it, but Ellie thought about it every day.

Was this the day she'd be gone? Was this the day that everything fell apart?

There was a reason Hestia had gone, and until Ellie understood it, she would wrestle with anxiety. Despite her aunt's insistence that she knew nothing about that missing time—and plenty of therapists telling Ellie that it was impossible to know—Ellie had doubts. More than that, perhaps, she had an irksome sense that there was an answer just at the edge of knowing.

As with every morning, Elleanor Brandeau was downstairs in the kitchen enjoying a bit of silence with a pot of overpriced coffee. As a teen, she would open Hestia's door, just to make sure she was still there. Now, she was an adult, so she'd watch the automatic pot brew coffee in silence.

And wait.

Every day, the coffee clicked on at 6:00 A.M. Hestia would wake by 6:15 A.M.

Those fifteen minutes dragged out with a pressure Ellie hated. She'd wait patiently for both the summons and the caffeine.

Fine, maybe not *exactly* patiently. Ellie watched the pot like a fox watched the hens that used to live in the coop out back. Unlike the fox that still crept around their empty backyard henhouse every so often, Ellie didn't paw at the coffee pot. She'd wait for the coffee and her aunt, busy herself baking—today was fresh lemon scones—and *wait*.

"Is the coffee ready, El?" Hestia called from her upstairs lair.

"On the way!" Ellie smiled wider. Life was normal, steady.

Hestia had some sort of internal timer. By 6:15, she was usually awake and calling to Ellie. Until recently, she'd call out to have Ellie pour her a cup and then come to the kitchen so it was the "perfect temperature" when she walked into the oversized room. Lately, she'd had to wait to have it brought to her.

Sixty-three years of sass and salt in a five-foot package, Hestia Brandeau was as energetic as a woman half her age—and twice as surly since she needed a hip replaced. Surgery was in a matter of days, and it was hanging over the household like a wet cloud.

"Coming!" Ellie sang out as she poured a cup for Hestia and shoved the second tray of scones into the oven.

A piping hot scone in one hand and coffee in the other, Ellie climbed up to the third floor where Hestia was propped up like a Victorian regent in a bed that was so immense that it had to be assembled inside the bedroom.

"Scones already . . . ?" Hestia eyed the plate.

"My, what big eyes you have," Ellie teased, wiggling the scone.

"Not your granny, you beastly child." Hestia grabbed the dark wood cane beside the bed and made to stand up. "If you won't hand it over, I'll go get my own damned scone."

"Nope." Ellie was there beside her in an instant. "Do you want to fall again?"

"No. I *want* to be on my feet in my own damn kitchen, but I'll settle for that scone and a cup of black coffee," Hestia grumbled.

Ellie handed her the breakfast and then went over to the recliner by the window. It was burgundy toned, like the curtains on Hestia's ornate bed.

"Almost there," Ellie reminded them both.

A few days until surgery. Then recovery . . . At least three months of Hestia testing the rules, and Ellie trying to convince her parental figure that not *all* rules were meant to be broken.

Hestia had raised her since Ellie's parents had died, but she wasn't a rule-follower by nature. Ellie had started filling that role for both of them by the time she was in her twenties—and Hestia had started testing any and every rule Ellie tried to impose.

Ellie took a long moment before saying, "If you fall down the stairs because you're being impatient, you're going to be sleeping in one of those rental hospital beds. That's the deal. You promised you'd follow the rules if I agreed to not rent one."

At that, Hestia cackled. There was no other word for it. The elegant little woman in her red damask four-poster Jacobean bed with its ornately carved posts and thick canopy cackled like a wily old witch.

"You're my favorite niece," Hestia said once her cackling subsided. "Lord knows, no one else in this world ever had the gumption to stand up to me."

Ellie smiled, despite best efforts. "I'm your *only* niece, and you are a cantankerous old goat."

"You're no fun, El." Hestia sighed. "When I was your age—"

"You were just as feisty as now, dating all over, but free as a bird," Ellie finished.

"Don't you want more out of life?" Hestia's teasing faltered. "A woman to settle down with . . ."

"Hestia." Ellie rubbed her temples. Sure, she *wanted* that—a great sweep-her-off-her-feet romance—but it wasn't in the cards. Not for her. She lived a quiet life in a quiet town with an elderly relative. It wasn't exactly prime conditions for romance. "I don't need that right now."

"Well, *I* do. Maybe we could go into Pittsburgh to a singles bar when I'm on my feet again." Hestia grabbed her laptop, presumably to start researching bars.

"I swear I'll take away the internet one of these days." Ellie ran downstairs to pull the second set of scones out of the oven.

The truth of the matter was that sometimes, when Ellie was alone and thinking about the future, she wondered what was left for her. Was this *it*? Would she grow old with her aunt as her whole life? There were no advancements to be had in the library, beyond the occasional pay bump, and she had no hobbies other than researching missing people.

She lived a life of stasis. Quiet. Mundane.

If I were to vanish or die, would anyone other than Hestia even give me a second thought?

That thought stung. She wanted something more—a woman who made her heart race and her words tangle. A romance that was book-worthy, dramatic and exciting. To have that meant being someone else, someone not mundane and uninteresting. So Ellie chose safety over dreams. Over and over.

It's better this way.

A few hours later, Ellie was still pondering her place in the world as she drove to work at the Ligonier Public Library. After Ellie's parents had died, Hestia had gone from field archaeologist to part-time teaching while writing cozy mysteries and the occasional romance that she passed out like Halloween treats at every possible chance. She'd rearranged her life so as to be both mother and father to a child who was anything but easy at the time.

How could Ellie even think about moving away or finding a relationship now that Hestia needed her? Sixty-three wasn't *old*, but it was old enough that Hestia sometimes needed help.

So Ellie got a degree by commuting the hour and change into Pittsburgh. She eventually got a job in Ligonier. She stayed home or worked. Sure, there were occasional flings over in Greensburg or in Pittsburgh, but nothing that could become serious and result in Ellie moving.

She needed to be sure that Hestia wouldn't vanish again. Despite what her last therapist said, Ellie was certain there was a reason why some people vanished. Not the usual reasons, like murderous spouses or criminals silencing witnesses, but a reason Ellie couldn't quite understand—despite her copious research. The only thing she had gleaned was the missing were all interesting, adventurous people.

So Ellie decided to be *uninteresting,* although she had a secret belief that she was far from uninteresting. She laughed it off most days. It was a sort of arrogance, a narcissism, to believe Ellie Brandeau—small-town librarian and quiet wallflower—was anything extraordinary.

And thinking otherwise made her feel like eels were swarming under her skin.

2
Maggie

Maggie Lynch was driving through the mountains of North Carolina at the end of her vacation with her son, Craig. By tonight, she would have to turn her son over to his father.

"Are you okay, Mom?" Craig folded himself into the too-small space of the passenger seat. He was all legs and arms, a teen athlete whose body seemed longer and leaner than he knew what to do with unless he was on a field or court.

"Not really," Maggie admitted. A part of her wanted to just keep driving, to go anywhere else. Fake identities. New lives. Maybe she could waitress or something.

"Something new bothering you?" Craig prompted. "Something Dad did?"

Maggie glanced at him and sighed. "All the parenting books say not to disparage the other parent."

Craig rolled his eyes. "Uh-huh."

She still wasn't ready to tell Craig that Leon wanted full custody—or how much of a criminal his father was. *Tell him I knowingly married a crook. What does that make* me *look like?* So Maggie had avoided the conversation the entire trip. Now she felt like something was rolling through her veins and making her feel queasy in the process. Lying always made her feel sick.

"We need to talk about something that came up last week," she finally said.

Craig deserved to know. His opinion mattered to *her*, even if Leon hadn't asked him what he wanted.

"Is it the part where you tell me the truth about Dad's job?" Craig sounded far too mature for his years. "Or that he's trying to cut you out of my life?"

"Maybe . . . ?" She glanced at Craig, trying to figure out how to tell him not to antagonize his father.

Would he really *hurt his own son?*

Then, a terrible snapping noise in the general area of her engine made her pause. Or maybe it was more that it *felt* like a snap. She couldn't explain it, but the brakes were squishy all of a sudden.

"Fuck."

The brakes weren't working. The SUV started going faster and faster. Mashing down the pedal did nothing to slow them down. *Leon, you bastard!* She knew her ex was lower than a possum's belly, but she'd thought he'd care enough to not hurt Craig.

"Mom!" Craig yelled.

"Hold on!" Margaret knew with certainty that this was how they would die if she didn't do something, and what felt like a protective bubble oozed out of her, trying to encase her body. She swore she could see it. *I don't want to live if Craig dies.* She shoved the bubble at him.

"Slow down!" Craig begged-asked-ordered.

"Trying. No brakes," she said, one hand tight on the wheel as the other fumbled for the emergency brake.

The imaginary bubble she'd shoved out of herself around Craig was now holding him motionless. She couldn't say how or why, but she *felt* it. She felt a sort of barrier that extended from her body to keep him safe.

The edges of the bubble leaked onto her, as if slowing her down, and she shoved it toward her son again.

If they could get around this curve safely, maybe she could try to stop the hurtling speed of the whole vehicle with a second bubble-cushion. If she tried arresting the speed *now*, they might flip tail over nose.

"Seatbelt tight?" was the last clear thing she was sure she said.

Maggie couldn't turn the wheel in time, couldn't get around the curve. There was a clarity, an icicle moment of stabbing comprehension, when she realized there was no way to avoid the accident. They'd gone too close to the berm. The side of the vehicle slammed into a guardrail with a screech of metal sliding along metal. The SUV flipped side-over-top, rolling like one of Craig's toy cars when he was a toddler.

This is where we die, she thought.

They were careening toward the bottom of a ravine, battered about as thick-needled trees sort of slowed them. They rolled down an embankment and landed with a shudder against a row of old trees. One branch jutted through the back window, and all she could smell was pine sap, overheating engine, and someone's blood. *My blood.* She knew with a sudden certainty that Craig was safe. She had always known when he was safe or in peril. *Craig isn't hurt.*

"Mom? *Mom!*" Craig sounded scared.

"It's all right." Maggie tried to reach out to him, to comfort him. He was alive. That was all that mattered now. She felt through whatever mom-knowing she had with Craig, had always had with him, that he was okay.

The pain was all hers.

She said, "It's fine. You're safe, baby. We stopped and—"

"*You're* bleeding." His seatbelt unbuckled with a clunk, and Maggie looked over at him.

He looked fine, completely uninjured. She felt no pain radiating from him. *Bubble. The bubble worked.* Her woozy brain insisted she'd protected him, that she'd wrapped him up in a bubble and kept him safe even now. He was fine. That was all she needed to know. She could let go.

"Christ. Mom, open your eyes." Craig's hand was on her cheek, like when he was a toddler and she'd had the flu. "Please, Mom? Look at me. I need you to stay awake."

Maggie reached up to pat his hand. "Mommy's tired right now. Go play with your trucks . . ."

He slapped her face. "No. Wake *up,* Mom! I need you to wake up."

As Maggie opened her eyes, she saw her son trying to get her seatbelt undone. "Come on, Mom. Help me get you out. Focus."

"Hey." She grabbed his arm, realizing too late that she was leaving blood on his arm. "I'm okay, sweetie. I'm okay."

"You're *really* not."

Maggie focused on clarity she didn't quite have, suddenly doubting herself at the sight of blood on him. "Are you hurt?"

"No, I'm okay. The blood's all yours, Mom. I'm fine. You need—"

"Just climb out the window. One step at a time. You get out, and then we'll get me out, okay? This is just a scratch. . . . Remember when you got that cut skateboarding. What did I say?"

"Head wounds bleed more. Thin skin," Craig repeated dutifully.

"Right. I'm okay. Just a cut." Maggie was fairly sure she was lying, but all that mattered was Craig being focused enough to be safe. Her chest hurt where a bone was broken.

My lungs hurt.

Craig climbed out the now-shattered back window with all the agility of a teen baseball player. Then he jerked on her door, shaking the entire SUV in the process. "It's stuck."

"Okay . . . but you're out there now, right?"

"*You* aren't, though, Mom." He looked like he was going to start crying. He'd stuck his arm through the window and tried to force the seatbelt to release her. Her increasingly mature son sounded like a small child now. "Your door's stuck. Your seatbelt. What do we *do?*"

"Phone?" she asked, pushing her panic as far down as she could. Her lungs hurt like there wasn't enough air getting in, and she couldn't tell if it was an injury or panic attack.

"No signal," Craig said finally. "I texted Dad, and Coach, and . . . that's it. I'm not even sure if the texts went and—"

"Shhh. Hey? Look at me. I'm okay. Just hit my head." Maggie tried to sound cheerful, calm, all the things you had to be when your kid was panicking. "I just need a little nap for energy. Then I'll think of something."

"I'll flag someone down," Craig promised, sounding calmer now that he had an idea. He really was more like her than his dad, and she was grateful for it. He nodded to himself. "I can climb up there. I'll get help, and then we'll get you out of there. Just . . . try to stay awake, Mom. Please?"

"Sure, baby."

"I can't help you if you don't cooperate," he said, sounding far more mature than his teen experience would hint. "Stay awake."

"Got it, but I need you to be careful with the cars up there! If there's anyone sketchy, you stay away from them. Don't get in a car with a stranger either. Just ask them to call the cops or ambulance." Margaret wanted to grab him, protect him. She was the mother, not a child to be rescued. "Then you come down here with me to wait. Stay with me while they come back, so I can protect you. I love you."

"You, too. Always, Mom. Always." He kissed her cheek, and then he took off.

He'd been swearing and darting worried looks at her when Margaret watched him vanish into the forest. That boy was the single greatest achievement of her life. No degrees or legal victories compared to the way she felt looking at the kindhearted man she was raising.

This trip, this escape to nature, was to be a time for clearing her mind. She'd realized she needed it when she starting debating running with Craig, kidnapping him really. That wasn't fair to any sports scholarships he might get. *Is that worth more than keeping away from his dad?*

In reality, she thought anything, any cost, was fine if it would keep Craig away from his father.

But now Margaret was trapped by the mangled door of the driver's side, which had bent into the steering wheel. *Leon will argue this is somehow my fault.* Maggie thought about the car careening out of control, the brakes not engaging. Someone had cut the line.

Leon tried to kill us.

My son.

He tried to kill my son.

She'd tried to force the seatbelt to let loose. She'd even tried tearing at it with her teeth. Nothing worked.

So she waited. When Craig returned, she'd get checked out, and they'd run. There was no other choice now. Leon was clearly dangerous.

But then, she fell asleep or maybe passed out. She couldn't say which really, but the sun finished setting, and her son hadn't come back. Was he in danger? Had he collapsed? What if he had internal injuries and was lying out there in the woods dying?

She felt stronger, though, like whatever exhaustion she'd had was letting up. She shoved at the car door, smacking it over and over as if she could do what her son couldn't.

"Craig! Where are you?" she yelled.

She needed to get out, to find her son, to get him to safety.

After a blink that made no sense, a knife was somehow in her hand. Maybe she was hallucinating, or Craig had left it there, but she'd forgotten . . . ?

Whatever the reason, Margaret sawed through the seatbelt to get free. "Craig! Can you hear me? *Craig!*"

Desperation to get to her son was mounting toward a panic attack as the car door exploded outward. She looked for Craig, expecting to see him with the paramedics or police or something.

"Craig?"

Silence greeted Maggie as she lurched out—ready to crawl through the forest to find her son. She landed on her hands and knees on the pine-needle-covered ground. No one was there. No vehicles. No Craig. No one at all.

How did the door rip off?

She looked for a . . . bear? Nothing else she could think of other than a machine would be powerful enough to tear the door off the SUV.

As Maggie tried to brace herself on the vehicle's wreckage, she realized it was gone. The SUV, the crushed undergrowth she'd plowed through, the broken glass—it was *all* gone. All she had was the knife.

"Craig! Where are you?"

But as she climbed the hill, she discovered that she was no longer near the road either. Nothing made any sense. She couldn't get to her son without finding help, though.

Somehow, Maggie was outside a *castle*. Tall spires and towers jutted into a blue sky, and balconies clung to the sides of the stone like hastily affixed iron ornaments. Windows taller than a person peppered the whole of the place in regular patterns. Some looked to be stained glass, and others were thick glass that looked opaque from here.

It wasn't the Biltmore, which as far as she knew was the only proper castle in the state of North Carolina. This was a building that had the look of ages and ages passing. The stone exterior was worn from rain, or time, or both. It was out of place here in the North Carolina forest, and she was not sure how such a thing wasn't on the map.

Maybe they can help find Craig . . . or maybe he's here, too!

Something about that answer was wrong, but she couldn't say what it was. Very few things made sense currently. All she knew was that she was separated from her son, and that was enough for her to press forward toward a misplaced castle in an out-of-season forest.

Because, although there was still a forest, her mangled vehicle was gone, and the trees looked different. Wrong species or whatever a person called types of trees. There was a castle, no car, and Maggie was certain something here was terribly amiss.

"Careful, now," a man in what appeared to be some sort of historical costume said. "The trip can make you queasy."

"My son—"

"Craig's quite fine," the man said. "Let's see to *you* now, Margaret, hmm?"

Maggie studied him as he helped her into a wooden wheelchair and rolled her along the bumpy ground right into the castle. Tall, muscular enough to rescue people from accidents—but he wasn't wearing a paramedic or firefighter's gear. He had on what looked like a graduation robe, sans hood. *Was there a university here?* He certainly didn't look like any professor she'd ever had with a tattoo on his throat and hipster hairstyle.

"Where are we?" Maggie looked around, expecting to see Craig or nurses or even hotel staff.

"Crenshaw." He smiled at her in the same way that she'd smile at victims on the stand, pity obvious. "You'll be okay, Margaret. Rest now. Rest and recover."

Maggie nodded, and despite the fact she was alone in a castle with a costumed stranger, she fell asleep right there in her wooden wheelchair.

3

Ellie

The Ligonier Valley Library, one of the various Carnegie libraries, was built in 1908. It was tucked in the same part of town as the post office, assorted restaurants, a coffee shop, antique and art spots, and The Diamond, a park with benches aplenty and a gazebo in the center. Honestly, if there were ever a Hallmark movie setting, Ligonier's main street was it.

Today, the brief drive through the wooded area where she lived toward downtown had been alive with color, as if painters had been set loose on the thick trees that lined the drive to work. No matter how many years Ellie had spent here, the coming of winter always felt magical. Change. It was in the cold morning air, and in the landscape around her. Pennsylvania wasn't far enough north that freezing weather came too early, but winter was edging near, and the air tasted of it.

"Earlier than usual today," one of the regular patrons remarked as Ellie went inside. She was as much a fixture as the park benches.

Years ago, Ellie had decided to keep her life orderly. Order was uninteresting. Uninteresting people never vanished. They lived quiet lives, perhaps even boring lives, not making waves or attracting attention.

Even if boring *doesn't come easily.*

Ellie, like her aunt, was anything but orderly. Impulsivity was her first reaction to most everything, but ordinary people don't go missing. So Elleanor Zelena Brandeau was *ordinary.* From the clothes she wore to the car she drove, Ellie was average. Basic brown hair. Not too thin, not too heavy, not too fit. She drove a nondescript white sedan—because three-fourths of all cars purchased in the U.S. were white, gray, or black.

She chose an average small town to work in, and she opted to live in an area outside town with no nearby neighbors. Missing people reports always included talks with neighbors. Ellie had created the most uninteresting day-to-day life that she could.

Her only exceptions were forays into Greensburg or Pittsburgh for dates *and* a job that was exciting to her. Some people might think being a librarian was uninteresting, but those people were Not Her Sort of people. Anyone who disliked books was suspect.

Possible kidnappers. Criminals. Generally questionable people.

On this topic, Ellie had strong feelings.

Her town—Ligonier, Pennsylvania—was a beautiful little colonial town with a pristine main street, a historic fort called Fort Ligonier, and an hour's drive away was Fallingwater, one of the most extraordinary of the Frank Lloyd Wright buildings. As far as places to live, it was both gorgeous and *quiet.* One might even call it uninteresting.

At least it had felt that way until today.

Today, walking through the stacks, Ellie found herself face-to-face with a black-clad, elegant woman who looked like she'd gotten lost on the way home from a noir film. *She* was a far cry from the usual patrons. Long flowing trousers hid most of her legs, and delicately heeled boots completed the unusual attire. She was white in the way of someone who had never seen the sun; porcelain or ivory or some such would be the tone if she needed to wear makeup. She didn't, though. She had a perfect complexion.

Her face was partially hidden behind a high-collared shawl and low-tilted hat with a short stark-white veil. The combination of the angle and the veil was such that it seemed she was forcing all gazes to her lips—which were painted a shade of red that screamed notice-me-*now.*

As if she wasn't already intriguing, she walked through the stacks with a floral teacup of all things.

"Excuse me," Ellie said, stalking after her. "No open containers in the library."

The teacup clattered softly as it was returned to a saucer the woman held in her other hand.

Who carried a saucer and cup with them in a library?

"But tea helps me think," the woman said, as if that were a reasonable explanation for carrying tea so close to the dozens of books that would be damaged if she tripped or was bumped or . . .

"Tea is dangerous to the books," Ellie pointed out. "Do you need help finding something?"

"Would you help me if I did?" the woman asked, cocking a hip against the shelf.

"That's my job," Ellie said.

"To help damsels in distress?" The woman removed her absurd hat and dropped it to the floor.

Ellie stared at her, taking in the elegant pantsuit and striking features. She looked much younger than her voice had sounded. In truth, she looked like a lost movie star from another era—or maybe a queen. What she didn't look like was a damsel in distress. She had the shape of a woman who could wander into a yoga or cycling class. Fit but not bulky. Tall and lean, painted lips, and flawless skin. She was breathtaking.

"Will you be my hero?" she murmured to Ellie. "Slay dragons for me?"

"We don't have an abundance of dragons here," Ellie managed to say even as her heart surged at the idea of being this woman's hero. She stepped farther into the aisle, trying to be quiet as she answered, "If you need *research* help, I'm a librarian here."

"Do you often help strangers, Miss Brandeau?" The woman cocked her head.

"I *am* a librarian." Ellie kept her voice professional, although it struck her that she had not shared her name. *Was she here for me specifically?* The thought of it was impossible; but in that way she always knew when people were lying, Ellie knew this beautiful stranger was previously aware of her for some reason.

She stepped closer. "What if *you're* what I'm looking for?"

Ellie felt like she was a bird caught in a snare. Her pulse sped, and her hands twitched as if she might need to defend herself. "I highly doubt that, Miss . . . ?"

"Prospero." The woman drained her teacup and sat it and the saucer on the nearest shelf.

"What an odd name," Ellie whispered.

Prospero placed a hand on Ellie's wrist, fingertips grazing the thin skin there so gently that Ellie swore she stopped breathing. "Miss Brandeau, I came here to find you. You're not quite like other people, are you? Secretly dreaming of *more*?"

Ellie shivered. "Doesn't everyone?"

"No. A great number of people are content," Prospero murmured, stroking Ellie's wrist. "You aren't, though. I wasn't, either, you know."

A little zing ran through Ellie, as if the gorgeous woman had an electric current in her skin. Everywhere they touched, Ellie felt a zing running through her. She stepped even closer to Prospero, so they were intimately close, although the surge of electricity felt real enough that Ellie's heart sped dangerously.

Who knew attraction could feel so close to a panic attack?

Prospero's free hand reached up to thread through Ellie's hair, setting actual sparks in the air. "Tell me, Miss Brandeau. What would you do if you had the chance to be a hero?"

Ellie laughed. "I'm a research librarian with a penchant for baking and reading excessively."

"And are you content?" Prospero stared into her eyes, as if she could discern hidden answers there.

"No," Ellie whispered. She thought Prospero was about to kiss her, so she angled her face upward.

"This might hurt, and I do apologize for that," Prospero said, hand curling around Ellie's hip.

"Hurt? Kisses aren't pain." Ellie brushed her lips over the bold red lips that were now so ridiculously close.

Elleanor Brandeau was not the sort to kiss strangers in the library. She was sensible, *uninteresting*. But Prospero's lips parted on a word or a noise, and all the sense Ellie possessed left the building.

She swayed toward Prospero. After a lifetime of secret dreams of a grand romance, it was happening. Here. Now.

Prospero's arm wrapped around Ellie's waist, and the electric feeling surged into something different. Ellie felt like the entire world was on fast-forward, her whole body glowing with some sort of energy that made no sense. Her heartbeat raced at a pace akin to high-speed trains, and her entire body tensed.

Was this love at first touch?

Was that actually possible?

Ellie's knees buckled suddenly. Her heartbeat sped in a way that was closer to terrified than magical.

Something is wrong.

"What's happening?" she managed to say, frightened and embarrassed all at once. She had an awkward realization that she might pass out. Her heart actually *hurt*.

Panic attack or heart attack?

Kisses didn't give a person—even one as mundane as Ellie—a heart attack.

Carefully, Prospero lowered her to the floor. She crouched down and gently tilted Ellie's face, so they were eye-to-eye. "Miss Brandeau? I fear this was a mistake."

Ellie felt Prospero's touch like a cool flush, and for one brief moment, nothing else mattered. "I don't know what that was. I don't have asthma or a heart thing."

"I shouldn't . . . I can't . . . *do* this to you. I thought I could. I came here to—" Prospero bowed her head, trembling ever so slightly.

At the sight of Prospero shaking, Ellie wanted to be the strong one, the hero, anything it took to put this back on the path Ellie thought it was going. "I swear I don't usually shake and fall over after a kiss—even when the kiss is from someone who looks like you."

Prospero gave her what looked like a sad smile. "I thought there were no lines I wouldn't cross. You've proven me wrong."

Ellie had questions, confusions, but as she pushed herself upward, trying for a more dignified position than fainted-at-a-kiss, all she could say was, "Can I see you sometime?"

Prospero leveled her a look that Ellie suspected was meant to be intimidating, but she also saw the hint of a smile that Prospero tried to hide. "Why would you *want* to? I've left you a jumble on the floor, Miss Brandeau."

"I kissed you," Ellie said, marveling at her own audacity. "I never do things like that, you know. Maybe that's why I panicked. I won't pass out if you kiss me. I'm safe."

"Unfortunately, I'm not safe, Miss Brandeau." Prospero gathered up her hat and stood.

Ellie was a sensible woman, one who didn't blurt out feelings and such, but she knew with a certainty that Prospero would not flinch away when she said, "I get this feeling of *rightness* or a knot in my stomach when I meet people. You feel *right* to me."

Prospero stared down at her. "Our kiss left you crumpled on the floor, Miss Brandeau. That's the very opposite of right."

"Fair. I felt faint, but I'm sure there's a good reason. I was over-whelmed, or my blood sugar is low or something." Ellie watched the beautiful woman wrestle with some thought or misgiving, and for a flicker of a moment, she thought she might get an answer.

"See your healer, please." Prospero straightened her hat, tugging the veil over her face more fully now.

"Over a panic attack?"

"Hopefully, one day we will share a meal and some truths, Miss Brandeau." Then Prospero swept away, leaving her teacup there like it was discardable.

See my healer? *Who says "healer"?*

Ellie stared after the mysterious Prospero, admiring the arrogant stride and the measured clackity-click-clack of her footsteps. Then Ellie looked at the underside of her wrist; fingerprints bruised the skin and tiny lines radiated out like bolts of electricity had been traced there. *Had that been a* real *shock, not just a panic attack?*

Ellie looked around. There were no loose wires in the library stacks. No lightning sparking through walls or shattered light fixtures.

That left the kiss.

But such things were impossible. Kisses couldn't be deadly. There was a rational answer. There must be. All questions had rational answers.

Had Prospero pressed too hard on my skin and caught a nerve under her fingertips in the process?

Ellie heart still thundered in her chest, but panic attacks and bruises notwithstanding, she couldn't help wishing Prospero would return. Meeting her was the single most interesting thing that had happened.

She made me *feel interesting.*

4
Dan

Maybe it was the backpack that caused all the problems. Honestly, it weighed almost as much as Dan did, but he needed *things*. Food. Dishes for the food. Soap for the dishes. Clothes. First aid. Sleeping bag. Fire starter.

And books. He had to have books.

Of course, pondering the contents of his bag as he fell arse over teakettle—he'd always liked that phrase—through the air, branches, and general end-of-life doom was silly. He ought to have had flashbacks. Dan expected a highlights reel of his life. Moments that mattered. Longing for the things undone.

"Are you broken?" a man prompted.

Dan looked up at the robed man. Taller than average with the sort of muscular form that made him seem menacing. Piercing ice-blue eyes. A black tattoo that barely showed on his throat. The only soft thing about him was a 1950s-retro hairstyle.

There very clearly was an afterlife, and Dan decided that all the years of lousy jobs and mocking coworkers were just fine if this was the reward.

"Hellllooo, nurse." Dan rubbed his mouth, as he felt like he was drooling embarrassingly. What he found was blood.

Dead people don't bleed.

The man murmured a word that Dan couldn't hear, and then sighed before saying, "Many of your ribs broke. Try not to—"

Dan scurried backward, as if he could escape his own blood.

"Something is very wrong," he whispered, wondering if the guy he owed money to had caught up with him. He'd been beaten pretty badly a few times before, so it wouldn't be unusual.

A man needs a vice.

Dan's was gambling.

Something was off, though. The idea of the bookie's enforcers following him to a hiking trail was funny enough to make Dan laugh—which made him wheeze and pass out.

☽ ✦ ☾

The next time he woke, Dan was in what appeared to be a hospital bed from the feel of the sheets. Maybe it was silly, but he thought coarse sheets were the worst. When he traveled, Dan always brought his own sheets. In fact, he had brought a set of sheets, including a pillowcase that was stuffed with his laundry, while camping.

He looked around and saw his backpack beside his bed. Hopefully, he wouldn't have to spend eternity lugging it around—especially as it still weighed as much as on the failed hike. Dan glared at the offensive bag and grumbled, "The afterlife is weird . . . and it smells like sulfur."

He looked up at the approach of a curvy woman in an old-fashioned hat and dress who held out a cup of something green and frothy.

"Is this hell?"

"No."

"It smells like it," he pointed out, scrunching up his face as if to erase the stench of sulfur that seemed to be everywhere.

"You get used to it." She wiggled the cup. "Drink this, dear. You'll feel better."

Dan drank it, and that was that. He was out cold again.

That cycle of wake, drink gross smoothies, and pass out was repeated several times, but each time he felt better and better.

Maybe I was dehydrated.

Maybe I hallucinated the fall and the blood.

But even in his flickers of awareness, Dan knew better. Lies made him feel peculiar—like ants in his veins—even when he was the one lying.

Finally, Dan woke to find the nurse—or *doctor?*—talking to Cosplay Hottie.

"He had a sickness in him," she said.

"How long to fix it?"

"Seriously, Sondre? I *already* repaired everything. As long as he stays here, he'll be fine. If he leaves . . ." She glanced at Dan.

"Hello?" Dan said, feeling awkward about eavesdropping.

The woman flashed him a smile, pivoted, and was gone.

"I have questions," he said, louder now. "Am I dead? And why does it smell like bad eggs?"

The man, Sondre apparently, rubbed his face and gestured toward the door. "Come with me."

Sondre slung Dan's backpack over one shoulder like it weighed nothing.

Dan stood, testing his stability, and in the next few minutes, he was back on his feet and escorted out of the hospital. After a lifetime of hospital visits, Dan still had a moment of relief each time he was able to walk out on his own. One more day, week, month, year of life was all he could hope for. The thought that the doctor was right—that she'd removed his "sickness" so easily—astounded him.

Dan followed Sondre as he strolled out of the infirmary into a court-yard that was straight out of the Middle Ages. Okay, maybe not totally. No horses. No swordplay. But it was a courtyard outside a castle, and in the distance, mountains loomed. It was if a European village had been restored to function.

And Dan felt better than he had in years. *Who knew nearly dying was the cure?* Dan grinned, almost giddy. His "sickness" was cancer, and from what he'd heard, it was gone. Not "more surgery/have some radiation/sorry about the new holes in your bones." Just gone.

"This is amazing," Dan whispered. There was an energy here, a sense of wellness that he hadn't often felt. He'd chased that sense of peace often enough via gambling. Betting on the horses and on games he didn't understand created a fleeting glimmer of joy. The peace he felt doing *that* wasn't real, though. It was like a quick buzz, but then it faded.

And then he'd lost and compounded the loss.

And then he'd been beaten by men who had no idea how brittle his bones were. A few pins and screws and plates later, Dan thought he'd learned his lesson—right up until the next tumor sent him back to a weekend casino trip.

"Thank you," Dan blurted. "For saving me."

"I didn't save you," Sondre said.

Dan looked at the man in the cloak as they walked through a vast stone doorway. "Is this a weird debtor's prison then?"

"No. You are alive and healthy and were in the infirmary."

"So I'm saved." Dan nodded. His ill-planned hiking trip ended abruptly with a tumble over the edge of a ravine, but all the people who said hiking would be the answer to his stress had been wrong. It wasn't exactly a cure for the debt back home, but look at where he was! By all rights, he'd expected to die this month one way or another. Instead, he was strolling out of a castle—which absolutely made no sense.

"Why a castle? Is this Europe? Is this like witness protection? Do I get a new identity here? I'll testify against my bookie. Where—"

"You're in Crenshaw," Sondre cut him off. "Mae—Dr. Jemison—has healed worse cases than you. Although, if not for that burst of magic you summoned to slow your descent, you'd be dead."

"Magic?" Dan stopped mid-step and stared. His rescuer had become even more alluring. "*I* did magic?"

"Yes. That's why I brought you here. All magic users are relocated to our world." The man paused. "Do you have questions or doubts or—"

"It's so 'Yer a wizard, Dan' or whatever." Dan looked around, hoping to see fantastic creatures or wizard duels or something.

Instead, there was still a regular-looking courtyard. The ground had a look of age, but the most interesting feature was a few bent trees and some stubborn grass that seemed to be attempting to shove through a thin layer of snow. There were no hints of anything extraordinary, but Dan knew the explanation his new hero had offered was true. His mother used to call it intuition, but mostly, Dan simply *knew* when people were lying. It made him an excellent poker player and a terrible date. Right now, however, it meant he was sure the most wondrous experience was really and truly happening.

He'd been cured by a potion and magic, gone from broken bones and coughing blood and slow-spreading cancer to feeling energized in a mere few days. If there were potions . . .

"Are there wands?" Dan asked. "Ooooh, tell me there are w—"

"No." Sondre straightened. "*Objects* can be imbued with magic. Stones. Jewelry. Some spells can be tied to the object temporarily. Also, the term is witch. Not wizard. Historically, witch was gender neutral. *Wizard* is, etymologically, the term for a 'wise man,' and pairs with the female term 'cunning woman.'"

"Sure, sure. Got it. Witch is gender free." Dan walked around the courtyard with a new curiosity. A preponderance of chickens roamed the courtyard, and two younger men were walking around scooping chicken poop. A third was gathering eggs in a giant woven basket. "What about the smell? Is it the, er, birds?"

"No. Gas leak from a ground vent we can't properly seal." The man sighed and motioned toward several piles of burning plants. "The outside world has done some drilling and spilling, and the noxious stuff seeped into the ground—" He held out his hands in a what-can-you-do gesture. "We *are* working on correcting it."

Looming over them was a castle. A real, honest-to-Pete castle. It could've been straight out of the Czech landscape, or along a Scottish tour, or watching over German forest. The towering stone edifice was neither ruined nor festooned with tour-guide trappings.

"So, er, what's your name?" Dan tried to sound smooth, but he felt like his geek heart was bursting. He knew the man's name from overhearing it, but he still felt like they ought to have an introduction. After a lifetime of Comic-Con, local cons, and this one furry con that was maybe best not discussed, he was in an actual magic city and strolling with a real witch. Dan wanted to do everything *right*.

"Sondre."

"Sondre," Dan repeated in a low voice. Louder he added, "Right. Well, Sondre, point me to the scullery or stables or wherever I need to work. Glad to be here. Ready to work."

"You're not here to wash dishes or shovel dung, Daniel." Sondre rubbed his forehead as if a headache was pressing on him, and Dan wanted to ask questions about potions for that or if they took regular pills like back home.

"You're in Crenshaw due to the awakening of latent magical traits," Sondre said in a tour-guide tone. "These traits mean that, in due course, you will decide whether to remain here or return to—"

"I'll stay." Dan interrupted the canned welcome-to-Crenshaw speech. "Shovel dung. Slay monsters . . . er, well, try to slay 'em at least. Whatever the bosses want. I'm your guy."

Dan scanned the sky. No giant eyes. No explosions. No militaristic space orbitals posing as moons, at least as far as he could see.

He glanced back at Sondre. "Is it dragons? Evil overlords? I'm *here* for it, man. Just aim me. Happy to serve the cause. Die for the nation of Crenshaw. Whatevs."

Sondre made a gesture and a teacup appeared in his hand. He downed the entire cup, sighed, and then stared at Dan. "You're in Crenshaw due to the awakening of latent magical traits. These traits mean that, in due course, there will be a decision whether you are to remain here or return to . . . What is your home location?"

"Baltimore," Dan supplied, wanting to be helpful—and not just because Sondre was handsome or because he was magical or because he'd brought Dan to a magical—

"Are you still listening?"

Dan blushed. "Er, yes. Choice. Staying. Not going back to Baltimore. I heard the other witch say I was healed because I was here."

"Magic self-repairs the *host*. Witches are, in essence, hosts to magic." Sondre looked at him, briefly seeming more approachable, but then he continued. "As part of this process, you will attend the College of Remedial Magic, after which you will be brought to court at several points, whereupon the Congress of Magic will determine *if* you can remain or be siphoned safely. *If* you are selected to remain, you will be a part of a magical house—from there you will earn an annual stipend—"

"What's siphoning?"

"Removing your magic." Sondre tossed back half the cup of tea in a gesture that looked like he ought to be in a bar with a shot glass.

"Can we *not* be siphoned? I mean, man, I want to stay here. If you siphon me, the magic is gone. It can't heal me then. So well, I'll do whatever . . . anything at all . . . clean the privy or—"

"We have plumbing here."

Sondre motioned him toward a massive door big enough to drive a rig into without scuffing the top. The doorframe was carved stone, but the doors themselves were wood with silver inlay.

They entered the castle, doors swinging open at a gesture from Sondre. The foyer was everything Dan had imagined. Massive arches swept up and met in a central dome. Beyond the foyer was a staircase that divided into two twin staircases that arced apart, as if they were inverted parentheses.

"I'm never going back," Dan announced. "Whatever it takes, this is where I belong. Seriously, I don't want to die. The radiation, the chemo, the surgeries. It's fucking exhausting. I was expecting to die this month, you know?"

Sondre started walking again, following a passageway that curved behind the staircase, so Dan followed him. The hallway had a row of open doors.

"As you aren't a noted flight risk like some recent arrivals, you can take a ground-floor room if you choose."

As much as Dan wanted to simply wander off, explore, he felt an embarrassing rush of emotions—too much to leave room for words.

Sondre continued. "The class will assemble shortly. Until such time, you are free to read, exercise, enjoy the sun—although I must warn you that the peacocks are moody. They lay an egg most days here, but they're loud and grumpy."

Dan spun around and hugged him. He couldn't help it. He was a hugger. "You're the best, man. You saved my life bringing me here."

Sondre stared at him, arms limp at his side until Dan let go and stepped back. Then, a small smile lifted just the corner of his mouth before he said, "No one around here hugs me . . . Better than a sharp stick to the eye, I suppose, but I *am* headmaster of the College of Remedial Magic, Daniel, and considered a warmonger."

"Still saved my life. Over there, my days are limited. So . . . are there textbooks?" Dan asked, stepping back a little more. "I could study, you know. How do I get money? Oh, and will I get a robe? All the boarding schools in books—"

"I will summon one of the resident hobs once you choose your chambers. The hobs will fetch your essentials so you can maximize your time here."

"Hob?"

"Hobs are a manifestation of magic, we think." Sondre shrugged. "They won't answer where they come from or why, but when the first witches arrived here, they found the hobs. Magical beings the size of squirrels, but as sentient and civilized as men."

"Are they like our overlords or . . . ?"

"No, Daniel. They are like neighbors with an ability to make things, change things, and generally infuriate the calmest souls." Sondre rubbed his forehead. "If they like you, they are willing to invade your house for a fee. Like grandparents who both meddle and cook, but who also will coat your undergarments in poison ivy if you anger them."

"Got it. Be nice to hobs." Dan repressed the host of new questions he now had. This was everything he had ever dreamed, even if it had started with a dismal attempt at camping.

"Room?" Sondre prompted.

Dan picked the third door because by then, he'd noticed that each room was alike. Not embarrassingly posh, but more luxurious than he was used to knowing. Antiques still in use, a massive fireplace, and, in the adjoining bathrooms, giant bathtubs with what looked like very modern plumbing. Beside the tub was a basket of dried flowers. To top it all off, there was a door-sized window with a terrace outside. The rooms were beautiful and inviting except for one detail.

"The tubs are sort of brown," Daniel said. "Big and all, but brown."

"The water in Crenshaw has gone foul," Sondre said. "Bathing is safe, but I limit my time in the water since it smells rather noxious. The herbs help mask it."

The room smelled like eggs and lavender; it was an odd mix.

Dan scowled at the tub. "Kinda weird, man."

Sondre nodded. "It's a recent situation, one we are working to fix."

"With magic."

"Yes, Daniel, with magic. Most everything of note in Crenshaw is done with magic." Sondre stepped closer. "As to money, members of each house—which is a group of witches with the same type of magic—are given an annual allowance by the head of that house. What you do with it is up to you."

Dan paused in his study of his new home. "Are there gambling spots?"

"Not legal ones, but yes." Sondre's voice pitched low as he added, "There are factions in Crenshaw, and choosing the right one can make a difference in whether or not someone of influence argues to reject you or advocates for you to stay."

Dan swallowed the terror of losing this world, of going back to a nonstop pursuit of dying, and looked back at Sondre. "Are you a person of influence?"

Sondre watched Dan with the kind of calculating look that made Dan tense. "For the right sort of people . . ."

Threat. Dan wasn't a stranger to threats—a gay man wasn't as imperiled in modern Baltimore as he was even a decade or two prior, but "not as imperiled" wasn't the same as always safe.

"Any issues with men loving men?" Dan was ready to fight dragons, but he wasn't willing to sacrifice his essential nature even to stay cancer-free.

"Not a one," Sondre said. "Not my path, but it's not an issue here."

A weight slid off Dan's shoulders. There was tolerance *and* magic *and* not-cancer. That was everything.

He held Sondre's gaze and declared, "Then, whichever side you support is my choice, too, Headmaster. I'm the right sort of people."

The smile Sondre offered made Dan suspect he might've chosen dangerously, but then Sondre nodded. "Welcome to the College of Remedial Magic, Daniel. I'll be expecting great things from you."

Dan was fairly sure no one wholly *good* sounded quite that deadly.

"And Daniel?" Sondre held Dan's gaze. "You will keep your silence about anything I share with you or request of you."

Dan swallowed. Then he grinned just a little, surprised by his own audacity. "Why do I feel like I just joined the dark side of whatever's going on?"

"Because you are astute." Sondre dropped Dan's massive backpack at the edge of the room, turned, and left.

5
Ellie

Later that afternoon, back in Ligonier, Ellie pulled out a list of search terms for the last two weeks. She ought to go home, but she was hoping the mysterious femme fatale from earlier would return. Oddly, Ellie had been thoroughly exhausted since The Kiss, although her heartbeat was no longer erratic.

The library closed early on Tuesdays, so Ellie was alone with her research. Typically, she updated her research on the missing every week. It was one of the many reasons she'd become a research librarian: she liked the peace and found comfort in sifting through old newsprint and journals.

Inside the century-old building where she worked, the sound of the air conditioning was punctuated by the whir and hum of the printer.

Once Ellie entered the usual search terms—missing, disappearance, or the name from whichever cases she was updating—she skimmed the results on the screen as she printed the articles. There was something comforting in the solidity of paper, especially when it came to something as ethereal as missing people.

Tonight, she was adding a new case, the latest entry in her printouts, to the binders that housed her research:

MISSING HIKER: YOSEMITE SEARCHERS HAVE FOUND NO CLUES

SAN FRANCISCO—The search for Daniel Monahan, missing three weeks, continues this week. "Even seasoned hikers can get lost, and Mr. Monahan was a novice with poor health. We aren't ruling out foul play, however," one park ranger explained. "The chances of finding him decrease every day. Nature can be unforgiving."

Monahan, an employee of a bank in Baltimore, was last seen standing alongside his backpacking gear. Several hikers saw him earlier that day. "We suggested he hire a guide." Authorities are hoping tourists saw Monahan after this and will reach out with information to narrow the search area.

Daniel Monahan would have a tab in Ellie's binder and a divider so he could be updated. Monahan joined the long list of people in the "National Parks" category, so his tab had a "NP" in the lower corner. Others had "accident" or "witness" in their tab corners. A few had "child" or "group" in the corner. Most missing people fit into categories, and often the likelihood of resolution was tied to that.

Monahan was likely to be found in a spring thaw—or at least, his remains were. His picture, as with many black-and-white images, implied a sense of time that was, in this case, a lie. Monahan was a thin man, certainly not in the shape to carry a lot of back country supplies. Bookish. Thick-framed glasses. He could've been in any era post-photography, if not for the fantasy-costumed people behind him in the snapshot. Monahan looked at home *there,* but he didn't look like an outdoorsman.

Was he trapped out of exhaustion? A bear or cougar victim? There were many possibilities, most of which meant he wouldn't be seen again—at least not alive.

The truth Ellie had come to embrace was that no one's disappearance was truly mysterious. Clues were obscured either intentionally or by time, nature, and error. Despite every television program or book offering scintillating tales of crimes solved by intrepid detectives and amateur sleuths—and Ellie adored such books—the reality was that not all crimes were solved in an hour or three hundred or so pages.

Many people were "last seen," but never resolved. The cases fell into the margins, forgotten and unanswered by everyone but loved ones—and Ellie.

The Missing files that Ellie maintained over the last decade had started as a way to comfort herself. If Ellie understood *why* it happened, then Hestia wouldn't vanish again, and the adult version of the little girl everyone said was "just like" Hestia wouldn't vanish either.

Back then, Ellie's efforts were pretty basic. Colonel Fawcett, Amelia Earhart, big obvious cases that a child could research. Ellie had been a child trying to make sense of a thing she still couldn't understand twenty years later. Statistically, 98 percent of the people who were declared "missing" were found eventually, often quickly and occasionally deceased. The remaining 2 percent, however, were the cases that filled her dark blue binders.

Ellie added three cases to the blue folder (unsolved). Sometimes, she was able to move a case to the white binder (found: alive) or the black binder (found: deceased). As each page printed, Ellie read it, slid the sheet into the three-hole punch, and then she added it to the correct page in the binders.

Her phone buzzed.

HESTIA
Withering away. Eagles will eat my carcass soon.

ELLIE
Eagles?

HESTIA

Sky burial.

ELLIE

I will not leave your corpse on the roof.

HESTIA

Then you better feed me soon.

Ellie packed up and went by the house to collect Hestia, who had texted they needed "a night out" before her "imprisonment." Honestly, Ellie didn't mind *not* cooking tonight. Whatever had caused her to collapse earlier left her exhausted.

By the time Ellie and Hestia were in the car and headed toward Fallingwater, where the restaurant was, Ellie had decided if she could find out about people who went missing, maybe she could find out about Prospero.

Is that stalkery? What were the rules after kissing beautiful strangers? Prospero had seemed to know that Ellie would be there, so really, this was just leveling the playing field.

It was just that Ellie felt . . . desired. It didn't seem like a huge thing, but it had been a minute since anyone had made her feel like she was interesting and beautiful. She felt empowered by the way Prospero had looked at her, spoken to her, kissed her back.

"I met someone today," Ellie blurted out. It was a little foolish because she had no intention of seeing Prospero again, of going to lunch with her or any such thing, but there was an innate *rightness* about her.

"Someone you like?" Hestia prompted mildly.

"I think so. . . . You know that click?" Ellie glanced over. "The opposite of the belly eels?"

Hestia nodded. They'd long since come up with words for the way some people made a person feel *right* and some felt innately *off*. Hestia called it intuition, although every so often she said "magic." Whatever it was, Ellie only talked about it with Hestia.

"She feels right, like I want to know everything about her," Ellie admitted. "No one ever has before."

"Tell me about her."

"She's pretty and has an elegance to her, and possibly a bit dangerous. Well, she said she was dangerous." Ellie paused at that thought. Prospero did have an edge to her that was hard to explain. She was risky in some indefinable way, and in that moment, Ellie was as certain of it as she was of gravity.

"Nothing says you have to stay in Ligonier," Hestia said gently. "I'm an adult, able to look after myself, and you have your whole life in front of you. Don't grow old before your time."

Ellie looked over to Hestia. "I'm where I want to be."

"If that changes . . ."

"I'll tell you. Promise." Ellie shook her head. "She's not for me, though. We kissed, and she left."

"Don't give up before you try." Hestia pointed at her with a shaking finger. "I met a man once. Thought he was the one. I sometimes regret not trying." She grinned. "I've enjoyed the hell out of the single life, mind you, but Walter was something else. He understood me."

"You never said anything." Ellie felt foolish. "But yes. That's it. When she looked at me, I feel like she *saw* me. Does that make any sense?"

"Perfect sense." Hestia sighed. She was absurdly romantic, although she channeled most of it into books rather than life.

Ellie expected her to wax poetic, but instead, Hestia yelled, "*Cows!*"

"What?" Ellie said, or at least she meant to say. She wasn't sure she said anything really.

A trio of cows seemingly appeared out of nowhere. She wasn't sure why they'd stepped onto the road just then, or *why* there were cows hidden in the woods beside the road.

If the cows had waited thirty seconds later, there would be no issue.

In that fractured second, however, Ellie realized swerving wasn't an option. She had to slam into the cows or risk killing the bicyclist who just as suddenly appeared on the opposite side of the road. *Who rides a bike in these temperatures?* A bicyclist wouldn't survive an impact with a car. Even forty-five miles per hour was fast enough to kill a person.

Cows, it is.

As the car careened toward the trio of cows, Ellie's brain felt like it was going slowly and logically. Adrenaline flooded her mind. It made the moment between *seeing* the cows and *hitting* the cows stretch out like wet taffy.

And in that taffy-slow moment, Ellie decided she wasn't ready for the death that would likely follow a cow-collision.

"God help me!"

She stomped hard on the brakes—which was *exactly* the wrong choice. Her brakes locked up, and the car started to slide into a spin.

"Hold on!" she yelled.

There was no one, nothing, to stop the accident.

Except

somehow

time

did

slow.

The moment of the accident was stretching. The taffy of the instant pulled, stretched, extended out so far that it was thin and showing holes.

If Ellie believed in things like magic, she'd realize she had, in fact, just slowed time. She'd know that she'd saved her own life with a reservoir of magic that she didn't even believe *could* exist. As it was, she didn't realize anything in that moment other than the dizzying lurch as the car went twisting off the road, executed several full spins through trees and brush, and shuddered to a halt.

The last things she saw were the eyes of the cow now half-stuck on the hood of her car. Huge brown eyes staring at her as something wet trickled down her face.

"Ellie!" Hestia cried.

But Ellie couldn't look away from the dying cow. She tried to turn her head to look at Hestia, but couldn't. *Nothing* moved. Not her toes, not her head. The fear that should come at that detail wasn't there, just the taffy feeling. The very air looked like it was stretching around the cow in her windshield.

"Time shouldn't be taffy," she told her aunt and the dying cow, trying to focus on that and not the fact she couldn't feel her legs or that sticky liquid was dripping down her face.

6
Maggie

Maggie glared at the man in front of her. *Was this Leon's doing? Had he hired one of the lowlifes he knew? Had Craig been kidnapped, too?*

Her captor was doing that thing Leon liked to do, the patronizing smile and calming tone. Being a woman didn't make her hysterical. That was merely a word used to quash a woman's voice. A man was bold, outraged, courageous for using his voice. A woman, especially a diminutive one with a Southern drawl, was called "hysterical" and treated as such.

"I want to go home," she repeated in her courtroom voice.

"Now, Margaret—"

"Don't you 'now, Margaret' me!" Maggie poked her finger into the man's ridiculous robe, meeting firm muscles that made her pause in a flicker of utterly inappropriate interest, before continuing, "I put up with that nonsense from my ex-husband, and I'll be damned if I'll hear it from some nutter in a castle that smells of spoiled eggs."

He looked at her with that implacable calm she'd already come to hate. "I'm not a 'nutter' as you so eloquently put it."

"You're holding me captive." Maggie raised one finger. "Wearing a robe like we're in some weird roleplay." She raised another finger. "And, oh yeah, we're in a fucking castle."

She shook the three fingers in his direction.

The man rubbed his forehead as if he were the one in distress. If he weren't holding her in a prison, she might feel a bit of sympathy. "You are at the College of Remedial Magic, Margaret. This is your temporary home—"

"Bullshit." She walked over to the door and jiggled the handle. Nothing happened. It hadn't any other time she tried either. "I'm in a *prison*."

Feelings boiled inside her—mostly rage with a generous dose of fear. Her captor seemed polite enough, but what would happen if she tried to escape? What would happen if she didn't give in to his delusions?

"Is Craig here, too?" she asked, finally turning to face him.

"No." Her captor gave her a pitying look. "He's in North Carolina."

"Is he okay?" Her voice broke on the last word.

"You don't need to worry about him now, Margaret." Her captor held out a hand as if to invite her toward him. "Let me show you around."

"Did Leon hire you?" Maggie crossed her arms. Something here was very, *very* wrong. "He cut my brake lines. Or hired someone to cut them. Was it you?"

"No."

For two days, she'd been in this room. There were meals, and the room itself was opulent. A thick rug with some scene that looked straight out of mythology spread over the stone floor. The ceiling arched upward, and a thick-hewn wooden beam that could've doubled for a telephone pole jutted out of the wall. From it, a metal light fixture—more candelabra than chandelier—hung from the pole. It was very much the ancient castle it had appeared to be from the outside.

How Maggie arrived here—or could depart from here—was another topic altogether. Her balcony door was locked, but through the arched windows she could see a village of sorts nestled at the foot of the hill. There were what she thought were shops or houses, and scattered around were a few taller buildings that seemed to defy gravity. As if this were an actual medieval town, the castle looked down on the village.

She had no idea exactly where the castle was, but the windows were cold to the touch, so she assumed it was somewhere northerly or at higher elevations because it certainly didn't feel like a Southern climate through the glass.

A sprinkle of snow that morning further clarified that detail.

She still had no idea how she'd ended up here. All she knew was her son was out there somewhere, alone in a forest, and she was trapped in this damnable castle.

Why?

That question plagued her far more than most things. As a lawyer, she understood that *why* was typically a secret to unlocking a case. Motives mattered. *Why* was she here? Understanding that would help her understand how to get out.

Maggie pushed all the unexplained details out of her mind for a moment and decided to try a new approach. "I appreciate the rescue. I really do, but my son is alone out there. His dad is a monster. You don't understand." She twisted her hands. "I need to get to my son. It's imperative."

The man walked over to the table where a steaming teapot sat. He poured two cups, and then added a dollop of milk to hers and a single sugar cube to his. He sat and met her gaze. "How did the door come off the vehicle, Margaret?"

"I have no idea. I'm assuming you used a winch and chain." She tried to keep her posture and voice both amiable, but it was a struggle. "I must've blacked out briefly."

"Mmm." He sipped his tea.

"*Mmm?* What sort of answer is that?" Maggie snapped. Then she lifted her teacup and sipped, determined to be polite. She'd managed it for years with Leon. Surely, she could do it for a few minutes now.

"What would you say if I told you that you were no longer in the American South?"

"The castle was a hint, Robespierre," Maggie muttered. "Maybe over here in Europe, castles are all over the—"

"We are not in Europe." He watched her with an uncanny attentiveness, the sort of doting gaze she'd once wanted from a man. Any man. Preferably one as delicious as this one, but all she seemed to attract were narcissists and delusional losers.

"Film set? Eccentric actor?" Maggie had been wondering where they were, so she had a few ready guesses. "Renaissance faire with a really good budget?"

He took another drink, one that looked like a person tossing back liquid courage, not tea, before saying, "Crenshaw."

Maggie lifted his cup and sniffed. "That's not tea. When did you—?"

"Watch." He pointed at the door to the balcony, which opened with a clattering noise.

"So . . . you're like a stage magician?" She looked around the room. "Is this a reality show of some sort? What are you? Some Houdini wannabe?"

He sighed again. "I am called Sondre, and I am not an illusionist. I am a witch."

"Sawn-dray" the witch?

Despite best intentions, Maggie snorted. "Uh-huh."

"You are here, Margaret, because *you* are a witch, too." He sounded so earnest, and she made a mental note to watch whatever show this was once her temper calmed. "As I've said several times, this is the College of Remedial Magic, where you will be a student and—"

"Sure it is." She snorted again; that and her braying laughter sounding anything but appealing.

"You are here in Crenshaw to attend the College of Remedial Magic, Maggie," said the affronted-looking "witch." It was a shame he was a raving mad kidnapper. He was a handsome man. "You are in the castle, which will be your home during your time as a student. Classes will begin this week."

When she was finally able to compose herself, she patted the man's hand. "I hate to break it to you, though, but man-witches are called wizards, and a few trip wires to open doors and sleights of hand aren't enough to make a rational woman abandon civilized society. Your television show has a few cool gimmicks, but—"

"This is not a television show," he stressed. "You are a witch, Margaret. This is a community for witches, and when you first arrive here, you must attend the college."

"Fine. I want to disenroll from your college." She shrugged.

Maybe it was the inflection in his words, or maybe it was the intuition she relied on in life and for her job, but she believed him. Maggie almost always knew when someone was telling the truth. She felt it in her bones.

"I still want to go home," she said again. "I have a *son.*"

Sondre stood, poured another glass of what smelled like mead from the teapot, and downed it before muttering, "You *are* home. And now that you are not a danger to yourself or others, you may explore the castle, Margaret. Take the day to see your new school."

Then he made a gesture as he headed to the door, which opened at his approach, and Maggie was left deciding if she ought to follow or stay in her prison.

Easy choice. She got up to trail after him. Exploring would let her find a way to escape—and get back to her son, her life. She wasn't going to let Craig stay in danger one day longer than necessary.

7

Ellie

Ellie blinked, trying to take in her location. Bright lights glared down. Steady beeps echoed. She yanked the IV out of her arm, and the beeping in her room became unreasonably fast, but she was convinced that time was lagging. What if whatever nerve was pinched in the crash worsened? What if that can't-feel-her-toes thing returned? Ellie wanted to explain the taffy to the doctors before it was too late to fix it.

"Where's Hestia?" she asked the empty room.

As Ellie thought about it, the pulling-taffy feeling in her belly started, stopped, and then started again. It was akin to dealing with an old push-mower she'd finally given away. Some days, she'd pull that starter cord a dozen times with nothing but a fuel-scented cloud in her face, and other times, it started on the first tug. It was infuriating with a mower, but it was something far worse with time.

The doorway darkened as a nurse entered. She stood, one leg raised like she was a full-figured flamingo clad in support hose, and slowly blinked at Ellie.

"What time is it?" Ellie asked, wincing as the skin and vein at the injection site responded finally to the jerk of needle and tape and tubing.

"Toooosday." The nurse shook her head and tried again. "It's Tuesday."

The woman looked around, as if she was also vaguely aware something was wrong. Of course, that was a projection. The nurse, undoubtedly, noticed *nothing* because time was nothing like taffy. Ellie knew that.

"What was in the tube?" Ellie motioned to the liquid now dripping onto the scratchy sheets and hospital mattress.

"Tramadol for the pain initially, but—"

"That explains it." Ellie watched the nurse move in jerky start-and-stop motions that made her seem robotic and glitchy. The woman took several halting steps, continuing to move in that mechanical way.

A robotic flamingo.

Ellie rubbed her eyes, wiping away the nonsense thought and, hopefully, the quirks in her vision. "How long until it wears off?"

The nurse patted her arm again. "We stopped the Tramadol last night, Ellie. You're just tired."

"Oh. The concussion—"

"No, dearie. You don't have a concussion." The woman beamed, flashing dentures that were a shade too white.

Ellie thought about the blood dripping down her face, the way her lower body wouldn't move at all, the sheer pain of it all. "I need to see my aunt. My passenger."

"She had her hip surgery scheduled for tomorrow, so she's in pre-op."

"Oh." Ellie thought about all the things she was supposed to do to get the house ready for Hestia. "I need to go home and get her bag. I'll be back and—"

"Once you're discharged," the nurse said. "You can't just walk out of the hospital!"

After the nurse left, Ellie dressed in silence. Her typical desire to follow the rules gave way under a strange new pressure in her belly. Something had changed when she hit that cow. Something *inside* Ellie was different.

She probably ought to stay in the hospital for now, but she needed to get Hestia's bag, and maybe call that home health company after all. Maybe no one would even know she left the hospital to fetch Hestia's things.

A few moments later, Ellie texted for a car pickup, gathered her things, and walked out of the hospital. It was, as a matter of record, one of the most adventurous, disobedient things she had done in over a decade.

Her bravado faded quickly as she stood in the midday sun, looking for her ride. Truthfully, Ellie wasn't quite sure she was ready to be inside a car at all, but there was no way to get home from the hospital without one—and her "things" included several heavy binders. Admittedly, she was proud of her years of research, but today the binders mostly felt like a weight she'd rather not carry.

But she also had over $600 in cash in her bag. She wasn't willing to drop her research or her cash.

Ellie looked again at the confirmation text on her phone as she walked around the front of the building, looking for an idling car. It wasn't an actual parking lot, so the car ought to be easy to find.

Ellie texted the phone number: "Where are you?"

"Keep walking" was the quick reply.

"'Keep walking' they tell the not-quite-discharged patient." Ellie stifled the rest of her complaint. It made her feel even more abandoned.

The angrier Ellie got, the more that taffy-pulling feeling grew. The pavement rolled and shivered. Twists of asphalt started to writhe and stretch.

No concussion, my butt! Ellie watched the ground imitate a sea of undulating serpents. They wriggled all over the ground around her, as if they were her own army of reptilian rage made manifest.

Time, of course, didn't stretch like taffy with holes, and grounds didn't ripple like enraged serpents. The only reasonable explanation was Ellie *did* have a concussion.

And the blood she recalled had been real.

If she did not have a concussion, the other explanation—the one

Ellie absolutely didn't consider—was magic. Magic, in fact, did cause parking lots to imitate serpents, and time to slow like stubborn taffy. Sometime later, Ellie would think about this, but not yet.

Ellie's practicality was a shield against any manner of unpleasantness, and both asphalt snakes and taffy-like time were quite unpleasant.

As her temper grew, Ellie watched the asphalt snakes peel off the hot ground and begin to wave around in the air. Ten-foot-tall serpents made of hot, stinking asphalt surged upward on either side of her. Where they ought to have eyes were voids, cracks in the asphalt, and gravel jutted out of parted lips like fangs.

Ellie glared at the forest of snakes. "Absolutely not."

They turned as if they were of one mind, absent eyes staring at her in curiosity, and sizzled. The sound of hot asphalt and the hiss of serpents mixed in their magical mouths, and the entire parking lot buzzed with the noise.

To anyone watching, Ellie's magic would seem rather remarkable—but also untrained, inexperienced, and above all else, *dangerous*. However, most magical folk were sequestered in their own world, and the sad truth was that—magical or ordinary—people tended to believe of others exactly what they believed of themselves. Ellie found herself rather ordinary, and so those about to meet her were predisposed to believe she was that and *only* that.

Ellie looked at her sizzling serpentine saviors and ordered, "If I don't have a concussion, you do not exist. *Down!*"

The serpents dropped but continued to shiver, so that the ground seemed to move. Ellie suspected she must be experiencing vertigo that her mind explained away with the fanciful notion of pavement snakes, and Ellie resolved then and there to call her insurance company to get authorization for an MRI, a CT scan, and a full blood panel. Clearly, something was amiss, and even though the doctors had overlooked it, Ellie knew herself. She was not fanciful.

For now, though, Ellie stomped across the pavement, squishing asphalt snakes under her sensible shoes. The serpents slithered quickly out of the way. However, as Ellie stepped off the long drive that was *not* filled with asphalt serpents, she found herself not along the road where she ought to be, but in what appeared to be a meadow suffering from neglect or over-farming. The ground was vaguely brown, as if nothing at all could grow here.

"Well, then, I suppose I've died after all," Ellie muttered.

A nearby bubbling well gurgled like old pipes in need of a plumber. There was no car or driver. In fact, there was no road.

"First snakes, now this . . ." Ellie pressed her lips together and debated her options. She decided she'd obviously had a concussion, no matter what the doctors had said. Now, her concussion had led to a stroke, a massive one.

But Ellie still had her bag of binders—and a not insignificant pile of cash.

Do you get to take your things to the afterworld?

Ellie looked down on a village with a castle jutting up in the middle and considered the weirdness of suddenly appearing castles and hills. She checked her pulse again; the stomping beat of her heart was to be expected. Nothing else here was, though. Medieval villages and castles didn't just appear.

And Pennsylvania ought not to vanish casually.

As Ellie watched the crowd in the streets swarm around the bustling village, she amended her ongoing observations. *People* didn't suddenly appear either. At least, they had never done so in her experience thus far.

Nonetheless, there they were. People were filling this lost-era-looking city, and the city was very obviously not near Ligonier—but Ellie's heart was beating. There was no rational explanation here, and Ellie was not prone to *irrational* explanations. She stood, watching the people and trying to find a way to make sense of it all.

"What do I do now?" Ellie dropped her bag.

After about an hour of pondering the matter from several angles, Ellie decided this was a coma dream, a figment of Ellie's imagination.

No other explanation made a lick of sense, despite the binders' familiar weight.

Then, the strangest thing happened. The femme fatale from the library strolled up the hill toward Ellie. *Prospero*. That was her name. Had she died, too? She looked far too lovely to be dead. Her hair was pinned up, and a top hat perched upon her head. A soft capelet covered her shoulders and upper arms, and she wore a sleek black pantsuit and sharp-heeled boots that were thoroughly the wrong shoes for pacing about a meadow.

Ellie's pulse was—she checked again—present and strong. Stronger, in fact, as she studied Prospero.

Ellie was, after several pinches, still awake . . . so, imaginative coma dream was the next best answer.

"Hello, Miss Brandeau," Prospero said. "Most witches wait until they are brought to Crenshaw. But here you are, all on your own."

Ellie frowned at her. Beautiful but perhaps a bit mad. "Most *what*?"

"Witches, Miss Brandeau; you are a witch." Prospero stepped forward as Ellie swayed on her feet.

Nothing Prospero said felt like a lie, but witches were nothing more than superstition.

Prospero wrapped an arm around Ellie's middle. "Not that I object to a beautiful woman falling into my arms, but what say we get you to somewhere less meadow, more fainting couch?"

Ellie nodded and let the strange woman lead her away.

"Witch?" Ellie echoed finally.

"Yes, my dear Miss Brandeau. We are witches." Prospero steered her toward the town at the bottom of the hill. "Welcome to Crenshaw."

8
Ellie

Despite the sheer oddity of the hospital's disappearance and the town itself, Ellie could only think about the woman in front of her. Logic tried to force its way to the surface, to remind her that nothing here made sense. She could not be a witch because witches weren't real.

Maybe Prospero isn't real either.

Abruptly, Ellie pinched her—or tried to do so. Her fingers had little purchase on the rough fabric on Prospero's side.

Prospero slanted a look at Ellie. "Did you pinch me?"

"Yes," Ellie said. "I think I'm dreaming. Gorgeous woman, magic, weird town . . ."

Prospero's mouth curved into a small smile. "You are not dreaming, Miss Brandeau. You are unsettled, but this will pass. You transported yourself to a new world without aid or direction. That is remarkable! Now, however, your body is adjusting. Sensible witches often sleep through it."

"I'm sensible!"

Prospero's expression made quite clear she disagreed. "You kissed a stranger in the library, arrived in a new world with a bag of books, and pinched me. Sensible isn't the word I would use. Intriguing? Lovely? Unusual?"

"I'm sensible," Ellie argued.

She glanced at Prospero, who was not wearing the veiled hat today. Instead, she had a pair of oversized sunglasses that had much the same effect: her face was half-hidden. Now, though, she had hair swept up into some sort of artful twist with a top hat on it, and she was dressed in a lovely black pantsuit, as if she were trying to mimic Audrey Hepburn in *Breakfast at Tiffany's*.

"You carry a teacup and wear a top hat, and I think time is moving wrong. Ergo, none of this is real—*including* you. So I pinched you. Perfectly logical test." Ellie sighed. "I fear I have a concussion or worse."

"You do not." Prospero pressed her lips together briefly, as if trapping more words inside. "I apologize, but we must hurry now. The street is too public. Can you keep up?"

Ellie nodded. "In a dream, I should have infinite energy."

"Not a dream, Miss Brandeau," Prospero rebutted. "There are quicker ways, of course, to travel, but your body is already in shock, likely nearing magical exhaustion, so walking will have to do."

Prospero lifted Ellie's hand in hers and tucked it into the fold of her arm, as if she were some old-world gentleman meeting a date. If the gesture had been the least bit affectionate, Ellie would've felt charmed by it.

Liar, her inner monologue whispered. She was incredibly charmed by this illusion of a woman. It made a certain sort of sense. Why would her mind create a fantasy woman who wasn't distracting?

Prospero removed her capelet from around her shoulders and draped it over Ellie, covering the strap of the immense bag Ellie carried with her. It was warm and smelled vaguely of lavender and something spicy. "You are shivering. Shock, I fear. It's not every day you travel to a new world and discover magic. We'll get you settled."

"I think at least one of us is confused," Ellie pointed out as they wound their way out of the barren meadow toward the town. "I'm expecting a rational answer, but that would be impossible if this is a coma dream."

"It is not a dream, and *I* am not confused." Prospero stepped in front of her, right there on the edge of an unfamiliar street, and smiled the sort of smile that most definitely did not belong anywhere outside of bedrooms or old classic movies. "You are in shock, but you are *also* rather remarkable."

"I don't think that this is a good idea," Ellie tried in a slightly less official-sounding voice. "Whatever *this* is . . ."

Ellie tried to ignore the three or four people surreptitiously looking at them. This, right here, was the sort of thing she avoided at all costs. Being a spectacle. Being the center of anyone's attention.

Being *interesting*.

Quietly, Ellie said, "People are watching us."

Prospero waved her hand as if she could make them all go away with the gesture. "You are obstinate, and you are a stranger in their town arguing with a powerful woman. Of course they stare."

Ellie laughed at the unexpected words. "Modesty isn't your strongest suit, huh?"

"I am a realist, Miss Brandeau." Prospero glared in the onlookers' direction. "They fear me, and they aren't sure if you are a threat or in peril."

"I'm not a *real* threat," Ellie quickly said. "I did not mean to make those snakes."

"Make snakes?"

"Out of the pavement," Ellie clarified. "No one told me I could do that."

Prospero gave her a look that could best be described as hungry, but she merely said, "Often the best learning happens when we are unaware of our limits. If I ran the college . . ." Her words drifted off. "No matter. You, Miss Brandeau, are going to be at my side, and we will see what you can do without the limits of small-minded people."

A flood of excitement filled Ellie at the thought of limitless magic, of magic at all, but she quickly tempered it. "I'm not sure what your agenda is, or if I even trust you, or if I'm awake for that matter. People don't walk into libraries with delicate teacups and leave helpless women in a heap on the floor and call them *witches*."

"Helpless?" Prospero echoed with a raised brow.

Ellie ignored her. "Women certainly don't walk into my life dressed like Hepburn or call me a *witch*."

"Well, why not? You're quite a lovely witch." Prospero looped her arm through Ellie's and started walking again. Her boots, of course, made a clattering look-at-me sound with each step.

Stunned, Ellie let herself be tugged along for almost half a block. Then she paused and said, "Why are we going so fast?"

"Time, my dear Miss Brandeau, is of the essence. I need your assistance with a matter of life and death."

Ellie shivered at the tone in Prospero's voice. "Seriously? Life or death?"

"Unfortunately, yes." Prospero looked older, wearier, and that humanity slipping into her confident visage was more effective than anything else she could've done or said or offered. "I find you essential in a problem that must be addressed."

"Tell me."

"Once we are at my house." Prospero tugged her forward again. "If we were seen, there would be consequences." She directed Ellie along the street, guiding her toward what looked like an elegant Victorian house. It was dark, somber, foreboding, albeit smaller than any Victorian home Ellie had seen in New England.

"Are you expecting violence?" Ellie whispered, looking around and noticing most people looked away from Prospero as if afraid.

"Oh, I can handle violence," Prospero said lightly as she led Ellie up the short set of stairs to what Ellie presumed was her front door. Prospero glanced at her briefly. "I have a reputation for being vicious that—while not precisely flattering—is not inaccurate. I can keep you safe if you permit it."

Swoon, Ellie's libido murmured.

Stop that, her common sense argued.

Prospero continued. "What I most need right now is you, so please come into my home."

Ellie hated that she saw herself as weak, but it was hard to fathom being the sort of person who could stand up to a force like Prospero.

Better to be swept in her wake, perhaps.

"Okay . . ." Ellie stepped inside the house, not taking note of much other than the exterior's somberness.

Directly inside, she saw a tiny woman in a bright red apron over a tailored jumpsuit. If not for the shocked look on her face, Ellie would have said something that might have been accidentally rude. The woman looked like a doll, perfectly shaped but tiny enough that an infant would outweigh her.

Prospero shoved the door shut, turning a series of locks as she said, "Bernice, I have a guest."

"You don't say," the miniature woman retorted. "I'm not so old that my vision's gone."

Prospero, fierce and assertive woman that she was, gave the woman a sheepish look. "I am anxious that we will be seen. I need no one to enter my home. No one at all."

"And who is *this* that we ought to be concerned?" The woman clapped her palms together, sending a cloud of flour into the air.

"A remedial witch who—"

"You snatched a *remedial witch*?" Bernice sounded horrified. Her voice grew higher and higher as she continued. "She's not even a graduate of the college? A brand-new witch? What were you thinking? That man's already trying to argue they ought to siphon you and—"

"What man?" Ellie interjected.

"The headmaster at the college where you are to be." Prospero took her hat from Ellie and hung it on a rack. "When new witches awaken, the headmaster and I go to retrieve them so they can attend the college."

"I see." Ellie sat down on the shoe bench. "So assuming this is not a dream, I'm truant before even beginning? Will they arrive here? The authorities, I mean."

"He'll go sideways looking for you when he realizes you're missing, then he'll come to me, and I'll magically find you." Prospero shrugged as she said it, but the look Bernice gave her was stern enough to make Ellie flinch.

"He'll know she vanished. He'll know you are involved." Bernice shook a flour-white finger at Prospero.

"And I'll truthfully tell him I found her over here in Crenshaw," Prospero rebutted with a harsher tone. "She was in the west meadow. Standing there alone and confused. What would anyone do?"

"Take her to the castle," Bernice muttered. "One of these days, you'll cross a line too far, young missy!"

Ellie leaned against the wall. This was all seeming a touch stranger than the coma dream she had expected, not that she'd thought overmuch about coma dreams, mind, but who hadn't imagined what sort of fictional dream world they'd inhabit?

"This really isn't a dream, is it? None of it?"

Bernice gave her a kindly smile. "It's not. This is your waking state. You simply feel a wee bit off because of the magic filling all your curves and corners."

"And the snakes, the pavement thing . . ." Ellie looked from one woman to the other. "That was all real. I made snakes."

"Quite a feat for a remedial witch, in fact." The tiny woman positively beamed at Ellie. "You are powerful—as is obvious in that you arrived without aid. Rare thing, *that* is."

Prospero cleared her throat. "I believe I owe you a meal, Miss Brandeau."

"And some answers," Ellie added. "Rather a lot of them."

Prospero gestured for Ellie to walk forward into a room that ought to be in a museum. The overfilled space held a Victorian-era sofa and chairs, soft oil lighting, and more tomes than even on Ellie's bookshelves.

"Come into my parlor, and I will tell you everything I can about our unique dilemma."

Said the spider to the fly.

9

Maggie

Sondre had seemingly vanished in the few minutes it took Maggie to decide to go investigate the castle. She wasn't entirely sure if that was a good or bad thing. If he was her captor, shouldn't she be relieved?

What if he was telling the truth about all of it . . . ?

Maggie was an attorney, though. Attorneys solved puzzles—because, really, that was what a legal case was. A puzzle. So she would approach this in a logical way.

She stood outside her door, seeing no one, hearing nothing. It was, in fact, a castle. Stone walls and floors, vast towering windows, and a chill that permeated everything. Against the walls were wooden benches, reminiscent of church pews.

As Maggie walked through the hallway, her steps sounded unnaturally loud. Too many scary movies had her expecting something heinous to pop out of one of the many doors that looked like hers. She counted twenty rooms. Several doors were closed, but the few that were open looked like her own room—large spaces with elegant furnishings. She debated knocking on a closed door.

"Har du gått deg vill?"

Maggie startled, having not heard the approach of the young man with the heavily accented voice. "I don't understand."

"Ah. *New*." He nodded, then he tapped his throat and under his ear, staring at her like she ought to understand.

"I'm sorry. I don't understand."

"Fix language." He tapped his throat and under his ear again.

Maggie stared at him, debating if she ought to echo that gesture as he seemed to want. He didn't *look* dangerous. He had a long thin ponytail that was bound by a series of silver clips every few inches. The hair was only from the crown and back of his head; the sides were shaved smooth. His beard was long and divided into at least three thick braids. Altogether, it gave him the look of a Viking TV show extra—except he was dressed in ragged jeans and a black T-shirt from some band.

He tilted his head and stared at her, as if she were the odd one. Forty-something-year-old attorneys were much more common than Viking-styled men. Then he smiled, and it transformed a handsome man into something near otherworldly. *He looks like someone who could be a witch. I do not.* The thought struck her as ridiculous. Witches were just people who were subjected to social injustice through history. Magic wasn't real.

So how do you explain Craig not getting hurt, her Logical Self asked.

"Unnskyld?" he said.

"What?" Maggie asked.

He tapped his throat and then under his ear yet again. Frowning, he carefully said, "To know other languages. Try now."

Maggie felt absurd, but she mimicked his action.

"Unnskyld," he said again.

Her expression must have made clear that she still didn't understand him. He frowned, stepped close, and took her hand in his. Directing her hand, he tapped her throat, the space under one ear, and then the other. "Igjen."

Maggie heard the word's translation—*again*—at the same time as the word "igjen." So she made the gesture he had demonstrated again.

"Pardon me," he said, waiting for her to respond. When she nodded, he asked, "Are you lost?"

Maggie's eyes widened. "Are you speaking English now or . . . ?"

"No. I still speak Norwegian. You hear your language; I speak in mine." He gestured between them as he spoke. "Now we can talk because of magic."

In that instant, she felt older than old. If this was real, what did that mean? She had already started over as a recently divorced single mom. She'd had to deal with being older than people who outranked her at the firm. She shook her head. Her life wasn't much, but that was where her son was. The sooner she figured this situation out, the better.

Maggie looked at him. "Are you trying to say you believe this magic stuff?"

"We are using magic right now." He smiled again, looking like she should recognize him from somewhere. "Come with me. I am exploring the castle. The acoustics are good in these halls. I can sing here." He closed his eyes and did just that, voice lifting in some sort of song she couldn't translate. As he did, drums thrummed from somewhere, and other instruments—not all familiar—wound around that thudding beat.

"Where are the other musicians?" Maggie scanned the hall for the hidden band.

"No others. More magic." The braid against his head waved slightly as he nodded, looking exceptionally self-satisfied. "This song in my head comes alive. Magic."

Maggie nodded. "Are you . . . new to here?"

"New witch? *Ja.*" He opened his arms. "Met a few other witches. I am Axell."

"Maggie."

"Come, Maggie." Axell walked away; his clomping combat boots seemed out of place in the castle's old-world elegance. "We are having grog in the village soon."

She looked around and saw Sondre leaning on a wall, watching them. She could swear he hadn't been there before this.

"Go make friends, Margaret." He smiled at her, seeming far friendlier than she knew what to do with, and gestured her onward. "Axell has been truthful with you, as have I."

Then, as she watched, he vanished like some over-muscled Cheshire cat.

"We'll learn how to do that soon, too," said another man, this one looking like he might topple from lack of muscle. He had a wiry look, as if he'd existed without ever seeing a gym or possibly the sunlight. "I'm Dan. Same witch class as you and Axell and the others. Are you okay?"

Maggie looked at Dan. "Doesn't this all just seem impossible?"

Dan shrugged. "Man, I had *cancer* and was dying so . . . I'll take impossible over death."

As Dan smiled, he still looked wan, like he had recently escaped a hospital bed, thin and pale. Mid-thirties at best. Hapless.

"Come," Axell called, poking his head around a corner that housed a suit of armor; it looked like the Norwegian's head appeared from within the metallic suit's ribcage.

Maggie said nothing as she walked toward him, taking in the stone walls and massive windows. A few had stained glass that cast bright jewel-toned light on the dark walls and floor.

Dan loped along at her side.

Axell smiled extra-wide as he saw them, but Maggie was fairly sure his smile was solely for Dan. Feeling like a third wheel, she asked, "How many others?"

"At least five we know of," Dan said. "There's a couple still in their cloisters."

"Cloisters?" Maggie echoed.

"Rooms." Axell shot a fond look at the sickly pale guy even as he corrected him.

"The main door is this way," Dan said. "Want to go grab a drink with us?"

The sound of her own heartbeat was enough to block out everything. Freedom? That easy? "We can just leave?"

"No, but he is friendly with the hobs," Axell said softly, his accent making his voice somehow more melodic.

"The *hobs*?"

"Ja," Axell said, and she realized he could choose to have his words stay untranslated, too.

Admit it, Mags, this is pretty cool, she thought.

Not without my son, she reminded herself. That was the crux of it: maybe magic towns were pretty amazing, but Maggie had passed on many things that were amazing. She made a vow to her son that he would always come first to her. *I will get back to him.*

Dan flashed them a grin and walked toward the massive door of the castle, what appeared to be the main door. It was a towering thing, stretching easily twelve feet tall, and the door handle looked like ivy vines had been dipped in iron. Sharp leaves jutted out.

As Dan reached for the handle, the iron leaves extended to hold fast around his wrist.

"Dan!" Maggie stepped up, maternal instinct rising like a sudden fire for this stranger.

"It's cool," he called out. "Clance?"

A miniature man appeared. No larger than a baby, but fully shaped and wizened. He wore a stylish pin-striped suit and fedora, like a tiny gangster, and Maggie could swear he winked at her.

"What did you do this time?" The little man snapped his fingers at the door, and the metal vine and leaves retracted. "This'un will be getting himself killed at the rate he tests the locks."

"Oh, was that locked, Clancy?" Dan widened his eyes as if surprised.

"You know it was." Clancy shook his head. "Go on with you. That man is already at the pub, so mind yourselves there. After tonight, there'll be all the rules and whatnots. And don't be telling the headmaster that I unlocked the door again, you hear?"

"You're the best, Clance." Dan tugged the giant door, which barely budged. "A little help?"

Axell pulled the door open, as Dan eyed the Norwegian's biceps in a way that made Maggie suspect Dan's true agenda had been met. The two young men were clearly interested in one another, and only Maggie's desire to figure out how to escape had her willing to tromp along with them.

Outside the castle were several steps and at their base was a path. It was lined with stones that had long since sunken into the ground, making it resemble an uneven sidewalk that stretched from the castle—where the path was easily six feet across in a V-shaped mouth—to a more reasonable four-foot-wide path that undulated down a hill toward a valley where lights from shops winked like an invitation. To the left and right were thick woods. There were paths into them, worn by footsteps, but the whole of the forest was overgrown like no one had ever entered there.

"I feel like Red Riding Hood," Maggie muttered.

"Axell could be the huntsman to keep us safe," Dan piped up cheerily. "I'm not suited for a heroic role."

Axell draped an arm over Dan's bony shoulders. "You would be the wolf."

Maggie rolled her eyes as she stepped in front of them. Maybe they were supposed to stay in the castle because there was something lurking in the woods. Maybe they were in danger, but so was her son. The first step to getting home was to get the lay of the land, so whatever was out there would have to deal with one angry mama if it popped out of the woods.

She snatched up a stick, thick enough to work like a baseball bat if she needed. Not her first choice for a weapon, but it'd do in a pinch. She walked a little faster as they cut through the woods, listening for sounds and scanning for movement.

Behind her, Dan and Axell spoke softly. About twenty minutes passed, and the woods gave way to barren fields and a meadow, and then the town began abruptly. She glanced back at the hilltop where the giant castle stood with its towers jutting into cloudy blue-gray skies.

As they walked, Maggie noted several smaller towers speared up out of the village, one with a decided tilt as if it had been constructed by children with blocks. If it were any taller, she suspected it would snap in half from the pressure of that tilt.

Here at the edge of the town, the streets were reminiscent of medieval streets, cobblestone or something, that would keep the mud somewhat under control. Not the sort of smooth paved sidewalks she was used to.

Wooden store signs announced a milliner, a shoe shop, a bakery, and a market. In the distance, she could see a bank, another bakery, and a shop labeled "bootie-tique." *Underwear maybe?* She wasn't sure, but she had little interest in staying in this Brigadoon knockoff to find out.

"Mead and wine this way." Axell stepped around her. Apparently, he had a goal. "When I was on tour in the band's early years, I played medieval festivals. Much more authentic, but this is good."

"He was famous, you know," Dan whispered. "Toured the world with his band."

Maggie nodded. She had zero interest in fame or tours or even mead—although a glass of wine didn't sound half bad. She followed the guys to a building labeled THE TAVERN OF NO REPUTE.

Inside, she came to a full stop at the wall of sound and heat. From outside, it hadn't sounded like it was busy. Inside was another matter altogether. The bar was reminiscent of any number of European taverns—dark by design, brick and stone walls that dampened the room and muffled the sound, and exposed rough-hewn beams that looked like they might crack at any moment. A crackling fire and raucous patrons added a sort of timelessness to the moment.

On the bar itself, people appeared to be rolling what looked like badgers. *Why are there badgers?* She looked around. This was weirder than the castle and the language thing.

"Where *are* we?" Maggie asked no one in particular.

"The tavern," a familiar voice said to her left. "Although I thought you'd be exploring the castle."

Maggie looked over her shoulder to see Sondre. He held out a stone mug of some sort of amber-hued liquid. She accepted it and took a long drink. She held his gaze. "I'm not apologizing."

He laughed.

"Magic might be real, but I'm not apologizing." She took another drink. "Seriously, what the fuck is going on? I'm in the wrong world and supposed to go to community college for witches? I did college *and* law school already."

He bodily blocked her from the rest of the bar. "Why do I get the feeling that you are going to be a problem, Margaret?"

"You're an excellent judge of character?"

Sondre shook his head. "I allowed three students to end up in a bar the night before classes started."

She looked past him, where loud cheers rose up as a badger did a double flip into a vat of something that splashed up out of the barrel. "Why?"

He held her gaze. "You interest me."

Maggie had to admit there was something tempting there. The hint of the tattoo on his throat, the sheer size of the man, the danger that rolled off him like a physical force—

Bad idea.

Her taste was remarkably consistent: Maggie Lynch liked bad men. Put her in a crowd of hundreds, and her internal radar led her unerringly to the worst idea in the room. Her entire life was a series of criminals of varying degrees—and then a law degree.

Maggie looked past Sondre to where Dan and Axell were watching the badger rolling. Nothing about this place made sense. The problem was she had no idea where Crenshaw was, how to get out, or anything else.

What she did know was the mountain of a man in front of her was giving her a look that wasn't hard to interpret. *What's the harm in seducing the answers out of him?* Anything it took to get home to protect her son was an option. Years ago, she'd come to terms with her ruthless streak, and the thing that made Maggie feel the most ruthless was the safety of her son. Nothing and no one would keep him from her—and if she was a bona fide witch? Well, that was just more skills to use to rescue her kid.

Leon tried to kill us both. Now Craig is with him.

"So man-witch, suppose I say that I accept that I'm a witch, what exactly does that mean?" She put a hand on his wrist. "And how do I use that to get out of here?"

"Use *me*, you mean."

"Maybe, but we can have fun along the way . . ." Maggie let her gaze sweep over him. "Both of us. Name your terms."

Sondre looked down at her hand, then back at her. "You're teasing the wrong person, Margaret."

"There has to be a way to *un*witch me." Maggie bit her lip and offered, "What would it take, Sondre, for you to set me free of this place?"

"I'm not that sort of man."

Maggie laughed. "Darlin', I've spent my life around people who broke the rules to get what they wanted. Turns out *everyone* is that sort of person given the right incentive."

Sondre wrapped an arm around her waist and pulled her close. "You are a menace, Margaret."

"I am a mother trying to get to my kid. No one is more determined than a mom." Maggie met his gaze levelly. "So are you going to help me, or do I need to go around you?"

The respect in his gaze told her all she needed. And as far as costs went, seducing a handsome man wasn't a steep one at all.

10
Prospero

There was something intrinsically nerve-racking about having Elleanor Brandeau in her sitting room, but Prospero had lived as a witch in Crenshaw for over a century. She should be able to share tea with a beautiful woman without feeling so unraveled. And Miss Brandeau's beauty was unassuming: soft brown hair, soft brown eyes, and enough delicate curves to her that Prospero wanted to get lost exploring the rises and falls of her body—but attraction wasn't reason enough to shift her priorities, even though that spark of mischief in Miss Brandeau's eyes promised a wit to go along with the beauty.

She's just another witch. Even if she was the line I couldn't cross, Prospero's mind whispered.

There was no polite way to say, "Sorry I considered making your heart stop," especially as Ellie had written it off as a panic attack. It hadn't been a malicious act. Prospero simply had tried to awaken her magic early.

What would Miss Brandeau say if she knew?

Currently, she sat on one of the overstuffed blue chairs that Prospero favored. Her gaze darted around the room as if she were cataloguing the oval mirror, vases with a few fresh flowers, thick silk drapes in a near-garish shade of violet, and assorted leather-bound books with no names on the spine. The latter held Miss Brandeau's eyes a little longer, although as she looked around the room, she paused and made note of the rest as well—and Prospero wanted to know what she was thinking.

"No one comes here," Prospero mused. "I welcome your thoughts."

"Your witch village?" Miss Brandeau teased, as if the idea was preposterous.

"My home." Prospero gestured at the tea carafe, then at the lid of the lavender Earl Grey tea she enjoyed on the rare occasions she had to indulge in luxuries. "I find myself breaking any manner of rules over you, Miss Brandeau."

"Because I'm a witch," Miss Brandeau filled in. "Surely, that's not so unusual in your witch town."

"Because you are a *singular* witch, an anomaly," Prospero corrected. "Magic itself is normal here. It is the way of your new home. Things here are done by, shaped by, managed by magic."

"Because we are all witches?" Miss Brandeau watched in curious silence as Prospero prepared tea.

"Yes, everyone in Crenshaw is a witch or a hob."

"But you don't usually steal new witches," Miss Brandeau clarified. "Your roommate"—she nodded in the foyer's direction—"mentioned that."

"New witches attend the college, learn laws and their magical strengths." Prospero debated how much to reveal so soon, but time was of the essence, and if the prophecy declared Miss Brandeau essential, the question before them was *why*. "There was a prophecy about you, however."

Prospero replayed the whole prophecy in her mind: *The woman who will change everything is called Elleanor Brandeau. She's in the Barbarian Lands, refusing her innate magic. If you don't awaken her, Crenshaw will suffer.* And though she was dubious of any one person changing the world, Prospero had yet to see any of Cassandra's prophecies fail. If she said Prospero needed to awaken this woman's magic, Prospero had told herself she *had to* make a serious attempt on her life. Magic only awakened if one was in imminent risk of death; no minor thing would work.

Prospero wasn't sure what to say to Miss Brandeau.

What about her is so unusual?

And how do I figure that out?

When Prospero said nothing more, Miss Brandeau ordered, "Tell me the crisis that's caused you to hide me here."

Prospero felt as if she were about to argue before their governing body. She smoothed her trouser legs down, sat taller, and pronounced, "Our water and worsening air pose a growing problem, a conflict that has no answer. We cannot move en masse. Where would we go? If we open our borders, we risk conflict with non-magic users—although there are others who argue for that very thing. The New Economists think we must go to *that* world, especially now that we are trapped in a poisonous place." Prospero's voice drifted off. "Witches cannot thrive around non-witches, however. That is my stance."

"And what are you called?"

"A Traditionalist." Prospero frowned. "The New Economists want to war with the neighbors, simply take what we need, but that way lies devastation of all witches in my opinion."

Miss Brandeau stood and paced as she listened.

Prospero swung her hand downward, as if to hit a lectern or table, but she stopped short of the gesture. "To add to the problem, we *must* have growth in population if we are to survive. We *require* immigrants so we can have the resources to purify the water we have."

"Resources means magic?"

"Yes, magic," Prospero agreed. "Some people who arrive here will have their magic added to the current of energy that sustains our community. Those who don't stay must leave their magic behind."

"So I could go home?" Miss Brandeau asked. "I could reject this whole witch thing?"

Prospero shrugged. She had little desire to tell Miss Brandeau that some people were too magical to be siphoned, so she deflected that question with, "There's a whole speech at the college."

Miss Brandeau laughed unexpectedly. "Not a fan of the college?"

"The headmaster would love to see me destroyed." Prospero kept her tone mild, but the fear she might be adding to his ammunition against her added a wobble to her voice. "Hiding you from them would not earn me grace."

For a moment, Miss Brandeau paused. Like any witch, she could undoubtedly hear the raw truth in Prospero's admission. "And yet here I am."

"Would *you* sacrifice yourself for a greater good, Miss Brandeau? For love? For country?" Prospero asked, although she suspected she knew the answer.

"Who wouldn't?" Miss Brandeau said lightly.

Then Prospero smiled. "That is why you are worth the risk."

Miss Brandeau paused her pacing, and for a moment, Prospero thought she might ask the normal sorts of things, focus on her own situation, but instead, she asked, "Are there options that have worked to improve the water?"

Prospero's smile widened. Perhaps it was her era of origin, but she found herself eternally attracted to women who looked at a problem as a puzzle to solve. Miss Brandeau's eyes sparkled as she analyzed the situation, which was rather more attractive to Prospero than those people who doused themselves in perfumes and wore scanty clothing.

Intellect was irresistible to Prospero.

Miss Brandeau sat down again, perched like a bird at the edge of the seat, and leveled a stern look at Prospero. "You aren't telling me where I fit in—or what your role is. Who *are* you, Prospero?"

Prospero felt as if that question struck her physically. "I am a witch who is feared, hated, and grudgingly tolerated. All witches have a propensity for a type of magic, but mine is frightening to many people here."

"You do not want me to know what you are capable of," Miss Brandeau surmised.

"I find that I want you to *like* me," Prospero admitted awkwardly. "Why?"

Prospero was not sure how exactly to answer that question, so she decided to ignore it. "I am hoping you will help me. This is my home and has been so for almost a century and a half. Crenshaw is home, cause, and country. I want Crenshaw to survive, and all of our current and future witches with it. And I know that you are a part of the solution . . . I just don't know how."

Miss Brandeau paused before saying, "So you knew I was a witch when we kissed. That day at the library. You knew. Was that why . . ."

Prospero tensed. *I came to try to kill you. Not really, but not* not *really* sounded like the wrong admission, but that was the crux of it. She'd been there to awaken Ellie's magic. Saying that, however, meant admitting how she'd attempted to do so. It made Prospero an enemy of sorts. That wouldn't do.

But then Miss Brandeau continued with, "You asked to see me next time because you knew I'd come *here!*" It was an altogether nicer conclusion than the truth.

"There was a prophecy about y—"

"*Me?* I'm not exactly a superhero." Miss Brandeau gestured at herself, from the top of her average brown hair to her average physique to her sensible shoes. She had no idea she was lovely, or at the least, seemed determined not to admit it. Instead she said, "I've read plenty of witchy books, obviously, but unless you need rapid alphabetization skills or semiphotographic memory or research prowess . . ." She finished with a shrug. "I'm not your person."

"You are, though." Prospero gestured and the tea poured itself neatly into two cups. "Sugar? Cream?"

"Black." Miss Brandeau watched the levitating teapot and cups intently, eyes wide with surprise.

Prospero directed the floating cup toward Miss Brandeau before she added two cubes of precious sugar to her own cup, stirring it with a swirl of her finger in the air. The whole process was done without touching pot, cup, or sugar by hand. "Prophecies are never wrong, Miss Brandeau. Perhaps it's your new perspective on the problem, or maybe it's the nature of your magic—"

"The nature?"

"As I said, all witches have an affinity for a different manifestation of magic. We can all do the basics—levitating objects, brief teleportation—but each witch has a skill that's rather *more*. Plus, we all have improved health that creates longevity." Prospero tried to keep her words calm.

Miss Brandeau sipped her tea, holding the cup in her hands and watching Prospero warily now. "So yours is a dangerous skill." She nodded to herself. "Good at violence, you said."

"True."

Miss Brandeau stood and paced to a drape-covered window. "You're asking me to break rules inside a world I don't even know so far." She glanced back at Prospero. "And maybe it's because I am a witch after all, but I can tell you're hiding things." She motioned to the drapes. "May I open this?"

Prospero stayed on her settee. "Of course. The windows are charmed to prevent others from looking inside."

"Of course they are." Miss Brandeau smiled. "Secretive. You are like this, then. Always?"

"Perhaps."

Once Miss Brandeau pushed back the drapes, Prospero tried not to stare at her as she watched the town bustle by. The city was rather medieval-meets-faux modern. Most residents never entered the Barbarian Lands from whence they came once they immigrated to Crenshaw. The town layout included an open plaza nearby, and the sidewalks and streets were cobblestone. The ground was worn smooth by countless feet, and the city center—where residents gathered and gossiped—took up a giant square space.

"You can explore once you are settled," Prospero mentioned when Miss Brandeau said nothing.

Miss Brandeau gestured to a small crowd. "They're all witches then. Those people."

"Yes."

Miss Brandeau let the curtain fall shut with a *thump.* The drapes were a heavy, muffling weight that enabled Prospero to still have her peace despite where she lived. Miss Brandeau stared at her as she added, "I feel like I ought to ask about the hobs or the witches or the crisis. But that's not where my mind keeps going."

Prospero's throat was dry. There was a bit of foolishness to the reaction. She'd bedded more women than she dared imagine back in her pre-witch life, but after a century of living in a witch community, there were rarely any *new* women of interest. There certainly weren't any who had made her unable to fulfill her vow to Crenshaw.

Until now.

"What do you want to ask?" Prospero whispered.

Miss Brandeau held her gaze. "If I will get to kiss you again."

11
Maggie

Maggie let herself be carried forward with Sondre, not bothering to suggest he slow his pace as they moved toward a shadowed alcove in the bar.

"I was confused when I arrived, too." Sondre gave her a kind look. "One minute I was feeling this stabbing pain, and the next . . . here I am. Strange place. Strange people. I understand how you feel. A lot of people *like* the weirdness instantly, but I wasn't one of them." He laughed in that way that sounded more irritated than amused. "My current job is a punishment. Typically that is not the case with work here in Crenshaw, though. You were a lawmaker, correct?"

Maggie stiffened. "Am. I *am* a lawyer."

Sondre sighed. "You sound a lot like me, Margaret. I was a soldier, but there's no call for that in Crenshaw. Perhaps, there are roles you could fill in the Congress of Magic. Taking notes or—"

"I'm not a secretary, Sondre. I'm a fucking lawyer, and a damn good one at that." Maggie shot the man a glare. Honestly, it wasn't fair he was both dreadfully handsome and infuriating. Was sexy and calming an impossible combination? Hell, she'd appreciate just sane and sexy.

"Then perhaps you would best understand if I explained in terms of contracts. You're in Crenshaw due to the awakening of latent magical traits," Sondre said in a dry tone. "These traits mean that, in due course, you will decide whether to remain here or return to your world. There is a contract that all witches must adhere to, and part of that is attending the College of Remedial Magic. After that, you will either stay or be siphoned—"

"That sounds barbaric."

"It can be."

Maggie swallowed her questions as Sondre swept an arm out to gesture toward the town outside the window. To say it was peculiar was the politest thing she could have managed. Up close like this, it looked like a cross between a film set and costumed theme festival or theme park, with people who were mostly embracing the chance to wear a costume but a few scattered folks who were thoroughly rejecting it. One woman had on a medieval-style dress, and another wore a Victorian-era dress but with tennis shoes.

"A lot of robes and dresses," she finally murmured.

"Fashion." He shrugged. "It shifts, but currently the trend is historic, ridiculous gowns and towering hats. Those of us who are more serious stick with some sort of robe."

He led her onto a deck that rather quickly emptied when he shot a round of glares at the people out there.

Once the drinkers were all gone, Sondre pronounced, "You must go through the college, Margaret. After that, if you choose to leave here, they'll send you back. Until then, this is where you are."

Maggie closed her eyes against a flood of tears. "My son needs me. Now."

She hopped over the railing and started walking through the town. There was an apartment building that jutted upward, laundry flapping in the breeze, and across the way was a building labeled "food distribution." A line of people stood there, shuffling and waiting. She glanced to the left and found a furniture maker, a potter, a clothing exchange, and an apothecary.

Maggie's knees were giving out. Nothing made sense. *How will I get home? What if Leon hurts Craig?* He'd been willing to kill both of them in that accident. *Why would I think my son is safe now?*

"I have you," Sondre murmured, catching her before she fell. "You can't get home to your son right now."

"He's in danger," she said. "Can't someone go get him or—?"

"We have people. A witch who can alter minds. I can send her to make sure his father—he's the threat?" Sondre paused until Maggie nodded. "I can send her to be sure Craig is safe. You just need to get through college, and then you might be reunited with him, forget us entirely, or—"

"Or he can come here? That could work, right?" Maggie looked at shops for baked goods and seafood, woven blankets, and odd hats. "Are there trade schools? Or what? I can't imagine there are full university plans." She paused, thinking about what that would mean for Craig.

What if we stayed here? Witch land or whatever might be okay. Then Craig wouldn't ever have to see Leon.

"If I do well at this college, I stay here, right?"

"Yes."

Maggie looked around again, thinking about the future. Crenshaw was nearly medieval, no modern universities or hospitals in sight, no cars or even skateboards. The youngest person nearby appeared to be in her twenties—not a baby in sight, or a pregnant person. It was evening, though, and they were outside a bar.

"I'd need to figure out a job, money, a place for Craig and me . . ." Maggie started to reassess the potential for a life here.

"We can go over that part later," Sondre answered quietly. "The College of Remedial Magic will cover not only magic but the society and laws here in Crenshaw, too."

She took a deep breath. Leon always complained she charged at problems and made things worse by not letting the dust settle. Maybe he was a little bit right? Maybe she should exhale and let her brain catch up to the fact magic was real.

"I have questions."

"And I will answer every last one, but not today. Right now, you're still at risk of becoming volatile," Sondre said kindly. "You wouldn't want to hurt anyone with a burst of unpredictable magic. Magic can be *deadly*, Maggie. So we'll sort your situation out—and the other students'—once we're all together. That's the point of the college. You'll learn about the rules and ways of Crenshaw, where you will each fit, and get a handle on your magic."

Maggie glanced at him. Nothing he said *felt* untrue to her, but at the same time, she wasn't an average trusting person. She was an attorney who had an ex who worked for the vilest of criminals.

"But my son isn't freaking out about my disappearance? Or in peril right now?"

"He is not," Sondre said. "There are witches who handle those details—any relations, jobs, anyone who might be panicking at a witch's awakening. Mind magic."

"Not like *kill* them, though?" she pressed.

"Adjust memories so they are calm," Sondre said. "There is a witch called Prospero. She owes me a favor, and if you want, I can send her to verify that your son's caretaker isn't a danger to him."

"I do want that. Name your price."

Sondre gave her an unreadable look. "What sort of men are you used to, Margaret? I would not exploit you to make your son safer."

His words still felt true, and the silver lining hit her then. "If I stay here, the custody battle will be resolved. Once we're both here, Craig won't have to deal with hopping between me and his louse of a father!"

Sondre nodded once. "That would be true."

Maggie pressed the topic a bit further. "So to be clear, all I need to do is adjust to this magic thing, and then we can discuss Craig's and my future?"

"Yes."

The single word also rang true, and so for now, Maggie put her questions aside. Maybe magic wasn't so terrible if she could protect her son from his father's influence. Maybe this could be like a holiday, especially if there was a witch who could do mind magic.

Sondre stayed silent and still, not leading her deeper into the town. His arm tightened around her, not to keep her from running but like a steady presence, and Maggie hated how much she liked it. She was strong, independent, and capable.

And he felt like a statue with marbled muscles.

Maggie took a deep breath, stepping away from Sondre. His gaze swept her from her slightly too-curvy hips to her not-at-all-flat-because-she-once-had-a-baby stomach. He said, "Once classes begin, there are rules, but to-day . . . I *was* hoping to share a drink with you."

Without the complication of thinking he was a crazed kidnapper, Maggie could admit that he seemed like he might not be a horrible person. She still suspected that Sondre had some darker traits she simply wasn't seeing yet; her taste in men was typically more monster than mouse.

But he didn't accept my offer of seduction in exchange for rescue.

"Coincidentally, if I have a night off, I was thinking of enjoying a drink and finding someone to burn the sheets up with," she said in that tone that worked wonders in court. Casual, as if it was no big deal. "I already had a drink."

Maggie felt like the girl she'd been when she was picking up men before she was married, bold and unembarrassed. Never mind the extra padding. Never mind the dangerous ex-husband or complications. She started to turn away as she said, "But you turned down my offer earlier, so maybe I'll go back in—"

He caught her by the hip as she was mid-pivot. "I am not interested in *coerced* sex, Maggie, but sex without strings? That is another matter."

She leaned in and put a hand on his chest. "I'm facing a custody battle, so I've been left to my own devices for over a year. Does Crenshaw have a motel? Or a back way to the headmaster's rooms?"

Sondre wrapped his arms around her. "Close your eyes."

She tilted her head up for a kiss, but instead she felt like her whole body was squeezed tightly and released. When she opened her eyes, she was in a larger version of her own room, one that smelled unmistakably of mead and sandalwood.

"Ho-ly fuck." She stepped out of his arms. This was the apartment version of her room, but more to the point, they had just . . . *popped*? *Magicked*? *Teleported*?

Sondre watched her warily.

"Did we—we fucking teleported, didn't we? That was magic," she exclaimed, walking forward to stare out the window to the village where they just were.

"Yes." He was still watching her, but he looked marginally calmer.

Maggie laughed. This was real. Absurdly, impossibly, undeniably real. Then she stalked toward Sondre, high on the possibilities in front of her—a holiday, a few orgasms, and then she'd rescue her son, and he'd grow up in a magical new world.

I deserve a holiday, she told herself. *What's the harm?*

"Impress me, man-witch." She reached out to grasp a fistful of his robe with one hand and wrapped the other around the back of his neck to guide him down for a kiss. Somewhere along the way, the cloth in her hand vanished, and she flattened her hand onto bare skin.

A pair of trousers and a shirt were on the nearby dresser, along with the robe she'd just been grabbing. Sondre was suddenly naked.

Not one to refuse a challenge, Maggie stepped back, stripping while she appreciated the man in front of her. A flicker of self-doubt threatened to rise up, but Sondre's visible reaction erased her doubt before it fully formed.

He lifted her, hands under her thighs as she wrapped her legs around his hips. "I take back every insult I hurled at you."

"I could be convinced to retract mine, too." Maggie leaned close to his ear and added, "One canceled insult for every orgasm you give me . . . but there were a *lot* of insults. You need to work for it."

Sondre tossed her onto the bed and stared down at her approvingly. "I love modern women sometimes."

12

Dan

Unlike Axell, Dan wasn't particularly good at drinking. In less than an hour, he'd come to realize that he probably ought to have stopped two drinks ago.

One drink drunk, that's me.

Dan half expected Maggie to come back, but then again, she had left with the headmaster—and Sondre wasn't acting particularly professorial when he'd been looking at her.

"We brought her out of the castle to a badger-and-witch-filled bar. And we misplaced her." Dan looked around the bar. The people here were a strange mix. One woman wore a dress that was a wonder of crystal beads that made a pleasant clattering this close, like she'd been born a century before him when bathtub gin was a thing. Another woman nearby was fanning herself with what looked like a hand-painted antique fan. Aside from that, she looked more modern than the rest of the crowd. Her navy shirtdress was faded with age, but there was a genuine vintage look to it. Tight at the waist, tighter on the bosom, and flaring from the hips, her ensemble looked like she'd walked out of a tavern from World War II.

"Should we go after Maggie?" Dan asked, looking back at his drinking partner.

Sondre is a bad guy, he thought. Exactly how bad was the question. He'd seemed nice, but also like he was on the villain team, not the hero side. *Do villains do only bad things?*

"She is fine," Axell said for the third time. "Grown adult, Daniel."

The way he said "Daniel" was as if all the vowels needed to be enunciated, not quite how American English worked. Dan stared at him from over a mug of draft beer, which he wasn't ever terribly fond of. This beer was a bit extra-watery with a strange eggy undertone.

"We probably shouldn't mention that they left together," Dan said after a few moments. "I don't think teachers are to . . . be *with* students."

"He is not a teacher." Axell spun on his stool and leaned so his back was to the bartender. He gave Dan an appraising look, one that almost made Dan want to offer the world to him, but it was an odd thing to have a Viking god look at him with interest. But then Axell said, "You would go with him."

Dan took a long drink of his beer. "I don't think so. He's pretty but straight."

"Move your glass this way more." Axell nodded at a badger who was on the bar stealing sips of Dan's glass. "The badger is drinking more than you."

We're drinking with a badger . . .

"You are like a hungry one," Axell added. "Waiting for scraps. Why not ask for the meal?"

Dan was mostly sure he understood what Axell said—asking for attention instead of everything—but he wasn't exactly built like Sondre or Axell or any number of witches in the bar. He was thin from too many years of illness. Not terribly sexy, in his opinion.

"There are probably other gay men in here if you are looking." Dan looked around the bar. "Sondre said it's cool to be like us here."

"I am not gay, Daniel. I am *pan*sexual, *all* sexual." Axell grinned like he'd made a joke. He was somehow sprawled over the stool like the uncomfortable wooden thing was a comfortable sofa. "Are you offering to help me meet people? Even though *you* are here at my side?"

"I don't know."

"A meal, Daniel. Not scraps. Why not ask for it?" Axell didn't exactly gesture at himself, suggesting he was the "meal" in question, but Dan was clear enough on his meaning.

Why can't he offer instead of telling me to ask?

Dan looked away from the splayed legs and complete lack of body fat. He wouldn't call Axell athletic, but he was tight. *Out of my league.*

"Did you run around a lot on stage?"

"This is what you ask me?" Axell paused and when Dan nodded, he continued. "Yes. And run in the street and park. I hate running but the studio liked a certain look." Axell shrugged, as if being told how to look was fine by him. "I was the object to them. Many times no shirts on the stage. Many photos of me with people after the show. Men, women, both. Good for sales. Good for not having stress." He grinned then. "No meals—no *relationships*—but plenty of buffets."

"Oh." Dan tried to keep the images of such things out of his head even as Axell grinned as if he knew exactly what thoughts Dan was trying not to think.

"Tell me about what you did in America." Axell had a way of phrasing questions like orders.

"Tried not to die." Dan shrugged like it was no big deal. To some degree, pretending was how he coped—*yes, I am constantly wondering if the cancer is back. Head cold? Or cancer? Flu? Or cancer?* Every ache was suspect. Every extra-fatigued day. Every low-energy day. Every new pain. And at the same time, he resented it, resented people who had their health and did stupid shit to risk everything.

"Magic stops dying," Axell said mildly. "What would you die of?"

"Cancer."

"Genetics? Did you lose family from a cancer?" Axell watched him as he spoke, not looking around at all the other witches in the bar, just at Dan.

"No. *I* had cancer," Dan clarified. People reacted to that sentence awkwardly, either fumbling words or blurting pity. After a lifetime of pity, Dan was over it—and he didn't want a pity flirtation.

"Cancer is bad," Axell said with a nod. "It is good you are a witch, ja?"

Dan grinned and echoed, "Ja."

Axell gave him a look. "You mock my words."

"You're built like a Viking god and are calm no matter what, Axell. I need to mock *something*, or I'll feel ragingly insecure." Dan shrugged. He glanced at a badger that was swinging from a trapeze overhead.

Axell shook his head. "There I traveled and sang, and had much sex, but here . . . I am a student. No different than you."

"So if we met there?"

Axell shrugged. "Depends on when. I had *much* sex. After a show . . . I had energy, you see, but when people said untrue things, I knew. So just the sex. Not dating. They did not say untrue things about my singing, ja?"

Dan chuckled. "Must be a witch thing. I could tell when people lied, too."

Axell caught his gaze. "So you know I do not lie to you now."

It was a simple statement, an obvious one at that, but it sucked the air out of Dan's lungs. He *did* know that Axell wasn't lying, that he was interested in Dan, and that made everything shift. The noise of the bar, the plethora of badgers, all of it faded in that moment.

"Ask me, Daniel."

"Would you like to go on a date sometime?" Dan said, feeling anxious that despite the conversations they had shared the last few days this was a setup of some sort.

Axell's answering smile made all the anxiety vanish. "It is just us here together, ja? This *is* a date, Daniel."

"Oh." Dan took a gulp of his beer.

"A date should move closer." Axell lifted his arm, inviting Dan to slide closer.

When Dan leaned slightly nearer, Axell sighed, tucked a foot under the rung of the barstool, and pulled it toward him, all but dumping Dan into his arms. "Better, Daniel. This is better, ja?"

"Ja," Daniel echoed again, gratified by the laugh that Axell let out.

I love being a witch. No cancer. A gorgeous man who seems to like me. Everything would be perfect if he could stay in Crenshaw. *Whatever it takes. Whatever the cost. I'm never going back to my old life.*

13
Ellie

There was something oddly energizing about the whole magic-is-real, here's-a-gorgeous-woman-hiding-secrets, and—oh yes—*there's-a-prophecy* business. Ellie stood in what appeared to be a Victorian sitting room with a Victorian witch who wanted to break all the rules to save this peculiar community. Bravery was obscenely sexy to Ellie. Passion for a cause? Sexy. The obvious battle Prospero was having with herself as she tried to sound reasonable and convincing? Still sexy.

And all Ellie could think about was kissing Prospero. "Dire straits, dangerous witch . . . it's all so very *much*. Seriously, though, I catalog books, bake scones, and sometimes, when I feel particularly saucy, I paint my nails bright colors."

"You're probably more overwhelmed since I didn't give you time for your magic to settle."

"Like sediment or something?" Ellie snarked.

"Yes, Miss Brandeau. You may feel a little tipsy, perhaps?" Prospero motioned her to the chair. "That explains the urge to ki—"

"*Or* I might just find you attractive." Ellie's desire to be swept off her feet was obviously going nowhere just then.

"Is there anything in your life that you care for enough to want to risk everything?"

"No. I don't think so. . . . Maybe my aunt. Hestia. She was an archaeologist, and she vanished for a few years until—"

"You're Hestia's niece." Prospero's eyes widened. "I haven't thought about her in years."

"You know my aunt?"

"Archaeologist with more attitude than caution?" Prospero laughed. "She was here for a few years until . . ." Her words faded. "She begged to go home. To give up her magic and go back for . . ."

"Me."

Prospero nodded. "Your parents had—"

"Died. Orphaned me. Yes, that." Ellie stiffened, expecting the wave of pity that usually followed, but it didn't come.

"Hestia adored you." Prospero offered her a small smile. "She spoke of you often."

"So you understand why I will need to go home once I help you with your 'save the witches' campaign," Ellie said in her most sensible voice. "I'll help, though, before I go home."

Ellie braced for arguments or objections, but instead, Prospero said, "I think we need to try to go over to the Barbarian Lands to find out why you matter to this world." Her voice was half a whisper, as if there were spies lurking nearby.

"Is that legal? For witches?" Ellie asked, knowing the answer.

"Not unless they are retrieving a newly wakened witch," Prospero admitted.

"Do you break a lot of laws?" Ellie thought about the fact that Prospero, by her own admission, was not to hop between worlds.

"For you? For Crenshaw's survival? I will break whatever law I must."

Swoon. Ellie's entire being—heart and mind and other parts—was smitten by the passion in that declaration. *Maybe I'll get my swept-off-my-feet romance for a little while after all.*

Prospero stood. She looked as if she wanted to say or do something to ease the panic that Ellie suspected she ought to feel right about now, but Ellie wasn't panicking. Instead she felt energized.

She stared at Prospero as the piece clicked into place. "This is where my aunt was. The missing . . . this is where *they* go."

"Yes."

"And I'm . . . missing." Ellie closed her eyes and counted to ten. It was one of the tricks she'd adopted to keep her very impulsive streak in check. It had always worked. The people who went missing were peculiar, bold, adventurous—like Hestia.

Like me.

Ellie opened her eyes and laughed. "I'm *missing*!" She continued laughing. "I'm missing over here, too. Ellie the Missing."

After all the years of trying to be sensible, Ellie had failed spectacularly. She was right where she'd tried to avoid—but from where she sat, sliding slowly to the floor and staring up at Prospero, it wasn't anywhere near as bad as she'd feared.

Giddiness washed over her now.

"Miss Brandeau," Prospero said, squatting down to pull Ellie a bit more upright. "Why are you in a heap at my feet yet again?"

"Magic?" Ellie suggested.

"Yes, actually." Prospero brushed Ellie's hair back. "Tomorrow when you're sensible, we shall plan."

Ellie nodded. "Then I'll have an adventure and go home."

"Is that what you truly want? What you dream?" Prospero asked, pulling Ellie into her arms with remarkable ease. "A regular safe life?"

"Honestly," Ellie confessed as she wrapped her arms around the witch carrying her up a surprisingly steep set of stairs, "I try not to think too much about what I want. I was being practical, uninteresting Ellie so I didn't end up missing. Except now I am exactly that."

Prospero didn't look at her as she asked, "If you had a dream, what would it be?"

"A sweeping romance seems like a selfish dream, right?" Ellie's cheeks burned as she realized a gorgeous, passionate woman was literally carrying her upstairs.

"Love is a goal most people have, Miss Brandeau." Prospero shifted Ellie slightly, so she could cause a door to sweep open.

Ellie burrowed her face against Prospero's throat. *Lavender and vanilla.* She brushed a kiss onto her skin. "Do you?"

Prospero said nothing as she lowered Ellie to a bed. She said nothing as she pulled a sheet and duvet up over Ellie. She said nothing as she looked down at her.

Already half asleep, Ellie caught her hand. "Do you?"

"What I want is immaterial," Prospero said. "I will do anything to save my home."

"But you *like* me," Ellie said. "I bet I'm not the only one thinking about that kiss."

Prospero looked guilty for a moment. "I apologize for that, Miss Brandeau. I was impatient with you, and . . . I shouldn't have come there or kissed you."

"I can't pass out if I'm already in bed," Ellie said, rather sensibly.

Panic flashed on Prospero's face as Ellie pulled her down, but this time there were no electric currents or fluttering hearts. Just a brush of lips too quick to even be an open-mouthed kiss.

Prospero pulled away quickly. "For now, Miss Brandeau, rest well. After you nap, we will try to save the world."

Then she was gone, and Ellie let sleep claim her.

14

Ellie

Ellie looked around the room. She was in a four-poster bed; overhead was a white canopy with what appeared to be tiny flowers stitched on it. Ellie fingered the matching bedspread. The flowers on it were lilac thread. The room itself was tiny, not much more than closet sized really. A washstand with a bowl of water sat to the left. A wardrobe with spirals and vines carved into the trim was to the right. A doorway led to a bathroom, and the partly open door revealed a massive black tub.

Curious, Ellie pulled open the wardrobe to see Prospero's clothes hanging there. "She gave me her room."

A smile came over her. The witch who had brought her here had deposited Ellie not in a guest room but in her own bed. Maybe it was a small gesture, but it made Ellie feel warm inside. She flipped past a number of rather austere trousers, jackets, vests. Prospero favored black, gray, purple, and deep blue. Not a lot of variety. All of it old-fashioned to the point of somber.

"And none of it fitting my shape," Ellie muttered. Prospero was lean with a few delicious curves. Ellie was rather soft in comparison. Not pinup curvaceous, but not hangs-out-at-yoga thin. *Average.*

Wearing the same clothes she had in the accident, after the hospital, and to sleep in was gross. Ellie took a sniff of herself, certain she smelled of hospitals and sweat. "No wonder she doesn't want to kiss me."

She closed the wardrobe and went to the bathroom. At least she could freshen up.

After a lifetime of not thinking about what she wanted, what she could be, all of it was swept away by the sense that every one of Ellie's cautious choices had been futile. She was exactly where she'd been trying to avoid, even after a life of caution, and it made her strangely reckless.

Impulsive, even.

She stood in a witch's bathroom, in a witch town, and tried to freshen her appearance, using a far-less-than-modern bathroom that had a vaguely eggy smell. The water from the sink, as she scooped it up to wash her face, had an unpleasant scent, and she wasn't sure what she could do about that. Bad water *was* the crux of the problem.

Fixing a world seemed impossible.

Ellie felt adrift even thinking about the problem that she was . . . kidnapped? . . . to help with in Crenshaw. How was she to ponder that when she couldn't fix her own life—or know what needed fixing! What she wanted, needed, craved—none of it was the same today. She was a witch. Magic was under her skin, and the possibilities felt immense.

Whatever I do now is not about staying uninteresting, not about avoiding going missing.

But Ellie had exactly zero experience in thinking about what she wanted out of life. Not a career. She liked being a librarian. Not a move. She had, apparently, done that accidentally. What she wanted, what she had always secretly dreamed, was to *matter*, to make a difference in the world. Well, that and fall in love in some sort of made-for-television overly dramatic affair.

As if Prospero would be dramatic.

Ellie stopped herself mid-thought. One kiss, despite being a knock-her-on-the-floor kiss, was not grounds for dreaming of romance. Ellie ran her hands through her hair, staring in the old mirror on the wall. It looked like an antique, silver framed, oval, and pitted with age in a few places.

"Miss?" A hob—not Bernice—had popped into the room. Levitating in front of the hob was a pair of black trousers and a gray sweater.

Ellie glanced over her shoulder.

"Lady P sent these for when you woke. I altered them for your shape," the hob announced and then vanished with an audible *pop*.

Ellie changed into the fresh clothes, pausing to take a deep sniff of the lavender scent that seemed to permeate everything Prospero touched. Then she went downstairs to find the woman herself.

After a few missteps, investigating rooms that were empty of witches, Ellie found her. Although Prospero was lovely, she had a drawn look to her face, as if her slumber had not been long or deep.

"You gave me your bed," Ellie accused.

"Yes." Prospero currently sat at a desk with open folders, notebooks, an honest-to-history quill, and a cup of half-consumed tea. "Are you feeling more together, Miss Brandeau?"

Ellie shrugged. "Still game to figure out how to help you. Still think kissing you sounds great. Still plan to go home after this whole magic college business."

Prospero gave her an unreadable look. "I see."

Feeling rather pleased by her uncharacteristic boldness, Ellie snatched a piece of toast with jam from a plate at Prospero's elbow. "What's the plan?"

"It is the middle of the night, Miss Brandeau," Prospero mused as she stacked her papers together and tidied her desk. "If you feel quite well enough, we will experiment a bit. Or go over to your original world and see if anything seems to draw your attention. . . . Prophecies can be muddled things, so a bit of a walkabout seems wise."

"So . . . more law breaking?" Ellie teased.

Prospero's cheeks pinked slightly. "A bit."

"Excellent." Ellie, rule follower extraordinaire for as long as she could recall, was excited to try on this new version of herself. "Show me what it means to be a witch."

After a few preparations, Prospero held out a hand. "I can take us to the rift first. Best not to walk about town, though. We ought to go there directly."

Ellie laced her fingers with Prospero's. "Do I need to do anything?"

"Hold tightly to my hand. Teleportation can be dizzying." Prospero's grip tightened, and then Ellie's world went blurry, as if the room and space itself had compressed and folded. Ellie had the general image of being a dot on a piece of parchment that was origami-ing around them.

She drew a sharp breath and closed her eyes.

When she opened them, they were standing alongside a series of gashes in the earth. The moonlight illuminated them, giving it an eerie cast. The ground looked as if giant claws had rent it, and as Ellie looked closer, she saw that the gashes had sunk deep through sod and soil.

Within the fissures were rock and an oozing, purpling substance.

"That's not natural." Ellie squatted next to it. She wasn't a geologist, but it didn't take much to realize that whatever the problem's source, it wasn't naturally made. "Magical?"

Prospero pressed her lips together as she nodded.

Ellie stared at the rows of gaping openings in the ground. The stench filtering out of it was stomach-turning. "Why not patch it?"

Prospero sighed. "It doesn't work. We've tried."

The futility of the moment washed over Ellie like a wave, and she thought back to the serpents she'd accidentally made. She glanced around her at the trees that were darkening near the opening—and she had an idea. Foolish? Maybe. She still wanted to know if it would work.

How did I make the snakes?

Honestly, she wasn't sure. She'd been angry, frustrated, and suddenly there had been snakes made of asphalt. What if she had known they were real and had tried to control them? What could she have done? The thought of it made her stomach squirm with anxiety and excitement.

Ellie closed her eyes and imagined caging that ooze, sealing it, covering it with a coiled tree, poised like the asphalt serpents. She stumbled slightly as she imagined the ground roiling, and then rising to fill that oozing fissure.

"Miss Brandeau!"

Ellie didn't open her eyes. She pictured the tree curling on itself, coiling like a serpent about to strike. She envisioned branches shifting into a jaw with sharpened teeth. She saw in her mind the fangs jutting from that wood-woven jaw.

Her knees faltered.

"Ellie!" Prospero's arms went round her as Ellie wobbled like a toddler trying to stand on unsteady legs.

Ellie opened her eyes to see a tree-wrought serpent curled over the fissure. Purple liquid pooled in its jaw, as if the foul goop was forcing itself through the wooden coils. "It looks like it's drooling."

As she watched, smaller trees leaned toward the faux serpent like baby rattlesnakes trying to cuddle close in a nest. Ellie pictured them with sealed mouths, hoping that would help trap the poison.

"You can't use *all* of your magic at once, Miss Brandeau." Prospero swept Ellie into her arms again. "You'll pass out, and I can't teleport you if you're depleted."

"So I'll try again"—Ellie yawned widely—"maybe later tonight. Smells better though. Jus' needed a bigger snake."

Her eyes were heavier than they ought to be. She forced herself to stare up at the serpent, and its mouth curved in a smile that looked a lot like the one she saw in her mirror. "I can make snakes, I guess . . ."

"I see that." Prospero shifted Ellie more securely into her arms and strode through the forest toward the town.

15

Dan

Dan leaned against Axell as they traipsed along the path to the castle. They had passed the barren meadow between village and woods. He was no longer at wow-those-badgers-and-tables-are-all-spinning levels of drunk, but he wasn't sober either. Axell, on the other hand, seemed perfectly fine.

And maybe part of it was the stench around everything in Crenshaw, and part of it was the shadows dancing under the trees, as if there were creatures in there after all.

Or people.

"How did you almost die?" Dan blurted, voice sounding overly loud in the eerily quiet forest. "I told you mine. Hiked my way right off a ravine. Yours?"

"A needle." Axell shrugged. "A bad day."

Dan stumbled to a stop. "A what?"

"Overdose, Daniel." Axell stopped and looked back at him, as if they were not at the edge of a creepy dark forest. "I was not good with limits. I was tired of being me, and the needle had more than my heart liked."

Dan gaped at him. "You *killed* yourself?"

"No." Axell backed him into a tree just past the path, a step or three into the woods.

"Are you *stupid*?"

"No." Axell was so close that Dan could feel Axell's exhalations, like the words were warm tactile things falling on his face. "I had a bad day. I did not die, though. I became a witch. This is better than fame and tours."

Now, Dan knew he was drunk, and he knew his brain was not following everything quite right because of the copious amount of booze—by which he meant four drinks—sloshing around in him. Had he been sober, perhaps the fact that a gorgeous man had backed him into a tree would filter into his brain. Instead, he fixated on the idea of someone with such a perfect fucking life wanting to die.

"Weak," Dan muttered. "I spent my life trying not to die, even when I was in pain, and you . . ." He pushed against Axell's chest as if he could dislodge him.

Axell didn't budge, and now Dan was standing there with both hands flat against the Norwegian man's firm chest. Dan closed his eyes.

"I was trying to find death, and you were trying to escape it," Axell said softly. "Now we are both here. Better."

He moved even closer, so there was no space separating them. Axell's thigh pressed against Dan's crotch, and Dan's eyes popped open in surprise.

Axell leaned closer for a kiss.

In a moment of bravery Dan wasn't sure he understood, Dan turned his face to the side.

Axell's lips landed on Dan's jaw. Dan heard as much as felt a laugh against his skin, before Axell asked, "Are you rejecting me?"

"Maybe?" Dan managed. "I don't know why you want me. Is it just that I am the only gay guy you met so far? Or you have a death thing, and since I was dying—"

"Truly? This is what you think?" Axell stepped away slightly, giving Dan enough room to duck under his arm and stand at his side.

Then Dan saw something in the woods, movement between the trees as if a shadow were running.

"Axell?" Dan whispered. "We aren't alone here."

Axell followed Dan's gaze into the dark woods. He moved so he was between Dan and whatever was out there.

The smart thing to do was likely to return to the castle, to the giant stone edifice with locked doors, soft beds, and space for Dan to hide away and think. And before discovering that he was a witch, that was likely what he'd have done. But tonight—whether because of excess drinking or a short wiring in his logic—Dan stepped around Axell and strode off into the woods.

"Wait!" Axell grabbed at his shoulder, but Dan dodged him and kept on walking.

Behind him he could hear Axell tramping after him, cursing and complaining as he pushed saplings out of the way. Dan didn't love being pursued. That, as much as an unhealthy amount of curiosity, propelled Dan even faster.

There was a noise, a distinct hissing ahead.

Suddenly, a hand covered his mouth.

Axell had caught up, one arm wrapped around Dan's chest so the palm of his hand muffled him. The other arm came across Dan's stomach, holding him still.

"Hush." Axell's whisper tickled Dan's ear.

Dan's body tensed as they watched a woman weave through the forest, holding an unconscious woman in her arms.

"Do you think she's dead?" Axell asked when the two were gone, lips still against Dan's earlobe. His arms remained wrapped around Dan, and the entire moment seemed surreal.

Dan reached up and caught Axell's wrist. He didn't resist as Dan tugged and removed the hand covering his mouth, but he didn't step away either.

"What are you doing?" Dan asked, glancing over his shoulder.

"Keeping you quiet. That one is deadly," Axell murmured.

Dan stepped out of his embrace. "Why do you say that?"

Axell nodded toward a lifeless man on the ground not six feet away. "Because of him."

The corpse was vaguely blue, as if the person had been frozen or suffocated. The witch was wearing fairly un-witchy clothes: trousers, boots, and a sweater. And the posture was as if they had been crawling through the undergrowth to escape the woods.

Dan looked in the direction the corpse was aimed. It was the same way the dark-clad woman had gone. "Should we go after her? What if the other one is still alive and—"

"They are *witches,* Daniel. What magic do we know yet? If that woman is a killer, we would be dead to follow her." Axell tugged on Dan's arm.

"I thought that was what you wanted," Dan said unkindly.

"Not now. I am choosing life, a second chance, here. I want this new world. I want to explore it with *you* right now." He glanced in the direction of the black-garbed woman and her apparent victim. "To follow her? That way is not life."

Dan swallowed hard at the thought of dying after finally being healthy. He supposed Axell was right. They shouldn't follow the potential murderess, so he pivoted and continued in the direction the woman came from instead. He wanted to see what the hissing was—and then he'd report back to the headmaster the next day.

He headed deeper into the woods, trying to be quiet in case there were other murderous witches in the shadows. Axell followed a step behind.

Dan felt oddly proud that he was taking charge. He was making decisions, marching—*or stumbling perhaps,* he thought as a tree branch knocked him into Axell, *but still*—into possible danger. He was, in brief, trying to be a Good Guy, even if he wasn't entirely sure how to do so. He felt confident, though, right up to the moment when they found the source of the hissing. Then, Dan was no longer so sure about his brief burst of bravado.

"It's a fucking monster," Dan whispered as they watched the wooden serpent shiver in the air. Purple goop dripped from its fangs. "Venomous snake monster. Do you see that thing?"

This time when Axell's arms came around him, Dan leaned into him.

"And hatchlings," Axell murmured, nodding toward the forest floor.

Dan followed his gaze to the half dozen or so tiny serpents twisting and rattling on the ground. "Do you think she brings sacrifices to them?"

Axell had no answer. He simply steered Dan in front of him and gently shoved. "We must leave here. You go first. I will follow."

"If they come after us—"

"You will run." Axell urged him onward with a firm hand on his back. "And we do not go into these woods again, ja?"

All Dan could do was nod as they sped back to the path and to the castle. He'd found out where the foul smell originated—in purple snake venom dripping from a monster.

No place is perfect, his mind insisted.

But somehow, the rattling and hissing of whatever monster those were seemed to echo around them, and Dan was no longer convinced that Crenshaw was as perfect as he'd been led to think.

As they entered the castle again, Dan had one last fleeting fear: *Is that where they send those of us who fail? Are we fed to the snake like that man was?*

16
Maggie

Maggie had a moment of panic when she woke in an unfamiliar bed. She was naked and aching in places that hadn't been made use of in far too long. The man next to her had the sort of tattoos that looked like they belonged on a grizzled soldier—or had been done in prison. Something about that niggled her brain.

"How old are you?" she asked as the rest of her orgasm-soaked brain started to function.

Sondre deflected. "Older than I look. Witches live a very long time."

"Not an answer." Maggie propped herself up on one arm, looking down at the man beside her. He didn't look a day over thirty, and she'd had an "Am I a cougar now?" moment earlier. Surely not, though. He was the headmaster for the college, so he was what?

She guessed, "Forty? Forty-five?"

"Ninety-six." He caught her hand as he answered, as if she'd bolt.

If not for her uncanny ability to tell lies from truths, she'd laugh. As it was, her mouth gaped open as she stared at him. He had the sort of gym body that rarely existed much over forty, and certainly didn't exist in men over ninety.

"You're old enough to be my grandfather." She stared at him. "You don't look—or move—like an old man."

"Witches live for a *long* time, Maggie." Sondre stared at her, clearly bracing for her panic. "You will look younger over time as your body heals the ravages of age. You'll feel younger, too. It takes a moment to adjust."

Maggie felt her stomach twist as she tried to make sense of the idea that she could live that long and not visibly age. Would her son inherit her magic? Or would he grow old and die before her?

"So the people I'll meet who look older are the non-magical relatives?" She had glimpsed a few people in Crenshaw, but no one looked anywhere near ninety. "Wait! Are any of the people here ones whose magic awakened when they were already old?"

"Sometimes. They un-age the first few years before beginning to re-age. Unsettling to see if you ask me." Sondre stood, rising out of the bed in a way that said he was stripper-agile. A random thought slid into her mind that since he was this fit and this lithe, maybe she could convince him to give her a show. Thinking about that felt better than thinking about the reality of her life as a witch.

"How do you feel about stripteases, man-witch?" She watched him pace to a window like he could hear or see something out there she couldn't.

He glanced back at her with an appraising grin. "I look forward to that if you're willing. We don't have that sort of bar here. Aside from one brothel, there are no half-naked women on display. A shame, really."

A chime echoed in the room, the sound bouncing around as if it were a physical thing seeking a person. Seeking Sondre.

In no more than a blink, Sondre was re-dressed—including his robe. Knowing what was hidden under it, she somehow found the shapeless fabric sexy. He might not be much for conversation, but Sondre was fit and had stamina.

But somehow old. Let's not forget that part!

He stepped out of the room, pulling the door shut. For a moment, Maggie considered getting dressed, but he was already back, frowning.

"The last student has apparently arrived," Sondre announced, staring down at her with an unreadable expression.

"I thought you had to go fetch them or whatever?"

"Typically." Sondre bent and slid his hands under her. "But this will save me time I can better use here."

He lifted her halfway off the mattress as his mouth covered hers in a kiss that was more possessive than he had any right to be, but Maggie's traitorous body had no objections. A great kiss was high on the list of reasons she'd missed dating. The others were what followed great kisses. The sheer truth was that orgasms were even better than meds at keeping her anxiety at bay, and he delivered enough joy that she felt blissful.

When Sondre released her from his kiss, she flopped back onto the mattress and shushed her mind.

Fine. Not captor. Not old. Acquaintances with benefits?

"I want more of you," he said.

Maggie was too much of an adult to play coy. "Same. If you keep delivering that many orgasms, I'm in."

He had a self-satisfied grin that ought to irk her. "I will get the new student settled, and then . . . I'd like to see this dance you suggested."

He was already to the bedroom door by the time her brain and mouth were on the same page. "Wait!"

He paused.

"I was asking *you* to dance for me, man-witch." She gave him the most lascivious look she could. "But I'm willing to negotiate to get you there, if you want."

His laughter was more lighthearted than she'd thought it capable of when he'd arrived in her room spouting what she'd thought had been nonsense. Neither laughter nor orgasms were enough to lure her into a relationship, but he wasn't mentioning such things either.

What was the harm in a little bit of no-strings stress relief while she took these magic classes? Once her son was here, too, that would have to change, but for now, she was content to wait in Sondre's bed.

She'd treat this like the most unusual spa weekend she'd ever had—and then she'd raise her son in a world far removed from her louse of an ex. Things felt like they were going to be fine. Better than fine. She nestled back in the bed and let her mind wander to the possibilities in this new future. Things like college and the rest were no longer going to be Craig's top goals. She'd need to make sure there was some sort of sport here, though. Her son had no pressing career goals, but a lack of sports might be enough to make him choose a mundane world over a magical one.

17

Sondre

As Sondre headed toward the door, the sudden thudding caught him off guard, especially as it was nearing morning. Very few students would have the audacity to hammer on his door, and the one most likely to do so was dozing in his bed. If things were different, Sondre thought he might like to keep her there, but Maggie had good reason to return to her world.

Sondre jerked the door open. "What?"

"There is a huge fucking serpent thing in the woods," Dan announced. He was breathing heavily as if he'd been running. "I thought you said there were no dragons and that failing meant going home, not being fed to a snake and—"

"Stop. Lower your voice, and then tell me what you're blathering about." Sondre didn't invite him inside. It was one thing to take Margaret to his bed, but it was something a lot less acceptable for there to be witnesses to the fact he had left a student naked in his bedroom.

The man at Monahan's side, another of the new students, nodded. "Snake with purple goo on the fangs."

"Excuse me?" Sondre stepped into the hallway, pulling the door closed behind him. It would be awkward if Maggie overheard this conversation.

Worse if she went into the woods. The rift there was fatal if a witch's magic wasn't strong enough. Maggie would be in danger. She likely could choose to go home, and though he wasn't ready to surrender her, he was planning to recommend that she be siphoned and returned to her world. She'd be furious anyhow once she realized he'd misled her about her son.

Sondre stayed in front of his door, watching the unlikely pair of men. Based on the observations he'd made of the new arrivals, Daniel Monahan was an overeager puppy, desperate for approval and attention. Thin, anxious, but with an accepting attitude that was useful. Axell Olsen was a different kind of person altogether: smiling as if everything was a great adventure, easily placated, and not eager for anyone's approval. Athletic build, unusual haircut.

"Why were you in the woods?" Sondre asked.

"We saw something and—"

"A woman carrying a body," Axell interrupted. "We saw her. A murderer."

"Is there a snake cult here?" Daniel asked in a low voice.

Sondre held up a hand. "You saw a woman carrying a body and a big snake with purple 'goo' on its teeth? So you followed it?" He looked into their pupils. "Did you have bad mead? Eat any odd mushrooms?"

Axell grinned. "We are not intoxicated." Then he glanced at Daniel. "He is a bit, but I am not. I drank professionally."

"Headmaster, there was a dead body on the ground in the bushes and a woman carrying an unconscious or dead woman toward town—"

"What did she look like?" Sondre asked.

"Top hat and black trouser skirt thing," Daniel started.

"Excellent vest," Axell added.

Only one witch dressed that way, buttoned up and prim as if still living in the 1800s and clad in her mourning garb. *Prospero.*

"You will tell no one of this," Sondre stated, making eye contact with them each in turn. "Unless you are looking for a quick return to the lives—and deaths—you escaped."

Daniel blanched; Axell quirked a brow. That one might be a problem. Sondre looked at Daniel again. "If he speaks of this, my kindness to both of you *will* vanish."

Then he swept past them in search of Prospero and the remains of the witch she might have killed.

I knew something was wrong.

Sondre hadn't been able to locate the last student quickly enough to reach her before she was undoubtedly carried to a hospital. In such cases, protocol would require him to take that beastly woman with him to adjust the memories of the staff at the hospital. In this case, Elleanor Brandeau had vanished entirely, which meant the remedial witch had teleported here or died.

Teleporting on one's own was very rare. Maggie had done so, but that was due to a burst of maternal panic. Had this other remedial witch teleported here on her own? Had she been wandering around the woods?

As Sondre stomped through the halls of Crenshaw Castle, he realized that the idea of any new witch appearing at that particular spot was highly suspicious. He'd known when the Brandeau witch's magic awakened—it was like that with each student—but hers was strong enough to catch his undivided attention.

When remedial witches arrived in Crenshaw on their own, they typically arrived near the castle. It functioned almost as a beacon. Unless she had a connection to someone or somewhere else, that was exactly where Brandeau ought to have appeared.

Mentally, he filed through his roster of students. There had been another Brandeau. *Hester or Heather or something.* She had demanded siphoning, though. So she was not here as a beacon.

So why had this witch not arrived at the castle? Why the woods? Or had that damnable woman fetched her without him because she knew Brandeau was strong? She *had* been friends with—*Hester? Helen? What was her name?*—Brandeau.

18
Prospero

Prospero desperately wished she could just teleport them. She would've ignored the risks if Ellie was . . . well, anyone else at all. Ellie, however, was someone to protect. She was essential to Crenshaw.

And possibly to me.

They had reached the edge of town, and Prospero had an arrogant hope they would reach her townhouse unseen. At least it was late enough—or perhaps early enough that not many witches would be out yet.

Just a few more minutes . . .

"Why are you holding a new witch?" a voice asked from behind them.

"Well, fuck," Prospero muttered, turning to greet the man staring at them. *Walter. Why did it have to be him?* The chief witch was an almost friend, a good witch who knew too many of her secrets already.

Prospero affixed a smile on her face and met his gaze briefly before saying, "Walter."

Ellie waved at him, lifting her head for a moment. "I made snakes." She pointed behind them to the woods where she'd fashioned a giant wooden serpent from the trees. "It smelled bad back there. So I made a plug, but then the ground was unsteady. This nice lady caught me."

"We have a new arrival, Chief Witch," Prospero said somberly.

Walter eyed the two of them suspiciously for a long moment, but then he nodded. "Let's get her up to the castle before this becomes a situation, Prospero."

"Prospero," Ellie echoed. "Hi. Your name is strange. I'm Ellie."

"Indeed," Prospero murmured. "Let's get you to the infirmary, Ellie. The doctor will want to check on you."

Not far past the edge of town, several other witches stepped up to help. One witch offered up a stretcher since there were no wheelchairs this far from the infirmary.

One offered, "I could pop up to the castle—"

"This is fine," Walter insisted.

So they began the walk along the path toward the castle, but then Ellie woke again. When she realized she was strapped down on a stretcher, she rose up. In a blink, she was crouched on the cobblestones, looking around at the crowd as if she were a madwoman.

When her gaze landed on Prospero, she lurched toward her, and Prospero caught her up in her arms again.

Walt gave her a look that said more than he would say aloud with witnesses, but in that moment, Prospero knew he'd realized she was previously acquainted with Ellie.

"She seems to want to attack you, Lady Prospero," Cassandra said from the growing crowd, offering an excuse the nearby witches might accept.

Because they hate me.

"We'll get the poor thing to the doctor," another witch said.

Why are they all awake so early?

Presumably drawn by the commotion, the crowd swelled. Several witches were still in their nightclothes.

Prospero followed along as they carried Ellie toward the castle. It was a curious procession: the incapacitated witch on the stretcher, the chief witch, Prospero, and assorted witches who joined them as they walked.

"Appeared all by herself," one said.

"Made a serpent," another added.

Somewhere near Prospero's house, Ellie had another moment of clarity. She rolled off the gurney, took a wide-legged stance, and looked around at them. When her gaze landed on Prospero, she charged again.

Prospero caught her, sweeping her up into her arms. This time she said, "Hush, now, Miss Brandeau."

"What's happening?" Ellie grumbled.

"You're a witch, my dear." Prospero held her gaze, which was easy now that she was cradling Ellie again. "This is a town called Crenshaw where witches live. You're going to the castle."

Ellie, thankfully, was alert enough *not* to say "I know" or some such thing. She merely stared at Prospero and announced, "I don't like this plan."

Prospero strode through the crowd of witches and lowered Ellie back to the gurney.

The chief witch side-eyed her, but Prospero's concern was on Ellie. "She needs to be seen at the infirmary."

"If she'd stay put, we'd be there sooner," Walter replied sourly. He held Prospero's gaze a moment longer. "We need to discuss this, you know."

Prospero gave a terse nod. She wasn't the sort of person to doubt herself. She didn't have that luxury. She made a plan, and she followed it. If there were bumps, she revised. Ellie being found by the chief witch was more of a massive explosion than a mere bump. Some witches found their way here, but it was rare. Some witches could strike out at a head of house, but that was rare, too. Ellie was proving to be an exception to quite a few rules.

"You can trust her," Cassandra murmured from somewhere behind Prospero.

"No." Prospero didn't look back at her friend. She'd stayed clear of the seer since that damnable prophecy. Cassie's advice was what had led Prospero to try to shock Ellie's heart.

Kiss her to near death like I was some sort of mythical monster.

"If you mess around with her mind, P—"

"Stop." Prospero glanced at the onlookers. They weren't near enough to overhear, and their attention was solely on the now unconscious witch on the stretcher. Ellie had risen up twice more, and she'd come damn near to launching herself at Prospero each time.

They all thought Ellie was "attacking" Prospero, and that was likely why everyone was surreptitiously staring at Prospero now.

Prospero, however, knew better. Ellie was trying to get back to Prospero, the only person here she knew. Foolish woman that she was, Ellie *trusted* Prospero.

My lovely witch.

Prospero repressed such traitorous thoughts. Who knew what Ellie would say to the others once she woke? That burst of power was reason enough to know Ellie would, in fact, be a force to be reckoned with once her magic was under control.

She already is.

What no one told the incoming students was their time in classes was also about giving them a chance to let their magic sink into their bones or muscles or wherever it lived. Many of the witches were able to balance their new gifts, and outbursts inside the castle were easier to treat because of the infirmary—and because of the castle's structure. The ancient stones were brought here intact. Both the castle and the Congress building had simply *appeared*, and as such the earliest settlers here came to understand that these buildings were important for magic.

Some witches never quite adjusted. Those witches were the first ones siphoned. Prospero shoved thoughts of the past away and glanced at Walter. The look on the chief witch's face was easy enough to read. He doubted the truth of Ellie's answer, and he knew damn well Ellie was going to be a force to reckon with.

Prospero ought to have warned Ellie not to try anything that extreme. Magic changed things, changed their bodies and minds. The new witches would undoubtedly shed a bit of magic during outbursts, and that would be absorbed into the stone that ran through the town, connecting those two central buildings. Each head of house could draw on it—as could the chief witch and the headmaster of the Remedial Magic School.

Prospero looked back at Cassandra, not wanting to tell her that she'd flouted rules, although there was a good chance the seer already knew. "I know what I'm doing."

"You are making a mistake." Cassandra's lips twisted in what Prospero recognized as disappointment, but the younger woman simply pivoted and flounced away.

Later, Prospero would need to make amends, but right now, she had a task to complete. She walked in the opposite direction of Cassandra and joined the crowd moving along the path to Crenshaw Castle. She'd only needed a moment alone with Ellie to erase the damaging details from her mind. The side effect, unfortunately, was erasing Ellie's knowledge of Prospero—erasing the burgeoning interest there.

That's what I get for having such a foolish hope.

Ellie was the one who would change everything. That was the prophecy, and Cassandra's prophecies were never wrong.

"Lady Prospero?" One of the teachers stepped away from the clutch of whispering women. She had a name. Prospero was certain of it, but without Cassandra there to remind her, Prospero had no idea what it was.

"The headmaster is ready to start the class once this one is settled. Would you be able to see if he still needs to go over to the Barbarian Lands? Or might that be something you could manage without him?"

The woman was asking her to invade Ellie's mind. It was what Prospero needed to do, but a flicker of anger still rose in her. Had they always treated the new arrivals so cavalierly? What if they were going to return to their lives? What if they rejected Crenshaw? Was it harder for them? Prospero didn't check on them, simply went back and altered the necessary memories.

"She's stronger than most." Several witches said versions of this, noting the fact that Ellie had arrived early and unaccompanied.

"Thought she was going to escape you," one added.

"I thought she might hit you," another said in an unmistakably gleeful voice.

"Too strong to siphon, for sure!"

The unspoken statement, though, was that Ellie was here to stay. She had seemingly attempted to strike Prospero while she was being subdued, and that sort of magic was impressive. Moreover, she'd managed to simply arrive here. That meant she'd ripped through the illusions that kept Crenshaw safe. It meant she'd exuded sheer brute force.

Prospero knew that and knew Ellie had spent a night recovering already, but they did not.

"I shall investigate." Prospero swept forward, moving abruptly, her cloak billowing out as she went. The effect was not accidental. Nothing about her persona was. Well over a century ago, Prospero had decided if she was going to be their boogeyman, their tethered monster, she would lean into that hurtful image.

I will be their monster.

But today, looking at the subdued woman on the stretcher, Prospero wished there were other options.

19

Dan

"Do you want to follow him?" Axell asked.

They were standing in the hall under a stained-glass window of a group of witches. It looked oddly religious, but the one thing Dan very clearly had not seen was a church, synagogue, mosque, or temple. If there were religious ceremonies here, he was unaware of them. He was, however, very aware that upsetting Sondre was dangerous.

"If he catches us—" Dan started.

"They are hiding things, Daniel. You see this, ja?" Axell put a hand on Dan's arm, and Dan had the flicker of a wish that he was more muscular. Axell stared in the direction the headmaster had gone. "If we are to choose this, should we not know the secrets?"

Dan shook his head. "If we leave, my cancer will return, and I'll die."

Axell stepped in, pulling Dan into a brief embrace. When he released him, he said, "Knowledge is power, Daniel. They have all of it right now. Do you want to let them have the power over us?"

When Dan thought about it, he might have just a little understanding of why Axell wanted to know what was happening. He seemed like he had been at the whims of his label and maybe his manager. Dan wasn't in the same place, but he'd been at the mercy of the cancer and the bookies. Both were pretty awful.

Still, Sondre is dangerous. Axell doesn't know just how much. And Dan had no desire to share what he knew. Not now. Maybe not ever.

He looked in the direction Sondre had gone yet again. "He might be going to the authorities," Dan offered weakly.

Axell's expression said what he did not. They both suspected the headmaster was going to the forest.

"Let us follow and see," Axell finally said.

Dan sighed. He wasn't the sort of person to race toward threats, and he definitely wanted to stay here.

Wouldn't it be good to know why there's a giant snake in the woods? his curiosity whispered.

"Fine," Dan muttered.

They return the way they'd come, slipping past closed doors where the other new students likely still slept. Dan wondered briefly if Maggie had made it to her room, but he wasn't entirely sure which was hers so he couldn't knock and check.

The front door of the castle was unlocked, and Dan had to wonder if the hobs were helping him. The sun was rising as they stepped outside the castle again. At least the woods wouldn't be as dark and dreary.

"Thank you," he said in a low voice to whatever hobs were near, looking around the castle entry before stepping outside and back on the path toward the monster in the woods.

By the time they reached the woods, they still hadn't seen Sondre. What they did see was a procession of people accompanying a woman on a stretcher. They were coming from the direction of the town, and the woman who had been carrying the limp woman earlier was at the front of the group.

"Hide!" Dan whispered.

The two men ducked into the woods, and Axell took his hand. Dan was briefly grateful for the brambles and shrubs that were at the edge near the path. It must be what enabled them to hide. No one so much as looked their way, even though they weren't very far into the woods at all.

But when Dan glanced over at Axell, he saw . . . nothing. No person there, even though he was holding what felt like another man's hand.

"Axell?"

"Shhh," a voice answered. Dan saw no one at all there; he appeared to be alone.

Then he glanced at his hand and saw nothing there either. He started breathing too fast, too deeply, and then he felt a second hand reach out and grab his wrist. He couldn't see anyone, and he hoped it was the man he'd been here with.

Did I imagine him? Imagine all of it?

Panic crept over him, but then the hand that had caught his arm crept higher, tracing up his arm and then across his chest. It was both the most unsettling and exciting thing that had happened to him in quite some time—aside from the whole becoming a witch thing.

He stared at the crowd of people passing on the trail as the invisible hands pulled him closer. He stumbled and fell into the invisible body he believed was Axell. *I didn't imagine him.*

Dan let out a small noise when his own hand landed on a taut stomach.

"Hush, Daniel."

"I can't see you *or me*," Dan whispered.

"Magic." Axell's voice, louder now that the people had passed, was slightly to the left of him, even as their hands were on each other's bodies. He was standing at an angle. "I did not want to be seen, and we are not seen."

"You made us invisible."

"I did!" Axell's laugh was right in front of Dan, but it was still disconcerting to not know where exactly he was.

"Super weird." Dan jerked away, and they both became visible again. "Okay, weird*er*."

"Together it worked." Axell stepped forward, took Dan's hand, and again they vanished. "We hold hands while we follow the headmaster." His grip tightened on Dan's hand. "Maybe we don't talk so much when we get near him."

Dan nodded, realized Axell couldn't see the nod, and suggested, "One squeeze for stop. Two for go."

"Three for yes," Axell added, squeezing Dan's hand three times.

They set off through the woods, wondering what exactly they would find in front of them. As they walked, Dan thought back on his first attempt at hiking. That one ended in his near-death plummet, but as far as he knew, there were no ravines here.

Supposedly no monsters either.

By the time they found Sondre, he was talking to a witch who looked like her hair had blood-streaks. She carried an ornate stick that she held out from her body like a weapon.

"Another one dead." The witch stared at the man on the ground, pointing toward the decaying corpse. "Damn fools refuse to stay away from the rift."

Overhead, the wooden serpent undulated like a snake-charmer had been playing songs. The little snakes shivered and shifted underneath the massive beast.

"Whose work is this?" Sondre asked the woman. He had an unmistakable hopefulness in his voice as he added, "Surely not Scylla's . . ."

The other witch cackled like she was embracing stereotypes. "As if."

Sondre walked closer, and one of the baby snakes lunged at him. Wooden fangs sank deep in his leg, and the red-haired witch slashed a sword down, severing the head of the creature. Purple fluid oozed down Sondre's leg, and the head turned into wood and vines. Lifeless. Still.

"Not an illusion." Sondre stared at the rest of the snakes. "What witch is keeping secrets, Agnes?"

"Go to the infirmary." The witch, Agnes apparently, pointed at his leg with the sword. "The poison is killing witches, you ninny. Tend that. I'll talk to the others while you see the healer."

She was pointing with the stick that moments earlier had been a sword. It shifted shapes at her will—which was undeniably cool aside from the fact that she was terrifying.

Agnes strode away, and then Sondre pivoted to look directly where they were standing. "Not bad."

Dan tensed. Axell squeezed Dan's hand twice.

Before they could take a step, Sondre's voice rang out. "Leaving would be unwise. Show yourself. I know someone is there."

"Someone," he said. He doesn't know it's us.

For a split second, Dan considered stopping, but instead, he squeezed Axell's hand again. Three times. They took off running.

Dan worried Sondre would catch them, but he was stumbling from his snake bite, and a few minutes later, he popped out of existence.

"Keep going," Axell urged.

So they ran all the way back to the castle, and when they got there, Axell didn't let go of Dan's hand until they were inside the castle.

Inside, Axell closed the door and said, "Stay with me, Daniel."

Despite the demanding phrasing, Dan knew it was a request, and today it was one he was happy to accept. "Your room or mine?"

20
Prospero

All the new arrivals received a health assessment. It wouldn't do to have people walking around in pain—and the beauty of magic was that it healed everything over time. They didn't heal people who weren't staying, though, so the intake was more of a patch and stitch. It bought time, rather than giving away near-perpetual health to every arrival. Magic sustained its host, but some of the arrivals would return to the Barbarian Lands with no memory of their time here.

Not Ellie, though.

Dr. Mae Jemison, the doctor in charge of all significant injuries in Crenshaw, was waiting for them. Despite the hour, the woman looked like a doll, perfect bow-shaped lips and a figure that had no need for a corset. It was a mask to hide a dangerously keen mind.

"Sondre will have kittens when he finds that you saw her before him," Mae murmured.

"Should've been paying attention then." Prospero resisted the urge to stroke Ellie's cheek. "Is she well?"

"Drained herself making snakes for whatever reason," Mae said. "She needs a bit of a recharge before her magic is able to focus."

"I will watch over her," Prospero announced. "I need to investigate her mind to see what I need to repair from her life over there. Please, pull the door closed behind you."

"I ought to be allowed to stay. She's my patient."

"I can't focus with anyone in the room," Prospero objected.

Mae crossed her arms, lifting her ample bosom upward in the process. "Anyone you don't trust, you mean. You don't trust anyone but the madam, do you?"

"Cassandra is my friend, and you just said that this witch"—Prospero gestured at Ellie—"was fine. So I would like to do my job."

"And you won't do it with me in here," Mae said. "Do you think I'll hurt you while you're skating around her mind?"

"No. I simply don't want interference." Prospero gritted her teeth.

"You know you could trust me, but you're as bad as he is." Mae shook her head. "You both use people up until the next victim comes along. I was nothing to you, then?"

Prospero stared at her for a moment before glancing at Ellie. It wasn't as if Ellie would remember anything about their almost-romance after today, but Prospero still felt a twinge about talking to her ex-lover in front of Ellie.

Fortunately, Ellie appeared to be unconscious.

"I never lied about my intentions, Mae." Prospero hated that their world was so tiny and lives so long that there was an extensive history of spurned exes for many of the residents. She lowered her voice even more.

Mae shook her head. "Fine . . . but you still used me to hurt Sondre."

"He's only hurt because he cares about—"

"Ha! I don't think so. He hurt because I was his possession and you bedded me. Nothing emotional about it." Mae's voice sounded wobbly, and Prospero felt a flicker of guilt. "You're both awful people, you know?"

"I do." Prospero nodded. "Now, I'm going to alter this woman's memory, so could we save any more of these accusations?"

"Bitch." Mae walked away, hips swinging and footsteps clicking in a way that would give Cassandra a run for her money.

She paused at the door and gave Prospero a chilling smile. Then she dropped a stone in a metal bowl. A *ting* as the stone connected with the metal echoed like a bullet. Then the spell ricocheted around the room, zinging Prospero, who physically lunged over Ellie to protect her from whatever it was that Mae tossed in her spell bowl.

"Prospero?" Ellie looked up at her, eyes wide and lashes thick like she'd added makeup to them. "Why are you on top of me? Why am I here?"

For a flicker of a moment, common sense seemed like it would prevail, but when Prospero opened her mouth, the truth spilled out instead: "I wasn't sure what spell the doctor just dropped so I . . . I wanted to protect you."

The stone was a truth encourager. They were used by the doctor often when the patient was stubborn. It should only last a few moments, so really all Prospero had to do was not talk. Surely, that could work!

"Are we alone?"

"Yes."

"Can we escape?" Ellie whispered.

Prospero shook her head, her teeth clamping her lips shut so no incriminating words leaked out. She knew she needed to erase the memory of her time over in the Barbarian Lands and Ellie's visit to her home—but she didn't want to.

"Did my snake help?" Ellie's hands slid around Prospero's waist, and one hands trailed up her spine. She teased, "Can I get a reward?"

If not for the fact this had to end, Prospero would be smiling. *This.* This was what she'd wanted from the first moment she'd seen Ellie.

Unable to continue resisting the spell now that Ellie had asked for the truth, too, Prospero angled her neck, so she was whispering into Ellie's ear. "I have to leave you here. You have to *not* know me. There are rules. I broke a lot of them to find you."

"I won't tell. No one here, and then no one at home when I—"

Her words ended as Prospero caught Ellie's mouth in a kiss. If they kissed, Prospero couldn't talk, and if they didn't kiss right now, they might not ever do so again. The chances of Ellie genuinely liking her after today were slim.

For a sliver of a second, Prospero thought Ellie would resist, but then the hand Ellie had been resting on Prospero's spine slid upward. In the next moment, Ellie was cradling the back of Prospero's head as she took control of their kiss.

What was to be a simple goodbye kiss flared into something else, and Prospero had neither the reserve nor the kindness to stop it. She felt Ellie try to unbutton her vest, and instead of stopping her, she leaned back to give her better access.

"Yes," she said, pulling back from the kiss and making her consent completely verbal in case her bodily clues weren't clear enough.

Ellie grinned, holding Prospero's gaze as she popped the first button.

By the second button, Prospero leaned back down and pressed her lips to Ellie's mouth again. This was a terrible idea, letting Ellie lead their kiss into something more—something that would leave them both with bee-stung lips and flushed faces. But Ellie's hand was on Prospero's hip again, and she shifted Prospero to the side so Prospero's leg was between Ellie's now-parted thighs.

No one would dare come in here. It's fine.

When Ellie moaned and her hand tightened on Prospero's hip, logic came screaming back to the forefront of her mind. For all that Prospero wanted this, wanted Ellie, she had to erase Ellie's mind, and erasing it after . . . however far they were about to go in this intimacy felt wrong.

Prospero pulled away and all but tumbled to the floor in her haste. "Stop."

"I already did." Ellie sat up on the cot, sliding backward and rolling to her side. "Did I misunderstand? I thought—"

"You thought the right thing," Prospero assured her, reaching up and squeezing her hand.

"Good." Ellie brushed back her hair and stared at Prospero with the same unflinching gaze she'd had when she'd told her not to drink tea around the books.

Prospero straightened her sleeves, rebuttoned the two vest buttons that had been undone. "You must understand what is at stake here. Your magic was awakened, but you *drained yourself* creating that serpent, Miss Brandeau. You're volatile, and if you tried to leave the castle unsupervised, you'd be a danger to yourself and any non-witches."

Ellie's gaze darted to the door of the infirmary. "So I'm to stay here? What's stopping me from walking out? I could come to your house and—"

"The door is magically sealed," Prospero said softly. "You can't leave Crenshaw Castle without going through the standard process of newly awakened witches. First, you need to be examined by the doctor, and then there's assessments, classes, and—"

"Nonsense!" Ellie's chin lifted in a way that was stubbornness incarnate.

"You'll attend the College of Remedial Magic and then—"

"No."

"Yes." Prospero stepped back and all but dropped onto the doctor's rickety stool. She was shaking, and no one could see her like that. Not even Ellie.

Then Ellie, beautiful and sweet Ellie, gave her a look that shook Prospero to the bone. "If I can do magic, good luck keeping me here."

"Miss Brandeau . . ."

"After you've had your tongue in my mouth, I think calling me Ellie is appropriate."

"You've identified yourself as a threat, Ellie." Prospero tried to reason with her, but the sensible librarian was gone. In her place was a witch unleashed. "They'll be watching you."

"Because I was at the rift with you—"

"No, Ellie, because you made a *giant hissing serpent.*" Prospero's exasperation filled her voice. "You could have been injured. I could've—"

"Not really. The snake was an extension of me, so it wouldn't strike you or me." Ellie came to her feet. "Although I'm not sure if it would read my unintentional thoughts . . . and you are really testing my patience."

If Ellie could still summon magic, Prospero would be afraid just then. There was something unholy about how much that fact excited Prospero. The edge of strength that had glimmered in Ellie was intrinsically tied to her magical core, and with magic's awakening, so, too, was Ellie's ferocity awakened. Prospero had felt that wondrous evolution in herself, but she'd rarely seen it so evident so quickly. Ellie would be a force to fear once her body adjusted to having magic.

"The Congress of Magic, our government, employs a witch to erase the memories of aberrant magic and other things," Prospero said lightly.

"Who does such a horrible thing? All of them or—?"

"Just the one witch," Prospero whispered. She looked at Ellie then, hating the pending loss of the memories they had, hating she had to do this to her of all witches. "With it comes an ability to travel to your world."

Ellie stared at her with horror clear in her gaze. "*You?*"

For Crenshaw. For my own safety. Prospero had no other choice. Ellie couldn't be allowed to have such power over her. *No one can. Never again.*

"I am sorry, Ellie. I wish I didn't have to do this," Prospero confessed, grateful this time that the truth enhancer was still working. "I already like you more than you'll ever know. I wish we didn't need to do this."

She gently pushed Ellie backward, so she was seated on the cot again.

"What are you—"

"Shhh." Prospero touched Ellie's forehead, letting her magic guide her to the memories they shared.

The process was as familiar as breathing. It should have been easy, but this time as Prospero reached into Ellie's mind, she met something new. Usually, she could sort through the person's details, filter, erase, shift nuances. Instead, all she saw was a black empty void, like looking into the night sky if all the stars were gone.

21

Ellie

Ellie felt the touch of Prospero's magic in her mind as surely as she'd felt the touch of her lips a few minutes ago. She knew without doubt that Prospero was trying to erase the memories of their meeting in Ligonier and their time at Prospero's house. But Ellie wasn't about to let anyone change her reality, and the beauty of not knowing the limits of her magic or willpower meant Ellie actually stopped Prospero's magic. She wasn't sure how or why or if she could do it again, but she wasn't about to admit that part aloud.

Better that she think I did it on purpose . . .

Tremors washed over Ellie so forcefully that she covered her mouth and looked for a wastebasket or something to vomit into if necessary. She scanned the room, taking in the oddity of where she was. There was a timelessness to the room, like it was a living mix of anachronisms. The walls looked like stone. The bed was carved of some sort of wood, and the thin mattress was filled with something that crunched—like dried husks or grasses.

"This is bullshit," Ellie muttered as soon as the roiling in her stomach lessened. "You tried to erase my memory." She stepped forward to slap the other woman with every ounce of betrayal she felt in that moment.

Prospero caught her wrist. "Stop."

"Do not touch me." Ellie jerked her arm away from Prospero's hold. "Not my body, and not my mind. If you try again, I will betray *your* trust as you've just tried to do to me."

Then Ellie stepped around her and marched to the magically sealed door. It opened at her touch, and she entered the hallway. She glanced back at Prospero. "Magically sealed, huh?"

A buxom woman was staring at Ellie.

She marched up to the woman. "Doctor? That's your role, right?"

"Yes. How did you do that?" She gestured toward the room Ellie had just left.

"I am told you must assess me, so I can attend a class before I can leave." Ellie decided she would not cry over being betrayed or mentally attacked. There was no time for any of that. *Great romance? Ha!* Ellie felt like the worst sort of fool. She trusted Prospero, risked her safety in this new witch world to help, and how was she repaid? By an attempt on her very mind.

Behind her, she heard soft footsteps, and even in that simple sound, she knew Prospero was hesitant.

Ellie refused to look back at her. Instead, she folded her arms and stared at the doctor. "Assess me so I can go home."

"It's not quite that simple." The doctor had the same soothing voice that every doctor did.

For a flicker of a moment, Ellie realized this absolute frustration that was bubbling in her belly was exactly what Hestia must have felt when she was being given a list of limits before her surgery.

I owe her an apology.

It was an odd thought, perhaps, given the circumstances, but it felt grounding. That world, *that* life, was her reality. This place was simply a detour, an inconvenience akin to going to urgent care.

Prospero walked up to stand beside Ellie, slightly behind her as if to catch her if she fled.

"She's fine, Mae." Prospero sounded completely calm, as if having life upended, lying, or even sudden bouts of lust and kisses were all perfectly mundane.

A disturbance in the infirmary drew their attention. A tall, muscular man half collapsed against a wall. "Mae?"

"Sondre!" The doctor gestured toward a table. "Sit."

As he half stumbled toward it, Ellie noticed he had a rip in his trousers, calf-high, and two punctures as if something attacked him. When Ellie saw the purple stain, she had a good idea what it was. *My snakes!* That wasn't what they were to do—unless he had gone too close. They were intended to cover and protect the rift.

Ellie looked at Prospero, and then back at the doctor. "Look. Find me the headmaster or a teacher. I'll answer your questions, and then someone can aim me toward the exit."

"That is the headmaster," Prospero said as she stepped forward. Her voice was almost gentle as she added, "You're tired, Miss Brandeau, because your body is trying to adjust to the magic. It'll pass." She paused, not looking away from Ellie. "When you are ready to talk, I'll still be here. I'm not hard to find. And if you have questions, I'll answer any and all of them."

Her words were loaded with things Ellie didn't want to hear . . . almost as much as she desperately did.

"Actually, as much as I hate to say this," the doctor started, "the headmaster needs me. Can you take Miss Brandeau to her room?"

"Of course," Prospero said, straightening.

Ellie's knees buckled, and the doctor directed her to a seat, which was probably for the best because Ellie felt rather like the floor might be swaying. Magical exhaustion was real, apparently. There was tired, and then there was this. Being sedated after the accident wasn't even this exhausting.

"I have her, Mae. Go patch him up." Prospero shot a glare at the man.

Ellie sighed. "Evil ought not be so damned beautiful."

"Witches are not evil, Miss Brandeau," Prospero murmured, almost too low to hear as Mae walked away.

"Being a witch doesn't undo whatever evil is inside you either," Ellie retorted.

Prospero shook her head. "Come, Miss Brandeau, or shall I carry you?"

"There's a chair," the doctor called out as she swished a curtain closed around her and her new patient.

"Stay," Prospero ordered before she walked away, swaying like a temptress trying to beckon Ellie toward certain disaster. That woman was a terrible person, a liar, a manipulator . . . and a terribly good kisser.

Ellie sighed again.

It doesn't matter. It can't. Ellie was going home, where she would slowly turn into a lonely old lady. Better that than pining over a woman who would try to erase or alter Ellie's mind.

But even as she reasoned with herself, Ellie touched her lips, still swollen from kissing Prospero, and tried to tell herself there were far, far more important matters to think about just then.

Unfortunately, neither Ellie's mind nor her body entirely agreed.

22
Chief Witch

A building not too far from Prospero's home and the Tavern of No Repute housed the Congress of Magic. The edifice looked like someone melded a great hall and cave-like warren. The stone of the building was old-fashioned to some people, and newer immigrants sometimes thought it was terribly foolish, but the *natural* was what transmitted magic: Stone. Wood. Water. Earth. Fire. Theoretically, air could be useful—as with blood and bone—but air was difficult to sustain, and the fleshly elements tended to be complicated in other ways.

So all meetings and ceremonies were held in stone rooms with a fountain and earthen bowls, and so it had been for as long as the chief witch could recall. In the land of Crenshaw, most buildings were stone or wood. Every third street had a fountain.

Tradition wasn't always foolish, no matter what the New Economists muttered and yelled.

Right now, it was hard to keep the fountains clean. The sulfurous water ran yellowish, and the stink of it had begun to permeate everything. Still, water conducted magic, and so they kept the fountains flowing although it looked more like something foul than pure.

Will the foul water pervert magic itself?

That was part of the reason the Congress of Magic was having another meeting in the seemingly endless array of meetings that went nowhere. Of course, getting nowhere took a remarkable amount of yelling.

And the odd curse.

The representatives from each of the twenty-six magical houses passed his job around like the steaming pile of garbage it was, and the current chief witch wasn't sure why he'd been tasked with this odious duty again. He hadn't done anything particularly ill-mannered before getting punished with the assignment.

Maybe it was simply because he wasn't the only witch who wanted a chief witch who didn't impose absurd costume regulations. He tugged on the ends of his massive beard.

On acutely unpleasant months, Walter would list the benefits of the job like a little song in his head, but it was a short list. The best— possibly the *only*—reason to take cheer in his responsibility was he was old enough that he wouldn't have to do it another time.

Witches lived for centuries, but they weren't immortal.

Definitely not lately. More and more, there were sudden deaths among the eldest of the citizens.

That decline in longevity was the biggest evidence of the problem. If the elders took centuries to die, why were they suddenly dying? Why was the water purification not enough? What were they to do when new arrivals came? They needed the immigrants, needed their magic, but they had a health and safety crisis in Crenshaw.

"Gil, if you wiggle that stone at me again, I won't apologize for what happens." The chief witch, Walter, modulated his voice so everyone in the hall heard him. Here, whoever held that position was in charge, and whether he wanted the job or not, Walter would have the respect that came with the damnable title.

"You can't excuse her ladyship from attending whenever the mood strikes her," Gilbert grumbled. He had been landed gentry a couple hundred years ago, not as old as Walter but old enough to shake off a few affectations. He was an uncommonly handsome white man who looked young still, perpetually dressed in a smart vest and coat, polished boots, and hat.

"Lady Prospero's hob said she was unwell," the chief witch started.

"Is it the miasma?" someone asked in a trembling voice.

"No. It's likely exhaustion from trying to come up with a solution," he assured them all.

Truth be told, Walter wasn't sure Prospero's absence at this month's meeting was necessarily a bad thing. That woman did what she wanted, when she wanted, how she wanted. When he wasn't chief witch, he rather quietly cheered her on.

"Thinks she's better than us. I came even when I had the boils. Not her hoity-toity-ness. You just excuse her, Walt?" Gilbert yelled.

"My title, if you will." The chief witch hammered on the table. Rules were rules, and when that officious duck pizzle had held the chair, he'd insisted on titles even at social gatherings. "I'd hate to have to badger anyone tonight."

Titters came from across the room, but Gilbert bowed.

"I apologize, Chief Witch." Gilbert cleared his throat and gestured across the room to the twenty-four other house representatives and assorted staff. "We all have days we are not well. Agnes has been passing gas since she walked in."

Agnes, Lady of House Grendel, made a rude gesture at Gilbert. "Because we're drinking poison!"

Her once red hair was slowly developing streaks of white almost as pale as her skin, but the streaks were such that it created the illusion that she'd run bloody hands over white hair. Walter wouldn't put it past her, but he also worried she was sickening. That all of them were. The symptoms varied.

"Prospero isn't here," Walter stated. "And as chief witch, I have commanded this body to carry on with the necessary plans, which she shall be notified of hereafter when she recovers. Where are we on the food stock?"

"Plenty of mead and beer!" Allan, one of the heads of the gardening and booze house, offered. Walter knew they had an official house name, but "House of Dionysus and Jörd" seemed painfully formal for the drunken man.

So they could drink away their hunger? As if that wasn't going to lead to more trouble!

"Six months on the shelf stable," said the other one, Jörd. She had a Northern European pale complexion to Allan's Mediterranean olive skin. She was typically the quiet farmer to Allan's boozy debauchery.

"And the crops?" another voice called out.

"Worse again this month," Jörd added. "The bad water . . . it's simply not good for the food."

"And a few of the fish we gathered the last month were odd in ways that meant I'm not sure that we ought to be eating them," another house head shared.

A quiet filled the building, feeling heavier than silence ought to be.

Walter put his hand on the wall, hoping for some spark of clarity or surge of magic or something. This was the building closest to a holy space in Crenshaw. The home of magical laws and acts.

"So we're in a pickle, and her ladyship is at home with the vapors? Not acceptable." Gilbert shot a glare at the chief witch and surreptitiously tapped a pattern on the heavy obsidian vein that was embedded in the floor.

The chief witch, who had turned 312 or some such number this year, had expected an outburst. He looked at his friend and mouthed, "Bad-ger."

Then he looked around at the group.

Gilbert, Lord of the House of Charybdis, folded his arms. "If she were here, she'd point out that if we open the gates, it'll be all our heads in jars in some doctor's laboratory! Mark my words. I hate to agree with that woman, but—"

Titters of laughter filled the right. Gilbert was the only one who managed to argue with *both* sides. It was a gift, really.

"And if you don't have a solution, maybe you ought to take a seat, old man." The speaker, a woman who was dressed in a newer fashion of robes, made a gesture that was akin to summoning energy. Her hair was as dark as her skin and twisted in a series of long serpentine beach waves, currently stacked atop her head.

"Now see here, Scylla—"

"*Lord Scylla*," the woman corrected, reaching into a pocket and drawing out a handful of tiny seed pearls. Each stone was undoubtedly loaded with a spell.

"I'll eject the both of you," the chief witch reminded them before Scylla could started hurling spells.

"I was only telling him that if he had nothing useful to say, maybe he ought to let those of us who have ideas do the talking," Scylla argued. She went out of her way to channel a Medusa-like energy, and if Walt spoke freely, he might even note that she started arguments as often as Gil and Agnes. *But perhaps not aloud!*

"We can do another food run," Scylla continued. "It doesn't help sufficiently with the water, but we can bring jugs of that home, too."

Gilbert rolled a fat piece of wood between his thumb and index finger. Being bound didn't stop him from throwing a pre-spelled bit of stick or stone at Scylla. Both House Charybdis and House Scylla argued with the same fervor as they did every meeting. They mixed as well as oil and water, and none of the other representatives in the hall tonight interceded. Only one house was invulnerable to their mutual churlishness, and the lady of that house was claiming illness so she could stay home with her research tonight.

Lady Prospero was the scariest witch in Crenshaw, and only a fool crossed her.

Perhaps, Walter admitted to himself, *that was how I landed in the chief witch position. Unlike most of the heads of houses, I'm not afraid of Prospero. The only other person who can say that is Scylla.*

At that point, Cassandra blew open the door to the hall with all the cheer and boisterousness that she did everything. She was as tan as the day she arrived here, and at a glance, she almost seemed unattractive. Plain hair, plain features, voluptuous in a way that some would find too heavy, but most found irresistible. The only seer in the whole of Crenshaw, Cassandra decided knowing everyone's sorrow meant she ought to comfort them, since no one wanted to hear prophecies, so she ran the sex work trade for the town and collected secrets like they were wildflowers.

"I'm late," she trilled out. "I'll hold Prospero's seat tonight so I can report back to her."

For several moments, the vast room—which was akin to a great hall from the era of castles in the Barbarian Lands—fell calm and blissfully silent. This lasted for all of thirty seconds or so before yells filled it. A cacophony of drunken hobs would be more soothing. Magic zipped around in small arguments as the factions erupted into accusations, screaming, and fistfights in one corner.

The chief witch pinched the bridge of his nose, but then he turned to the topic at hand. "We can buy ourselves more time if we siphon a few of the incoming remedials. As chief witch, that is my recommendation. Mark the four or so weakest for siphoning, and we'll proceed. Yemaya can try cleansing the water at the latest fissure."

Prospero had sworn to him that she'd find a plan, but the border that held the line nearest the Barbarian Lands was becoming more porous by the month.

"And we can buttress the southern wall again. The last thing we need is hapless barbarians wondering into town," Scylla said, as if the strength that would take was nothing. Undoubtedly, Prospero had pre-warned her about the border.

"Soon?" the chief witch asked.

"I'll get my house on it tonight," Scylla offered. The House of Scylla was skilled in the sort of illusion work that was as sturdy as rock—which meant that Scylla was almost as bad as Cassandra and Prospero about making her own rules. *Case in point, deciding she preferred being called Lord over Lady.* No one argued with her long.

Each house had its particular skills—that was what divided them into their respective houses. Water witches went to Yemaya; illusionists went to Scylla. Another witch was responsible for growing crops, another for medicine, and still another handled the planning of the town. Others were gifted in sport or music. One witch manipulated minds. One handled money. Every house had a purpose, and the magic seemed to know which houses needed more witches.

Every year, new witches filled the gaps in the houses.

Until recently, Crenshaw was idyllic. Sure, they had factions that argued. And maybe their justice system—turning witches into badgers—seemed a wee bit primitive, but it wasn't like they *killed* people for infractions like people in the Barbarian Lands did.

That peace ended when the water turned foul and witches started dying.

Now fear festered. Quarrels erupted. Politics became dangerous. Ultimately, Walter thought they all quarreled more because of the shared fear—death if Crenshaw collapsed. One faction thought they ought to drop the barriers and step into the light, and the other side thought any means necessary should be used to uphold the barriers.

Both are probably wrong. But Walt was damned if he could think of a third answer. So they'd muddle through until someone else did.

"Medicine?" Walt asked.

"I have sent one of mine over to retrieve it from a hospital," Mae said.

The path ahead was deadly. Witches would continue dying unless they found an answer. Crenshaw couldn't go on as it was, and they *also* couldn't survive without new witches. The water was now toxic, and after centuries of farming, the land had begun to yield questionable produce.

Can't support what we have, can't support new blood, but we'll die without new blood.

There was no solution that worked, and the situation grew more dire by the month. Perhaps it was time to accept the defeat of their hidden world.

Unless the new witch who made snakes at the rift was on to a plan . . .

That one had given Walter a reason to hope, but not so much that he was ready to tell the other Congress of Magic members.

Not yet.

23

Ellie

A day later, Ellie walked into a meeting hall in what appeared to be a fully functional, semimodern castle. The stone walls and floors held a chill that was like natural air-conditioning, and an echo hampered the ability to speak freely, making whispering preferable.

Voices carried, despite the numerous gorgeous tapestries on the stone walls. Ellie suspected the inability to speak quietly wasn't accidental. For a town that seemed to have an identity crisis as to what year it was, Ellie had no doubts that there were canny minds at the helm.

The reality of her situation was somewhere between "I'm fucked," and "I can figure this out."

"Welcome to the College of Remedial Magic," pronounced the robed man in the front of the room. *The headmaster.* She'd glimpsed him briefly in the infirmary. Menace seemed to ooze from his skin like sweat.

Not unlike Prospero.

Ellie's gaze darted toward her briefly, and she realized rather petulantly that on *her*, danger looked like how a fairy-tale candy-made house had to Hansel and Gretel. It was bait for some trap Ellie was certain she should avoid. Her initial instincts had been right: Prospero was temptation made flesh.

Prospero looked like her clothing here was a kind of armor, a second skin she wore into battle. Currently, she was dressed in trousers and a vest. Over them she wore a flaring suitcoat that draped over her back and stretched to her knees. Her coat was fitted in the waist, but there was an almost gender-free cut to the top half of the coat—double-breasted, satin lapels, and what Ellie suspected were bone buttons.

The bones of her enemies, Ellie mused. It shouldn't be sexy, and yet . . . it really, really was.

The man continued speaking: "I am Headmaster Sondre, and over the next few months, I'll be in charge of your education. You will meet the heads of several houses. These individuals were drawn here as they feel a magical pull to someone within our group. If you succeed here, you will join their houses as citizens of Crenshaw."

The assembled class, roughly a dozen other people, had expressions somewhere between intrigued and irritated. One woman was practically bouncing on her toes. Another had her arms crossed over her chest in a fearful pose. One man—with a long thin ponytail that was bound by a series of silver clips against his shaved head, a braided beard, and a black T-shirt—seemed only to have eyes for the scrawny man next to him, who was watching everyone warily.

"Take your seats, please, and we can begin!" Sondre's delivery was more resigned than energetic, and Ellie watched him pointedly not look at the students.

The oldest-looking person Ellie had seen so far stood. He moved slower, and Ellie had to wonder how many years it took to reach *old* as a witch. She had no intention of finding out, but her brain was a librarian's brain, so collecting answers was her thing. She thought he might have been the witch to approach her and Prospero at the rift.

"Welcome to Crenshaw." The man paused and let his gaze drift over them, meeting eyes directly as if he were reading something about each of them. He stroked a cloud-white beard and announced, "I am the chief witch, head of the Congress of Magic. In due time, you will stand before me to be assessed."

That's him.

"For what?" Ellie asked, feeling ready to argue with anyone, but especially with him.

Every eye in the room turned to her. The reactions were a mix of politeness, curiosity, shock, and envy.

"I didn't sign up to come here," she added. "I don't want to be here—"

"Yeah!" someone interjected. "What she said!"

"So how about you just send me home? I don't want to learn your history and whatever. *Nothing*"—Ellie resisted glancing at Prospero—"about your Brigadoon witch land is going to change that."

The chief witch rubbed the bridge of his nose. "Miss . . ."

"Brandeau," the headmaster filled in when Ellie didn't.

"Miss Brandeau, there is a process. You will attend classes for the next several months. After the first session, some students may be returned from whence they came."

"I don't want to wait," Ellie said, crossing her arms and glaring at the old man. "I want to go home now. I volunteer."

"That's not how it works. You will stay until you are assessed. At that time, if you fail out of our program, your memory will be altered so as not to expose Crenshaw to the Barbarian Lands, and—"

"Suppose you can't erase my memory?" Ellie continued to resist looking at Prospero.

"Lady Prospero"—he gestured toward her—"has a unique type of magic, Miss Brandeau. No one here or there has ever been immune."

Ellie now turned her gaze to Prospero, who looked rather like she was trying not to speak. Their eyes locked, and, for a moment, Ellie pressed her thoughts at Prospero. "*So what happens? Do you lie to them or trust me?*"

Prospero's eyes widened as if she heard Ellie.

Prospero's voice slid into Ellie's mind. "*This is . . . new.*"

Despite her best intentions, Ellie looked away first. Maybe that was normal? Maybe it was just another side effect of why Prospero couldn't steal Ellie's memories? The truth, however, was Ellie didn't want the other witch in her head.

"We aren't your enemy," the chief witch said, expanding his conversation to the assembled group. "You are special, born with a genetic ability that some trauma awakened, and to exist in their world as you are *now* would inevitably result in persecution of our kind. To protect you, them, and us, there is a process we will follow. This is a necessity."

The headmaster cleared his throat, loudly. Another witch, an exceedingly pale one who had bone-white hair with red streaks in it, snorted.

"Allegedly," the woman said.

"Over fifty thousand people, Agnes. Murdered as witches." The chief witch pinched the bridge of his nose again.

"For being odd or old or outspoken," the red-and-white-haired witch snapped. "Most of them weren't actual witches, and you know it, Walt."

"They are still dead, Agnes." Prospero's voice rang out loud and clear. "So are plenty of lesbians, gays, transgender people. So are people whose skin is different, whose faith is, whose—"

"Well, they didn't have magic," the red-and-white-haired witch, Agnes, retorted. "We can defend ourselves. I could fold them inside out and—"

"Order!" the chief witch called out, cutting off the argument.

There was obvious dissent here, and if this was the leadership on their best behavior—as one would expect in front of the new students—Ellie wasn't sure their worst would be tolerable. She recalled the things she'd learned from Prospero. She didn't want to expose this world to the non-magical world, and others—including the headmaster and Agnes—did.

The chief witch continued, "We have a system here in Crenshaw. It works. So you all will attend the College of Remedial Magic. Should your magic be too weak, you might be selected for siphoning. This would allow you to return to the Barbarian Lands without magic or memory of your time here."

"And if not? Someone will look for us and—"

"Not necessarily." The chief witch took a deep breath. "Any connections you had there will be induced to forget you, or they will futilely seek you. There is no travel permitted between the worlds other than by the acting headmaster and Lady Prospero or those they send to assist them."

Every student seemed to be hit by this revelation.

"But my fiancé—"

"Nothing there for me."

"I'll fail out anyhow."

"The band will profit." The Viking-looking man nodded. "This is good."

"Who wants to go back to life without magic!"

"My son!"

The last one was more scream than word. The speaker, an angry-looking auburn-haired white woman, seemed to deflate, as if the weight of her loss was too much. She glanced at the headmaster, who steadfastly did not look her way.

The chief witch, however, was moving on to the next item on his agenda. "Some of you have magic that has called out to specific heads of houses. They will be taking turns instructing you, and should you succeed, you may find yourself under one of their umbrellas." He motioned to the very pale witch with the white-and-red hair. "With us today is Agnes, Lady of House Grendel, head of our house of justice. She studies the laws we have here—as well as patrolling the borders in case our walls falter."

He then gestured to a Black woman whose hair was a series of long waves that fell to her waist. "Lord Scylla is a master of illusion. The House of Scylla primarily keeps the walls in place to protect Crenshaw from discovery."

This time, the murmurs were a few quiet sounds asking why Lord Scylla, who dressed in feminine garb, used the male title. The only answer forthcoming was Scylla saying, "Because I like it."

"All of you have met Dr. Jemison." The chief witch beamed at the doctor, who merely nodded.

"Allan, current Lord Dionysus, head of our plants and drinks. His associate, Jörd, who fulfills the gardening and food production part of the duties when Allan is, er, resting." The chief witch looked vaguely awkward as he glanced at the woman, Jörd, who sprawled over a chair like she was bored with the whole meeting.

Jörd, who was barely clothed and had deep red scratches all over her muscular arms, grinned. "I handle the earth's fertility. I won't be found inside classrooms."

"Welcome!" Allan said cheerily, lifting a horn overflowing with some sort of liquor. "If you stay, please stop in at the Tavern of No Repute for celebration!"

A glance too long at Jörd had Ellie ready to blush at the thoughts that rose unbidden.

Magic, she reminded herself, jerking her gaze back to the chief witch.

"Omer and Fatima, Heads of House Hephaestus, who manage building, roads, and general infrastructure." The chief witch motioned to a brown-skinned man and a woman with a hijab covering her hair and neck. "They repurpose housing materials, too."

The pair murmured greetings, but they seemed distracted.

For a moment, the chief witch looked like he needed a stiff drink, but then he gestured at a group of people currently arguing. "The house of . . . which of you is currently the name of the house?"

"Xochipilli."

"Nike."

"Lugh."

"Hermes."

"Takemikazuchi," said an Asian man.

The five answered simultaneously—and loudly. Ellie wasn't sure which name was the person's name and which was the god or being after which they were arguing the house's name ought to be.

"The entertainment house," the chief witch muttered. "Not arts, but—"

"Sports!" Xochipilli, who was as Latinx in appearance as the god whose name he carried, cheered in a husky voice. "We have a gaming space with—"

"Races," said Hermes, who was a short man with calves so overdeveloped that they appeared carved.

"Combat sport," Takemikazuchi added.

"I won that last bout," grumbled Lugh, who was ginger-haired and stout.

"You cheated," argued Nike, a non-gender-specific person with a slight tan.

"*I* do not cheat," Takemikazuchi said simply, hand on the hilt of a sword.

"House of Takemikazuchi," the other four all answered as one.

"Excellent." The chief witch smiled wider. "We lack for nothing in Crenshaw, including sporting events for entertainment! There are music houses, as well, but . . . punctuality is not always the current head of house's priority! You will meet him and others of the dozen or so houses as time progresses, but we don't want to overwhelm anyone." The chief witch gave a chuckle. "No sense setting off any magical panic."

For all that Ellie was ready to go home, she took a moment to pause and acknowledge that Crenshaw had a governmental structure covering many key elements—farming, infrastructure, security, and order. They had a program for education. It seemed like a well-run, inviting place.

Aside from that purple sludge at the rift.

A part of Ellie, the part that she kept in a box filled with hidden urges, whispered that she should stay here.

Prospero says they need me.

At home, however, was Aunt Hestia. At home was security and quiet. At home was everything she knew. She belonged there, not here where witches erased minds at a whim and illusion was so common that it was part of the introduction to the world. She'd lose nothing by leaving.

Except Prospero.

And maybe a grand romance.

And magic.

And a chance to save lives if I can help with the rift.

24

Dan

After deciding that the best move was to avoid mentions of the snake, the dead witch, and the bloody-haired witch, Dan was trying to focus on how to stay here. If he could avoid whatever that drama was, he could build a life here.

Maybe with Axell in it.

Today, he was at the back of the queue of students now traipsing out of the castle toward the village. He was assessing them with a more mercenary gaze than he'd thought himself capable of having. He had no intention of being removed from this weird, wonderful place—and if that meant that he had to work against his classmates, he would. Sabotage wasn't his default setting, but if needs must, he decided he could—and would—be ruthless.

Except with Axell. Dan wanted him to stay. Maybe he was trusting too fast, but he thought they had something.

Were there a set number of students who had to leave? No one mentioned *that*, but surely, there was more to the process than simply, "You fail, you leave!" And where did the siphoned magic go? Did they *need* siphoned magic? What was the process of siphoning? Was the magic redistributed?

Not Axell. Not Maggie since Sondre likes her . . .

Dan had more questions than they had answered, and after a lifetime of dealing with microaggressions—the inevitability of life as a member of the "Alphabet Mafia"—Dan tended to pay as much attention to what was left unsaid as what was said. So far, the chief witch was focusing on a few basic details, and Dan felt confident there were reasons. The government lied. It didn't matter *which* government; they all did. He didn't need to finish his abandoned history degree—one of several incomplete degrees—to know that.

"Do you think they'll make us do something awful?" a woman whispered to him. "I bet they're all perverts. Liberals."

Dan rolled his eyes and pointed at himself. "Gay. Democrat."

She scurried off.

Maybe a little bit of sabotage could be fun.

He looked at a few other people. There was one woman who looked to be about sixty. She had the sort of figure that spoke of someone who enjoyed good meals with no guilt, and her hair was caught in a long braid that was looped into a bun. At first glance, she seemed like someone's sweet abuela, but the glint in her gaze when she turned to him was assessing.

"Not everything is a competition."

He nodded. "How'd you end up, er, almost dying?"

"Monsoon when I was walking." She shrugged. "My husband had died, and I was thinking about him. Mourning. So I wasn't watching the skies or checking the weather apps. Flash floods are deadly sometimes in the Southwest. You?"

"I tried to go hiking. Fell." Dan tried to match her tone. "Broke my . . . well, my everything."

She grinned. "Lucky you're gifted. You're too skinny to last long if you ended up in a ravine. I'm Ana."

"Dan."

"I won't be going back, Dan, so set your eyes on others." Her smile was harder than the rocks he'd mistakenly tried to hike. Even ancient glaciers wouldn't carve her edges away. She added, "I will be joining the agricultural house."

He gaped at her. "How do you know?"

Ana put a hand on her heart. "I know who I am." She looked him up and down. "Some of us have to figure that out to exist in that world, eh?"

Despite the competitive impulse he'd felt, he looked at her and grinned. "You're a little scary, Ana."

"You're wiser than you look," she answered with a laugh.

When she laughed, he felt warmer, happier, as if there was something about her that was innately nurturing, but in his brief stint in pursuing a degree in Comparative Mythology, he'd quickly learned that most people saw nature goddesses differently in the past. Creator and destroyer, that was what a nurturing woman was at her heart, and Ana was a living, breathing reminder that nature—the source of his own near-death experience—was far more scary than direct violence. Natural disasters were destruction on a scale that mere humans couldn't accomplish often.

Ana cut a path through the other students, clearly ready to get to know more people. She was wasting no time in getting a sense of her peers. It made him like her even more.

Dan was one of a dozen—Ana, Maggie, Axell, the nervous woman, and the angry one.

I guess that makes me the gay one.

He grinned, eying another person who definitely signaled as possibly nonbinary. The *majority* of the people in his class were not your standard white-bread boring. Not always in the same way, but there was definite variety among the new witches.

Everything about today felt far more exciting than his first go-round in college had been. Magic. Pass or get kicked out of the entire magical world. Intrigue between faculty. And that woman with the attitude . . . *oof.* He was pretty sure avoiding *her* at all costs was the wisest choice he could make.

He was making his way toward Axell, who was staring at him now, when he was stopped mid-turn.

"Mr. Monahan? Daniel?" Sondre called out, sounding so formal that Dan could almost pretend they had never spoken.

Maybe that would've been better.

Dan saw the witch he was hoping to avoid glance his way. *Ellen Brandeau or something.* She had looked startled, like she recognized his name, but he'd never met her.

Dan put a larger gap between him and Axell. Sondre was dangerous, and Axell was without filters. It seemed wisest to keep them apart.

In a level voice, Sondre added, "I try to check in on all the students individually. One per day as it were."

Dan nodded and fell in step with him, hating the creeping itch of Sondre's cover story, but still smiling and saying, "Sure thing."

"Get to know the mouthy one," Sondre whispered. "I *do* need to talk to everyone."

"Sure thing," Dan repeated, optimism flagging more. Nothing good could come of this request. Dan knew it in that fundamental way that he knew a lot of things, but just as clearly, he knew there were a lot of things Sondre could ask that would be worse.

Honestly, Dan suspected there would be worse things.

"Settling in well?" Sondre asked louder. "I like to be sure you're all adjusting well to our world. It can be a lot."

Dan gave him an are-you-serious look, before saying, "Castle? Hobs? Magic? Yeah, I think it's pretty much ideal. How are *you* doing this week?"

Sondre faltered slightly. "You're an odd one, Mr. Monahan." He frowned at Dan. "No one asks me that."

"Well, I just fucking did, so . . . how are you? I bet all these new arrivals at once is stressful." Dan tried to ignore the flicker of joy he felt at Sondre's surprise. "I'm staying, you know. Then I'm going to be your friend. Friends ask, 'How are you?' So *how are you?*"

Sondre glanced at Maggie. "I hate this job."

"Really?"

"It's a punishment, meant to keep me busy." Sondre's gaze swept the group. "At least I get to meet all the incoming witches." He looked at Dan. "Even those who unilaterally decide to be my friend."

"Could be worse. 'Least you're not a badger," Dan said quietly.

Sondre laughed abruptly, seemingly surprised by his own burst of chuckles, but then he nodded and clapped Dan's shoulder. "Right you are, Danny Boy. Right you are. Could always be worse!"

Then he wandered off, greeting several other students and seeming far more jovial than he had appeared thus far in Dan's experience. It was an act, though. Dan was sure of that. He doubted much brought genuine smiles to Sondre's face, but he wanted the grumpy man to like him.

Build a new life. Make friends. Connections for when I am guaranteed to stay.

Dan glanced at Axell, who was chatting with Ana and Maggie, and made his way toward them. They were staying, too: Ana because he couldn't imagine anyone telling her no, Maggie because Sondre liked her, and Axell because . . . but Dan would ask Sondre if he had to. He *liked* the Norwegian man.

"Daniel!" Axell called.

Dan rejoined him. Maybe it was as simple as being told Sondre could make it so Dan could stay. Maybe it was being treated like he was important. It didn't really matter, though. Dan would do whatever Sondre asked to stay here and healthy.

And far away from that snake.

He felt certain it would be fine as Axell's arm reached out and pulled him close. No one had ever acted like that, like Dan's presence mattered, like his nearness was exciting.

I fucking love being a witch.

25

Prospero

Walter and Sondre were the only two people at the tea shop when Prospero arrived. No one questioned their odd collective, but she knew without doubt that they were being watched. Such was the nature of a town on the edge of panic.

"Lady Prospero," Walter said, standing at her arrival.

"Chief Witch." She nodded her head in greeting. The old Scotsman was probably the person she most trusted other than Cassandra and Scylla—the difference was that Cassandra was cagey, and both Scylla and Walt were very direct. It was why she called in favors to appoint him chief witch. Crenshaw was at a crossroads, and someone able to be objective had to be the balancing voice.

Sondre did not stand. He kicked a chair out and slid an empty teacup toward her.

"About the new witch . . ." Walter started. "She should've been taken to the castle immediately."

"She was creating a plug, trying to cover the rift—"

"Why would a stranger do that?" Sondre interrupted.

"Because it stinks?" Prospero offered with a tight smile.

Walter looked between them, as if he were a suspicious parent. He wasn't wrong to look askance at her, and they likely all knew it. "Do you have anything else to explain how you were the one to find her?"

Prospero sighed. "Look, she appeared here. I tried to talk to her. Then she was making a damnable serpent whose fangs dripped poison. What else would you have me say?"

"You should have summoned me," Sondre said, not wrongly either.

"And leave a remedial witch alone at the rift?" Prospero bit out. "Sure, and while we're at it, why don't we just widen the rift, let the poison out, and allow widespread death?"

"Prospero." Walter's quelling look was enough to make her stay in her seat.

"Fine." She took a calming breath. "And the witch who died? Eric? I couldn't get to him and get her out of there."

"How are we to be sure you didn't kill him?" Sondre asked sotto voce.

"Sondre." Walt glared at him. "Prospero is not a killer."

"Are you sure?" Sondre crossed his arms.

Prospero smiled slowly. "Since *you* are still alive, I suspect Walt has a point."

Walter made a sound that was more growl than word and slapped his palm on the table. "Enough."

For a moment, no one spoke. Their animosity was all Sondre's fault as far as Prospero knew. He still blamed her for his life—as if dying would've been better.

"What's the verdict on supplies?" Prospero looked at them both, noticing the grim turn of their expressions at her question.

"We need another run." Walter's lips pressed into a tight line.

Prospero, despite her issues with Sondre, met his gaze. That was worse than she'd expected. "Already?"

"Housing is problematic as well. We simply don't have enough suites or apartments for the new arrivals." Walter poured her tea, and she noticed with a not-insignificant flare of guilt that the water was crystal clean. There were perks to Walter's station—and to hers and Sondre's.

She still felt bad knowing others didn't have that privilege simply because their magical ability was of a lower level. All witches had basic gifts, and some had a lot more magic than others. Then there were the heads of houses, the witches who ran Crenshaw. She was one of them, and so her safety would likely not be imperiled soon. It would eventually: poisoned water would sicken all of them.

"We could stretch out the length of the classes and keep the students at the castle for at least six months," Sondre offered. "If not, we're looking at having most of the new arrivals move in with existing households."

"And if most of them do stay in Crenshaw, we will have to decrease food and clean water distribution even more." Walt rubbed his forehead, as if he could wipe worry away. "We can try to tell the citizens that there's a mead sale."

"They'd know why. Honestly, we ought to tell them before they decide if they want to stay here or be siphoned." She stood and began to pace. "What if I start bringing back water only? Or we could do half supplies and half water?" Prospero made eye contact with Sondre as she added, "We could both go together every Monday. We just need a second truck."

Sondre crossed his arms over his chest. It was as close to relaxed as he ever was around her. "Steal even more from some family because we have a need? Is that *right*?"

"They have 'chain stores' now, Sondre. Not a person or family, just a big company. We can get a second truck." Prospero squirmed a little at the awkwardness of the idea. "Gemstones could work if we need to pay. I don't know the exchange rate, but one of them still ought to be worth enough for a pile of food or a few barrels of water. We could create a food committee. You and me. We take the volunteers over, and I can . . . make the people accept the stones."

"It's not a terrible idea." Walt beamed at her. "Maybe we can import other new things, too? Surely, there's something you miss."

"Steak," Sondre muttered. "I miss steak."

It was odd the things many citizens of Crenshaw missed, and Prospero wondered yet again if there was something broken in her. The only things she missed were newly issued books. New, just-printed books. She didn't have access to as many as she wanted, and her brief time over in the Barbarian Lands when she'd debated an attempt on Ellie's life had reminded her all too well that Crenshaw had a lack of new things to read. *A library of new releases.* After a century or so here, Prospero had read all the books they had on hand. Sometimes a new arrival brought a book or two, so there were additions.

Not that I have much free time of late.

The responsibility for her home—her whole world, really—weighed her down. The citizens were adults, every last one of them, but she spent her waking hours trying to find ways to stretch out their time here, extend their space, expand their ability to gather provisions.

And with literal mountains on either side, there is only so much even a witch can do.

She shrugged. "We can try to work together."

Walt looked cheerful at the thought. "We'd need volunteers to carry the extra supplies. Trustworthy ones who could . . . pass for modern and not wander off into the wilds."

Sondre nodded to himself. "I'll get the hobs to collect the clothing from the latest arrivals and modify it to fit the volunteers."

Walt's head hob popped in with another garish scarf and hat. He dutifully stood and donned the fuchsia and orange knitwear. "Shall we go to the warehouse?"

The unlikely trio walked to the food reserves.

"Back in the beginning, we brought in most of the supplies to build houses and everything," Walter said, voice low in that conversational tone he adopted when he was carefully politicking. "Food wasn't a problem then. Water either. Hell, we were even allowed a child per couple if we wanted one."

"You brought in *all* the supplies for the houses at the beginning?" Sondre asked.

Prospero thought about all the things that had once been common knowledge but were no longer part of the remedial witchcraft classes. No sense talking about frequent transfers from the Barbarian Lands when it was so dangerous. With the new technology over there, trips to gather supplies had been reduced to food only.

"More or less," she said. "There was a village here. Abandoned for whatever reason—"

"Plague," Walter interjected. "But that was a couple hundred years ago. Before both of your times. It was easier to slip into their world and liberate things. These days, we repair what is here. Magic evolved to fit our needs."

They walked to the old kirk that had become a food reserve. The guard stepped aside, not remarking on the oddity of seeing Sondre and Prospero walking together. Word of it would spread, though. They'd been spotted sharing tea and now this.

Maybe it will ease worries. That was likely Walt's plan. For all that he said he hated politics, he was damn good at it.

The short walk passed in silence.

"If this works, we can continue to import extra food." Walt closed the door behind them.

The scarcity of food on the towering shelves made Prospero's stomach clench. Barrels, sacks, and bunches of dried herbs were to one side. Jars of pickled and preserved food were to the other. A small bit of meat was drying, and salted fish hung on looping strings. The river only provided a few varieties, but they were prized.

There was one cold room, kept so via magic, but most of the food was the same temperature as the outside world.

"It's worth a try to bring more, especially water," she suggested, staring at Sondre. It was as close to an olive branch as she'd ever given. "We could do great things together, you know."

"It's not a real solution," he argued, but his gaze darted over the food reserves, too.

"Neither is a bandage, but it can help. Can we try to cooperate?" She didn't touch him, but she started to raise a hand as if to do so. Her brief time with Ellie had already made her weaker, softer.

He flinched.

She dropped her hand. "Recon. That's what it's called, right? We do recon. Maybe if we go over there more than the few trips a year we typically do, you can convince me I'm wrong—or maybe you'll see I'm right."

Sondre scoffed, but he said, "I'll change clothes. We'll do a food and water run today."

Then he walked out, leaving her alone with Walt.

The door had barely dropped closed before Prospero sagged a little, feeling as if her strings had been abruptly cut. She could relax more around the chief witch.

"He seems more amenable." Walt scratched his head through the blindingly colorful hat he still wore.

"If we go over there, we'll be hunted, Walt. You know that." Prospero didn't understand Sondre's drive for conflict. She could, obviously, lean in toward violence as necessary, but it wasn't her first thought.

"Staying here will kill us slowly, though," the chief witch pointed out. "I'm not sure there is an answer."

"Slower buys us time. If we expose ourselves to the people there . . ." Prospero touched her cheek. On the day she arrived here, the occipital bone had been shattered, and her eye was barely attached. By the time her husband had paused and left her for dead on the sitting room floor, she had welcomed the idea of death. Instead, she'd woken up here. "I can't live over there."

"Agreed." Walt stroked his beard. "I don't miss the bloodshed, lass. Even now, the memory lingers too clearly."

"Same." Prospero felt her emotions well. "We'll figure it out."

"Perhaps," Walt demurred.

26
Prospero

Prospero added a long coat over her clothes, but she didn't bother with a costume. Since he was the person who drove and interacted with people, Sondre was dressed in his jeans, a button-down shirt, heavy black boots, and a leather jacket.

"We'll need to use more magic if it's just the two of us." Sondre gestured her forward. He never agreed to her walking behind him.

They each rolled a barrel in front of them.

"We will be bringing a load of supplies today," she told the barrier guards as she and Sondre stepped through the wall that protected Crenshaw.

The wall wasn't solid, simply a very convincing illusion with repelling magic woven into it. Non-magical folk would think it was a slick mountain face with briars decorating the slope. Not a place to cross, or climb, or really even think about it. Scylla's magic was nearly infallible.

As they walked to the giant truck hidden in a cave near the border, Prospero wondered how hard it was to drive. She'd been in vehicles, often in the back of the truck where she slid around the trailer.

"I'll ride up front today." She jerked open the passenger door, stepped up onto the metal step, and grabbed a handle alongside the door to hoist herself into the truck's main carriage.

"You never ride in the cab," Sondre said as he climbed into the driver's seat.

Cab, she mentally corrected herself. *Cab, not carriage.*

"The back is uncomfortable," she admitted.

He said nothing as they drove toward the warehouse they visited. It wasn't ideal as they could only select from whatever was there, but the imported foodstuffs were enough to offset the bad growing seasons.

By the time they arrived, Prospero was worrying the barrels they'd brought were not enough.

"How do we fill the barrels?" she asked as Sondre backed the giant truck up to the building's loading dock. It reminded her of the dock at the harbor when she was still living in this world. Ships would unload cargo ranging from sugar to bolts of fabric.

"Let me go first," he said, shucking his jacket so his work shirt was obvious. "Unless you need to, I don't want you messing with his head."

Prospero sighed. The argument against her gift grew tedious no matter how many times they'd had it. "It doesn't hurt them."

"Says you." Sondre hopped out of the truck and sauntered up to a man with a pen and clipboard who had stepped out of an office at the back of the dock.

Prospero couldn't hear their discussion, but she could tell the man was angry and suspicious. He was gesticulating in wide sweeps. Sondre was still wearing his affable expression. Objectively, she could see why people found him charming, but that friendly demeanor was never turned toward her.

She opened the truck's door, hopped down, and walked toward them.

"No record of a scheduled pickup." The man jabbed a meaty finger at the list on his clipboard.

"We're early. They were to call and—"

"No name on the list, no loading. It's not a new rule, Sean." The man clearly wasn't open to negotiation. He used the name stitched on Sondre's shirt. "So unless I have a call from logistics—"

"Is there an issue?" Prospero asked as she strolled up to join Sondre.

She could see by the clench of his jaw that he was not asking for her to help, but he obviously needed her to adjust the man's mind. If not, they'd be left with either resorting to violence or returning with an empty truck.

So she reached into the man's mind with her magic and snagged the memory of their last trip where he saw "Sean's" name on the roster. She pulled it forward to the now, as if the sheet in front of him had the name at the very bottom.

"Isn't that us?" she asked, stepping close to the dock supervisor. "Right there."

Sondre looked away, but the dock supervisor squinted at his list. There was, of course, no extra name there, but he saw it there all the same. "Sorry, man. I swear it wasn't there before. Long night last night."

"No worries." Sondre held out a hand to shake.

After the quick shake, the dock worker pushed a wheeled trolley at them. "Go ahead in and load her up."

Obviously embarrassed, he turned and walked toward his office.

"You're a monster," Sondre grumbled as he snatched the trolley. "How many times can his mind handle that invasion before it's mush?"

She grabbed a second trolley. "I don't hurt them. I've said as much dozens of times."

"Tell that to my brother. Dementia. That's what you did." Sondre stomped forward, hefting a bag of rice and another of dried beans.

"I did not cause your brother's mind sickness," she said to his departing back.

They continued on, gathering flour, sugar, salt, pasta noodles, oats, peas, more varieties of beans. While one of them rolled the cargo into the truck, the other continued to load the supplies for their "grocery store."

It was true to a degree—they were gathering provisions for Crenshaw's grocery supply.

She added crates of tinned fruit and vegetables, powered milk, and some hard cheeses. They worked forward with a combination of a list they always had and odd items that weren't always in stock. Today, they added paper goods, several bolts of fabric, wood, metal bolts and nails, some farming tools, pots, and a pan.

"Bed linens?" Prospero asked as he swept a pile of blankets and sheets onto his trolley.

Sondre ignored her.

Prospero reached the fresh produce area. It was such a treat for the residents, but they didn't always have room in the truck. She topped her next load off with fruits, lettuce, onions, and potatoes. Maybe healthier food would help their eldest members resist the water sickness better.

"Any ideas on the best plan to fill the liquor barrels with water?" she finally asked.

"There's hoses on some of the faucets." Sondre pointed to a red nozzle poking out of the wall. A long green tube was attached to it. "I'll bring the barrels in."

He didn't make a point that she wasn't strong enough to lift them, and she was silently grateful for that.

While he was getting the barrels, Prospero turned a corner and found herself face-to-face with a tower of plastic-wrapped bottles. By the time Sondre was back, Prospero was eying a machine with wide metal tines like a fork.

"Can you drive that?" She pointed at the small yellow machine. "I've seen them move these pallets with it."

"The forklift? Yeah. Why?"

She pointed at the stack of bottled water. "I want that."

He walked away and grabbed what looked like tines on wheels. "A pallet jack is easier." He slid it under the water cases, the tines entering the openings in the pallet, and then with seeming ease, toted the entire tower of water off to the dock.

She looked around for a second pallet jack.

"You fill the barrels and work on the variety," he said when he returned. "I'll take all of this out to the truck."

"All?"

"I hate to say it's a good idea since it's your idea, but it is." He rolled away with the second pallet of water before she could reply.

The flicker of hope that they could move past their conflict, that they could work together rather than against each other, made her walk deeper into the grocery storage warehouse to where they kept the meats.

At the far back corner was a cooler stocked with meat. They didn't generally take as much of that. It wasn't essential, as they'd always had fish aplenty—until the water had gone bad recently.

She stacked trays of ground meat, roasts, and the like on the trolley. On top of all of it, she added the best-looking steaks she could find. Then with as little remark as Sondre had made, she rolled her trolley filled with meat to the truck.

Sondre straightened and eyed her suspiciously. "That wasn't on the list. It doesn't store well."

"Well, maybe it would make *some* people happy." She kept her back to him as she moved the meat to the stacks in the truck bed.

From behind her, Sondre finally said, "This doesn't mean we're friends, Prospero."

She looked over her shoulder. "Agreed. Wouldn't it be nice not to be enemies, though?"

He said nothing as he walked away into the warehouse for more water.

It wasn't perfect, but as she'd told him about this plan: bandages help. And if bringing back dead cow would appease her adversary, she was willing to try.

More and more, she had begun to think the chief witch was right:

there was no good solution. If the water was turned, and the air was unhealthy, and the space had become too small, continuing to cling to the past wasn't the solution.

Unfortunately, mixing into *this* world was too dangerous. The most logical solution was to move the whole town, but even with magic, she wasn't sure such a thing was even possible.

27
Maggie

The first day's long class appeared to be on medical magic, and Maggie was surprised to find the whole thing was genuinely interesting.

"I'm Dr. Jemison," the witch at the front of the room said. "You've all met me in the infirmary for your intake exams. Everyone has basic healing as a result of the magic in your veins."

Dr. Jemison had the most approachable manner of all the witches Maggie had met so far. Maybe it was because she was a healer. Maybe she was simply charismatic.

The doctor explained how their internal magical flow would unage them to some degree and that basic illness and sicknesses were historically a nonissue in Crenshaw. Maggie's stomach tightened at "historically." Her experiences seeking legal loopholes meant she focused instantly on that detail.

Before Maggie could ask a question, the doctor said, "I need a volunteer for—"

The Norwegian band guy, Axell, spoke. "I will do it."

"I didn't say what I needed," the doctor pointed out.

"I am willing." He stood, and Maggie had to give him credit. He was still wearing a pair of his tattered jeans, and whatever his shirt was, it was cut low in the chest, revealing an intricate tattoo. That was not unusual. What was *odd* was that Axell was one of those who had taken to wearing robes. His were draped over him like a long suitcoat. The open robe flared out as he strode forward, and the sides of the robe were a giant elegant frame around the tattooed, muscular man. Though it ought to look contrived, it was natural on him, as if he had always worn such absurd clothes.

"What do you want of me?" He stared at their instructor in a way that made him seem in charge.

"I will ask them to assess your health," she said. "Then I will injure you."

Axell nodded. "You will? Not . . ." His gaze drifted toward Ellie Brandeau. "Anyone else?"

Dr. Jemison said something too low to hear, and Axell nodded once. Then he took off his jacket, revealing a sleeveless shirt. Then he peeled off his shirt, too.

"When your patient is on your table . . ." The doctor paused as a table appeared.

Axell dutifully sat on it. He gathered his robe into a bunched-up thing and held it in his lap. As he did, he stared straight forward, not making eye contact with anyone in the room.

Dr. Jemison continued. "You need to be aware that a pleasant exterior—which most witches develop—is not proof that there is no injury." She held up a hand, and they all watched as she lifted her palm, which visibly darkened. "What we do when we assess an injury is to first project our magic gently into their skin. Think of it as throwing a ball that you know will return to you."

"Like a boomerang," Daniel, an increasingly vocal student, said. "Or something you drop on a trampoline!"

The doctor nodded. Her hand brightened like it was a hot coal, and then the light she'd generated pulsed out like a strobe and sank into Axell's skin.

"My patient flinched because I have warmed my magic so you can watch it." The doctor directed the energy over the student's chest, but she stopped at his belly button. "For your exercise, you will stop here, no lower, *or* you may start at the ankle and work only to the area above the knee."

She looked at Axell, who grimaced and gave a single nod.

"Does it hurt?" a student asked.

"The opposite," Axell answered tersely.

"I do not typically select a male volunteer for this, as it is apparent when they react to this spell." The doctor's expression was bland, but as her meaning became clear, more than a few people's gazes went to Axell's bunched-up robe.

Axell, for his part, simply looked at the room's ceiling. He didn't appear embarrassed—or arrogant, for that matter. There was no smirk, but now that she understood what was happening, Maggie could see the tension in him.

"Why does it feel that way?" she asked. "I was healed—a lot of us were—but it didn't feel *good.*"

The doctor smiled like Maggie had answered a question correctly. "Because you were in so much pain that the pleasure was not obvious. The pleasure counters a measure of the agony if you're legitimately injured, so it offsets the limits of pain relief options in Crenshaw."

It was a clever system, and Maggie could give credit where credit was due. It didn't change her opinions. She still wanted to go home, *needed* to go home, but she was vaguely disappointed that once she did, she wouldn't remember all of the adaptations magic allowed.

"Right. You see the basics, and so each of you will try your hand. I'll help you with the words you need to utter while you direct the magic into the volunteer's body." The doctor motioned them forward, and Maggie joined the group.

She cast a surreptitious glance at Dan. He was too close for comfort, but he seemed vaguely anxious. *Maybe because Axell was the one at the front of the class.*

They waited their turn, and Maggie was unpleasantly surprised to see two of her classmates intentionally push the boundary.

Maggie started to notice that they were being called on in a not entirely random order. If there was a strong magic—and there were two—the next couple were weaker. It was as if Dr. Jemison could already tell who was and was not adept.

When it was Daniel's turn, he had a tiny spark like a few specks of glitter in hand, and for the first time, Axell looked disappointed.

"He really likes you," she whispered to Daniel when he came back to stand at her side.

Dan looked back at Axell and smiled. "That's what he tells me."

Two more students went, both lower level, and then it was Maggie's turn. She stayed as far back as she could, not loving the idea of being the center of this sort of attention. Arguing in court was one thing, but this felt uncomfortably personal.

Maggie felt a low hum, like a tiny vibration in her skin, as she said the necessary words.

Carefully, she directed that glow into Axell's foot. She could feel the callus on his second toe that another student mentioned.

Then she glanced over her shoulder at Dan, who had stepped too close and stumbled into her.

She felt her magic surge as his hand touched her spine to steady himself. She was glad not to fall, but the pulsation she felt surged like switching a vibrator from low buzz to atomic level.

Maggie tried to step forward, away from Dan's touch, but he followed—and the magic just kept building.

"Everyone out!" Dr. Jemison yelled.

The room filled with scurrying sounds. Chairs falling. Words blurted. Maggie had only the sense of noise and chaos, but after a moment, Maggie felt Dan finally withdraw, too.

It was all she could do to hold back some of the magic.

She could see as well as feel the magic flowing from her into Axell, a wave of energy rushing at him. He was writhing and making noises she wasn't sure she ought to hear. "Sorry. Didn't mean . . ."

Then her teacher stepped in front of her, like an extra junction in the magic that was insisting it needed to flow.

"Let it go, Maggie," Dr. Jemison ordered. "All of it."

So she did.

Maggie looked away from Axell, away from Dr. Jemison, and closed her eyes against the lash of magic that ricocheted through her own body. She bit down on her lip and swayed, still pointedly not looking at either of the two other people still in the room. Sharing unplanned magic-induced orgasms was not something she had ever considered in her life.

When Maggie opened her eyes, Dr. Jemison was looking directly at her, relatively composed, even though her shaking voice betrayed her. "That was unexpected."

"But not unwelcome," Axell said calmly. "I am not upset with you, Maggie."

"I tried to . . . to stop the magic from . . ." She glanced from the Viking-looking man to her teacher. "I am *so* sorry."

Dr. Jemison smiled. "Oh, Maggie, we can all use a little joy, can't we? I felt how much energy you were trying to contain, and I apologize. I had no idea you were so powerf—"

"I'm not."

"Beg to differ." Axell squirmed slightly. "That was a lot, er, of the magic sex. Doc? Any magical napkins or towels?"

"I would suggest returning to your rooms to clean up." The doctor gave him a sympathetic smile.

"And a nap," Axell joked as he stood, robe still gathered in front of him. Then he caught Maggie's eye. "No regrets, Miss Maggie. No guilt." His words felt like an order, but he was so *young* that she felt guilt all the same. Then he added in a soft voice, "If I wasn't pursuing Daniel, I would ask you to join me in my room . . . to hold you after that."

"Thanks for saying that," Maggie managed to reply, face flaming in embarrassment.

Once he left, she turned to the teacher. "Daniel is some sort of battery booster pack. When he touched my back, it was like a jolt sizzled though me." She caught Dr. Jemison's eye. "It wasn't *my* magic."

Dr. Jemison sighed softly. "The headmaster needs to know about Mr. Monahan and about this incident."

"I can go tell him. I needed to speak to him anyhow." Maggie crossed her arms, now feeling guilty for an entirely different reason. Whatever she'd done with Sondre was no more than friends with benefits, acquaintances with benefits really, but she had a flicker of a thought that he might not be pleased with what just happened.

It was an accident, and I'm not staying here anyhow.

☽ ✦ ☾

Maggie had been hunting Sondre for several hours. She'd confronted hobs, students, and finally just grabbed a blanket and decided to sleep outside the man's door. The ground was uncomfortable stone, indented in the way of stone that had seen innumerable steps, but it radiated a low warmth that she hadn't noticed initially, as if there were in-floor heating lines in it. Was that intentional? Or was the warmth she felt an embedded spell?

Maggie flattened her palms to the floor, feeling no clear answer, but somehow shifting the hard stone into something vaguely squishy.

"I broke the castle," she muttered, but she wasn't entirely sure how or what she'd done.

She waited for hours, but finally, Sondre stomped toward her. Oddly, he was carrying a stack of what looked like meat in his arm. Over his shoulder was a bulging sack. At the top, she could see a bag of pretzels of all things.

When he noticed her there, he rubbed his head with his free hand in a way that was already familiar to her from her initial imprisonment. "What are you doing here, Maggie?"

"I have some words for you." She pushed to her feet, not particularly graceful with the cocoon of blankets she was currently wrapped in. "You lied to me."

"Not directly." He held out a hand to her. "There will be no back and forth between parents for Craig."

"Because he'll think I abandoned him!" Maggie smacked his hand away. "Why? Why didn't you tell me?"

Sondre sighed. "There are rules, Maggie."

"Ms. Lynch," she interjected. "Headmaster."

He said nothing for several moments, simply stared at her. Finally, he motioned to his door. "Come in for a moment."

"I'm not here for tha—"

"Obviously." Sondre dragged the word out as he made a gesture, and his door clicked open behind her. It was as effortless as swatting a bug, and she wondered what he—what *any* of them—would do if they were suddenly without magic. Would it be as awkward as it was to discover that magic was real?

A guilty voice in her mind whispered, "*It wasn't awkward. It was exciting.*" But she shoved that detail down deep into wherever unpleasant truths went.

"I also need to tell you about class . . ." She felt her cheeks warm. "I had an incident."

"Are you injured?"

Maggie swallowed awkwardly. "Not at all. It was the medical class and—"

"Plenty of students find that arousing," he murmured, looking at her with an assessing stare that made her thighs clench. "Let's discuss this. It's safe here."

"Safe?" she echoed.

"They can't hear us in there," he whispered, nodding toward his door. Maggie flinched. "Who?"

He shrugged, but in that way that was dismissive more than not knowing the answer. "Any of them."

She stepped over the threshold, pointedly not looking at the open door that led to the bed where she'd enjoyed him. Unlike her room,

Sondre's included a sitting area and what she would call a kitchenette. It was like a tiny apartment inside the castle.

Sondre tripped on the threshold as he followed her.

He turned, frowned, and said, "Why is my doorway spongy?"

"I was uncomfortable, and I didn't mean to and . . . it doesn't matter. I'm here to yell at you, not apologize for spongifying—"

"Spongifying?" he echoed, a small smile twisting his lips.

"You lied to me, you oaf." She crossed her arms to keep from smacking him. "I *slept with you,* and you lied to me."

"Maggie—"

"Ms. Lynch," she corrected again with a scowl. "You will not call me something so personal."

He sighed and gestured at an extremely battered L-shaped sofa. It was covered in cowhide of all things, white and black splotches. "Please. Have a seat, *Ms. Lynch.* I gather you are not here to address the consequences of volunteering in Mae's class."

"I wasn't her volunteer. Another student was." Maggie sat on the edge of the sofa, perched to stand and attack as needs be.

"Did something happen?" His voice was gentle, but there was an underlying core of steel. She could almost see it, and her logical mind argued such things were impossible even as her recent experiences reminded her that magic wasn't logical.

"I had a lot more magic in the medical magic assessment lesson than anyone expected," she murmured. "The result was that someone was . . . satisfied."

"Ah. And you?"

Maggie looked away. "It wasn't my choice."

"So you're here to say that you're going to join Mae's house?" Sondre surmised. "Are you sure? That's a respected choice."

"Actually, it wasn't my magic. Something—someone—else interfered." She filled him in on Dan's boosting ability and omitted the detail about the doctor's involvement when the magic went sideways.

"So you think you were altered by Monahan's involvement," Sondre deduced.

"I think so. And I don't want to stay, you know, so I need you to figure out how to make it clear that it's not *my* magic. If they think I'm powerful, they won't siphon me." Her voice rose until she sounded angrier than intended. She took a moment, resettled her emotions. "I can't stay, Sondre. I *can't*. If they think I am powerful . . . what if they make me stay?"

He looked pensive, and that did more for mollifying her anger than anything else could—short of sending her home. She didn't know much about magic yet, but she realized now that she'd used it to protect her son in a cocoon of it, burst a door off her vehicle, and spongify the floor of an ancient building.

She was not as weak as she needed to appear.

"If I got out of the vehicle before you found me, could I have escaped?" She'd been thinking about it during the last few hours. Craig wouldn't have gone far, and she would've caught up. There were ways she had been mentally replaying events, things she mentally shifted so in the end she wasn't here without him.

"The initial arrival of magic is exhausting," he said gently. "You passed out, but you saved your son as a result of your magic. That's something."

"Someone tampered with my engine."

"Yes."

"Was it you? Someone here?" Maggie hated the likelihood that it was her ex-husband. Surely, Leon wouldn't be so awful as to do something that could kill his own son.

"It was not me or any witch." Sondre gave her a sad look. "Based on what I know, I suspect it was personal."

"How would you kn—?"

"I learn a *lot* about the incoming students, Maggie." Sondre gave her another sympathetic look, and she opted not to correct his use of her name.

"I need to rescue my son. You understand that, don't you? I like it here, but he's my priority." She twisted her hands together as she spoke. "His father . . . his own father is likely the one who tried to *kill us.*"

"Yes. That is my assessment, too. But without needing to pay money to you, he's unlikely to hurt his son right now." Sondre said these words as if it was at all reasonable that a man could want to kill his own child. It wasn't. It just wasn't a decision she could fathom.

"*My* son."

"Yes," Sondre allowed.

"I just want to go home," she whispered. "I belong there."

"I don't have the power to send you back, Maggie. I would if I could." For several moments, Sondre was silent. Finally, he nodded. "I am part of a group of witches arguing that we ought to be able to move between worlds. You are a perfect case of why. I will argue for you."

"So there's a chance?"

"Right now? No. In time—"

"I don't have time!" Maggie crossed her arms, holding herself together. "He's a teenager. He needs me *now.*"

"We can go over periodically for food and water and assorted other things, but that's only a few authorized people who can do so. Maybe I can eventually get you added to that task and—"

"Then I want to be siphoned. I want to go home," she insisted. "Look, I get that you don't know me. We had a friends-with-benefits night . . . or a 'one-off,' or whatever the term is these days."

Wryly, he said, "I'm not the authority on current terms in your world for our evening together."

She stood and paced away from him. Without looking back, she asked, "Tell me how to get them to let me go home."

"Fail," he said softly.

She turned to face him again.

"Fail every task you can. Be inept. Be difficult," Sondre continued. "Treat them all the way you treated me. Make them *want* you to leave."

"Thank you." Maggie looked at him, realizing for all that she wanted to leave here, she wished she could take him with her. She wasn't going to admit that, but she'd spent her life looking for someone who *saw* her, who made her feel complete, who made her feel protected.

And I'm going to leave him before we even try.

He gave her a look that she couldn't interpret before simply saying, "Siphoning can kill you."

"So would living here without at least trying to rescue my son." Maggie wiped a tear away at the brief thought of abandoning him to his father. "Leon tried to kill me and our *son*. My baby. I can't not try to protect him."

"Fail spectacularly, then, Ms. Lynch." Sondre walked to the door, opened it, and gestured for her to leave.

She paused and looked at him. "You'll tell them about Dan, so it doesn't make them think I ought to stay?"

"I will, Maggie. I promise I'll tell them that I think they should let you go home." He touched her cheek softly. "And I'll think of you after you're gone."

"I'd have liked us to become friends or something," she whispered. It was the truest thing she could say. She had no hesitation about leaving, but she thought—despite other evidence to the contrary—that Sondre was actually a nice guy.

Not a good guy, but a nice one.

As she walked out, he murmured, "Good luck at failing; I'm betting it doesn't come easy to you."

28
Ellie

Over the next few days, Ellie had decided to make a statement about her intentions regarding Crenshaw—and she wasn't the only one. A couple students had already started wearing robes, apparently determined they were going to stay. One older woman, Ana, had a big blue feather jabbed into her hair. They were signaling their intent—and Ellie supposed she was, too.

Her intent was not to give in to anyone who decided to make decisions for her. Not even sexy Victorian witches or prophecies.

She refused to change into whatever witch-world fashion was. She'd growled at a hob who tried to take her shirt. "Duplicate it or get me similar ones," Ellie had demanded. "I'm not dressing like them. No robes or weird hats. I'm not staying. So . . . what do I pay you with? Is it on the school's bill?"

"No charge. It's worth it." The hob laughed, but Ellie didn't get the joke—or an explanation.

Today, Ellie was sporting a garish green T-shirt that announced, "Never cross a librarian. They catalogue everything." It felt remarkably on point for her mood.

Aside from the hobs, though—who seemed unanimously lovely—

and that ill-fated kiss and grope with Prospero, Ellie was far from charmed by Crenshaw.

Creating snakes was pretty cool, but I haven't felt safe trying anything like that in the castle.

The classes were tolerable. The food was uninteresting. The other witches were intriguing. In fact, one of the students, Daniel Monahan, was in her binders.

MISSING HIKER: YOSEMITE SEARCHERS HAVE FOUND NO CLUES

SAN FRANCISCO—The search for Daniel Monahan, missing three weeks, continues this week. "Even seasoned hikers can get lost, and Mr. Monahan was a novice with poor health. We aren't ruling out foul play, however," one park ranger explained. "The chances of finding him decrease every day. Nature can be unforgiving."

Monahan, an employee of a bank in Baltimore, was last seen standing alongside his backpacking gear. Several hikers saw him earlier that day. "We suggested he hire a guide." Authorities are hoping tourists saw Monahan after this and will reach out with information to narrow the search area.

She had been surreptitiously looking in her binders and trying to find the rest of her classmates. Quickly, she had also realized Dominique was one of the women who kept to themselves on the periphery of the group.

PUBLIC ASKED FOR HELP IN LOCATING MISSING MOTHER

ALBUQUERQUE—The New Mexico Police have requested the public be on the lookout for Dominique Rodriguez,

mother of three, who disappeared from her home in Angel
Fire last Saturday. Ms. Rodriguez was due to pick the children up from their grandmother's home late that afternoon.
Police were called when Rodriguez's car was found abandoned along U.S. Hwy 60.

Dominique had been quiet during the few history and rules classes
they'd had, and Ellie caught herself wondering more about her than
about the rules of Crenshaw. She felt weirdly guilty, though, wondering
if all of the people she'd meet out and about were in her binders.

She began looking at older cases. *How long had the missing been vanishing to Crenshaw?*

Was Prospero one?

Ellie mostly ignored the classes themselves and spent her evenings
rereading her binders, trying to match people with her news clippings.
She didn't bother with the class readings or practicing, since she wasn't
planning on staying in Crenshaw. She had no desire to learn things that
would be *literally* erased from her mind as part of the siphoning process
according to the chief witch.

But will they?

That question nagged the back of her mind. Prospero had failed to
alter Ellie's memories, so Ellie would probably have to pretend they had
been erased. That would be much easier if she skipped learning things
she didn't need to know—and would be expected to forget—in the future.

Not *actually* forgetting Prospero . . . that was a more complicated
topic. The Victorian witch took up much of Ellie's thoughts. There
was something about her. She felt like home, like everything Ellie had
dreamed of finding in a woman. Not just the physical stuff, but her passion for protecting her home, her courage, her hints of a wicked sense of
humor, her earnestness.

But she tried to erase my memories. Ellie kept looping back to that.

Prospero had broken rules, and Ellie knew there were dire

consequences—but she'd also tried to mess with Ellie's actual memories instead of trusting her. *But we were in a panicked situation, and she's desperate and . . . does it matter why, though?* Ellie couldn't quite decide, and since she was trapped in this damnable castle, she couldn't show up at Prospero's step to hash it out.

Instead, she was forced to listen to witches drone on about this or that. It was ridiculous. They never talked about essential things like the poisoned water or why Ellie had a habit of fashioning serpents.

Their first class that was actually interesting to her was something called "Maintaining Illusions." Currently, she and her classmates were in a room with four benches that looked like church pews arranged in a horseshoe shape. The pews had a thin red cushion, but they were far from comfortable. More interesting, however, was the intricate mosaic on the floor. A hydra writhed there, held fast by many chains that were being hammered into the ground. Other people were erecting a massive wall around it. The mosaic was stationary, but Ellie caught herself wondering if it had to be. She'd peeled strips off the asphalt and bent trees to her will, so could she make this move?

The teacher, Lord Scylla, prowled the room. As the teacher was speaking, the curls that looked like thick coils on her head started writhing like the hydra on the floor.

"Ho-ly fuck," an older woman called Sunny whispered loud enough that Lord Scylla grinned as her hair writhed like Medusa's serpents.

Another woman, Claribel, made the sign of the cross over herself. "Our Father . . ." She mumbled the rest, but a few moments later blurted out, "Deliver us from evil. Amen."

Axell, whose Norwegian accent was melodic enough to make everything he said seem vaguely authoritative, nodded. "Like smoke and mirrors. She is there and not there."

Lord Scylla smiled. "Exactly. If you reshape the thing, it is still that, but it is something other, too."

Axell nodded again.

Ellie silently agreed, but she was hesitant to speak up.

Claribel began praying again. Louder this time. There wasn't much doubt on where she stood on the whole return home thing. Forgetting would be a blessing for her.

"You will it, shape it with the hands you can't see," Lord Scylla explained to a mostly rapt class. "Hold the image." She pointed at the mosaic. "Chain. Wall. Serpent. . . . And make it appear."

At least four of the students—including Dominique, who was much prettier than the photo in her missing persons article—were staring at their teacher like she'd actually become Medusa. They were frozen in shock as their teacher smiled at them.

"You want us to *make* a monster?" Ellie asked. This, unfortunately, seemed exactly in Ellie's wheelhouse. She'd made multiple serpents so far.

Lord Scylla shrugged. "Find the well of magic in here." She put a hand on her low belly. "And give your illusion breath. Don't worry about failing. Few of you will create a sustainable illusion."

"Why?" asked a woman whose eyes were red rimmed from weeping.

"Why *what*, Ms. Lynch?"

"Why do you say we'll fail?" She had the sort of edge to her voice that made Ellie take notice. It was the kind of woman-pushed-too-far sound Ellie recognized, and she wondered what her Missing story was.

"Because you are new. Because magic takes practice. Because most witches here are not going to be in my house." Scylla looked around, meeting gazes. "Every witch has a skill that is unique to them. Everyone can do low-level magic of some other houses. Holding an illusion is rare, though. But if you can, I have work for you to do. So"—she opened her hands widely—"impress me."

Impress her? Ellie hated that she wanted to rise to that challenge, but after a lifetime of trying to be ordinary, the urge to be *more* whispered temptingly.

Why not? Just this once.

Ellie looked at the hydra and searched for that strange cauldron of energy in her belly. There was no way she was going to fail. She only had a few weeks here before she'd surrender whatever magic was in her, and so she decided to make the most of it.

She unfocused her gaze, as if she could fall into the mosaic, become part of it. She didn't focus on the hydra, though, but on the people restraining it. They were stopping the creature from being who it was, reducing the unfamiliar to Other, making a monster of it.

They are monstrous. With their chains and their rules.

Ellie visualized them, and in the process, she felt like she became the mosaic. She wasn't the hydra but the one with the chains. She felt the cold metal in her hands, the weight of the chain as it tried to stop the many-headed creature struggling to escape.

The links were golden, but not gold. *Bronze.* Strong and thick and—

The hydra tugged back, pulling in all directions.

"Miss Brandeau!" A voice was calling her away from the monster, but Ellie's eyes closed as she tried to hold fast to the illusion.

A hand came down on her wrist, and the chains felt thicker, heavier. Ellie's arms were weakening from the hydra's resistance, and for a flicker of a moment, she considered opening her eyes—but she was afraid the illusion would fade completely if she did so.

"Ellie!" Prospero's voice cut through the illusion of screams. "Miss Brandeau, look at me. Now."

Ellie opened her eyes and discovered she had chains clutched in her hands, and they snaked out to everyone in the room. Some were barely visible outlines, but others were as tangible as the woman staring at her in shock.

"Hey," Ellie managed to say. She felt limp as the illusion vanished— and took all her energy with it.

Just like the serpent in the woods.

Her classmates all looked at her warily, and both Lord Scylla and Headmaster Sondre were now standing in the front of the room. The headmaster looked intrigued. Lord Scylla looked like she'd just discovered magic was real, but then the woman's scholarly expression returned as she pointedly looked at Prospero and lifted one brow.

Whatever communication they exchanged was one written in tiny gestures. The result was that Prospero stepped nearer to Ellie.

The headmaster was now scowling.

"That will be all for today," Lord Scylla announced with a booming voice. "Let's walk down to the infirmary."

"Field trip," Daniel Monahan said awkwardly as the Norwegian guy wrapped an arm around him.

Ellie tried to step forward with the rest of the class, faltering instantly. If not for Prospero's quick thinking, Ellie would have hit the floor. Instead, she sagged backward into Prospero's body.

Again.

She's always here to catch me.

The thought of that made Ellie's heart speed; she looked away.

As she took in the red marks on several throats, Ellie was awash in guilt. *I did that?* Magic was dangerous—or maybe Ellie was.

"I'll have a refresher sent to her room, Prospero." Lord Scylla motioned to one student who was shaking all over. "Headmaster? Would you mind assisting Claribel?"

Then, in a matter of moments Ellie was alone with Prospero, who still had both arms around Ellie's waist. "Can you walk at all?"

Ellie shook her head. "Not far."

"Let's sit then." Prospero lowered Ellie to the floor, but still half supported her. The feel of Prospero's curves, of her row of bone buttons, of her strength, was enough to make Ellie think a different sort of dangerous thought.

Could I magic away buttons?

Common sense reared up, and Ellie considered pushing her away, but that would mean toppling over. That was the only reason she leaned against Prospero. *Really.* Just to be sure at least one of them believed that lie, she muttered, "I would accept help from anyone right now. You aren't special, you know?"

Prospero chuckled. "You *are* special, Ellie."

Ellie met her gaze. "But you abandoned me to them and—"

"Did you see what you just did, Ellie?" Prospero shook her head. "Whatever magic your family has, most of it was dormant. Maybe it built up? Maybe you're just rare?"

"You said *most*. Not Hestia, though. She had this magic, too." Ellie might be exhausted and far too attracted to Prospero, but she also wanted a few important answers.

"No. Not Hestia. She chose to be siphoned to return to you, Ellie." Prospero gave her a sad smile. "She tried tearing down the thickest of Scylla's walls, nearly succeeded in escaping, and when we found her, she demanded siphoning. I still don't know how she survived having so much . . . having her magic removed."

So much?

Ellie caught the slip, the almost-admission, and asked, "Not all of it, then?"

"She was my friend, Ellie. I . . . interceded," Prospero whispered. "I couldn't bear the thought of her dying, and I was afraid that if we took all of it, she would. Some people have so much magic that siphoning would be death. I would die if I were siphoned. I worried that she might, too. It was no effort to make the others think they'd siphoned her, and she was weak enough that it seemed like it was all of it."

"You're quite the rule breaker," Ellie murmured. The truth of what Prospero had done kicked Ellie's heart in dangerous ways. *She saved Aunt Hestia.* If not for Prospero's disregard of the laws she was sworn to uphold, Ellie would have been sent to a foster home. She'd have grown up without Hestia.

"So you erased someone *else's* mind without permission?" Ellie guessed.

Prospero shifted awkwardly. "No one, witch or regular person, has been immune to my gift before you."

"That doesn't make it okay that you tried to erase *my* mind." Ellie pushed away from her; thinking about what she'd done was enough to make Ellie's anger return.

"If anyone here learns that I was over there or that I hid you . . ."

Prospero looked smaller somehow, her fear evident in her expression. "You don't understand, Ellie."

"You could've tried trusting me." Ellie slid backward, so there was more space between them.

Prospero said nothing at first. Then she offered, "I am not used to trusting people."

"Try harder," Ellie retorted.

They sat there for several silent moments. Then Prospero stood and held her hands out. "You won't be able to reach your room unaided. Let me help you."

Ellie knew she was right, but she had the rare opportunity of having a Prospero at her side who wanted to make amends, so she asked, "Tell me something about you, and I'll take your hand."

"No one here likes me much," Prospero said lightly. "Except Cassandra, the Prophet of Crenshaw, and Scylla. Sometimes the current chief witch. Walt."

"That's about other people." Ellie folded her arms over her chest. "Try again."

"I like you . . . ?"

"The kiss before trying to mess with my mind already clued me in on that," Ellie said, unable to stop the laughter from her voice. "Not subtle."

Prospero smiled briefly. "I was born in the 1800s, and my husband beat me regularly. When he realized that my friendship with another woman had become . . . clarifying for me, he beat me until I was near dead. If I hadn't been a witch, I would've died that day. Crenshaw saved me, and I'm terrified of losing this town."

She said all of it in a quicker than usual pace, but her voice was flat, as if explaining something mundane. The combination made it all the more heartbreaking.

Ellie took Prospero's hand and let herself be pulled to her feet. She was well aware that some men, even now, found the thought of a woman finding happiness with another woman terrifying. The thought that someone as strong as Prospero almost *died* over love made Ellie's heart hurt. She couldn't fathom living in a world where marriage to a man was the *only* choice; she couldn't imagine a life where death was a not-insignificant possibility for being a woman who loved women. She knew her history; she knew some countries—and parts of her own country—were still backward on gay rights, but it boggled her mind to imagine it being the only lived reality for the confident woman in front of her.

Until she became a witch.

Prospero slid an arm around Ellie's middle again, holding her upright.

Ellie said only, "You are far braver than most people realize, you know?"

They made their way to the classroom door before Prospero paused. "Could I transport us to the resident quarters?"

"I thought you were already doing—"

"With magic," Prospero clarified.

"Sure." Ellie rested her head against Prospero's shoulder briefly. This was a level of exhaustion she hadn't known existed before magic, as if the act of speaking was the extent of her ability.

Barely a moment passed before they were at the end of the hallway where Ellie's room was. She didn't try to step away as she admitted, "Honestly, I wasn't sure I could make it up the staircase even *with* help."

"That's why Scylla suggested I help you. Translocation is easier than walking for me. Most witches can't do so easily, but I have to be able to do so for my work." Prospero half shrugged as if to dismiss her own talents. With a wry laugh, she added, "I'm most useful at being forgettable and escaping awkward situations."

Later, Ellie would blame it on her exhaustion or Prospero's confession, but in that moment, she simply said, "Oh, I don't know. You're pretty good at kissing, too."

Prospero stilled like she was afraid of an attack, and Ellie glanced at her.

"Does that mean I could kiss you again, Miss Brandeau?"

"Just to be clear: I'm not totally forgiving you, but . . ." Ellie gave a small shrug.

Prospero escorted her to the door of Ellie's temporary room.

Ellie added, "I'm only here until this absurd Remedial Magic thing is over, but when I go home, I *won't* forget you. You know that."

"If they knew I couldn't erase—"

"It looks like we both have blackmail material then," Ellie said levelly. "I'll keep your secret if you keep mine."

"That sounds fair." Prospero smiled. She didn't step forward, though.

Ellie sagged slightly against her door. She wasn't going to let Prospero escort her *into* her room. She wasn't convinced either of them had the self-control to make that a good idea, but she wanted something more, something that made her feel good.

When Prospero did nothing, Ellie tilted her head. "This is when you should kiss me."

Prospero's usual arrogance returned, and the predatory look on her face did almost as much to make Ellie's pulse skyrocket as the demanding kiss that followed.

A kiss is not enough reason to stay, Ellie's mind whispered.

Hestia would argue with me on that, Ellie's heart reminded her.

More. Just need more, lower parts of her body demanded.

And to that, both heart and mind agreed. More kisses. More time. More touching. More talking. More Prospero. On that, all of Ellie agreed.

29

Maggie

The students filed through the infirmary. Little pockets of conversation were mixed with the doctor calling, "Next."

Each time, a student stepped behind the white curtained area to be examined. So far only three students had gone through the exam. One was Dan, the sickly pale white guy who had taken Maggie to the bar. The other two were a super-religious white woman who seemed to be reciting prayers on a loop and a Black guy called Karl who was keeping to himself so far.

Maggie rubbed her throat and the back of her neck absently. She could feel the abrasions, as if she'd been tugging back against an actual chain and collar. The skin on the left side of her throat was no longer bleeding, but that didn't erase the burning sensation. The edges of the collar were unfinished, as if the metal hadn't been polished.

Of course, there was no *polish* involved. The metal was an illusion, a phantom image that ought not have felt solid enough to injure. The dried blood on Maggie's skin was real enough to prove otherwise; Ellie's illusion drew blood. The class itself was proof things that were supposedly deception could feel damn real.

What was the cost? That was the lawyerly question that now crept into everything Maggie thought. Negotiation was about what a person was willing to give up in order to get what they needed, and asking the right questions was how one figured that out, at least that was Maggie's opinion. Being with Leon had cost her a lot of self-respect, a loss in career advancement, but what it had gained her was an amazing son. She'd sacrifice a lot more to have her son safe with her again.

Which is why I need to get out of here.

Initially, she hadn't asked Sondre the right questions. She'd heard his answers and thought they would mean Craig came *here*. She'd thought everything would be ideal. Instead, she realized there would be no custody case because Maggie was going to be considered missing.

Fuck that.

Maggie pushed that rage down. One of these days, her habit of swallowing her anger would give her ulcers. Today, it let her find focus. The witch responsible for the tactile illusion was Ellie. She had collapsed, but that was likely because she was a brand-new witch, untrained, just working from a few words and some instinct. No one else came anywhere near that level of creation. Dan had accomplished nothing. Axell and Ana had managed wavering illusions, like creating ghosts.

I need to get to know Ellie.

Power was an asset, and Maggie was fairly sure the degree of power that she wanted wasn't inside her. Admittedly, she hadn't truly tried. She'd been going through the motions in classes, doodling absently, and waiting for the moment where she could say, "Siphon me!" because as cool as magic was, it wasn't enough to make her abandon her son to the man who had tried to *kill them both*. Not now. Not ever.

Maggie was still kicking herself over hearing what she'd wanted to hear when Sondre had answered her question. Yet again, she'd let sex cloud her logic.

"Are you well?" Dr. Jemison asked as Maggie stepped forward into the little cubicle for her exam. "Please, stand still for a moment."

There was a red X on the floor, faded but still visible. Maggie stepped onto the mark.

The doctor stared at her from toe to top, closing her eyes after a moment but still facing Maggie.

"Pivot ninety degrees," the doctor ordered.

They repeated this three times more, and then there was silence.

Maggie squirmed, shifting from foot to foot awkwardly, and studied the part of the infirmary where they now were. No sounds filtered into the space, even though the only visible barrier was a thin white curtain. The hum of conversation had vanished. The room itself was not as old-fashioned as a castle, but it was more 1940s than modern. No laptops or other technology was visible. The worktable was wooden, scarred with age, and the patient table reminded Maggie of a hotel room service table but long and wide enough for an average-sized adult to recline.

"Nothing internal," the doctor pronounced as she opened her eyes several moments later. "Do you have any concerns to report? On this or any other health-related matter?"

"It was an illusion, but . . ." Maggie gestured to her throat. "I still bled."

The doctor held out a tiny jar of teal goop. Unlabeled, obviously homemade, the stuff wouldn't have been put through any sort of FDA analysis. No scrutiny. *Who knows what's in it, what carcinogens or—*

"It's a cream with white willow bark and arnica, otherwise known as wolfsbane." The doctor smiled in a reassuring way. "Arnica is used in your world for bruising, as is willow bark's primary ingredient, salicin. There's some magic in it, too, but the base is familiar."

"How . . . ?" Maggie shook her head and rephrased her faltering question. "Did you read my mind?"

The doctor laughed. "Just your expressions. I've been handling the new students for over a decade, so it was an informed guess. A very, *very* well-informed guess gleaned from the questions of the students who came before you."

Maggie offered her a sheepish smile. "It's all so weird, you know? I don't know what's make-believe and what's real here. Are potions even a thing?"

"Yes. Herbal remedy has been recorded for literally hundreds of years, but in Crenshaw I can add magic as a stabilizer or booster." Dr. Jemison gestured to a wall that was filled with what looked like ancient glass bottles and vials. "We reuse the containers, so when you run out, please return the pot."

Maggie nodded.

"How are you breathing?" the doctor asked.

It was an odd question, but Maggie took a deep breath. "Fine. The sulfur stench is a bit much still, but it's not as bad."

"Good. Good. If you experience any breathing issues, come see me at once. If you notice anyone with breathing struggles, I expect to know that same day." The doctor seemed less kindly and more intense for a moment.

"Sure. Any reason why that—?"

"Other health concerns?" the doctor interrupted.

For a moment Maggie hesitated. *I'm too damn old to feel self-conscious about sexual health.* She squared her shoulders. "Are there any STIs I need to worry about?"

The doctor sighed. "No. It's not wise to have relations with your peers, though. I know this is a time of heightened emotions and—"

"I arrived early. He wasn't a student."

"May I ask?"

"No." Maggie shook her head. "I escaped, went to the village. . . ." She shrugged. It was better that than point the finger at the man she actually had sex with. They likely all watched out for one another. "It was consensual. My idea, in fact."

"Doctor-patient confidentiality is a thing here, Maggie. You don't need to lie," the doctor said gently. "If you escaped, Sondre is failing in his responsibilities, but he's taken other students to the tavern, so . . . you don't need to lie if he took you into the village, too."

He took others?

Maggie felt extra stupid for trusting him. Was this a thing for him? Did he just go around sleeping with all the remedial witches? She had plenty more questions, but suddenly, the doctor called, "Next."

So Maggie exited the cubicle on the opposite side from where she'd entered. Outside, Dan was waiting for her.

He practically bounced, rocking forward onto his toes and then back to flat feet. He paused, looked around, and then asked, "Do you know anything about the witch that Ellie left with? Or about Ellie?"

"Why?"

"Because that was intense," he said, and while Maggie knew he was omitting things, he wasn't completely lying.

"Her magic changed when *you* touched her arm. Just like with me. You touched my back that day," she said bluntly. No one else might be calling it out, but Maggie wanted to be clear that something weird had happened—and it was Dan's fault. Her job as an attorney was to see the details, and this one was as clear a clue as any that had opened a case for her.

"Nah," he said. "Probably just spells take time to build up, or she hit her groove."

"Or you scared her, and she lashed out magically." Maggie crossed her arms and glared at him. She wasn't old enough to be his mother, but she certainly felt like it as she ordered, "Don't touch people when they're doing magic. Definitely don't touch her, or *me,* ever again. She didn't seem to be as connected to the room we were in, and people got hurt as a result."

"Whoa! That's on her, not me! I'm not the problem here!" He stared at her like he was insulted by her words.

"Touch her or me or, hell, *anyone* else whose magic goes sideways after you touch them, and I'll make you regret it." Maggie could do without yet another man who couldn't take responsibility for his own damn messes. She mentally washed her hands of him and walked away.

30
Chief Witch

Walter was sick of politics, which was rather unfortunate as this was his current responsibility in Crenshaw. *The peril of life in a magical world,* he supposed.

Childhood stories of magic always seemed so glamorous . . . or exciting, at the least. Being snatched by faeries. Outwitting trolls. Facing dragons to steal an artifact from their hoard. Instead, it was gossip and dire proclamations, ego and sensitive feelings.

I'm tired of being an adult, Walter thought for the 412th time. He didn't want to be involved in potential mutiny. He didn't want to be privy to all of his friends' and neighbors' secrets. And he certainly didn't want to be the one to try to stop them from making stupid choices.

Like creating a thrice-damned serpent in the woods.

These days, of course, all clandestine meetings that might get dangerous involved either Sondre or Prospero, so the alternative to meeting at the Congress building—and Walter shuddered at the thought before he even had it—was allowing them into his home. He'd rather kiss an angry bull than let those two into his haven. The Congress building also increased Walter's innate magic, a benefit to being the current chief witch.

"Perish the thought of letting them both in here," he muttered, as that particular thought continued to worm around his brain. His home might not be fancy, but it was exactly the way he wanted it to be.

Unlike some of the residents, Walter's home was an intentionally modest place staffed with three well-paid hobs. He had a kitchen, a water closet for the necessary deeds, a bedchamber with both a bed and an armoire, and a sitting room with a peat-burning fireplace. It was positively mundane. Gloriously so.

His bedroom window was charmed with images of angry waves and green hills, but that was his one and only concession to admitting he lived in a land of magic.

After all this time, he loved being in Crenshaw, but he remembered his early years of rage. He remembered wanting to burn it all down and go home. In fact, he remembered hating every witch he met because he couldn't go home—so he understood the witches like the current headmaster. Sondre was piss and vinegar, fists and fucking. He was like a much, much younger Walter, which meant dealing with him was emotionally exhausting.

We are irritated by our own flaws in other people.

Grumbling about having to go anywhere at all, Walter hauled himself toward the front door and snagged one of the dozen scarves hanging by the door. This one was a rich purple, like the darkest part of an iris petal, and several spring greens. It was pointedly *not* in a plaid pattern.

Walter draped it around his neck, and then he pulled on a more or less matching cap. Wearing it made his hobs happy, and it kept his balding head warm. Sure there was magic for such things, but nothing beat a good woolen cap.

Once of his hobs, Grish, appeared and held out a mug and a chunk of bread coated in honey and a wee bit of butter. Butter was a rarity what with giving up their limited space in Crenshaw for cows, but every so often, Lady Prospero would hand him a container of the stuff. Blackmail was beneath her, but bribery? That was her domain. She bought his patience and understanding with butter—and who could blame him?

"Hidden under the honey, boss," Grish said with a grin. "Since you're walking and eating."

Walter nodded as he accepted his breakfast. "Good man, Grish. Good man."

His hobs were akin to family. He had no wife. No kids. No siblings. No parents. Those people had all been left behind a couple hundred years ago when he'd been swept from the slaughter on the field and into Crenshaw. When magic woke, it was in a person, not a family, so witches arrived with no ties. No one here had non-magical family members. And since they lived so cursedly long, no one had babies anymore. There simply weren't resources to support little ones.

Somewhere in a box was a bloodstained bit of plaid he'd worn when he'd arrived here. Walt had left the blood in the weave. The fight had been lost, and even if it hadn't, Walter thought wearing a plaid without a clan at his side felt like a never-healing wound.

This was his home now, and he understand the whys and ways of it. That didn't mean he liked all the rules. Sometimes, all it took was "it's always been that way" for many people to accept things, but the elders remembered the changes. They were sentenced to mind the law because they understood, remembered, and could explain it.

As he pulled the door closed behind him, Walt walked into the heart of Crenshaw in search of the witch who had summoned him.

C. W.

THE SNAKE STILL STANDS. SHE MADE CHAINS, TOO.
THIS IS A NEW MAGIC. WE NEED TO CALL THE CONGRESS.

PROSPERO

Crenshaw felt more like home than he ever thought it would. He stepped to the right, knowing from hundreds of walks that the third stone from the wall was loose. The edges of this world were deteriorating. There was a cracked window in more than one house. The little details weren't getting attention because the world seemed to be fracturing. It hadn't been like that when he first arrived.

A metal-framed window opened from the bakery at the corner.

"Bit of a chill today," Colleen said in her way of greeting. That one was the queen of the obvious. Heart as big as a dinner plate, but not a gifted conversationalist at the best of times.

"Thankful for hobs who knit!" Walt said cheerily, flinging the edge of his garish scarf over his shoulder. It made his beard puff up as the bottom bits were now under the scarf.

Colleen laughed. She had returned with the supplies Mae had needed for the people with lung complications. Walt considered stopping by to get one of the "puffers" as people had taken to calling the containers of medicine to inhale, but that would mean people knowing he was falling to the sickness, too.

That won't do.

He was well aware that it was coming, and he wasn't terribly convinced that fighting it was what he wanted. The first woman he loved was long gone. The witch he loved, Hestia, was back in the Barbarian Lands—and he was not sure continuing on after more than three hundred years was necessary.

"Walter!" Cassandra practically skipped past him, and he couldn't help but smile. As long as she wasn't sharing words of doom, the madam was a joy. She seemed cut from bliss itself, and the fact that she barely remembered to cover herself in any semblance of proper clothes didn't hurt matters.

"Miss Cass!" he called back, but who knew if she heard. The woman barely paused most of the time, as if wherever she was going next was always urgent.

At the corner nearest the tavern, Scylla nodded as he looked up and caught her gaze. *That* one would be a force no matter what, but Walt was grateful every day that she'd not pitched her lot with Sondre. Her illusions were all that kept them safe from hikers on trails or some sort of devices in the sky that the last batch of new arrivals called "sat-lights." Giant all-seeing cameras up in space like stars.

In my day—Walt stopped himself mid-thought. *This is still "my day."*

He was still on this side of the sod, and until he disappeared into wherever witches' bodies went when they died, it would stay his day.

Walt pondered the issue that was the heart of the ongoing factions: to tear down the walls or to keep trying to create a self-sustaining world of their tiny hidden home. Neither solution worked, but staying here without some kind of plan for the problems of the water and the noxious air wasn't an option. That was akin to waiting for all the witches to sicken and die.

So what's left?

Some people waited for the magic to offer an answer. Others waited for the heads of houses to figure it out. So far, though, there wasn't an answer on the table.

Unless we move the whole damned town . . .

But to where?

How?

Could magic move the castle? Would *it? Magic brought the castle and Congress building—and hobs—here in the first place . . .*

All Walter could say for certain was staying would mean dying and trying to live among the non-magical folks would also mean death for quite a few people.

Walt understood far too well that some sorts of ignorance were too ingrained for people to surrender. Scylla understood it because of her skin. Prospero understood it because of her love of other women. When both women had come to Crenshaw, they were near death from the violence of racism and homophobia respectively. Sure, things had changed the last century or so, but the Barbarian Lands were still a place of inequity. Change *did* come. The English were no longer killing Highlanders or stealing their lands as they'd been in and after the Battle of Culloden when Walt had died.

But change was slow, and the benefit of centuries of living was that Walt saw that some changes were slower than others. So if Walter *had to* choose a side, he'd not be on Sondre's. For all that the rage Sondre felt made sense, his way in the world had been an easy one. White. Male. Straight. Handsome. Athletic. Able-bodied. Jovial. Men like Sondre couldn't always understand that the path they had walked was lined with privilege—and Walter had no desire to prove it by showing Sondre and his ilk how poorly the world would react to them once they landed in the category of outcast.

The non-magical in the Barbarian Lands would include *some* who accepted the magical, but here in Crenshaw, they'd built a community where race, gender, sexual orientation, faith, and culture were not grounds for prejudice. Surrendering that safety wasn't a thing he could accept. But neither was poison from their own water and air. It left a quandary that was seemingly impossible as both paths ended with the death of witches.

As Walter approached the turn to the road toward his destination that morning, the leader of the more reasonable of the two factions approached.

"How would we decide who had to go back if we are out of space?" Walt asked Prospero softly as she fell in step with him. "Would we start with the newest arrivals? The straight white men? It's not our fault we were born straight or white or male."

Prospero sighed. "I know, Walt. I don't want to send anyone back."

"No water, no room, what else is there?" He shoved the last of his honey and butter bread in his mouth. "Don't think I am unaware of your trip over there, Prospero. I know where you were, lass."

She paused. "I don't know what you m—"

"Ha! That lie will work on everyone but me, girlie." He poked his chest with a recently wrinkled finger. "Chief witch. This devil-wrought job of mine comes with perks. I know you went there, even if I don't know why. I feel your comings and goings. *Any* of you."

The look of abject terror in her eyes was enough that Walt felt guilty. The woman was a thorn in everyone's side, but he'd known her since she arrived in Crenshaw. Back then, he was the headmaster, the one who retrieved her nearly dead body.

The woman cringed away. "No more. Please."

One eye was swollen shut, and the other mangled. At least a few teeth were missing. The then-head of the infirmary had muffled a cry. "That poor creature."

"You're safe, lass." Walt had stepped backward, instinctively giving her space. "Drink up. It'll ease your pain."

The vial the healer had given her was slick with blood from her hand and her mouth when she handed it back. Several fingers had been so broken that the bones pierced the skin.

"No one will hear your secrets from my lips or hand or actions," he said softly, echoing words he'd said more than once since her arrival in Crenshaw. "You can trust me."

He watched her mask slip into place, cold and unfeeling. Deadly. That was the image she'd created over time, and it was easier than it should've been thanks to her propensity to slide into minds and shift the memories of those around her.

"I had to try to find an answer," she admitted. "Bringing back supplies isn't enough. People are dying."

"I am aware." Walt sighed, hating the lack of a good answer.

He didn't ask if she used her gift over there. Hers was rare enough that it left no trace, no mark, no proof. It made her a bit terrifying to most citizens—and invaluable to the safety of Crenshaw.

"Did you *hide* that remedial witch when she arrived?"

"Don't ask me," Prospero begged.

Walt stared at her. That was as good as an admission.

"And she made a snake at the rift because of what you said?"

"My spine and my belly both say it's unsafe for our people to go there," Prospero said defensively. "So we need to fix our home."

"Do you still contend that the creation of the rift was intentional?" Walt asked. That was the part that twisted him up. It was one thing to argue they needed to move from here; it was a wholly different thing to tear a hole in the earth and poison their own people.

"I am going to find proof," Prospero said. "I now have spies in place."

Walter stopped mid-step and stared at Prospero. Around them was the hum and mill of the village, but the flow of Crenshaw's citizens just shifted around them. Bakeries to visit. Milliners to patronize. Grocers to see. Walter lifted a veil around them, blurring their appearances and babel-izing their words.

"A spy in the New Economists?" he asked.

She gave a small singular nod.

"Not her?"

"Correct," Prospero said.

"Did you . . . *influence* her awakening?" Walter's stomach twisted at the thought of tormenting a potentially unmagical person to see if they were latent.

"I was going to stop her heart . . . but I couldn't go through with it."

"Say no more. I am duty bound to report you if I even hear this." Walter scrubbed his hand over his face. "Erase that memory, lass. I cannot know this."

"One last thing, this one not a secret. Her aunt is Hestia." Prospero whispered the words.

"*My* Hestia?"

Prospero gave another single nod.

"Well, that is something to bring up with the Congress, isn't it? Has Miss Brandeau spoken of Hestia here? Can someone witness that detail? Not you." Walter, for all that he tried to stay objective, wasn't eager to prosecute the nominal leaders of either faction, but proof that magic could run in a family was something they had to address. "This could change things. If we prove magic is familial, perhaps the rule against children—"

"Still no space for them," Prospero said sharply.

Nodding and smiling at people as they passed the last few buildings, Walt thought about all the complications this new knowledge created. *What are we to do?* If magic was familial, should they bring whole families? Where would they live? How would they be fed? Would they need schools?

By the time they reached the austere halls of the Congress building, Walt was no more settled than before.

He gave her an inquiring look but said nothing as he walked to the main hall and, with a word, lowered the entry restrictions on the building.

"I . . . like her." Prospero squirmed like she'd confessed to a crime—a reaction, he noted, she rarely had when she *did* commit a crime.

"Hestia's niece?"

"Yes. Her name is Ellie." Prospero looked poised to say more, but the rest of the invited members of Congress started filing into the building now that he'd unlocked it. She joined the throng in taking a seat, and in less time than it took to exhale, Prospero looked as cold and calculating as everyone thought she was.

"Headmaster . . ." Prospero began, respectful to a degree that grated on many of the new arrivals. History was different if you'd lived it.

"Devil." Sondre flashed her a look of pure loathing. "How preemptive of you to notify the Congress of my student's—"

"Miss Brandeau could have killed the entire group." Prospero's expression did not waver. "She is something more than illusion, and that requires prompt address."

Lord Scylla strode to the center of their gathering. "Concur."

Ten sets of eyes locked on her as she created what looked like a ghostly reproduction of a memory hovering in the air, complete with sound. They all watched the new witch manifest tactile illusions.

"She created actual chains," Scylla said as the image disappeared. "Thick, deadly chains. Not illusions."

"We can use this," Prospero said. "Once she has control of it, we can make use of a fabricator."

"To do what? Turn Scylla's walls solid?" Sondre scoffed. "And what then? We're trapped here with poisoned water?"

The room was uncharacteristically silent.

Walt sighed. "With that much power, she stays in Crenshaw. It's not negotiable. Elleanor Brandeau, first Lady of the House of Thesis, named after the primordial creation urge. Perhaps the magic will offer her more such creators to add to her house."

He'd need a full Congress to make it official, but there was no other option. This was what Crenshaw needed. If not, the magic wouldn't have brought her here without escort. If not, this new type of gift wouldn't happen. There was order, and he'd be damned if he allowed one woman's opinions to be a factor.

"We haven't had a new house in years." Fatima's voice was hesitantly excited. "The magic wouldn't create a new house if we were going to die, would it?"

"It would not." Prospero glanced at Walter and said: "She'll change things."

31

Dan

Within the castle halls, Dan and Axell exchanged a look. The murderess had been in their classroom. *Lady Prospero.* She'd carried a student— Ellie—away.

"To my room to talk?" Axell asked.

Dan shook his head. "Somewhere else?" He crinkled a note in his pocket as they walked past the rows of rooms used for classrooms. One room had rows of beakers and high desks. Tiny bowls sat in hollows of the desks, and tubing ran along a contraption that was akin to a Rube Goldberg machine, or an elaborate chain reaction machine.

They paused in the doorway. In one corner, an experiment was simmering over a low flame. A flask that looked like a lightbulb with a flat bottom and no way to open it was bubbling slowly like a geyser or tar pit, as if occasional air bubbles leaked out.

"Are those feathers?" Axell asked.

Dan nodded. "Mad scientist class? Chemistry for witches?"

"Alchemy or potions," Axell offered.

All Dan knew of alchemy was that it seemed to focus on turning things into gold or extending life. Reading comics and books had taught him that much. "The magic here is about intent, though."

"So far." Axell stayed at his side, and Dan wasn't actually sure whether he was asking to be protected or to be Dan's protector. Either way, Dan was in favor of it.

"Do we talk here?" Axell asked.

"In the mad scientist room?" Dan eyed the tube of bubbling stuff. The bubbles had increased as if the stuff was starting to reach the "add pasta now" boiling water stage.

"Is that snake venom?" Axell asked.

Dan had the same question, but he wasn't entirely sure he was ready for an answer. "Not all purple things are venom, right?"

Axell looked unconvinced, and Dan didn't blame him. He also wasn't sure if he ought to share this discovery with classmates or ask Sondre or—

"Daniel?" Axell bumped his shoulder into Dan. "Let us go somewhere not here."

They backed out of the room, pulling the door shut. A pair of students in the hallway glanced back at them curiously. Everyone here was still trying to figure out magic, their roles, their futures.

One of the hobs, Clancy, blinked into an alcove ahead and gestured. In such moments, Dan wondered why the hobs were so friendly to him—and why he was so sure they were trustworthy. He was, though. Nothing any hob had said or done registered as a lie. He couldn't say that about most humans.

Once Dan and Axell reached the alcove, Clancy mimed placing the palms of his hands on the seemingly blank wall and closing his eyes. Dan watched the small man's mouth as he silently said, "I need answers."

Dan did the same, vaguely aware of people walking up behind him as he did so. When he opened his eyes a moment or three later, he intended to look over his shoulder, but he couldn't look away from the sight behind the wall.

There, in front of them, the wall had vanished. Behind that recently vanished wall was an enormous room. Floor-to-ceiling bookshelves, complete with rolling ladders, lined the room. Circular shelves jutted out like ribs. There were tables with cushy seats. Other tables seemed designed for tabletop gaming, others for drawing, and a few for puzzles. Then in the back were upright easels and desks that appeared to have a translucent bubble over them.

Three separate examples of Ramelli's sixteenth-century bookwheels sat at other spots. The first looked very much like a cherrywood Ferris wheel wherein instead of carts for people there were trays for books—complete with wooden place holders. The other two reminded Dan of old-fashioned spinning wheels with less ornate book trays.

"There's a library?" a voice asked from behind them.

Ana stood there with three other people: Maggie, Karl, and a student Dan didn't remember. They filtered around him into the vast, empty room. As they walked in, it almost felt as if the room stretched, being somehow larger on the inside.

"How did you find this?" Karl asked, one hand moving the spindled Ramelli's wheel slowly.

Dan shrugged. "We've been exploring."

Maggie just scowled at him. Then she gestured her fingers from her eyes to him in a very obvious "I'm watching you" way.

Once they passed him, Axell whispered, "No privacy anywhere here either."

Dan decided that maybe the best plan was to go elsewhere and leave these three in the library, but then he saw one of the bubbles around a desk glimmering like a beacon. "Come on."

Axell kept pace with him until they reached the bubble. "Door?"

Inside, Dan could see a book on the desk that was open to a page called "Earth Magic." The article was on plowing the ground, and the image etched there looked a lot like the hole around the snake.

"Do you see that?"

"Gardening?" Axell asked. "Is this really the time to—?"

"Look." Dan pointed. "That's like the ground where the snakes were."

He didn't have any better answers than he'd had before the library had appeared, but now he had new questions. If the snake appeared because someone had supersized their garden furrows, he wasn't entirely sure that the *snake* was the real issue after all.

"Someone made that hole the snake came out of," Dan said.

"Did it come out of the earth or is it guarding the hole? Or keeping people away?" Axell asked.

Clancy appeared and gave a single nod. Then the hob was gone again. If that book was on doing farming magic, was the villain actually a gardening witch, not the snake itself? And why was someone experimenting with the venom?

And was staying in Crenshaw the best answer? Will I die soon here, too? Just in another way than cancer?

32

Ellie

Ellie woke to a knocking noise. For a flicker of a moment, she thought it was Hestia needing her, but then she focused her eyes and saw her room—*prison cell*—in Crenshaw. Even after everything, she was still here. She'd hoped Prospero would argue that she could leave here, or rescue her, but instead she was still in the castle.

Maybe I will have to rescue myself.

Maybe I'll have to rescue the whole town.

As Ellie yanked open the door, she did find a woman there waiting, but she wasn't the woman Ellie was hoping to see.

"Maggie." The woman held out her hand. "I'm a lawyer from North Carolina. And *you're* the witch who tried to kill me yesterday."

"Not on purpose!" Ellie stared at her with a sort of stunned feeling. That was going to rank high on the weirdest greetings ever for her.

"Ellie, right?" Maggie made a sweeping gesture toward the room and the hallway. "Talk here or in the courtyard? Where do you think they are less likely to be listening?"

"Do you suppose the rooms are bugged?" Ellie asked, scanning the ceiling as if there would be an actual item physically identifiable as a bug. "Magic ears or cameras?"

Maggie flipped both middle fingers up and lifted her arms toward the ceiling. As she turned in a slow circle, she said, "If so, I hope you all enjoyed the show." Her shoulders slumped a little as she lowered her arm and looked at Ellie. "I was in my room yelling at the headmaster for days . . . until one of the others broke us out of the castle. Dan—the bookish guy who smiles a lot."

"Monahan," Ellie supplied.

"Good with names?" Maggie asked.

"Something like that," Ellie hedged.

There was something remarkably inviting about Maggie. She was older, not old like mother or grandmother age, but about a decade older than Ellie. Her hair was reddish, but darker red, not ginger. And she had fine lines at the edges of her eyes. This was someone who had smiled a lot, although she currently had an edge to her that felt wild and dangerous.

"What do you think of Dan?" Maggie asked.

"He seems nice enough." Ellie shrugged. Honestly, she wasn't going to see any of these people later, so the urge to be overly social hadn't struck her. Maggie, though, seemed interesting.

Ellie weighed the danger of revealing too much.

Do I tell her about the Missing files?

If Maggie was sent back, she'd be brainwiped. Everyone who went back home would be. If she stayed, she deserved to know. Ellie grabbed one of her binders and opened it to the page with the article about the missing hiker—their new classmate. She pointed at his photo. "He's a missing person."

"Damn . . ." Maggie looked up at Ellie and then back at the news clipping. Quietly she read it, and then she started to lift the page. She didn't flip it. Yet. Finally, she met Ellie's eyes. "Are we all in here?"

"Some." Ellie looked at her and decided there was no way to backtrack, not really. Again, either Maggie would be brainwiped or she'd be here—and if she was here, maybe Ellie would have someone to leave the binders with when she went home. The idea of passing on her work appealed. She'd long thought of letting go of her project, but now that her curiosity over missing people was sated, she could.

"Do you want to read yours? If not, it's—"

"Yes." Maggie handed the binder back. "Show me."

Ellie flipped the pages to one of the newest entries, pages that had been unsorted before Ellie's cow collision. She'd only read it once, but she hated Maggie's ex already.

MISSING LAWYER

RALEIGH—The search for 44-year-old Margaret Lynch continues this week. "Ms. Lynch careened off the road. Evidence suggests the mother of one was day-drinking," local sheriff Bill Bamberg explained. "Maybe she caught a ride with someone. Maybe she planned the whole thing."

Lynch, an attorney, was last seen by her teen son, who was knocked unconscious in the crash. Several campers saw the two that weekend, but there were no witnesses to the accident. "Maggie was in over her head at work, but there were no cases likely to lead to foul play," her ex-husband explained. "I think this was her cowardice. We were in a custody discussion, and I wouldn't be surprised if she was trying to kidnap our son." Authorities are hoping someone will reach out with information on Ms. Lynch's situation.

Maggie slammed the binder shut. "What an absolute lying sack of shit waffles."

"At least you know your kid is okay," Ellie said, trying to find a silver lining to the character assassination in that clipping.

"Leon knows Bamberg, so there's no way that fool would be honest either." Maggie made a muffled sound that was still loud enough to make a hob appear. "The old boys' network is alive and well in the South."

Ellie shooed the hob away with a smile. She looked back at the older woman and thought about the rambunctious patrons at the library on occasion. "Hey . . ."

Maggie looked at her.

"So maybe we could walk or something. I'm not here to make friends. I'll likely be going home, but—"

"Same. I have a kid back there, one I would never abandon." Maggie tensed, staring out the window. "If he's not here, I'm not here. Simple as that. You?"

"No kids." Ellie shuddered. The thought of being responsible for a small human in a world filled with violence, school shootings, and political idiocy was enough to turn her off from even the hint of reproducing even if she found a person with whom that was an option. She didn't feel compelled to say any of that, though. Some people wanted kids; some didn't. Neither path was wrong—but one was wrong for Ellie. She was certain of it.

They stood awkwardly for a few moments.

"Er, so why did you ask about Monahan?" Ellie finally asked, assuming the going-for-a-walk idea was dismissed. "Do you want a chair or something if you're going to be here?"

Maggie flashed a grin at her. "Not much of a hostess back home?"

"Librarian. I can lead a book club, story time, guided meditation, or help you research, but I don't really do parties for work or personally." Ellie shrugged. "I like my privacy."

"Fair. Well, I'm pushy . . . in case showing up here wasn't enough to make that obvious."

"Pushy is good." Ellie held her hands out in a welcoming gesture. "Welcome to my prison cell."

"Looks just like mine," Maggie said lightly.

It wasn't really Ellie's room, but it wasn't not hers either.

"You wanted to say something about Dan?" Ellie prompted.

"Several somethings," Maggie replied. "He seems like an okay guy and all, but when he touched you, the chains got a lot heavier. I don't know, maybe no one else noticed, what with the trying not to die thing—"

"Do you think I really could've killed—?"

"I do. Definitely. I felt that weird boost when he touched me in the healing magic classes, too, and the poor guy—"

"Got happy?" Ellie interjected. "Gossip is that he wasn't the only one."

"Truth. Me and the doctor. Honestly, if she hadn't kicked everyone out . . ."

"Daaaaamn."

"Yes, but you're already strong, *and* he boosted that." Maggie folded her arms over her chest. "That's why I'm here. I want an alliance. Even better? We both want out. This whole thing is weird and freaky, and I just want a friend who isn't going to try to convince me that staying here and polishing cauldrons is the future I want, you know?"

Ellie grinned. "One who is on your side so if I start choking people again, you're safe?"

"Yeah. Something like that wouldn't suck either." Maggie opened the balcony door. "Wanna practice? Make us a ladder or fireman's pole or . . ." She gestured. "Magic it up, Ellie. Let's take that walk."

Ellie paused. *Could I?* She tried to think about what she'd done before, how she'd managed. *What if Maggie is right, and the real magic was that scrawny guy? Dan?*

"Only one way to find out if I really can, right?" Ellie glanced at the woman who boldly declared that she was there to form an alliance. In a world where everyone had an agenda, it was pretty cool to have anyone be transparent.

She weighed the maybes. Fire pole seemed problematic. What if it wasn't anchored? They'd grab it and tumble. Ladder could work. Steps?

Ellie met Maggie's gaze. "If I do anything dangerous, knock me out. I really didn't mean to hurt anyone."

"Entire group had to go to the infirmary. You're the real deal, Ellie, a *bona fide* fucking witch." Maggie shook her head. "And my goal is to hide in your shadow. I need to show them that I am a failure at this, so I can get siphoned and go home."

Ellie saw a twig on the ground and thought of the snake she'd made in the woods. She visualized that bit of wood growing. It was an odd feeling, because she had the definite sensation of tugging and shaping the wood with invisible hands.

I need more steps, though.

She could make a solid wooden staircase if she had enough wood. She pictured stacking each step one after the other until it stretched from the railing of the balcony to the ground. When she opened her eyes and looked, there was a plain wooden staircase.

"Let me go first, so I don't drop you or something," Ellie suggested.

"Side by side," Maggie countered. She linked her arm with Ellie's, and they stepped forward onto the first step.

Ellie didn't feel any surge when Maggie touched her arm, so it wasn't like some trick where contact with her made the illusion stronger. Still, she concentrated. If there were two of them walking on this, she wanted the steps to be steady.

She imagined the steps growing roots, as if they were actually shaped trees, living things that belonged here. She pictured roots sinking into the soil and the long branches curving outward into a playground of sorts for adults. There were swings and a set of rings. A couple branches straightened into uneven bars. The steps twisted and circled so the tree was more of a spiral staircase than plain steps.

And over it all, she imagined leaves. Blossoms. Fragrant blossoms and apples, simultaneously.

"Look," Maggie said.

Ellie opened her eyes again as Maggie stepped in front of her and hurried to the bottom. She looked up at Ellie, who stared at the fruit and concentrated—eyes open this time—on the apples that were ripening and hanging from the branches.

"Holy . . ." Maggie reached up and grabbed an apple that had just grown and ripened. She rolled it in her hand as she looked at Ellie and then back at the apple. "That was amazing, Ellie."

Ellie held her hand out, and Maggie tossed the apple to her.

Carefully, Ellie bit it, hoping it was real. Crisp, juicy tart apple. It didn't vanish. It didn't fade to smoke or air or whatever magic turned into after it was made. It tasted of fresh apple. Perfect in the way an illusion could be, and a flicker of awe kindled in that instant.

I made this.

"It's really good." She paused before she admitted, "It'll be hard to leave this behind."

"Not as hard as staying would be." Maggie pressed her lips into a tight line. "I can't abandon my kid. I'll be going back this week when they ask or fail us or whatever."

"Same." Ellie took another bite of the apple and stared up at the oddly shaped tree-steps-gymnastic structure. "Might as well enjoy it while I'm here, though."

She plucked a couple more apples and stuffed them into her pockets. Eventually, they'd vanish, and she'd know how long illusory magic lasted, or she'd eat them before they did.

Do the calories stay if the illusion vanishes? Does the hunger resume?

Ellie had more questions every hour she was here, but at the heart of what she most wanted to know was whether this longing she felt for Prospero would linger or vanish like the rest of this world. There wasn't a clear answer on the permanence of magic so far, although admittedly Ellie wondered if it even mattered.

"Where to next?" Ellie asked. "If we're going to slip off our 'campus'"—she made air quotes—"where do we go?"

"Lousy day. That calls for booze or dessert or shopping in my book," Maggie said with a cheery tone. "Village?"

"We're off to see the wizard," Ellie sang quietly as they set out for the tiny village of Crenshaw.

33
Prospero

Before Prospero could escape to her home to weigh the emotional crisis of Ellie staying—against her will—Mae caught her, her hand clamping around Prospero's wrist.

"We have an issue."

"Of course we do." Prospero would sell a few years off her life for something mild to address, but Mae's tone wasn't merely a surly or combative one.

"Thirteen people." Mae stepped in close, so no one could hear her. She smelled of camphor and rose, sick and secrets. Mae usually covered up the scent of sick and decay with a heavy rose oil.

"All dead?" Prospero whispered.

"Yes. Blue skin. And it was just so sudden . . . They all knew each other, obviously. Several lived in the same building. It was just . . . *thirteen* at once.

"All at once." Mae shuddered. "I don't know if they're contagious or if I'm contagious or . . . did I infect this whole street?"

Prospero pushed down her own flicker of panic. "Did you talk to or touch anyone?"

"Just you. Did I just kill you? I'm sorry. I just—"

"Hush." Prospero affixed her calmest smile on her face. Now was the time to manage the crisis, not let the possibility of her own illness rise up. "It was likely the water, Mae."

"They lived nearer to the vent than we do." Mae frowned. "Do we need to investigate or relocate any of the other residents near—?"

"Sleep." Prospero slid into Mae's mind, starting to tuck and trim the things the doctor knew.

"What?" Mae scowled.

"You need to sleep, Mae." Prospero reached up and cupped the side of Mae's face with one hand. She stared at Mae as she gently erased the memories of the thirteen dead witches.

In the next moment, Mae would think that the witches were fine, magic removed but fine. Her new memory was that she had exhausted herself siphoning so many at once.

"You've been working a lot, Mae, too much. It's a lot. And you were with Sondre for a long day. Naked and happy, but now you are exhausted." Prospero found a memory of Sondre with Mae and tugged at it until it seemed recent. Then she said, "I think you need to go to your chambers for the next four days and rest. You shouldn't let anyone in, and you shouldn't go out. Obviously, Sondre will understand and cover for you."

Mae nodded. "Siphoning that many people was exhausting, especially after reuniting with him again . . ."

"You deserve some space after all of that. Probably think about whether you made a mistake trusting him. Maybe you're better off as friends." Prospero stroked Mae's cheek with her fingertips, wishing they were actual friends and wishing she didn't need to do this. "I'll lock up the infirmary."

"What if the students need me?"

"There are others in your house, Mae. I'll have three of them on staff. You aren't the only doctor here." Prospero stepped backward until her back was flush with the storefront where the groceries were distributed.

Behind it was the warehouse where all the groceries, water, and sundries had been stockpiled.

"You're right." Mae nodded, looking calm and resolute. "I'll send a hob to fetch a few people to mind the infirmary."

"Starting tomorrow," Prospero suggested, deftly weaving the detail into Mae's mind as if Mae had made that decision.

"Correct." Mae smiled. "You're not entirely awful."

"Thank you?"

"I was exhausted and not thinking clearly. This talk helped." Mae reached out as if to hug her.

Prospero caught her forearm and squeezed it briefly. "Not a hugger."

"Right." Mae frowned slightly as if trying to remember a thought—likely one Prospero had erased. Then she turned away and left.

Prospero walked around the side of the storefront, past the guards, and let herself into their warehouse. The old kirk had a feel of age and solemnity that had her occasionally longing for a childhood faith that had died a century ago when she'd been beaten and bloodied by the man who'd sworn before God and their community to cherish her.

"Bernice?" she whispered.

The tiny magical woman who ran Prospero's house appeared.

"Thirteen dead witches in the infirmary," Prospero said, not wasting time with politeness just then. "Can the hobs remove them?"

"As always." Bernice vanished then.

Wherever the bodies of the dead went, Prospero didn't know—or want to know. Crenshaw had no room for graves or memorial services, and right now, the thought of a mass death was too dire to do anything but create panic.

She'd notify the heads of houses, the chief witch, and Sondre. She'd consult with Cassandra. Then, she'd try to think of a solution that wasn't "stay and die" or "hide scattered throughout the Barbarian Lands."

First, she would take a moment to sort through the terror she felt welling up inside her. They might not all need the panic and horror, but she couldn't erase the truth from her own mind. Hers was—until Ellie—the only mind she couldn't erase or alter.

I just need something good to ease my panic, she thought as she straightened her jacket and stepped back outside.

The last thing Prospero expected, however, when she stepped into the cobblestone street outside the old kirk was to hear Ellie laughing. For a sliver of a moment, she thought she was imagining it, but there she was giggling with another student.

Something good.

Ellie is my something good.

Despite every bit of logic, Prospero was fascinated by the librarian witch. Jealousy sliced deep, not in a "who is that other woman" way, but that Ellie was so relaxed. Prospero stayed at the edge of the building where she could see them, but they couldn't see her.

"Does it bother you that you'll forget all this?" the other woman asked.

"Why?" Ellie made a sweeping gesture. "Seriously, Maggie? What's to *miss*? I can visit medieval villages in Europe. Maybe the costumes are fun, but I love my life."

Maggie looked a little less convinced. "I don't know. I guess I thought this life could be pretty cool. If not for my kid . . ."

Ellie squeezed the woman's forearm in a kind way, a way she'd done with Prospero on more than one occasion. "But they destroy families. Plus"—Ellie looked around—"there are secrets. I have no doubt. Every city has them, and add that to the witchy longevity?"

"The doctor slept with the headmaster. I feel like I shouldn't know that."

"Ugh." Ellie shuddered.

"Riiiiight, but *I slept with the headmaster, too.*" Maggie rushed the words together, so they were something of a blur.

"Oh." Ellie paused in a way that Prospero had grown fond of. It was her thinking face, her weighing words look. Finally, she said, "I think that's sort of unethical of him."

"Yeah." Maggie sighed, looped her arm through Ellie's, and started walking. "He lied, but . . . I still had fun. He's actually sort of nice. Not that I'm staying, but if I did, I think we could end up friends."

"No guilt," Ellie pronounced. "Sometimes, you need to scratch an itch. That doesn't mean anything, right? It's like the rest of what we do here—forget and move on."

Then Ellie looked over her shoulder and met Prospero's gaze with a grin, as if she knew exactly where she was somehow.

Prospero smiled at her, not quite sure how Ellie knew she was there—or what Ellie would do when she discovered that *she* was going to be staying in Crenshaw whether she wanted to or not. She'd be angry, no doubt, but in time, she'd see that it was the right choice.

As long as I figure out how to keep us all safe.

Cassandra said Ellie was essential, and even if she weren't, a selfish part of Prospero would want Ellie to stay no matter what. *Get to know her. Get to kiss her.* Prospero shoved those thoughts aside. Ellie needed to stay to save Crenshaw. That was the most important thing.

And her magic is remarkable.

Magic wouldn't create a new house if it wasn't critical that Ellie stay. So the key was figuring out how to make that happen. For starters, Prospero would do whatever she could. Be whatever she had to. She genuinely liked Ellie already, and if the way to make her stay was to offer things that Prospero swore she never would, so be it.

Maybe this Maggie person would be good to keep here, too, to ease Ellie's stress. Friends were important.

Friends. A partner. A nice home. Prospero started a list of what was needed. She mentally labeled it as "List for the Care and Feeding of Ellie Brandeau."

If Prospero had her way, she'd be doing her best to convince Ellie that her life would be better if she stayed here. Affection and desire were more of a basis to a relationship than Prospero had experienced when she'd first married. She already had those things with Ellie, so, really, there was no harm in encouraging more. It was for the good of Crenshaw—and it wasn't a hardship to romance Ellie.

Step 1: Seduce Ellie so she chooses to stay.

If Ellie didn't choose to leave, she'd never know it wasn't actually her choice to stay.

34

Ellie

Maggie had tensed as they'd passed the forest, and Ellie considered telling her about the rift—and the big serpent she'd made—but why worry her if she wasn't staying? Neither of them were staying in Crenshaw long enough for the bad water to poison them.

She'd been wrestling with her responsibility for telling other people. *Who? The doctor? The headmaster?* They knew. *The other students? Which ones?* If she told the wrong people and they reported her to the chief witch, would the Congress try to make her stay? *Should I just stay to help?*

Making that snake had been amazing—almost as good as kissing Prospero.

Ellie shot a look in the direction where she'd seen the Victorian witch. Maybe she had to take the initiative to have her sweeping romance. Maybe while she was there, she could . . . try.

Maybe being essential and having a romance without the responsibilities of a job and my aunt is exactly what I need.

She looked over her shoulder again and let her gaze sweep over the well-dressed witch. Those damn bone buttons were a temptation that made Ellie want to give in to any manner of bad ideas.

Maybe magic had an effect on libido.

Or maybe it's just Prospero.

Ellie had liked her life in Ligonier. The farmhouse. Her grumpy "roommate." Her job. The library patrons. A lot of people looked at their lives and found them lacking. The only thing Ellie wanted was a partner, a woman she could laugh and love with, a person who shared her joys and sorrows. On some level, she'd decided that she couldn't find that.

Until I met Prospero.

Ellie kept walking, but she glanced back a few times, feeling a bit like a siren trying to lure Prospero toward her. It was working, too. Her stomach was squirming with a tangle of excitement and guilt. Common sense said letting anything continue to happen with the beautiful witch was a terrible idea, but common sense kept getting washed away by the memory of having Prospero in her arms.

Maggie leaned in and whispered, "Are we pretending not to see the woman staring at you like you're her favorite dessert and she's been on a diet for a while?"

Ellie let out a bark of laughter. "I think it's a shame we won't remember each other when we leave here, Maggie. I think we could have been great friends."

"We can be friends until we leave." Maggie grinned. "Let's go to the pub and see if there's some sort of witches' brew to make the stench of this town more tolerable."

"How are we to pay for it?"

"Bat our eyes and plead ignorance?" Maggie quipped as she fluttered her eyes like she was trying to dislodge fake eyelashes. "Buy a lost witch a pint?"

"Not exactly my top skill set." Ellie laughed at the absurdity of the idea, but she didn't change her course. She darted one more look at Prospero, but she stayed at her new bestie's side as they headed toward a place calling itself the Tavern of No Repute.

It was decidedly grungy, looking like it was straight out of a low budget pirate movie. Nothing here seemed likely to pass a health inspection.

There was a viable possibility that the floor hadn't been swept in a month at least, and there were some sort of furry rodents sitting on barstools.

"Are those . . . bar weasels or something?" Ellie asked as she looked around.

"Badgers." A man in a tunic, tights, and combat boots lifted a full glass of something vaguely cloudy and gestured. "That one's m'wife."

"Your . . . wife?" Ellie asked. "Your *wife* is a badger?"

"The little one with the star-shaped patch on her head." He gestured again with his drink. "Her sentence ends in twenty-seven days. I miss her more 'an I expected. Even cleaned the whole room where we live."

"Your bedroom?" Maggie asked. "You only cleaned the bedroom?"

"Sure. We have jus' the one room that's our own. Not enough magic in us for a bigger place, but"—his voice became very loud—"that's fine because my honey bear is coming home."

"The *badger*?" Ellie asked.

"Only for another twenty-seven days now." He sat up straighter, but his words were very much a slur. "Then she's gon' be all soft and woman shaped."

"But currently, you are trying to tell me that your wife is a badger?" Ellie asked, trying to verify what he was saying. Was he drunk enough to be thinking lusty thoughts at a mustelid? Was there some perversion that made a person aroused by otters, ferrets, and badgers?

Ellie stared at him, trying to understand both why he thought he was married to a badger—which hopefully was a drunken delusion—and more importantly, why there were badgers in the bar at all.

"We don't have the space for a jail here," said a familiar voice from behind her. "So when extreme infractions must be addressed, a person is transformed."

"Wait. You turn people into *badgers*?" Ellie took a moment to erase the flicker of longing the mere sound of Prospero's voice elicited, and then she turned to look at her.

"Yes, the term is 'badgering.' We badger them," Prospero said with a wry grin. "The responsibility is part of the chief witch's duties."

"It's so weird here," Maggie muttered. "I can't wait to go home, even if I did find a very cool library in the castle tonight."

"Library?" Ellie echoed. She looked from Maggie to Prospero. "There's a *library* in the castle?"

"Sometimes," Prospero said. "No rules on teacups either."

Maggie frowned. "You two have in-jokes already?"

Ellie squirmed. *What do I say?*

Luckily, Prospero saved her from trying by saying, "Oh, my eyes and ears tell me that Miss Brandeau isn't the only one who has found herself captivated by parts of Crenshaw." She paused, looking at Maggie for a long moment, before adding, "Libraries and escapes to pubs and who knows what else. Remedial witches always break some rules figuring out whether or not to stay. Witches are rarely the best at abiding by rules, historically."

Maggie looked like she was trying to decide whether to defend accusations that hadn't been made or simply walk out of the tavern.

"Prospero . . ." Ellie started.

"Have you found nothing—other than a library—in Crenshaw to tempt you to linger in our magical village?" Prospero asked, holding Ellie's gaze as she spoke.

Ellie swallowed, but she didn't look away even as Prospero smiled in that damnably sexy way that said Ellie was not misunderstanding the question.

Ellie smiled. "It's hard to say."

"Oh?" Prospero was already standing closer than a stranger would be, and she looked like she was dressed to erase any doubts Ellie still had. The vest she wore was nipped at the waist, fitted in the chest, highlighting Prospero's slight curves perfectly.

Maggie cleared her throat, and when Ellie looked at her, she gave her a decidedly disapproving look.

"Have you ordered drinks?" Prospero asked, pulling Ellie's attention back to her. "Miss Brandeau and . . . ?" Prospero glanced at Maggie expectantly.

"Maggie Lynch." Maggie extended a hand as if to shake. "Just passing through your town."

Prospero laughed lightly and took her hand in a brief squeeze. "Not a fan of witches, Ms. Lynch?"

"Not a fan of leaving my kid behind." Maggie sounded friendly but stern.

Prospero's hand landed on Ellie's low back, making her tense like something was coiled there ready to erupt. Ellie took a moment to push down the memories she had of talking to Prospero, kissing Prospero, and doubting her.

Pulling her shoulders back as if a stronger spine would erase the heat on the small of her back, Ellie smiled tightly at Maggie. "Would you mind going up to the bar, Maggie?"

Maggie raised a brow questioningly, and Ellie gave a single nod.

"Just get me whatever looks good," Ellie suggested. "I'll grab a table."

For a moment Maggie was silent, and Ellie felt a strange flicker of excitement. She had never been the person whose judgment needed to be questioned. She was always the careful one, the quiet one, the smart one. Designated driver. Clock-watching friend. The one who took notes and studied early. Being in Crenshaw continued to bring out a new side of Ellie.

I like this version of me, Ellie thought. After a lifetime of self-control, Ellie no longer had to follow the rules so she wouldn't go missing, and it was dangerously freeing. She stared at Prospero. *Is this what it was like for her?*

"You sure you want me to go up without you?" Maggie prompted.

"I am." Ellie pressed back into Prospero's hand slightly and then moved so her hand naturally slid to Ellie's side.

Prospero's face was expressionless, but her fingers curled around Ellie's hip.

No more refusing me. Not since the failed memory thing.

"I'm not back home yet," Maggie said baldly. She pointed at Prospero. "Just know that while I'm here, I have my eye on you. Ellie's my friend. And you?" Maggie shook her finger at Prospero. "You look like a problem about to happen."

Prospero nodded. "Duly noted."

"Bad idea," Maggie mouthed at Ellie. "Very bad."

Then she walked off, slipping between two badgers who were sprawled on the floor passed out and a man with a wreath of flowers in his hair. The bartender was staring at Prospero, who gave him a wave.

"What was that all about?"

Prospero pulled a chair out for Ellie. "He wanted to know if your drinks are on my bill."

Awkwardly, Ellie sat and let Prospero push in the chair slightly. Prospero took the opportunity to lean down and whisper, "Anything you want is on my bill, Ellie. Name your desire, and I'll do my best to give it to you."

Ellie frowned at Prospero. "I won't be here long enough to need a sugar mama, but thanks."

Prospero made a soft noise, a laugh of sorts.

Ellie repressed a shiver at Prospero's breath against her neck, but she felt the loss when Prospero stepped back and pulled out a chair for herself.

"Sugar mama?" Prospero asked.

"A person who provides gifts and money for someone in exchange for affection. I'm saying that I'm not here to be seduced by you in exchange for drinks or whatever else you want to pay for," Ellie explained.

"What if I want to seduce you for purely carnal reasons? For my own desires?" Prospero held Ellie's gaze. "Would that be preferable, my dear Miss Brandeau, if I seduce you simply because I crave you?"

"It would, in fact." Ellie tilted her chin up, deciding that she was done being meek. "That's the best reason for a seduction, I expect."

"Not for promise of forever? Building a life to—?"

"If you were in Ligonier . . . or anywhere over there . . . maybe," Ellie interrupted.

Prospero leaned in closer, her hand landing high up on Ellie's thigh.

"But we are *here*. Both of us. Together in Crenshaw, and I could take care of you. I am . . . comfortable. I could give you everything you want, Ellie."

"Not my home. Not my aunt. What I want is not just comfort." Ellie hadn't intended to be so serious, but here they were, talking about relationships. Bluntly, she added, "It would take a grand love, Prospero, to leave my family."

"What if I could . . . give you *that*?" Prospero looked incredibly uncomfortable, and Ellie had to remind herself that she was from another time, one where women's lives were different, one where women like them typically couldn't have everything they wanted.

"My family? Hestia?" Ellie lowered her voice and sat up straighter, noticing how many people were watching them now.

Prospero looked pained. "No. The *other* part."

"Love?" Ellie stared at her.

"Yes. That." Prospero's voice sounded strained, as if she'd tossed back a harsh drink too quickly. "Hestia is a grown woman, Ellie. She could live her life without you. You know what she'd tell you to do. I do, too. I remember her spirit. So, what if you could have the love you want by staying here with me? Am I worth the risk?"

Ellie was at a loss as to the right words to say. *Do I want that? Want her?* This felt a lot more serious than a simple date or kiss. How had they gone from talking about a drink to talking about love?

"Bartender says these are on you," Maggie announced as she placed three stone mugs on the table with a *thunk*.

The liquid in them was sloshing over the edge, but Prospero still took one and lifted it to her mouth. In a far from delicate gesture, she emptied half the glass.

Maybe she was as nervous about her offer as Ellie was stunned.

The thought of Prospero's nervousness was strangely charming. Ellie had never been the sort of woman to enchant beautiful strangers, but the way Prospero was acting had Ellie doubting everything she thought she knew.

Maybe it's not just about saving her town.

Either way, Prospero stood abruptly. "Enjoy your escape from the castle." She looked at Maggie and nodded. "It was good to meet you, Ms. Lynch."

Then she lifted Ellie's hand, turned it over, and brushed a kiss over the inside of her wrist. "I'll be here if you are willing to give this a fair try . . . give *me* a fair chance. I live in Crenshaw, Elleanor. Sacrificing my magic would mean dying, so I cannot move to your world even though you are remarkably tempting. I'd be dead within a month there. So if I am to have a chance at this, you would need to choose me. I'd very much like that chance. Stay with me, Ellie. Let me show you what we could be together."

Ellie's mouth gaped open, but she had nothing close to intelligible to say. She needed to ask if the accident with the cows was magically prompted. A person who would put her in the hospital wasn't high on the list of "good ideas to date," even if there was a prophecy.

But Prospero pivoted and left before Ellie could ask her anything.

Ellie stared as she strode out of the bar. The Victorian witch was moving with the sort of authority that made the people in the room part for her as if a tiger stalked toward them. More than a few of those people were staring at Ellie now, assessing her with looks that said she'd gone from average to fascinating in those few moments.

"Well," Maggie drawled. "She moves fast, and you seem genuinely tempted."

Ellie couldn't explain that it wasn't as quick as it looked, that they'd had an unexpectedly magical kiss, that Prospero had found Ellie when she'd arrived here and steadily wormed her way past Ellie's defenses. To say any of that was to expose Prospero's crimes—and the lovely witch had made it quite clear that her lawbreaking came with serious consequences.

All Ellie could do was meet Maggie's gaze and say, "Did you ever meet someone who felt like the answer to a question you had never been willing to ask?"

Maggie raised her brows.

"She was the one to stop me when I arrived in Crenshaw and was attacking everyone near me in my panic. She was the one at my side when I opened my eyes at the infirmary . . ." Ellie paused, weighing the next words. "I thought I knew her when I woke, and I kissed her."

"And . . . ?"

Ellie sighed. "I'd fight small nations to do that more often, but I have a *plan*. Over there, I have a home. A career. Everything I want is back home."

"Except her," Maggie added.

"Yeah, except her." Ellie looked toward the door. "Honestly, I'm not sure if it's better to knock on her door and say, 'Ravish me, please?' or just steer clear of her. I thought I knew, but she shows up here talking about wanting to take care of me, love me, and . . . *Argh!*"

"You'll forget her, though, so what's the harm?"

Ellie wished she could answer that truthfully. Instead, she said only, "I think a part of me would always long for her even if I forget."

"Damn. That's no good at all," Maggie murmured. She patted Ellie's hand consolingly. "The sooner we get out of here, the better."

And Ellie nodded, despite the little voice whispering, *We could stay.*

35
Sondre

Sondre was settled in his quarters, wondering what fresh hell was demanding attention when he heard the thundering knocking on the door. He wasn't sure whether it would be more frustrating to have Monahan or Maggie there. Dealing with this crop of damnable students was wearing him down.

"Keep your trousers on!"

He stomped to the door, jerked it open, and stopped silent. Of all the guests Sondre expected in his rooms, the last person he ever thought to see darken his door was the snake herself, but there she was.

"Prospero? Stealing me a few steaks didn't turn us into friends," he said, not moving to welcome her into his private space or slamming the door.

"I am well aware of that, but this is not a social call, Sondre. I am here to speak to the *headmaster*. No matter the witch in that position, I would have had to come here. As it turns out, you are the witch in that role currently." She strode past him without invitation.

"We can go out to—"

"No," she interrupted. "Not on this matter."

Sondre closed the door. His hand fisted anxiously at the fact that she was in his space. "So why are you *here*?"

"No choice."

He noted the pinch at the corner of her eyes. He used to cherish that pinch. It meant he was getting to her, upsetting her, and he took pride in that victory.

But then she said, "No student can go to the infirmary, Headmaster. I need you to shift classes, if you must, so as to protect the new witches from any mishaps that might require help, especially with Miss Brandeau's unpredictability."

For a moment, he simply crossed his arms and stared at her, marveling at her audacity. "You might be able to give orders on the street and in Congress, but at the coll—"

"There are thirteen corpses." She crossed her arms, mimicking his posture, posing as if she had actual emotions. He had always thought that was highly unlikely. Anyone who spent over a century erasing lives and altering memories was a monster. He was fairly sure of that much.

Prospero's voice wavered slightly as she added, "Thirteen dead witches today, Sondre. Our people. Dead."

"What?"

"Thirteen sudden deaths of Crenshaw witches," she clarified. "I wanted to speak with you personally before we convene the Congress."

Sondre stomped over to the case of beer he'd brought back on their last supply run. Beer didn't solve anything, but it brought him a sliver of calm in a way that only fighting or fucking typically did. And he didn't have time for either if there was a mass casualty. He pulled a can out.

That wasn't to happen.

The uptight Victorian witch across from him held out a hand. "May I have one, too? I could stand a drink or three tonight, Sondre, and I don't think I can be at the tavern around everyone right now. I was there, but I couldn't stay. Not tonight . . ." She shrugged.

Mutely, he pulled a second can out of the case and handed her one. The beers were as cold as he could manage, considering where they were, so he was sharing lukewarm beer in a can. To him, it was still delicious. He couldn't imagine Prospero as a beer-in-a-can person. To Sondre, she had always seemed too uptight for such normal things.

He gaped a little as she cracked the can and took a long drink. Whatever details she had on the deaths were clearly upsetting.

"Mae had thirteen witches die on her today for no reason. Blue skin. Rapid aging." Prospero took another drink. "I don't have time to negotiate. Neither do you. Our people are dying and I . . . I cannot fucking figure out what we should do. You and I both know that neither of our solutions is the right one. We need something else."

"Wait." Sondre clutched his drink. "Is Mae *sick*?"

Did we kill Mae? His stomach churned at the thought. The rift was only to injure the weakest witches. *No kids here to risk. And our oldest have lived for centuries.* It was a calculated decision.

Prospero sighed loudly. "I don't know. I sent her to her chambers to rest and quarantine—"

"She agreed to that?" Sondre couldn't picture Mae being compliant, even if she were sick.

Prospero gave him a look, and he felt foolish. *Panic is clouding my mind.* Mae agreed because Prospero messed with her head. That was the only way the dedicated doctor would hide willingly. And Prospero altered people's minds with no remorse, as if she were entitled to control what people thought and felt.

"Mae might be sick. She might be fine. I have no idea how we'd know, though. She had no idea what caused everyone to die," Prospero said with an edge to her voice. "What I know for certain is that she was traumatized and panicking. Perhaps she was seeking the chief witch or maybe she was looking for you. She found me. I handled it."

Prospero was an excellent liar; framing lies as "maybe" or "perhaps" allowed her to lie convincingly, so Sondre didn't point out that if Mae wanted to see him, she wasn't going to be roaming the streets of the town. She knew exactly where to find him. The infirmary was here, in a wing of the castle, not somewhere away from where she was when the witches had died. Mae was seeking either the chief witch or Prospero—who was trying to spare his feelings for some reason.

Gently Prospero added, "Maybe she just needed to walk to clear her panic."

Or maybe she knew Prospero was cold-blooded enough to handle the crisis.

Or that it's my fault.

Sondre nodded but held his tongue.

"If the sickness is blood- or airborne, I needed Mae contained," Prospero explained, obviously reading his silence as anger, not guilt. "If it's not via our air or water, if it's something else, I needed to keep this secret, so our people are calm. I didn't *hurt* Mae, Sondre. I simply did what seemed most likely to keep the crisis—or knowledge of it—from spreading. If she's caught it, she would spread it through the whole castle. I need her in quarantine, and I need that to be a secret."

"But you're telling me," Sondre pointed out; the reminder that he was not her usual confidante seemed important in the moment.

Does Prospero know what I've done? He honestly wouldn't be shocked if the Victorian witch had figured some of it out by now. *It's more of a hammer than subtle as far as plans go.*

Prospero took a long drink before answering. "We just had thirteen healthy witches go from a cough to death. Is this a plague? Did the water or the foul odor in town kill them? Probably the latter, but . . . it doesn't matter what it is. We are dying unexpectedly of late. Now, with these deaths, we've lost several *dozen* people, Sondre. *Dozens.* In Crenshaw. It's unheard of."

She's here because Mae works in the castle where the students are, he reassured himself. *Just informing me because of the students.*

He shoved down his guilt and finished his beer before replying, "And you think Mae might be sick, too?"

"Yes. Maybe? I have no idea, honestly. She didn't *seem* sick so far." Prospero looked away. "I wanted to contain her—and hopefully the illness—if she was carrying it, but I hope she's not. She's a kind witch, and, honestly, we'll need her if this continues. But I had to quarantine her. Please, don't fight me on that."

"She likely expected it, probably agreed with quarantine, but felt guilty not being available to help," he suggested. "I wouldn't have done it if she came to me."

"You don't know th—"

"You're colder than me, Prospero. We all know it." Sondre didn't mean it as an insult this time. That ice-cold blood of hers was useful in a disaster—and if Mae was sick, it was a disaster.

"True, but this could be something contagious. We could *all die*." Prospero's voice was far from cold now.

"Maybe. I was a kid when they cured TB, and the cure for polio was right around when I left . . . and in between, I was in a war in Korea." Sondre shook his head. "I think expecting to die of something awful was normal. So, no, I don't know that I would've quarantined Mae."

He sat on the sofa in his suite and stared up at the woman he often thought of as his nemesis. Not that he was completely shifting his stance—he still thought they needed to change the way they lived, the location, and a lot of things. He could admit—briefly, privately, in this moment—that Prospero was not completely without redeeming qualities if she had saved Mae.

"Are you and Mae entangled?" he asked awkwardly.

Prospero laughed humorlessly. "No. In fact, I may have made her think she was exhausted from having sex with you."

"Oh."

"She had quite the detailed memory of you," Prospero said lightly. "I pulled it forward, so it seemed recent. It was a hasty patch so I could convince her to rest." She paused and lifted her can in his direction. "To never seeing that much of you naked again."

He chuckled.

She drank quietly, and Sondre couldn't decide if he was proud or embarrassed. Either way, it was far down the list of things he needed to ponder. "Mae may be sick, and the students are to be kept in the dark longer. Anything else?"

Prospero stared up at the ceiling for several moments. "We need to work together, Sondre. Table my plan and yours. Figure something out."

They sat in silence for several moments until he finally stood and walked to the counter. *Am I doing this?* If he turned against the rest of the New Economists, if he revealed what Prospero likely suspected, he was signing his own assassination order.

He grabbed two more beers, crossed the room, and held a can out to her. "While we're sharing, you need to know that Monahan is an amplifier."

"Damn it." Prospero rubbed her forehead. "No one caught that?"

"I caught it. He boosted both Lynch and Brandeau that I know of, so far." He watched Prospero as he added the next words. "I withheld that detail because he's loyal to me."

Very softly, so quietly he wasn't sure he heard her at first, Prospero asked, "Are you confessing things now?"

He paused, increasingly sure she knew he was at the thick of the rift's cause. *Do I tell her?* Sondre still believed they ought to let people have families, let them choose to live normal lives, but had they gone too far when they polluted the water table? *Was the rift a mistake?*

He couldn't answer that, so he said, "Step one: we keep the students locked down in the castle."

"About that . . ." Prospero gave him a guilty look. She explained two of his students had been in town, and for the first time since he'd come to Crenshaw, he saw a hint that the woman he'd thought of as reptilian had a heart. A flare of possessiveness washed over him since the students in question were Maggie and the overly strong witch.

"How?" Sondre asked. "How did they get out the castle without anyone noticing? There are spells and . . ." He shook his head. "Elias?"

The hob, Elias, popped into the room. He was one of the least objectionable of the creatures, dressed in miniature blue jeans and a button-down shirt that looked identical to one of Sondre's own shirts. Though he'd not had the urge to ask Elias why he mimicked Sondre's clothes, Sondre hoped it meant this hob was less adversarial to him than most.

Maybe.

"How did the students escape?"

Elias grinned in that nerve-racking way hobs had of smiling, as if they were laughing at a person but not out loud. Then he said cheerily, "Built a tree. Summoned it from nothing to fruiting. That one's a strong witch, Headmasher."

"And you didn't think to tell me?" Sondre asked.

"Thought about it. Decided not to." Elias bobbed his head, nodding in affirmation to either his own statement or a thought he wasn't sharing.

"I see." Sondre pinched the bridge of his nose. "That will be all."

Elias vanished.

Prospero gave Sondre an amused look as the hob disappeared and echoed, "*Headmasher?*"

"Hobs. Who knows why they say or do anything?" Sondre shrugged, not feeling like he and Prospero were now or likely ever would be at the sort of friendship where he'd confess that he had been falling-down drunk often enough that he'd stumbled and whacked his head into doorways or furniture. Sondre suspected a few of the castle hobs purposely shrank door lintels to injure him—but he had no proof.

Instead of saying any of that, he settled on, "This way."

In mere moments, he strode through the castle with his former nemesis at his side. They stepped outside. Springing from the ground outside Miss Brandeau's room was an enormous tree.

"Damn." He plucked a perfect apple. Rolling it in his hand, he marveled at the sheer immensity of what the new witch had accomplished. He was more than adept at a lot of things, but to create a full, mature tree out of thin air? Not even the House of Dionysus and Jörd, who managed plants for Crenshaw, could create such a thing.

She could heal the rift.

Do I tell the others? Do I let her heal it? Do we try to send her back?

Sondre stood side by side with Prospero and marveled at the tree that now stretched from soil to balcony.

"Plan?" she prompted.

"You go see the chief witch. I'll deal with the students. Bring these two back to the castle, and make sure Brandeau's balcony doors are sealed. Tomorrow, we'll select which students we siphon and which stay. I'd rather get that managed before anyone has a sickness that their magic is too weak to heal."

"Logical."

Sondre tossed her an apple. "Why didn't you bring them here when you saw them?"

Prospero bit the apple, chewed, and swallowed. "I have no authority over students." She held the apple up. "It's as good as the fresh, perfect fruit that it resembles."

He ate part of the one in his hand, buying time for her to say whatever was on her mind. He'd been at odds with her long enough to know when she wasn't done speaking.

Several silent moments later, she spoke. "Miss Brandeau is friends with Ms. Lynch, so I recommend keeping that one here, too." Prospero's lips curved into what he would consider teasing if anyone else did so. "I know that you can already tell which of them is powerful enough to stay here. It's not been *that* long since I held your position at the castle."

Sondre sighed. "I'll share my thoughts with the Congress. That's all. I won't suggest any of them have to stay or go."

Prospero's smile faded. "As you will."

In the next moment, she swept away toward the town. He wasn't sure if she intended to cross paths with his students after all or seek more drinks in the tavern. Tomorrow was going to be a helluva mess, even without the chaos of their town knowing so many witches had died all at once.

First, we siphon a few of the new arrivals, and then I talk to the others and figure out a new plan. Sondre wasn't sure they wanted the all-out war that would result from Brandeau being here and fixing the rift, but he wasn't sure he could convince the Congress to let her go back to her world either.

36

Dan

Dan was trying to practice magic in his room, but all he'd managed was a small illusion that looked more like an image projected onto fog. It was wavering and ephemeral, and he was irritated. Even with focus, what he could do was a far cry from the sort of thing Ellie had done in their class with Lord Scylla.

"Don't exhaust yourself tonight," Sondre said from the doorway. He strode into Dan's room, making the space seem significantly smaller. "You're going to need your reserves tomorrow."

"What's tomorrow?"

"Congress," Sondre said, but quickly and visibly dismissed that topic with a raised hand. "No other student knows yet, but *tonight*, I need you to go into town and retrieve Lynch and Brandeau."

"The one you, er, talked to at the pub and the strong witch?" Dan paused, feeling fairly sure there was something not being stated here that he probably ought to know. "They'll both pass, I think, but Lynch doesn't want to stay anyhow, so who—?"

"Tonight is a bed check, according to a *rumor*," Sondre interrupted.

"Where did you hear the rumor?"

Sondre gave him a look that was almost parental. "I'm here to tell *you*, Daniel. What you choose to do to help your friends that you saw leaving the castle earlier . . ."

"I saw—" Dan caught himself. "Right. I saw that. Sure did." He nodded, feeling acutely aware that subterfuge wasn't his skill set. "A friend would tell people, so they didn't get caught. Where did I see them?"

"Leaving through the balcony."

"Oh." Dan forced a laugh. "Better go get them then, huh?"

"You should know that there will be consequences for you being in town," Sondre said quietly.

Dan muffled a noise of frustration. He really had no choice but to obey Sondre's requests. He knew that. To be sure he was secure here, he had to obey his master. That was how it worked. A host of sci-fi and fantasy franchises flittered in his mind, and in every last one, the whole "obey the bad guy" thing ended poorly for them.

Except Sondre's not entirely bad, right?

Something of Dan's struggle must have been evident in his expression because Sondre added, "Trust me, Daniel. Go to their rooms, and then use the tree there."

"The tree?" Dan echoed.

But Sondre was already gone. The only answer was the soft click of the door closing. He, obviously, was fine with subterfuge.

Dan tugged on his robes, reminding himself yet again that this was the path he'd chosen, and the ends justified the means. *Unless I get expelled.* He was hopeful Sondre wouldn't do that, but hopeful wasn't the same as certain.

Focus on the now.

Focus on the goal.

Dan had taken to wearing robes over his trousers and shirt any time he left his room. He *would* be staying here; Sondre had as much as promised it. Hopefully, the headmaster wasn't reneging on that by sending him out to break the rules.

"What tree?" Dan asked the empty room, half hoping a hob would appear with an answer. "This is going to be fine. Find the tree. Find the witches. Earn Sondre's respect. I can do this."

With as much stealth as he had in him, Dan made his way to the rooms of the two witches. The first room, Maggie's, was locked.

"There's a bed check tonight," Dan told one of the people in the hall, a student whose name he hadn't bothered to learn. "Pass it on."

Then as the woman went off to knock on another door, Dan went to Ellie's door. This one was—conveniently or not—unlocked.

"Hello?" He poked his head inside, leaving the door open behind him. "Hello? Ellie?"

He was loud enough that others might hear him, providing an excuse for why he was there. At the balcony, he stopped cold in his tracks. He wasn't under any illusion that Ellie Brandeau was *average,* but the sight before him was next level.

"Holy bat balls," he whispered.

Unfamiliar envy suffused every inch of him at the sight of a perfect tree—and with stairs, too! There was no way she was leaving Crenshaw. Ellie was going to be—to quote Sondre—"a person of influence."

And Dan was going to be her friend.

Debating briefly the risks—and maybe getting Axell, who seemed able to make them invisible—Dan decided he'd be better off tackling this on his own. If they both went, he had no guarantee Axell wouldn't be punished.

Dan descended the tree and walked toward the village. He had a bounce in his step at the thought of the influence he might have if he had powerful allies like Ellie Brandeau. It wasn't quite as good as if he had the power himself, but all he really wanted in life was to be here. In Crenshaw. Everything else he'd ever thought he wanted came second to that.

No one witnessed the way he practically ran past the woods, where he could swear he heard the hissing venomous beast. He'd dreamed about the nest of serpents chasing him the other night, and so he said a silent prayer to whatever deity witches prayed to that he would not need to go into the woods tonight.

He'd barely reached the tavern when the two witches came outside, giggling and holding on to each other.

"Don't let him touch you," Maggie said as soon as she saw Dan. She stood with her arms stretched out as if she were on a tightrope. Then she stepped in front of Ellie.

Dan held his hands up in surrender. "Whoa!"

People nearby were giving them suspicious looks, maybe because of Maggie's loud words and the other things such words could mean or maybe because they were students and ought to be in the castle.

Or maybe they all knew about the snake and the hole under it.

"She thinks I can change people's magic," Dan said in a low voice. He shook his head. "I'm not your enemy. Either of you. They're doing a bed check tonight, and I saw you head to town—cool tree, by the way—so I thought I'd come tell you."

Ellie took a tipsy step toward him. She extended her index finger and leaned forward but didn't touch him. Her words sounded like each one had a long pause after it as she jabbed her finger in the air toward him and announced, "You went hiking. Now you are missssing. Didja know?"

"*What?*" Dan stared at her. As far as he knew, only Sondre knew about his near-death adventure. Well, and he told Ana. Maybe—

"Hiking. Ravine. *Aaaaaah.*" She made a gesture in the air like her fingers were walking and then fell. "Plop. Dead Dan . . . except you're not dead. You're a fucking witch."

Nope. I didn't share all that with Ana.

"Did I know you over there?" Dan stared at Ellie, finding her knowledge of his near-death unsettling or maybe embarrassing.

She shoved at his shoulder. "I'm a remedial witch, Daniel Monahan Who Hikes. Like you and Mags. We're all fucking witches in this poisonous place."

Ellie spun and grinned at Maggie, who was staring at her as if she'd sprouted horns or something. Maggie said nothing, and Ellie was grinning at him like a cheerful drunk.

"Right, well, bed check you know . . ." Dan gestured toward the path to Crenshaw Castle. "We ought to get back, so no one is in trouble."

But Ellie stepped closer. "If you touching someone when they do magic is a thing, I want to experiment. On me. Not on Mags or anyone else." She no longer sounded drunk or even vaguely tipsy, which set off more alarms for Dan.

"I don't think—"

"So when we get back," Ellie interrupted, "*you* are going to help us figure it out. Call it science. We're going to test this."

Dan sighed. "She's wrong. I'm barely able to do the spells. The only thing I'm really good at is ending up in the wrong place."

"Didn't we all do that?" Maggie muttered as they started toward the school.

And Dan wasn't sure what to say about that, as he hadn't meant *here*. He liked here. He wanted here. Saying he meant more "under thrall to the whims of the headmaster" and "facing a weird purple slime venom serpent over a hole in the ground" wasn't really an option, though, so he kept his mouth shut.

"At least if all you can do is boost other people's magic, you'll be able to get back to Baltimore," Ellie said finally.

He stayed silent. That was exactly his fear, and he was no longer sure he could trust Sondre.

"What if you tried to make something?" Maggie suggested. "Let him grab your arm after you start."

Ellie walked away and came back with a big rock. "Okay, so here's the plan. If I go dangerous again, Mags, you conk me on the head."

"Are you sure?" Maggie asked, accepting the rock with both hands.

"They can heal me. Just do it. Hit me hard." Ellie gave one nod, as if to emphasize to herself or maybe to Maggie that it was a good plan. "He'll cooperate. Won't you?"

Dan swallowed awkwardly. "This is a bad idea."

"But then you'd know if you're stuck here. Although I guess you want that with the robes and all . . ." Maggie looked oddly resolved, even though everything in Dan said this experiment was a terrible idea.

"If I agree to do this, then we can go to the castle?" Dan actually *did* want to know about his magic, especially if he had to go before the Congress of Magic tomorrow.

"Sure." Ellie started walking toward Crenshaw.

The path back wasn't overly long, and once they got past the woods, Dan felt like he could relax.

When they reached the edge of the open space around the castle, Ellie came to a full stop. She nodded toward the tree that now stood beside her balcony. "It's still there."

"The castle is like a fairy tale," Dan murmured.

Maggie gave him a dangerous smile. "Lacks thorns."

Ellie laughed. "Maybe I ought to add them. Make it clear that I'm too much trouble to try to keep me here."

"Berries. There's no berries here." Maggie looked like she was enjoying this far too much.

And all Dan could think was, "*Please don't let me get expelled.*" So he said, "But you already proved you can make that. Chains, too. Don't you want to try something else?"

Maggie deflated slightly.

"Clean water." Ellie nodded. "I just want a bath that doesn't smell like eggs."

"Pool?" Dan suggested. "Hot springs?"

Ellie closed her eyes; she'd done that in class when she was envisioning the chains that nearly choked them all. Dan flinched a bit at the memory, but in front of them was a small opening in the earth. As he watched, it grew to be a size slightly smaller than an Olympic pool.

"Now," Maggie whispered. She gestured toward Ellie. "Her shoulder."

Dan reached up and rested his hand on her shoulder. He felt a slight buzz in his skin, but that was it. It didn't *feel* like he was really doing anything. But as he looked at the pool, it suddenly lined with what appeared to be white tiles, and crystal-clear water burbled out of the ground like a fountain and splashed into the pool. Steam rose from it.

"What in the hell are you three doing?"

Sondre stomped out of the castle door. Dan jerked back at the sight and sound of the headmaster, and Maggie raised her rock just as Ellie muttered, "Done."

Then Ellie tumbled to the ground, seemingly unconscious.

"Well, shit," Maggie muttered.

Dan offered as an answer of sorts, "Experimenting?"

Seeing Sondre looking so angry made Dan step back. At the same time, Maggie stepped forward, placing herself between the headmaster and the unconscious woman. "I was trying to look after my friend." She gestured to Ellie. "Care to help? Those muscles of yours ought to be good for something other than trying to look intimidating."

Dan winced, but Sondre's eyes widened in surprise.

"I'll carry her to her room," Sondre said. "You two get inside. You know you aren't to leave the castle without perm—"

Maggie walked up to him and jabbed his chest with her index finger. "I'm a grown-ass woman, Headmaster. No *man* tells me what to do, even if he is wearing a dress."

"Robe," Dan corrected her. "These are robes."

But she was already headed inside.

Sondre gave him a friendly wink. "Inside, Monahan. I'll be by to speak to each of you once I get this one settled."

Dan scurried after Maggie, who looked at him and said, "Told you."

Then she was gone, and Dan headed to his room.

I have magic! He grinned. Tomorrow, the Congress of Magic would surely let him stay. He went into his room and let out a cheer of joy.

I. HAVE. MAGIC.

37
Ellie

Ellie opened her eyes to find Prospero staring at her from a chair across from her bed. A quick glance verified they were alone in Ellie's room at the castle.

"Hi . . . ? Where is everyone? Why are you here?" Ellie felt her cheeks warm.

"I swear you need a minder, Miss Brandeau." Prospero stood and came over to the bed. She brushed a hand over Ellie's cheek "The others are all over at the Congress of Magic. So I volunteered to stay with you."

"How long was I asleep?" She sat up abruptly, not thinking about the fact that doing so would put her face-to-face with Prospero.

Ellie's experiment was apparently a bad idea. Or maybe magic after booze was?

"Is the tree still there? The pool?" Ellie tried to stand to go look out her balcony window.

Prospero put a restraining hand on Ellie's arm. "Slow down. Your creations are still there, and this is the morning . . . well, the *afternoon* after your visit to the tavern where I tried to convince you to let me . . ."

Ellie couldn't help herself. "Love me? Seduce me? Ensnare me?"

"Yes." Prospero closed the distance, capturing Ellie's mouth in a kiss that was surprisingly tender.

When Ellie brought one arm around Prospero's back to pull her closer, Prospero pulled away from the kiss.

"You, my dear Miss Brandeau, are overdue for a meeting with the heads of houses. And you are magically drained." Prospero leaned in and dropped tiny kisses along Ellie's jaw and throat. "And, might I add, remarkably forward."

Ellie chuckled. "Not all of us can be polite Victorians."

"Whatever made you think I was polite?" Prospero whispered. "Patient, yes. Polite, not truly." She pulled the edge of Ellie's shirt aside and kissed her collarbone.

Ellie shivered. "If you aren't planning on seducing me, you might want to stop now."

"Oh?" Prospero leaned back and looked at her, holding her gaze. "And if I was planning on doing so?"

For a flicker of a moment, Ellie's common sense took control. *Bad idea. Very, very bad idea.* But then, Prospero caught her bottom lip in her teeth, looking vulnerable and unsure, and Ellie's hesitations vanished entirely.

"I'd suggest you get on with it since the castle is empty enough that no one will hear you moaning." Ellie tugged her T-shirt off and tossed it aside. She reached back to unhook her bra.

Prospero stopped her. "Let me unwrap you."

"You do know I still might not stay in Crenshaw," Ellie reminded her as Prospero leaned in and kissed the now-exposed tops of Ellie's breasts. "Just because I sort of like you doesn't mean . . ."

"You do know you might not even like me if you get to know me." Prospero sounded like she was trying to make light of it, but Ellie heard the doubt.

"Hey?" Ellie caught her chin and tilted her face up. "I like you enough that I'm no longer ready to decide if I want to stay or go home."

"Truly?"

"A gorgeous woman walked into my workplace and *kissed me*." Ellie carefully began to unbutton Prospero's vest. "And then I appear here, only to find *you* again, wanting me to help you save your world . . ."

Prospero shrugged off her vest, and with a gesture and muffled word, her shirt was gone, too.

"Neat trick." Ellie plucked the strap of the corset-looking contraption that was still in her way. "You forgot this, though."

"I believe I was to be the seducer here." Prospero looked at Ellie's bra. "May I?"

"Yes please. All of these clothes can go." Ellie was breathless as Prospero removed her bra and gently pushed her backward onto the bed.

"You were so magically depleted that you were unconscious for almost twelve hours, Ellie." Prospero's voice wobbled. "You scared me."

"I made a tub of *clean water,* though." Ellie preened a little.

Prospero stared at her, seeming far too serious. "You are a hero, Ellie Brandeau. Now, let me make us both feel better."

Her hand slid along Ellie's breast and along her hip, pausing to clutch her hip bone like it was a handle as her mouth lowered to draw Ellie's nipple into her mouth. A sigh escaped as Ellie arched upward. She felt Prospero's mouth curve slightly, smiling before she gently bit.

But Ellie really wasn't great at patience. She pushed down the sheet that divided them. "Skin, Prospero. I want to feel yours on mine. I want you touching me."

A tingle of magic washed over Ellie, and she noted that she could *feel* Prospero's magic when their bodies were touching. But then silky skin glided over hers as Prospero shifted the rest of the way onto the bed.

Ellie stroked her hands down Prospero's spine, but as soon as she reached Prospero's low back, Prospero slid away out of reach. She dropped kisses on the underside of Ellie's breasts, the edge of her ribs, the curve of her hip bones.

"How impatient are you, Miss Brandeau?" Prospero asked, gazing up at her.

Ellie widened her legs, so she was cradling Prospero between them. "Very . . . but I can't touch you when you're so far away."

"Shall I stop?" Prospero let out a low laugh. The heat of her breath over Ellie's underwear made Ellie bite her lip to stop a moan.

"No. No stopping."

"Good." Prospero pressed a kiss to Ellie's right thigh and then another kiss to the left thigh. She whispered a word against the covered but now aching and damp part of Ellie, and the thin cotton barrier between Ellie's body and Prospero's mouth vanished.

The only magic in play after that was Prospero's clever mouth and hands, and in far less time than Ellie had thought possible, she was shaking with pleasure. A part of her logical mind said she ought to be embarrassed at her utter lack of self-control, but both her mind and body were trembling.

And Prospero didn't stop.

When Ellie finally tugged her upward, she gave Prospero an awed smile. "Give me a moment to catch my breath and then—"

Prospero kissed the rest of her words away. "As much as I want that, I need to take you to the Congress."

Ellie narrowed her gaze in a glare. "Are you serious?"

"Unfortunately." Prospero pulled her into an embrace. "We only have a few . . . Ellie?"

"Hush." Ellie parted Prospero's legs a bit more and after only a few moments, discovered Prospero wasn't far from finding her own release. "I want to put my mouth here, but if you're going to be difficult, this will do for now."

"I'm . . . fine. You don't need—"

"Hush." Ellie slid two fingers inside Prospero's already dripping body. "I *do* need. I most definitely need. And so do you."

Prospero whimpered.

"I'd rather be late than leave you wanting," Ellie whispered as Prospero shifted to give Ellie better access.

☽ ✦ ☾

By the time they were dressed again, Ellie almost felt guilty for the obvious worry on Prospero's face.

She caught her hand. "Hey."

Prospero looked at her.

"I'm going to tell them I can't decide yet. We both know they won't ask me to leave," Ellie admitted.

"You made clean water, Ellie. They will beg you to stay," Prospero said, her voice light despite the worry in those words.

"So we just need to go over, tell them that I am staying for now, and that when I'm feeling recharged, I'll make more pools, and then maybe you can take me to your home where noise isn't such a worry?" Ellie laced her fingers through Prospero's. "We can figure things out."

The look of relief on Prospero's face made Ellie tug her into an embrace, but then Prospero straightened and stepped backward. "I would very much like that. All of it."

"Good." Ellie felt victorious. She'd bought time to figure out both the witch thing and the Prospero question. She'd helped Crenshaw, too.

Everything will be fine.

After an awkward moment, Prospero took Ellie's hand again. "I am not interested in hiding what's happening between us, but for your own safety, we will walk into the Congress without contact."

Ellie frowned. "And after?

"I will dote on you as much as you—and my own comfort—allow." Prospero squeezed her hand. "I'm not particularly good at relationships, Ellie. I need you to know that."

They walked through the hall and out of the castle in comfortable silence. By the time they were beyond the edge of the town, Ellie ask-ordered, "Tell me about your last serious relationship."

Prospero shrugged and didn't make eye contact. "My husband who nearly killed me? Or the woman who died for kissing me? There's no good story there, Ellie."

Ellie stopped walking. "Wait. You didn't date *anyone* in Crenshaw? Ever? In like a hundred years?"

"Or more," Prospero corrected.

"My goodness . . . so you . . . I mean, not that there's anything wrong with self-satisfaction." Ellie paused. "Are there, you know, magical vibrators?"

Prospero almost stumbled. "Somehow, you are never what I expect, Miss Brandeau." She gazed at Ellie. "I have not been *celibate* for that century. I simply haven't been in any relationships."

"Ah. That makes more sense." Ellie looked at Prospero.

"I have never promised anyone a relationship, Ellie. Not once since I became a witch."

"Right . . . so . . ."

Prospero stopped in the middle of the sidewalk, stepped in front of Ellie, and took both of Ellie's hands in hers. "Make no mistake, though. I was not suggesting that *we* have a casual dalliance. I want *everything* with you; that means I am going against more than a century of habit. I am, in fact, suggesting a relationship. Now. With you."

"Oh."

Prospero lifted one of Ellie's hands and kissed the very edge of her knuckles. "I am interested in knowing you."

"Define knowing," Ellie whispered.

Prospero's smile was a beautiful, wicked promise. "Thoroughly. Your mind, your foibles and victories." She lifted Ellie's other hand, gently flipping it as she did, and pressed a firm kiss into the palm of Ellie's hand. "And what makes you sigh and quiver and gasp."

Ellie stared at her. "And will *you* let yourself be known? You . . . earlier you seemed hesitant to let me look after your needs."

"I have been rather celibate since our first kiss," Prospero whispered. "Then you resisted my magic, and it made me uncomfortable. I do not like giving anyone power over me, and I am at your mercy *already*, Ellie. That makes it hard to surrender."

Her rather proper phrasing made Ellie smile. It was quite the contrast to her enthusiastic and somewhat aggressive actions in bed. It made Ellie want to be uncommonly honest. "I haven't really dated in a while either. Not as long as you, of course! I was always afraid. . . . It sounds weird to say, but I was afraid I'd vanish, becoming one of the missing if I did. I tried to be different than Hestia, so I wouldn't go missing like she did." Ellie gestured around the street. "But here I am."

"On my life and magic, I swear to you that I had no idea that you were her niece."

"What about the cows?" Ellie asked. "Did you cause the accident to make me come here? Near-death experience and all that?"

Prospero frowned. "I didn't."

"Was that why you kissed me?" Ellie felt vulnerable the more they talked.

"*You* kissed me," Prospero corrected. "But yes, I was there to . . . attempt to hurt you."

"Right . . . the shock." Ellie glanced around, and as much as she realized Prospero was making a statement by doing this in public, Ellie was over others watching them.

"I stopped, Ellie. I couldn't *hurt* you." Prospero gave her such a vulnerable stare. "I wanted to bring you here, but I couldn't."

Ellie's heart thrummed at the longing in that admission. "We should discuss this somewhere more private. I don't need all these people overhearing us."

Prospero froze, looking more exposed in that moment than any other time outside the bedroom. Softly, she asked, "Are you ashamed to be seen with me?"

"No." Ellie leaned closer and brushed her lips over Prospero's in the ghost of a kiss.

Then she stepped back and looped her arm around Prospero's waist.

"I want to kiss you. Talk more. Maybe convince you to let me put my mouth on you," Ellie said in a low voice. "And I don't want an audience while I say those things. I'm not an exhibitionist, Prospero, so telling you that I want to taste you and have you at my mercy seems like a private conversation. Would you agree?"

Prospero made a noise that did little to help Ellie's self-control. "Let's go to the Congress. So afterward . . ."

"Good girl." Ellie watched Prospero's eyes widen and made a mental note that she'd need to see how those words worked in other circumstances. Maybe they weren't going to end up perfect or meant to be, but right now, it felt like they actually might be.

And that was worth a lot of risks.

38

Maggie

The Congress of Magic building was reminiscent of the castle. It had the feel of somewhere ancient, the kind of place that was constructed by medieval European people. It was not an ancient Americas structure, neither a stepped pyramid or cliff dwelling.

And castles were typically European. So what was *this*? Though castle-ish, it lacked the towers and spires and levels. There were no fortress walls either. Ultimately, it was like someone started to build a castle, but stopped after the bottom floor and instead added hallways that branched off to unseen locations.

One by one, the students filed in to whatever was beyond the giant doorway. Until their turn, they sat on old-fashioned stone benches so uncomfortable that Maggie wanted to pace.

"Ms. Lynch?" Sondre called.

She stood and glanced at him.

"You and Daniel will be last. Ideally, Miss Brandeau will be here by then." Sondre's voice was loud enough that the remaining six people all heard.

But Maggie wasn't keen on saying her piece in front of everyone, so she gestured him toward the door that they'd entered. Sondre's promised visit to chastise her last night hadn't happened, so whatever punishment she was to face had not materialized.

He quirked a brow at her, but then he gestured her forward to walk in front of him. She wanted to say goodbye and apologize for any problems her actions caused.

When they both reached the back of the room, he stood facing the exit door. Maggie was between him and the door, so she stood sheltered by his body.

She looked up at him. "Did I cause you trouble last night?"

He mouthed, "No."

She interpreted that as "Be quieter still" or maybe "The walls have ears." It was hard to tell in Crenshaw, so she nodded and decided to phrase everything cautiously. She said quietly, "I'm going to request leaving. You know that."

He nodded.

"I appreciate the kindness you've shown me." She gave him a sweeping look and tilted her head appreciatively.

He choked on a laugh, and Maggie was grateful he shielded her body with his larger form.

"Take care of yourself, Headmaster Sondre." Maggie ignored public protocol for a moment and put her hand flat on his chest long enough to say, "I wish I'd remember you."

Sondre covered her hand with his. "I hope you find joy over there."

Then she stepped around him and returned to her seat. Her eyes burned slightly with unshed tears. Today had come faster than any of them were expecting, and while she was excited to get home to Craig, she felt more than a twinge that both Sondre and Ellie were going to be gone from her life so soon.

And I won't even remember them.

"Axell Olsen," the bodiless voice announced.

The Norwegian stood, looking at the remaining people in the room. "I hope to see all of you tomorrow."

The door to the assembled heads of houses opened, and he went through it with a small wave over his shoulder.

Maggie waited through two more people. Then, the doors at the back opened and in walked Prospero and Ellie, looking remarkably cozy. They separated, and Ellie came to sit beside Maggie.

"Well, you look like someone who ignored her own advice," Maggie whispered.

Ellie shrugged, but she was smiling. Her gaze darted toward the Victorian witch. "Decisions were made."

"I'll miss you," Maggie said, no longer whispering.

"You won't remember me," Ellie pointed out.

"In my heart, I think I'll miss you. We could've been excellent friends." Maggie glanced at Sondre, who was watching her, and hoped he understood that she meant him, too.

"Margaret Lynch," a voice echoed through the waiting room. "Elleanor Brandeau."

It was odd that they were both called in together. Maggie glanced back at Sondre.

He shrugged.

The door opened.

Maggie reached over and squeezed Ellie's hand. "Let's do this."

Together, they walked into the room. It was an odd assemblage of people, ranging from those in towering hats who were somber faced to those who looked so anxious there were no other details Maggie could notice.

The witches were all seated such that they were looking down on them as they stood side by side. Something about it reminded Maggie of being in court, and that made her more confident.

"I'm leaving Crenshaw," Maggie said. "No need to debate. I want to be siphoned. No matter the risk. My son is there, and no amount of magic is more important than that."

Several witches exchanged looks.

"Siphoning you could kill you, Ms. Lynch," one said.

"I'd rather be dead than without my son." Maggie realized she sounded melodramatic, but it was the raw truth. If she didn't have a son, she would stay, but Craig was her guiding star, her reason, her heart. "I absolve you of guilt if I do die."

Before anyone else could reply, Ellie said, "I, er, don't know long-term, but for this round, I'd like to stay." Her hands were held loosely at her side, and the typically tense librarian looked uncommonly relaxed.

She's staying for Prospero.

Maggie looked back at the Victorian witch, who was staring at Ellie with the edge of a smile on her lips. Maggie pressed her lips together tightly. She didn't trust that woman any more than she trusted the rest of them.

"Siphoning you would certainly kill you, Miss Brandeau," the chief witch said, drawing Maggie's attention back to Ellie. "I would recommend you make a permanent choice to stay."

Ellie tilted her head. "As it's my decision, my life, my body, I'll make my own damn decisions. For *today,* I am willing to stay, but if I do, I expect a bit more autonomy. I'll not accept being trapped in a castle like a Rapunzel or Sleeping Beauty."

Her hands were no longer held loosely. Ellie had crossed her arms over her chest in a clearly judgmental pose.

"My decision is permanent," Maggie blurted out. "Where do I go to get siphoned?"

For a moment, no one replied. Then the chief witch answered, "After we finish these meetings, those who are to be siphoned will be gathered." He paused, stroked his face absently, and then his voice dropped to the kind reserved for bad news. "Ms. Lynch, do you recall the accident?"

"Yes."

"Your son did not survive, Ms. Lynch." The chief witch held her gaze as he lied to her face.

Maggie was baffled that he could utter the lie so convincingly. *I can tell when someone lies.* She knew damn well that this was a lie, but it didn't make her stomach tense or skin itch the ways lies did.

"Craig is no longer in that world or ours," the chief witch continued. "I am sorry for your loss, but I would ask you to consider your choice further. There is no sense returning to someone no longer there."

Maggie opened her mouth, but no words came. She glanced at Ellie, who quickly wrapped her in an embrace. The act of doing so hid Maggie's face from the assembled witches.

"Hush, Maggie." Ellie patted her back as if consoling her. Her voice grew louder as she announced to the Congress of Magic, "I'm taking her back to the castle."

"We are sorry for your loss, Ms. Lynch," one of them said.

"Please take a few days to grieve before making any choices," the chief witch suggested.

"I'll escort them," Prospero offered, stepping up to Ellie's side. "I'll make sure they are safely back in the castle and return to you for the siphoning."

No one replied, and in mere moments, the three women were striding out of the Congress of Magic.

Maggie had a moment of wondering if she could speak freely, but then Prospero said, "They should have told you sooner." She awkwardly patted Maggie's shoulder. "I am sorry for your loss."

"Did you know?" Ellie asked, her voice sounding strained. "Most of us only know what we recall. I do have articles about some people—like Dan—but most of us don't know what's going on back there."

Prospero stood as if frozen, and then she said, "I should have said something. There are rules, of course, as to what we can tell you and when. We don't want volatile magic hurting anyone! But I'm sorry I didn't mention it to *you*, Ellie. I will do better in the future."

Ellie's smile looked strained, but she leaned closer to Prospero. "Thank you for saying that. It helps."

Maggie opened her mouth, but Ellie grabbed her again. "I'm so sorry. Let's get you back to your room." She stared into Maggie's face, and then she cut her eyes toward Prospero.

And Maggie realized Ellie was well aware they were being lied to both by the Congress of Magic *and* Prospero. So Maggie kept her mouth shut and let her tears fall. They were not tears of simple grief, though. Much like Leon, these people were trying to stand between her and her son.

The witches of Crenshaw were about to learn the same thing Leon had been figuring out: no one stood between Maggie and her son.

39
Maggie

"Your room." Maggie gestured toward the hall to Ellie's room once they were inside the castle. The memory of Sondre saying the castle wasn't secure, that people might listen or watch, made Maggie want to see Ellie's notes. Saying that out loud was dangerous, though, so she just said, "I need my friend."

What I need is that article!

Once the door to Ellie's room closed, Maggie turned to Ellie. "Do you have a notebook?"

Ellie nodded.

Maggie wrote, *I want to see the article again.*

Without a word, Ellie opened the binder and handed it to Maggie. The words were the same. Her memory wasn't faulty.

MISSING LAWYER

RALEIGH—The search for 44-year-old Margaret Lynch continues this week. "Ms. Lynch careened off the road. Evidence suggests the mother of one was day-drinking," local sheriff Bill Bamberg explained. "Maybe she caught a ride with someone. Maybe she planned the whole thing."

Lynch, an attorney, was last seen by her teen son, who was knocked unconscious in the crash. Several campers saw the two that weekend, but there were no witnesses to the accident. "Maggie was in over her head at work, but there were no cases likely to lead to foul play," her ex-husband explained. "I think this was her cowardice. We were in a custody discussion, and I wouldn't be surprised if she was trying to kidnap our son." Authorities are hoping someone will reach out with information on Ms. Lynch's situation.

She pointed at the damning words: "teen son, who was knocked unconscious in the crash." Even if her memory was flawed and Craig hadn't been able to escape the SUV, even if he had been knocked out—which was not what she recalled—the article wouldn't reference him in the *present* tense if he had died.

Ellie traced her finger on "wouldn't be surprised if she was trying to kidnap our son." Then she took the notebook and wrote: *It's as if there is still a son. If Craig had died, they'd mention it.*

The Congress lied, Maggie wrote.

Ellie nodded.

Prospero lied, too. We need to leave. We can do that. Right? Maggie stared at her only friend. *Or can you help me escape?*

Ellie looked away, and Maggie felt like a nest of wasps had set flight in her stomach. She wasn't sure how to do this. How was she to escape on her own?

After several moments, Ellie took the pen and wrote *Prospero is the one who makes people forget things. The only one. So she knows he's alive IF he is.*

Maggie mouthed, "If?"

Some concussions or internal bleeding aren't immediately obvious. Ellie gave Maggie sad eyes before writing, *There is a chance they aren't lying.*

Maggie knew that. She did. However, her heart was certain that if Craig were actually dead, she'd know. No one understood when she said that sort of thing; they chalked it up to sentimentalism. Maggie realized now that it was part of her magic. Like her uncanny ability to hear untruths in most cases, her foreknowledge of Craig's well-being was rooted in magic. She'd known his tibia was fractured before the X-rays had confirmed it. She'd known he had the flu the moment he'd caught it—before symptoms. They'd had endless fights about her overprotectiveness.

It was always magic.

Careful of her words, she took the notebook and wrote, *My magic feels his health or sickness. It always has. He's alive.*

Ellie sighed and mouthed, "Okay."

I have an idea, Maggie wrote. *Stay here?*

Once Ellie nodded, Maggie said, "I need to go to the headmaster. Tell him I need a few days alone to grieve. That you agreed to stay with me."

"Are you sure?" Ellie asked, and Maggie was pretty certain she meant that more in terms of trusting Sondre—what with her knowing Maggie had slept with him—than the larger plan.

"He's a good man. I trust him." Maggie walked to the door. "I'll be back soon."

She made her way through the quiet halls of the castle until she stood before Sondre's door. She debated knocking and waiting, but she was done waiting. For anything. For anyone. She knocked once and then turned the knob. "Sondre? Headmaster?"

He sat on the sofa inside, looking defeated with his head bowed. At her appearance, he looked up. "I tried, Maggie. Before you yell at me, I want you to know th—"

"Am I safe to speak freely?" She looked around. They were apparently alone, and he'd said previously that his room was not bugged in any way.

Once Sondre nodded, Maggie blurted out, "My son isn't dead. I am certain."

"Maggie, the chief witch said—"

"Fuck that." Maggie started pacing. "When Craig was in the car, I made a bubble . . . a magical bubble-wrap, I guess, and I wrapped him up. He wasn't even scratched. He crawled out of the SUV and went for help." She stopped and made eye contact with Sondre. "I didn't *know* I was a witch, but I am a lawyer because I can tell when people are lying. Even before I was a witch, I could."

"Typical of many of us," he murmured.

"Right, well, I don't know how the chief witch lied, but I know he did because I can also feel when my son is hurt or sick. I always have. My arm ached when his broke. My throat was tight when he was sick. Not like I caught it, but my body is tied to his. Intrinsically connected."

Sondre stood and took a step toward her. "Witches are dying. We are dying here—miasma or viral or bacterial. I have no idea. Thirteen of us dropped dead yesterday. So they are desperate to sort the weak from the strong, and then send them back to save them."

"So because I'm stronger they want to expose me? What sort of fuckery is—?"

"They think the strong have a better chance of survival, and Crenshaw needs new witches if it is to exist." Sondre pinched the bridge of his nose. "I wanted you to go back so you were safe. I was overruled."

Before she could think better of it, Maggie was flinging herself into his arms. She looked up. "I told you that you were a good man."

"If I were a good man, you wouldn't be here." Sondre's arms tightened around her all the same. "Not in Crenshaw. Not in my room. Not in my arms."

"What about your bed?" Maggie suggested. "You seemed pretty good there."

Sondre chuckled. "You're dangerous, Maggie Lynch."

"I don't think anyone else thinks so," Maggie admitted. "I like that you do."

"I definitely do." Sondre stared at her as if he could will her clothes away with a thought. She'd seen similar looks on other men's faces, but Sondre was a witch.

"Why are we still dressed if you are looking at me like that?"

"You're never predictable," he murmured. Then he held Maggie's gaze and asked, "Would you like me to change the clothing problem?"

"Yes." She ought to go now, figure out a plan, but after today, she'd never see him again if things went right—and because she was leaving Crenshaw with her magic and memories intact, she wasn't going to forget him. "I want one more memory for lonely nights."

He whispered a word, and they were both naked. "I'd teach you how to do that, but you can't use your magic over there or they'll be able to locate you." He paused before admitting, "It's altogether possible I wouldn't teach you if you stayed either. I don't want anyone else undressed by you. Or with you."

"Possessive."

"Exceptionally." He pulled her into his arms and lowered his mouth to hers. A lot of men could kiss, in theory, but Maggie had never felt like a mere kiss was devouring her. Not until Sondre.

When he pulled back, she teased, "So give me something to remember, man-witch."

He had the look of a man on a mission as he dropped to his knees and lifted one of her legs over his shoulder. "With pleasure."

Time seemed to melt as her world was reduced to Sondre's agile mouth. Almost a century of living might be a factor, or maybe it was him, but she was muttering unintelligibly in mere seconds, knees shaking, body trembling.

Several moments later, she managed to say, "Can't stand. Too much . . . Sondre. I'm . . . going to fall."

But he didn't relent.

Her hands dug into his shoulders.

"I need . . . I'm . . ." She didn't fall, even as her whole body trembled and went limp. Sondre lifted her as her orgasm washed over her, and, in a blink, she was sliding down his body.

Maggie wrapped her legs around his hips as he walked to his bed. She rested her head on his shoulder for a moment to catch her breath.

"You're a god," she whispered against his throat.

"Does that mean you plan to worship me?"

When he leaned forward and let her fall the slight distance onto his bed, Maggie grabbed his hips and slid to the floor. "Yes. I think it does." She licked her lips and looked up at him. "I can't hold you up, though, so if your knees grow weak . . ."

He laughed. "I think we can find a solution. Maybe I won't even . . ."

His words died on a moan as she drew him into her mouth and set about proving him wrong.

When he stopped her, pulling away, he wasn't the only one who made a noise of regret. "Bed," he demanded.

Maggie obeyed, kissing her way up his body, and then crawling onto the bed.

Sondre pulled her forward, standing alongside the bed, and lifted her legs so this time her ankles rested against his shoulders.

Maggie let out a whimper as he slid home. The depth at this angle had her certain no man would replace him in her future. No one had ever left her so satisfied.

Then Sondre leaned forward, bending her in a way that made her grateful for all the hours of yoga over the years. He pushed her wrists over her head and pinned them there with one hand. He had her pinned, unable to move, unable to do anything but wait.

"Please. Please, Sondre." She thrust her hips upward, urging him deeper.

But he held her immobile for several more moments, as if he needed to prove he had control. "Memorable yet, Maggie? Should we stop—?"

"More."

He caught her mouth in a kiss and set about making the memories she'd asked for.

☽ ✦ ☾

Afterward, Sondre held her to his chest, wrapped tightly to him, and she knew that she wasn't the only one with regrets about their parting.

He gave her details on where to hide, how to get out of Crenshaw, and ended with, "There's a truck there that we use for supplies. Use it to get to town, but leave it there."

"Come with us," she whispered, her words muffled against his bare chest. "We could be something."

"If I did that, they'd come after me. After my years of saying witches ought to be able to return there, they'd think I was starting a war." Sondre shook his head and then dropped a kiss on the top of her head. "You ought to know that they *may* come after Ellie. She's the first head of house in decades."

Maggie shifted so she could stare up at him. "Head of house?"

"Some magic is strong enough that the witch possessing it becomes the founder of a new house," he explained. "Crenshaw creates what it needs, almost like it's sentient . . . or the hobs do. I have my doubts about them."

"Does Ellie know?"

"Unless Prospero told her, I doubt it." He made a noise that sounded like a grumble and a sigh all at once. "And I don't see that one sharing all her cards."

"She propositioned Ellie," Maggie told him. "I'm not sure . . . I think . . . Not that it's my business! I'm not the sex police." She laughed awkwardly. "I just don't trust her, and Ellie's so nice . . ."

"Prospero likes power. Ellie *is* power."

"I'm not going to tell her she can't come with me," Maggie said softly. "If they come after us, we'll run faster. I just can't abandon Ellie here. She's my friend."

"I can pretend to do what you suggested and believe you are in your room grieving," Sondre offered. "At most, it'll give you a three-day head start."

"I wish you were coming with us." Maggie rolled on top of him, leaned in, and kissed him until her body was at distinct odds with her mind. "I should go."

He released her.

Once she re-dressed, he said, "I hope I never have the pleasure of seeing you again, Maggie . . . but I think I'll miss you."

"Same." She smiled at him, barely resisting the impulse to lean in for just one more kiss. The sad truth was no number of kisses would be enough. Not with him. "I finally meet someone I want to get to know, and I can't. I hate this."

"Less than two hours until shift change at the gate," he said, repeating the instructions yet again. "If you want to get out, that's the best option. I'll have people attempt a break-in at the warehouse. That will, in theory, draw both the new guards and old shift guards away for about ten minutes."

"Thank you."

"Go gather your partner in crime. It's not a plan that will work twice, Maggie. You have one shot at this." Sondre stood and with a word, he was fully dressed again. "I'll shield your rooms. Give me about fifteen minutes after you leave here. You'll feel a sense of something dripping over you. It's not perfect, and it could make them suspicious, but if not . . . they'll know it's empty."

"Who watches?"

"There's a staff of low-level witches who are assigned to observation. Not constant, but every few hours they check in."

Maggie shuddered at the thought of that sort of invasiveness. "Bathrooms?"

"No, and they close the viewing window if anyone is . . . having relations." Sondre sighed. "They report it, but they don't *watch*."

"So you know who . . ."

"Yes, and who takes their pleasure alone." Sondre glanced at her. "I get reports."

"That's illegal in my world," Maggie said, reminding herself that *this* was not her world. "It ought to be illegal here, and how do you know they don't watch? There's no way to tell."

"Agreed." Sondre paused as if he shouldn't say more, but then he added, "You need to know that Prospero was with Ellie in her room at the castle. She won't let Ellie go easily, and if you wait too long to escape . . ."

Maggie hugged him, and then she fled toward her room. She needed to tell Ellie enough to convince her to leave.

40

Ellie

Ellie paced her room; she felt like the world's biggest fool. Not that she hadn't had *doubts* about Prospero, but she'd thought they were on the edge of something real . . . so when Prospero said she wanted to love Ellie, she'd believed it. When Prospero had taken Ellie to bed, when she'd confessed her vulnerabilities and that she wanted a relationship, Ellie had thought Prospero was telling the truth.

But she's a liar.

If it were true, Prospero would know. She was the one and only witch who erased memories, so she had to know if Craig was still alive.

Ellie felt like her heart was physically aching.

I should ask her. I could go to find her and ask and . . . then she'd know I have doubts. Then she'd watch us, and escape would be impossible.

So Ellie reread the article on Maggie and the accident. Nothing there said the boy had died. Maggie deserved to know for sure. If he was dead, they'd come back. If not . . . the weight of Prospero's second betrayal would mean there was no way Ellie could live here.

By the time Maggie returned, Ellie was calmer, and Maggie looked surprisingly resolved. She walked over to the notepad and wrote, *They watch our rooms. We have a few hours until Sondre stops that in this room. Temporarily. Then we run.*

Ellie flinched. All she could focus on was the "They watched the rooms" detail.

Maggie wrote, *I know about Prospero. So does Sondre.*

Someone watched Ellie have sex with Prospero—and Prospero *knew.* She had once been headmaster, so she'd known they had an audience. Was she making a point? Staking a claim?

The wave of betrayal washed over Ellie so intensely that her stomach turned. She dropped her hand to her stomach, pressing against it like she could stop the squirming feeling.

"I feel sick," Ellie whispered.

"I'm sorry. I understand . . . when I heard that my son . . ." Maggie covered her mouth, as if to stop a sob. "I just want to hold him again. He is my only child. I wanted more . . ."

"There are no children here. At all." Ellie looked away from Maggie. "I mean, I never wanted them, but . . ."

"Can you imagine raising a baby here?" Maggie laughed, although it sounded more like a cry. "In this stench?"

She scrawled, *The stench is part of something worse. 13 dead witches yesterday.*

Ellie realized the meeting with the Congress of Magic was because of that. More secrets. More lies. She just shook her head.

She shoved her binders back into her bag. "Sorry, I just want to tidy up." She forced a laugh. "I guess I'm not used to guests."

"Thank you for letting me stay here. I just . . . I don't want to be alone." Maggie stared at her, as if there were other layers in the words. "I'm scared."

Ellie looked up at her and nodded. They sat in silence for several minutes until a hob popped into the room with a tray of food.

"Headmasher says you need to eat even if you're having a sad."

The little man vanished a moment later, and Ellie looked at the food. "I don't know if I can eat."

"They brought sandwiches and things we can carry," Maggie said.
Ellie gaped at her.

"I felt the shield. He did it. No watchers now, Ellie." Maggie crossed her arms. "If we use magic over there, we'll be found. He'll cover for us as long as he can, but he doubts it'll buy us more than three days . . . less if Prospero comes looking for you."

Ellie wrapped her sandwich up and stuffed it in her bag, hoping it wasn't going to leak all over the binders.

"We can go down the tree. There has to be a border we can find. I know what it looked like when I walked in but—"

"I know where to go and when." Maggie looked excited, glassy-eyed with it, in fact. "I just need your magic to get us there. Once we're there, we probably ought to split up."

"Fuck that." Ellie went to open her balcony door, only to find it sealed. She closed her eyes, visualized the door being gone. When she opened them, it was exactly as she'd pictured.

"Let's go." They stepped through the empty door.

Holding up a hand, Ellie closed her eyes, visualized the door being intact again, and reopened them. The door was back. She gestured to the steps in the tree. "Let's get out of this place."

They saw no one at the tree's base, and in a few moments, they started to run toward the copse of trees that was alongside the path to the village. Maggie directed their route until they came to the gate Sondre had mentioned.

"We wait," she whispered to Ellie.

Ellie wasn't sure what they were waiting for, but she trusted that Maggie knew. It occurred to Ellie, though, that there was another option. "I can manifest ropes," she suggested in Maggie's ear. "Tie them up."

Maggie's eyes widened, but after a moment of obvious contemplation, she nodded.

Ellie stared at the two guards, studying the look of them, the shape, the location. When she'd caught the details, she closed her eyes and pictured them bound and gagged.

"Blindfold," Maggie whispered loudly.

So Ellie pictured that, too. The guards were incapacitated when Ellie opened her eyes, flopping on the ground like angry caterpillars.

"They're fine," Maggie said quietly, but not whispering now. "Change of guards is soon. That's what I was waiting for."

Ellie didn't ask how she knew that. *Sondre.* The headmaster had made this escape possible, and even if Ellie wasn't sure why, she was grateful for it. She shouldered her bag again and stood. "Let's get out of here."

They stayed away from the bound guards as they hurried to what looked like a shimmering space in the air. Ellie knew without asking that it was the marker of a well-crafted illusion. She'd learned as much in Lord Scylla's class.

Both women took a deep breath and stepped forward.

"Look," Ellie said, gesturing at the space behind them. On this side, it looked like solid rock, like a cliff face. There was no doubt that this was the work of the head of House Scylla.

"Come on." Maggie strode forward to another shimmery rock. "There's a truck here. Keys under the mat."

Ellie shook her head. There was a necessary arrogance to hide a truck *with keys* behind a bit of illusion, but according to their class, only witches could see the gleam in the air that said there was an illusion present.

Inside the cab of the truck, Maggie was in the driver's seat. "More gears than anything I've driven. Fucking hell, I'm not sure I can drive—"

"Then we drive in low gear." Ellie adopted a calm voice, hoping it worked. "No magic now, Mags. No going back. Your son needs you, so woman up, and grind the gears if necessary."

That was precisely what she did. The truck's transmission objected with awful grating sounds more than once, and they lurched awkwardly more than a few times, but within the hour, they were in a tiny town.

"Any idea how to boost a car?" Maggie said as they pulled into a shopping plaza. "He said to ditch the truck."

"No." Ellie pulled out her wallet of cash she hadn't expected to ever use since she'd been trapped in a magical world. "But I have this. If we find someone who we can pay for a ride . . ."

"That works."

They went inside, and Ellie found herself scanning the crowds as if Prospero, or the chief witch, or some robed stranger would appear. She wasn't foolish enough to think there were no consequences to what they'd done. They hadn't hurt anyone, but witches weren't allowed to be in this world—not that Ellie would reveal Crenshaw if she got caught. The reality, of course, was that people weren't quick to believe in magic even if she did tell them.

Times have changed.

There was no harm in living here with magic as long as they didn't use it. Just in case, she whispered to Maggie, "No magic."

Maggie nodded.

They paced around for a good ten minutes, long enough that Ellie was going from nervous toward panic. Then she saw a young college-aged woman and pointed her out to Maggie.

"Let me talk to her," Maggie suggested.

Ellie shrugged, and they approached the twenty-or-so-year-old woman.

"Excuse me." Maggie stopped her. "Are you busy the next few hours?"

The young woman looked suspicious. "Why?"

"My friend is on the run from an abusive ex," Maggie said. "If we use our credit cards or she travels under her name, we'll be caught, and she'll be dead."

"What does that have to do with me?" The woman looked sympathetic, but wary.

"I need to get us as far south as possible. Fast. All we need is a ride." Maggie smiled warmly, kindly, hopefully.

Ellie held up the six hundred dollars in her hand. "We can pay you."

The woman sighed. "My car isn't worth much more than that, to be honest. If you had another hundred, I'd just sell it to you."

Maggie reached into her pocket. "Diamond ring?"

"There's a pawnshop here," the woman suggested.

"Let's go." Maggie gestured her forward, and in about fifteen minutes, the pawnshop had offered a mere $680.

"It's worth a helluva lot more," Maggie argued.

The man wouldn't budge, so Maggie turned to the girl. "If you're smart, you'll sell it instead of pawning it. My ex paid over four grand for it."

The young woman, Tammy, thought and apparently agreed. "I'll trade you the car for the ring and a hundred in cash."

Maggie looked at Ellie, who nodded.

"Deal." Maggie held out a hand to shake. "We need a written contract, and it ought to be notarized."

After borrowing paper, Maggie wrote a very legal-sounding contract that they both signed—and the pawnshop owner notarized.

Deal complete, Ellie bought an inexpensive burner phone and minutes, and soon they were in the car headed south to the Carolinas, where Maggie would miraculously return from being missing and rejoin her son. Hopefully. They didn't have much of a plan beyond that, but it was a start.

"What if he's not alive?" Ellie asked as they pulled onto the freeway in their new car. She kept her eyes on the road.

"He is," Maggie insisted. "He's probably a wreck being stuck at Leon's house. We'll show up, and then I'll have my son with me, and we'll go back to my place."

"They know where we live, Mags. We need to run." Ellie paused before adding, "I want to pick up my aunt Hestia first, though."

"So we'll get Craig and Hestia, and then . . . I know a guy who can get us fake IDs. And I have money at the house for an emergency. We'll grab it. Get the IDs. Then we start over. New lives."

The reality—that doing this meant no more library for Ellie and no more law for Maggie—hit Ellie then. Their lives as they knew them were over, all because of their magic waking.

"People over there are dying, Ellie. This is better," Maggie insisted, staring at her.

Ellie nodded without taking her eyes off the road. "It's just all . . . settling in on me, I guess."

"They lied. They're dying and didn't tell us. And Prospero? She used you." Maggie sounded so sure that Ellie had to remind herself that her new friend was a lawyer. She was trained to be convincing.

Unfortunately, Ellie had no reasonable doubt. All she could say was, "I know."

41
Prospero

Prospero worried she was ignoring Ellie, but she wanted to get a sense of the scope of Crenshaw's risk. Her first stop was to find Cassandra, who was unusually difficult to find. She wasn't at her place of work or the tavern or the agriculture fields. By the time Prospero got back to her house, she was starting to worry her friend was sick.

Instead Cassandra was perched on Prospero's steps like a particularly odd bird. She quirked her brows. "Do I know you?"

"Cass . . ."

"Hello, stranger who has ignored me . . ."

Prospero gave her a withering look and stepped around her. "I cannot do this right now. Either come in or don't. I could use the help, but I have no patience for drama."

"Well, you're no fun." Cassandra huffed and stood with a swirl of skirts and hair. She jingled as she moved, and in a few moments, she was right behind Prospero and resting her chin against Prospero's arm. "So . . . you need a bit of prognosticating?"

Prospero glanced back at her. "It would be helpful."

"The water is not going to improve. I've looked at dozens of maybes . . .

all bad." Cassandra sighed. "We need to relocate, P, unless Ellie can patch the rift."

"Relocate a *town*?"

"I know it seems—"

"Impossible?" Prospero shoved open her door and stepped away from Cassandra.

"The miasma is from the water, and it'll keep getting worse." Cassandra sounded cheery despite her dire predictions. "Death. Paralysis like death. No good outcomes . . . and soon."

"Even though Ellie is staying?" Prospero didn't look back at Cassandra as she asked. If she avoided eye contact, it was easier to pretend the answer wasn't important to her personally. Thinking about it in terms of Crenshaw's good was how she kept herself from looking too closely at how honest she'd been when she'd told Ellie she wanted to love her.

It's better to think about the reasons.

"P?" Cassandra's hand came onto Prospero's shoulder. "It's not that easy . . . or guaranteed."

"She said she was staying when we were at the Congress the day before yesterday." Prospero glanced back at her friend.

"And you still lied to her."

"A little but—"

"You *lied*." Cassandra gave her a pitying look. "What was she researching over there, P?"

"Missing . . . The folders of information!" Prospero felt like her stomach was in her throat. "I know Monahan was in there."

"And so was Maggie Lynch." Cassandra leveled a stern glance at her.

"I need to talk to her." Prospero pivoted. "You come. Talk to Sondre. I'll go see Ellie and explain."

Cassandra closed her mouth and gestured to the door, and after so many years of friendship, Prospero knew there were more sentences that Cassandra wasn't sharing—but asking was futile when she had that look on her face.

After Prospero exited the house, she exhaled in frustration. If Ellie wouldn't or couldn't fix the rift, Prospero had to convince the entire Congress of Magic to relocate the town. It was an undertaking she couldn't fathom—could anyone move the buildings? The people? Where would they go? Could the hobs help? Would they?

"Cass . . ." She faltered in her steps. "Ellie can create. She fabricates from nothing. If she goes back . . ."

Cassandra tucked her hand in the fold of Prospero's arm. "I know. We need her, or we live without shelter while we build . . . or we stay here in the town, hoping not too many people die while we wait for her to fix the rift."

"I'll explain everything to her." Prospero picked up her speed. "She'll understand. If she knows what's at risk—"

"You will need to tell her how you feel." Cassandra glanced over at her. "I sent the demon beasts into her path, but—"

"You *what*?" Prospero stopped and glared at her best friend. "You caused her accident? The cows . . . Cass, what were you thinking? She could've died. She could've not had magic and—!"

"She was essential to us, P. Of course she had magic." Cassandra tugged on Prospero's arm. "People are staring, dear. Don't raise your voice. Do you know how many people I had to blackmail to bring her here?"

Prospero felt like she'd been betrayed in ways she couldn't even explain.

"If you'd handled it, I wouldn't have had to fetch her," Cassandra muttered. "I told you she was essential. You didn't awaken her magic. One simple shove into danger, P. That was all you needed to do. Where's my cold-hearted friend? Where's the woman who would do anything to save our home?" Cassandra shot her a glare. "Then, then she's here . . . and you blew that, too. Seduce her. Enthrall her. No, you waited and obfuscated. You *care* for her, but you delayed telling her. And then you lied to her."

Prospero was uncharacteristically silent until they were at the castle door. She glanced briefly at a giant pool of water that hadn't been there until a drunken witch—*my witch, I hope*—created it.

Prospero looked at Cassandra. "And you thought trying to kill her was the answer?"

"She didn't die. I told you she needed to come here." Cassandra rolled her eyes. "I wouldn't have prophecies if there were no need to act, and honestly, you were bungling it. People are dying, P. I had to bring her here before too many witches died."

Prospero couldn't answer.

"This is a war, Prospero. They are killing us. The rift wasn't an accident," Cassandra snapped. "You know it, and I know it. So we needed a weapon. This witch is our weapon."

She's not a weapon! She's a person!

Part of Prospero understood the logic of Cassandra's actions, but another part—a softer part—could only picture Ellie in pain, Ellie dying, Ellie angry.

Cassandra just strode off toward Sondre's quarters, and for the first time in decades of friendship, of trusting Cassandra, Prospero felt dangerously alone. She tried to remind herself that the good of Crenshaw was her guiding light, but she didn't think she would've been capable of putting Ellie in the hospital. Other people? Sure. Not Ellie, though.

Even though she'd been healed, Ellie had been in pain.

And Cass did that.

Prospero needed to see Ellie. If she thought everything was a lie, she'd change her mind. She'd leave. The entire town would need to figure out how to relocate, or they'd continue to die.

☽ ✦ ☾

Prospero knew many things had to happen to protect their home, but the pressure to clear up the lies she'd told Ellie—and maybe tell her that Cassandra was the cause of her accident—filled Prospero like a swarm under her skin.

Too late.

Why would Ellie believe anything Prospero said now? If she said, "I lied" and "But not about the accident," she'd sound foolish. Moreover,

Ellie would feel foolish if she believed the next words out of Prospero's mouth.

Prospero sped up as she wound her way to Ellie's door. She knocked. "Ellie? Miss Brandeau?"

When there was no reply, she pounded her hand against the door. Still nothing.

In a flare of uncontrolled magic, she burst the door open. It thunked onto the floor, and Prospero flinched, hoping the door hadn't landed on Ellie. She couldn't stomach the thought of hurting her.

Or that Cass has done so!

But the room was empty. Completely and totally empty.

"She's gone," a voice said from behind her.

She glanced back to find a hob in the hallway.

"The funny witch left us," he said.

Prospero rounded on the little magical man. "There's no way that the Congress of Magic siphoned Ellie without telling me!"

"Didn't say they sent her away." He gave Prospero a look reserved for the daft or drunk. "Said *she* left."

Prospero put a hand on the shattered doorframe for support. "On her own?"

"Nope. She took the one that likes the headmasher," the hob said in a cheery voice. "A day or so ago. Clever witches went away from the poison water . . . but at least our Ellie Witch left us a clean pool first!"

Prospero opened her mouth, but as she was not sure what to say, she closed it.

Ellie left.

This was disastrous in ways that Prospero could not fathom. No one simply *left* Crenshaw. There were attempts, but mostly since they'd begun asking people if they wanted to be siphoned, no one really tried to escape anymore.

The hob vanished, as hobs tended to do. Prospero wasn't sure how much she could trust any of the castle hobs. Her own? She'd trust them with her life. There were others she'd known and trusted, but if Sondre had allowed Ellie and Maggie to vanish . . . if they really *had* gone to the Barbarian Lands . . . any truce with Sondre was void.

He sent them. They couldn't escape on their own.

Prospero stormed through the castle, her shoes rat-a-tat-tatting like a warning. Students veered out of her way. Heads of houses that were near exchanged looks, and, in short order, fell in behind her like an unplanned entourage. She winced at the thought of dealing with them all at once, but there was no way around it.

When she reached the headmaster's quarters, Sondre's door was open in invitation. She stepped inside, glancing at Cassandra, who was perched on the edge of a sofa.

"What did you do?"

Cass cut her eyes at Sondre, lips pressed tightly, but she said nothing. Behind Prospero, several witches filed into the room.

"Did you know that Brandeau and Lynch were missing?" Prospero watched his face. Sondre had tells; everyone did. His were wider eyes and friendly smiles, as if happily surprised.

"Ms. Lynch, Maggie, asked to stay in Miss Brandeau's room while she grieved." Sondre's expression gave nothing away. "We all know damn well that the woman's son is alive, so what was I to do?"

"He felt guilt," Cassandra supplied, as if Prospero was suddenly daft.

"You can take yourself out of here, Cassandra." Prospero gestured to the door. "You are neither invited nor a head of house."

A heavy silence fell over the room. Cass was, perhaps, the only person present who had not been on the receiving end of Prospero's temper, but now Ellie was gone and thought Prospero had lied about everything.

"Mind yourself, Lady Prospero. You have enough enemies without adding me to the list." Cassandra was still smiling, but that smile felt like daggers now.

From the doorway, Walt's voice rang out, "One of the castle hobs disturbed my tea."

"If Ellie Brandeau isn't brought back from the Barbarian Lands, we will all die." Cassandra's voice had a depth that was a side effect of prophesizing in public.

Then she stood, shook her jingling skirt out like there were crumbs on it, and gave a cheery wave around the room. "I'll see myself out. Oh, and I hope I can trust that someone here has the cold heart necessary to do what needs must . . . and the battery booster will make you actually able to erase *anyone's* memories, Prospero."

Then she slipped between the eight people now in the room.

"What in god's teeth is that one on about now?" Walt asked the room. "And what battery booster?" He pointed at Prospero. "And since when do you need aid fixing anyone's mind?"

Prospero walked over to Sondre's kitchenette and grabbed two beers. She opened one and walked to Sondre, holding it out. "Still a truce?"

He lifted it in a toast. "Truce holds."

She might not trust him, but any allies were useful in a crisis. She cracked open her own beer. "I need a retrieval unit. We have two escaped witches."

"Damn it," Walt muttered. "*That* witch? Our new head of house?"

"That one," Prospero confirmed. "And the one we lied to. Ellie Brandeau had been researching missing people, apparently, before she came here. Her aunt Hestia Brandeau was once 'missing,' so . . ."

"We have a plague *and* escaped witches." Walt stomped over and snatched the can of warm beer out of Prospero's hand. "I am resigning as chief witch as soon as this pickle is sliced."

No one said a word. Walt threatened to resign regularly, but no one actually succeeded at it.

After a moment, he yelled, "Well, get over there! Prospero! Sondre! And someone get me a report on the status of Dr. Jemison. *Now!*"

42

Ellie

By the time they reached Virginia, Ellie was ready for a nap. She'd driven for the first six hours, hating the fact she'd zipped through Pennsylvania without at least stopping to check on Hestia.

Maggie took the wheel for a few hours. Their vehicle was far from luxury, and the noise of every rig or SUV that passed rumbled through the car.

By the edge of North Carolina, Ellie was driving again. Country roads took more focus, so Ellie took over.

About two hours later, they were approaching Durham, and the car was silent but for the increasing sounds of traffic zipping by now that they were near the city.

Maggie finally said, "You know this means a lot."

"We need to know. If he's not . . . if they *didn't* lie, I don't want to fight all of them." Ellie finally admitted that part to herself. Sure, living without magic was possible, but fighting an entire town of witches who were determined not to be exposed? There was no way Ellie wanted to deal with that.

Part of her felt like she'd lost her life either way. There was no way Prospero wouldn't look for her in Ligonier. She knew where Ellie worked. From there, it was easy to know where she lived, where she grabbed coffee or lunch.

"I can't go home again," Ellie whispered.

"Pull over." Maggie pointed to the narrow shoulder. "I'll finish this bit. You did more than your share."

"Ha! It was that or let you drive. I'm a lousy passenger," Ellie admitted.

"Control freak."

Ellie didn't argue against the truth. She'd made her life's mission all about staying in control, focused, calm. Now that she was running from Crenshaw—and Prospero—that was who she had to be again.

As Ellie steered toward the shoulder, Maggie added, "I'll go around. You climb over the middle. It's dark, and you're tired. No sense getting hit by someone."

Ellie nodded. Once Maggie got out, Ellie clambered over the middle console of the car and situated herself awkwardly in the passenger seat. When Maggie got in, she said, "We need to think about where we can go. No magic means they can't track us, I think."

"We can't fly anywhere or access our bank accounts or—"

"Could your aunt empty yours?" Maggie asked. "I could get Craig to draw mine out. I mean, I'm dead to them, so he's my kid . . ."

"Underage."

"Yes, but with my ATM card. Hell, maybe I could transfer it to our new names. Wire transfer like we are paying a bill and—"

"Our accounts are likely closed if they think we're dead." Ellie kept her voice calm. Ever since they'd found out about the way the Congress of Magic lied to them, Maggie seemed to be a razor wire. Not all the way dangerous, but close enough that Ellie couldn't decide whether it would be better or worse if her kid was dead. Obviously, his death would be tragic, and Ellie wouldn't wish *that* on Maggie—but finding him alive? That was a new set of grief, betrayal, consequences.

And I want Prospero not to have lied to me.

While Maggie had her own baggage, Ellie was feeling a betrayal she couldn't name. The woman she was falling for hadn't even cared. If she lied about Craig, did she lie about the cows that sent Ellie to the hospital? How much of her "let me love you" was a lie?

And how dare she let strangers watch them have sex—because it clearly wasn't making love if she was a liar and put Ellie on display like that.

"If we don't get a hotel, your ex will be there . . ." Ellie tried to weigh her words. "We need a hotel, Mags. If we arrive in the middle of the night, what are we going to do?"

Maggie deflated. She looked like she shrank in size. "Can we drive by the house?"

"Once."

"I know you're right," Maggie muttered. "What about ID? I know a guy . . ."

"And if your son is—"

"He's not dead." Maggie shook her head, shooting a glare at Ellie. "It's not like regular currency works over there. We get the IDs, and if we don't need them . . ."

"Fine." Ellie was fairly sure they would need them, but she wanted to leave room for the possibility that the people in Crenshaw hadn't lied.

Because I want Prospero to be the real thing.

What about the spying on rooms, though? The thought that the students were under observation wasn't shocking, and if the headmaster told Maggie, it was likely true. *So why would Prospero be with me like that in my room if we were being watched?*

Ellie shoved that mental quagmire away. "Let's call your guy."

Maggie recited a number, and Ellie tapped it in. She put it on speaker, and after the third ring, a rough voice—like the speaker had smoked all the cigarettes in the state and paused for moonshine between them—answered with, "How did you get this number?"

"What's the news, Charlie?"

"My girl! Wait. I heard you was dead . . ."

Maggie laughed, sounding strained. "I need a few full sets. What's your timeline?"

"For you? Tomorrow night if you get me photos tonight."

"Cash."

He made a tsking sound. "Doll, your money's no good with me. You know that. I'll see you where I see you."

The phone went dead.

Ellie reassessed her travel partner, who apparently had a direct line to criminals. "You know where to go?"

"I do." Maggie glanced at her. "You have a photo of Hestia?"

"We're getting her—?"

"Look. You can ask her. Stay without ever seeing you, or come with us. It's her choice . . . unless you'd rather she stay. We can avoid seeing her if you think—"

"She's a witch. Siphoned," Ellie blurted out. She felt like Maggie deserved to know. "Siphoned to get back to me."

"They let her go? Why not let me go, then?" Maggie's hands tightened on the steering wheel. "Sorry. I know you don't know why they won't. Ugh."

They zipped along the road a few minutes before Maggie said, "Four sets of ID or three?"

"Four." Ellie's stomach twisted. The odds of pulling this off weren't great, but she wasn't going to abandon Hestia. She had come back for Ellie, and now it was Ellie's turn.

"Charlie isn't my cousin's actual name. It's Hector. Charlie is a fake name in case anyone's listening." Maggie glanced over. "He's family, though. We're safe."

Ellie didn't point out that if they were safe, no one would be listening in on his calls, and they wouldn't be running from a town filled with witches. If they were safe, they'd be in their old lives, blissfully unaware of potential magic, lying witches, and hidden towns. There was no point in saying any of that, though, so the rest of the drive to Hector's was quiet.

When they pulled into what looked like an abandoned service station, Ellie had the distinct feeling that this was why seemingly rational people carried a gun.

Across from the lot, in the shadows alongside the building's ruins, an El Camino was parked. Gold or bronze or something. It was idling there, and Ellie wasn't sure either of them ought to get out of their car.

"This is a terrible plan."

Maggie laughed quietly. "Hector's my cousin. My *actual* cousin. I trust him."

That didn't do much for Ellie's anxiety, but she still handed Maggie their recently acquired phone. On it was the headshot of Hestia that Ellie had downloaded. The benefit of Hestia's archaeology and book-writing notoriety was that finding a good portrait of her online took all of two minutes.

Ellie stared at the quietly idling car. "How do you know it's even him?"

"I know his car." Maggie flashed a grin and got out. "Be right back."

Ellie watched her walk away into the shadows. She'd left the keys in the ignition, and that felt like a hint that Maggie might not be as sure as she'd said. Minutes ticked by as Ellie debated following or getting in the driver's seat at the least. Maybe they'd need a quick getaway or—

The gold El Camino drove off, slow and steady, not even kicking up gravel. Maggie lifted a hand to wave at the car's occupants. Then, she sauntered back to the car to join Ellie.

As she slid back in, she said, "Noon tomorrow."

Ellie felt foolish, but honestly, she wasn't exactly used to clandestine meetings at abandoned gas stations. She stared at the window. "We need a hotel. A little sleep. Maybe an actual meal."

43

Maggie

Being in a hotel after living in a castle was a surreal experience. It ought to be easy to slip back into this world, this set of details that made things "normal," but there was some saying about not being able to un-know things. Now that she knew magic was real—that she was magic—the Kozy Komfort Motel seemed wrong. The beds were new, and the blankets were standard motel fare. She'd stayed at such places in her younger years, and she'd even met clients or witnesses at them when they were skittish.

"Are you okay?" Ellie asked as they climbed into their beds that night.

Maggie turned out the light. Sometimes confessions were easier in the dark. "I wanted to stay there. Raise my kid there. Build a life where he was safe from his father and the darknesses of this world."

Quiet stretched. Then Ellie said, "If he's not alive . . ."

"He is." Maggie sighed. Explaining her connection to her son was one of those things that seemed beyond words. Now that she knew she was a witch, she realized she'd been using some low level of magic her whole life. "We're witches, Ellie. Magic is fucking real . . . and my connection to my kid is *magic*." She heard the vibrating frustration in her own voice, so she took a moment before adding, "He's alive. I know it as truly as you know your aunt was siphoned for you."

"Why would they lie like that?" Ellie asked. "I don't get it."

Maggie shook her head. She'd circled that question in her mind like the lawyer she was. Rolling over details was her process. It was how she found holes in a case. "Either because he's not magic so he's not welcome, *or* because he's a kid. There were no kids there. None. At first I thought they were in school or something . . ."

"I hadn't really thought much about that." Ellie rolled on her hip to stare at Maggie across the gap between their beds.

Maggie glanced at her. "The other possibility is you."

"Me?"

"Maybe they thought you needed me because there was no way they'd let you go willingly." Maggie rolled to face her. "And by 'they,' I mean Prospero. I don't trust her."

Ellie flopped back onto her back. "I get it."

And for a moment, Maggie felt guilty. She was accusing Prospero of lies because she knew Craig was alive, but she saw in Ellie's reactions that Ellie was hoping Prospero hadn't lied, that Prospero could explain herself, that she could make things right. Maggie had seen plenty of women in Ellie's position, desperate to believe despite facts. Few of them ever had the kind of happy-ever-after ending they wanted.

"Tomorrow, you'll see," Maggie whispered.

"Goodnight" was all Ellie said.

☽ ✦ ☾

The next morning, after a quick breakfast of bad coffee and stale pastries, they headed to the car. Maggie was bouncing in excitement.

"Too much coffee?" Ellie asked.

"I'm going to pick up my kid." Maggie shot a look at her friend. Honestly, people without kids never understood the bond a parent formed with her children. Sometimes, Maggie wanted another child, but sometimes, she suspected her stress and heart couldn't contain two such bonds.

Ellie was silent as they drove through the early-morning streets. Finally, a block from Leon's house, Ellie said, "I hope you're right."

Maggie glanced at her only long enough to smile. She knew she was, but knowing something—even knowledge that was marrow-deep—wasn't the same as being able to explain it to another person.

Leon's neighborhood was one of those overpriced, carefully manicured developments that could be anywhere in the U.S., no soul, no substance. Every driveway was paved; every house was the same basic model. Even the shrubs were matching. *Behold my wealth*, the neighborhood's design said clearly.

Maggie slowed the car so they crept up on Leon's house. He ought to have been gone, and his wife was always off to the gym earlier—that had been her routine when she was Leon's employee, and Maggie doubted it had changed much. Craig would likely be home alone. "I'm going to park in the street in case Craig and I need to get away quick. You slide into the driver's seat and—"

"They lied," Ellie said. She gestured toward the front door of the McMansion in front of them. "That *is* him, right?"

Craig was walking down the steps of the oversized front porch.

Maggie nodded, swiping at the tears that were dripping down her cheek. Then, she was out the door. "Craig!"

She started running toward him when her son stood as if frozen in the very manicured front lawn. "I'm so sorry. I was trapped after the accident and . . ." She wrapped her arms around him and kissed his cheek and forehead. "I'm so sorry I didn't call or—"

"Who are you?" Craig pulled away and stared at her.

"What? I'm your mother. What do you mean—?"

"My mother died. What sort of sicko are you?" Craig glared at her like she was monstrous.

"It's me." She reached out to her son.

Craig took another two steps back toward the house and shoved a hand in his pocket. "Look, I don't know who put you up to this, but you're sick. . . . I mean, pretending to be my dead mother? You don't even *look* like her."

"I *am* her. I'm me, I swear. I didn't die, obviously. I was held captive, but as soon as I could, I escaped so I could find you." Maggie knew in some part of her mind that his reaction was because of magic, but she *felt* her son's fear and rage. He was wrecked emotionally, and it made her want to wail.

She noticed his pocket light up. He'd shoved his hand into his pocket to use his phone.

Craig yelled, "Dad? There's someone at the house—"

Maggie knew better than to react with violence. She did—but she still tackled her own son to the ground and tried to get the phone away from him.

"No! You have to listen." Maggie tried to get the phone even as he tried to twist away. "Listen to your mother!"

Her ex-husband's voice came through the phone. "If you stayed in the damn house, this wouldn't be an issue."

Apparently, she'd turned it to speaker phone when she'd tried to take it.

"Help!" Craig cried out. There were tears on his cheeks. Her son was terrified.

Of me.

"*Craig?*" Leon continued to yell. "I've called the police. Get inside."

From somewhere behind her, Maggie heard Ellie's voice, a car door slam, but all she could think was her son would believe her if she explained well enough. He *had* to. Once he did, they could escape Leon.

Instead, Craig punched her and scrambled away.

Craig was at the front steps of Leon's house when Maggie said, "I carried you in my body, Craig. You're my son. We were camping, and then there was an accident. I was hurt, but you crawled out of the window and went for help."

He paused.

A burst of hope rose up inside her, and Maggie pushed to her knees.

"That part was in an article." Craig sounded horrified. "Then I got back, and my *actual* mother was gone. So I'm stuck here . . ." He gestured at the house. "I wish my mom was still alive, but she's not."

Craig fumbled with the lock on the door, looking over his shoulder at her repeatedly.

"I'm not dead," she said, tears and what felt like a broken nose making her voice thick and wrong. "I came back for you. I'm right here. Craig!"

The door closed behind him, and Maggie was sobbing full-out now.

"Come on," Ellie urged. She grabbed Maggie's upper arm and tugged her to her feet.

Sirens wailed in the distance.

"Seriously, Mags. I don't want to sit in jail."

A flash at the window made Maggie look up, and she realized her son was doing exactly what she'd taught him. He took pictures of them and the car.

And he punched me!

He might not remember her face, but he remembered her lessons.

"Once I can talk to him longer, I can convince him." Maggie stared at her son through the window. He wasn't safe *or* happy here. She was sure of it before, but hearing his words made that doubly clear.

"Right now we need to get out of here, or we'll be in jail." Ellie pulled on Maggie's arm again, and this time, Maggie went willingly.

They ran to the car, and as Ellie started it and pulled away, Maggie glanced back. Another picture. Their license plate was in his photos.

"He'll turn those in," she told Ellie.

"No shit, Mags. No fucking shit." Ellie was speeding away, randomly turning whichever way seemed likely to be the opposite direction from the police.

When they finally got to an intersection with a red light, Maggie took a steadying breath. "Fabricate it. Change the number on the plate. The color and shape of the car, too. Do it."

"If we use magic, they'll come here and—"

"If we don't, we'll be in jail by morning or trapped here with no car because we need to abandon it because my son smartly photographed the car and plates." Maggie winced at the thought of leaving her son.

It's only temporary.

She'd come up with a plan. She'd get through to him. She would. That meant staying out of jail, though. Jail made them vulnerable—to the law and to the witches.

"If we're sitting in jail, they'll find us and return us to Crenshaw anyhow." Maggie swatted at the tears that kept falling. "I can demand siphoning, especially since I know he's alive, but there's something over there killing people, Ellie. Do you want to go back there and die?"

Ellie's hands tightened on the wheel, but she closed her eyes.

As Maggie watched, the hood of the car became black. The shape shifted slightly. The compact car grew into an older-model sedan.

Ellie opened her eyes. The shifting was either easier or she was better at it. Either way, she wasn't passing out this time. "If you drive, we can go faster. I'm tired from . . ." She gestured around the car.

"Pull over." Maggie nodded. It took a lot of willpower to stop the lingering tears, but wrecking wasn't an option any more than jail was. They had to get away, figure out the next step, avoid any police—including magical police if there were any—and rescue Craig.

He's alive.

Maggie wasn't sure how they were going to do all of that, but they were. There was no way in hell she was letting some witches—*or her* ex— steal her son. "We need to get our IDs, make some sort of plan, and—"

"We need to get the hell out of here before we get arrested, or witches pop up to take us back." Ellie pulled over and got out of the car.

Maggie got out and ran to the driver's door.

When she reached Maggie's still-open door, Ellie slid into the car. She glanced at Maggie, now in the driver's seat. "And I need to rest and recharge."

Within moments, Ellie was sound asleep, and Maggie was left with her thoughts—and avoiding the sirens that were zipping through the streets.

Passports and ID.

Get to Ellie's aunt.

Maggie twisted her way through side roads until she came to her cousin's shop. Hector wasn't a bad guy, not really. He was a good guy in his way—family first, money second, law somewhere down the line. When Leon took him on as a client in exchange for staying away from Maggie and Craig, she should've stepped in and said no. A lot of things Leon wanted were things she ought to have refused.

She rolled up to the garage. One man with a barely concealed gun gave her a look, and she spotted three others at various places. The first was tucked between two towering stacks of tires that had to have come from rigs or construction machines. Another was sitting in the doorless frame on the second floor, kicking his feet into the open air and smoking a cigar that was likely as illegal as whatever else Hector had here.

Leaving the door partly ajar so as not to startle Ellie, Maggie stepped out and waved at each of Hector's guards.

Then—hands held palms out and raised—she strolled toward the open garage bay as if she had all the time in the world. Once, his guards would've all known her, but she was a long way from that life.

"Hey, cuz!" she called out. "Charlie?"

"Charlie, my ass," Hector muttered as he swooped her up into his arms. He twirled her around in half circle before letting her feet touch the ground. The result was that his back was to the door, and his lackeys had seen his exuberant greeting.

"Hector." Maggie stared at her cousin. It hit her then, just as at the gas station, Hector knew her. Carefully, she asked, "You recognize me?"

"Hell, girl, it ain't been that long." He scowled. "You're a little skinnier, and a lot less dead than I expected. I read how you died. Drinking, they said. As if."

Maggie couldn't understand why he recognized her, but Craig didn't. His words made it click though. He wasn't in her life in a way that anyone knew, and likely, a witch wouldn't seek out every person—just the closest ones.

Magic took energy.

Prospero—because it had to be her since she was the only mental magic witch—couldn't alter all people's memories, just those closest to the vanished person. Maybe Leon really did believe Maggie was a drinker! Craig obviously now thought she'd died. Had that changed when the Congress of Magic decided Maggie couldn't leave? The article was proof that, at first, the common belief was that she was missing. Craig, however, had said she died.

Who knew what lies Prospero had woven into their minds? Or when? Maggie wanted to know, but right now, her pressing concern was escape.

"Did he hit you or something?" Hector asked. "This is some abused wife shit you're doing. Vanishing like you did and then showing up asking for new identities for you and the kid, and these other two . . ."

Maggie started crying again and found herself in her cousin's embrace.

Hector's hand patted her awkwardly. He might be adept at fake identification, but he was lousy at crying women. "There, there," he muttered over and over, patting her back like it was a drum.

It was awkward enough to make her smile.

"Whatever you hear about me, it's Leon's bullshit. I need to get Craig away from him, to somewhere safe. And if anyone shows up here asking about me, just think about taxes or gadgets or something real hard, okay?"

Hector gave her an odd look.

"They can get info out of most people, so do your best, but if they do get you to talk, I forgive you." Maggie pulled back and caught his eye. "Try, though, okay?"

"What kind of shit are you into? Spies? Treason? Talk to me, Maggie girl!"

She shook her head. "Just get me the papers. I need to get out of Carolina. Fast."

Hector stared at her. "You call if you need anything at all, you hear me?" He led her to his workshop. Behind the predictable auto mechanic's garage was a locked room, and inside it was a gleaming sea of technology. Printers and scanners, whirring computers, and humming monitors. It was a geek's dream.

And it was where Hector did his real work, the stuff that paid for his assorted children's private school tuition and his indulgent gifts to at least three on-and-off-again exes. He was devoted to family, and that included the women he never quite married but continued to impregnate. Not a one of his girlfriends needed a job. Not a single kid they claimed was his wanted for anything. "Good guy" wasn't as easy to define with men like Hector. But good to his family? Every single time.

He handed her a fat envelope. "I took the liberty of adding a credit card for each of you."

Maggie hated to say "thank you" for the identity theft she knew that required, but she also hated to be penniless as they all tried to start over. She clutched the envelope.

"Don't look at me like that. I took your life insurance money from the jackass," Hector said quietly. "Maybe a little extra."

"How much?"

"Two fifty." Hector grinned. "That was the policy. The other hundred was pain and suffering." He tapped the envelope. "Stacks of prepaid cards, Maggie. Some cash, too. Craig's a growing boy, yeah?"

Three hundred and fifty thousand dollars. They could build a new life with that.

"Made you a college teacher. Lawyer is too easy to trace." He shook his head. "Made her a sociology teacher, too. Degrees. Money. Cards. ID. Figured the old lady was that one's mom." He gestured to the general direction of the lot. "So that seemed like a thing she could do . . ."

Tears burbled over in her eyes again. She wished she had been better to him. "I'm sorry I let him cut you out of our life."

Hector shrugged. "Love makes us all a little stupid. You need help, you call, though? Okay?"

Maggie nodded. "You really are the best."

He shook his head once. "Just family being family."

"I wish I could stay. Tell you everything. I need to go, though, before the police catch up," she whispered.

Hector's brows rose. "Police?"

"Chasing a dead lady who was careless today," she said with a forced laugh.

"Cuz?"

Maggie paused.

Hector pulled out a 9 mm and held it out. "Unregistered."

When she accepted it, she stared it. Quite a few years had passed since she'd carried a gun, but magic was no match for bullets as far as she knew. As she continued to stare at it, Hector walked away and came back with two spare clips and an extra box of ammunition.

"Take care of yourself and the boy," he said.

"I will," Maggie promised. She wasn't sure how to undo the magic that made her son forget her, but she had as many tools as a woman in *this* world could ask for. Now she just needed to figure out how to kidnap her son.

If he was in his own mind, it's what Craig would want, and that truth only added to her determination.

Maggie walked away, back to her magically altered car and sleeping friend, and hid the gun. She wasn't sure of Ellie's stance on guns, so hiding it from her felt wiser.

44

Dan

Dan and Axell walked into the library, lights turning on to illuminate the vast open space. Behind them, the door sealed, trapping them alone in the chilly room.

"Why would anyone hide books?" Dan muttered.

Axell gave him a quelling look. "Books are dangerous, Daniel. They give people ideas, make them rise up against lies and intolerance."

"So witches are fascists?" Dan scoffed.

"No, but someone—or maybe several someones—hides this for a reason. We must ask *why.*" Axell walked deeper into the library, looking at the shelves. "Maybe it is opened once we finish more classes, but . . ." He shrugged. "We should ask."

Dan knew Axell was right, but he wanted to believe. Maybe he'd always wanted that: to believe in something. Coming here had felt like it could be perfect. A world with acceptance. A place with magical healing. It had sounded like utopia. But there were humans, and every place with people was a place where there would be lies and jockeying for power.

He trailed a hand over the backs of chairs as he followed Axell. "We should tell the Congress about the snake and the hole in the ground, and we should tell our classmates."

"Yes, when we—" Axell's words died abruptly. Like Dan, he'd obviously thought they were alone in the library until they heard a faint *pop*. It was louder than hobs.

"Take my hand," Axell whispered loudly, extending it toward Dan.

As Dan took Axell's hand, they both became invisible. "Don't move," Dan whispered.

They stayed still in the library as two people popped into the room. The headmaster was there with Prospero, the witch who had been carrying Ellie out of the woods.

"Look, I don't know why you brought me—" Sondre stopped, looking around. "The library?"

"Privacy. I know the New Economists created the rift." Prospero folded her arms over her chest. "How involved are you?"

The headmaster said nothing, mimicking her posture and glaring.

"Ellie made the snake in the woods," Prospero added. "I took her to the rift and she . . . was irrational. Injured herself to try to plug it."

"You know better than to ask me things," Sondre started.

Prospero held up a hand. "You, Agnes, who else?"

"I don't know what you—"

"Lynch and Brandeau will be brought back, Sondre. They'll be here, and if you think that killing witches is not going to get you badgered or *worse,* you're wrong. Walt knows. Scylla knows." She took a step toward him. "What if I told you I had a spy?"

The headmaster's eyes widened.

"My spy told me about Agnes," she continued.

Sondre shook his head.

"Mae could die. Maggie could die," she continued.

Sondre's shoulders slumped. "Allan. Lord Dionysus. He made the rift. It was to be our evidence that we had to move. He wants to go back. A lot of us do."

Prospero shook her head. "Fools. Our magic is unstable over there.

If we're there too long, magic lashes out, and then we're looking at witch hunts. That's not a myth."

Finally, Sondre seemed to straighten, to rebuild his confidence. "Prove it."

"The escapees are already proving it. You'll see." Prospero shook her head. "I'll have to erase memories, hide the proof. And there's *one of me* so I couldn't do that if everyone went over there to live. We need to fix our home. Miss Brandeau has the magic to do it, but now she's angry and—"

"So tinker with her head. That's what you do." Sondre turned away like he was going to leave.

"I'll need Monahan," Prospero called. "Since he's your lapdog, let him know to obey me."

Dan's heart sped dangerously at the thought of doing anything with her. She was fucking terrifying.

Then Sondre's voice grew louder. Not turning back to her, Sondre asked, "Who's the spy?"

"You are. You just never remember," Prospero said.

The room went silent as she did whatever her magic was to alter the headmaster's memory and thoughts.

"So everything seems in order?" Sondre asked.

"It does. You and I will retrieve the escaped witches," Prospero said. "Thank you for meeting with me. I didn't want to talk about their retrieval in front of everyone."

"You know our truce is still temporary," Sondre muttered.

"I do." Prospero gave him a strange smile. "Wouldn't it be nice if we could work together, though?"

"Mmph. As if." Sondre popped out of the room.

A moment later, she followed.

Dan and Axell were alone together in the library again.

"Do we tell him?" Dan asked.

"Do *you* want to fight with the scary witch?" Axell countered.

They were quiet for several moments, and Dan thought about the things he knew—things that seemed dangerous to know. Then he shook his head. "Sounds like they'll fix the water problem."

"Eventually." Axell was still holding Dan's hand. "Are you still wanting to stay here?"

"Yes."

Axell nodded. "I would like to not tell them that I can vanish us."

"Seems wise." Dan looked around the library, not quite sure what to do or think. Then he noticed that the door was back. "Let's borrow a couple books and hide away for a few hours."

"Excellent idea," Axell agreed.

It wouldn't undo any of the horrible things, but sometimes getting lost in a story was exactly what Dan found was the best medicine for his fears or anxiety. Apparently, that hadn't changed even though he was living in a magical world.

45

Ellie

Ellie woke with a crick in her neck from sleeping in a moving car. She blinked, looked around, and realized that they were darting between cars at a speed that seemed anything but legal.

At least we're on a freeway.

"Mags?"

Her friend had what Aunt Hestia used to call "bad idea eyes" as she glanced over at Ellie.

"Are we being chased?" Ellie stretched, trying to pull out the pinch in her neck and tightness in her shoulders.

"We are whether we see them or not. I got the IDs, and you were asleep, so I decided." She sounded as manic as she looked. "My cousin liberated my life insurance policy. Added that to our stuff. We have plenty of cash. If we need we could get a new car, maybe an RV. I thought about that for once we get your aunt and Craig and—"

"Where are we?" Ellie interjected, trying to make sense of where they were.

"Headed north again. If we can get to your place, we'll know if they messed with her head the same way or—"

"Walk into a trap?" Ellie was wide awake now, adrenaline chasing the last of the sleep away. "If they realize we were at your son's house, they'll know—"

"Why do you think I'm driving so fast?" Maggie shot her a mad-eyed look.

"Watch the road!"

Maggie continued unperturbed. "Well, that and the espresso and other caffeine drinks." Her hands white-knuckling the wheel, voice sounding somewhere after dangerous, Maggie looked like a woman who found the proverbial do-not-cross line and gleefully zipped past it.

"Maggie . . ."

"Might be easier to kidnap your aunt, too, if they messed with her head. Old lady and all," Maggie offered with a grin. "I was thinking about cult deprogramming. No way that witch erased everything. Once I can get Craig to sit and listen, I could explain enough things that only I would know."

"Maggie."

"Then we could go to Alaska. . . . Get an RV. Go to Alaska. No one can find you if you get lost there. I had a client who was going to be found guilty. She sent a postcard from Alaska. I don't know where she is out there, but I think that's where she went."

"Maggie!"

Maggie glanced over.

"Pull off on the next ramp," Ellie said, adopting the tone that every librarian, bartender, and security staff had to learn. The everything-will-be-fine voice, the no-sudden-movements voice. "We need to get a bite to eat, and I need to pee. And you need to get something in your body other than caffeine and sugar."

As Ellie watched Maggie's hands tighten harder on the wheel, she added, "If you want to rescue your kid, you need to think clearly."

Without a word, Maggie exited the highway.

They were in a stretch of Virginia where the amenities were not immediately off the exit. Roads like the I-95 were financial lifesavers for dying towns. Speeding tickets brought in revenue, as did convenience stores and diners.

"We should go back. It looks like there's nothing for several miles," Maggie complained.

"So this won't be busy." Ellie folded her arms. "Seriously, I just woke up in a car that I modified with magic after watching your kid punch you. Can I get five minutes to think and eat?"

Maggie sighed, but she kept going. "You could pee beside the road. No one would see."

"Call me old fashioned, but I'd like to wash my hands, too, especially if I'm going to eat."

"I have bottled water, energy drinks, pretzels—"

"How long did you drive?" Ellie asked pointedly.

"We're in Virginia. Craig is in North Carolina."

"Exactly." Ellie saw the shining silver of what looked like it was vying for the tackiest diner in the South. "Over there."

Maggie slid into the lot with a spray of gravel. "I should've asked you to make this a sports car or an SUV. I've had the pedal down as far as it goes the last few hours."

Ellie shook her head and got out of the car. When she looked back, Maggie was shoving a thick envelope into a canvas bag. She paused.

"Three fifty and ID. I'm not leaving it in the car."

"Three fifty?" Ellie echoed.

"Three hundred fifty thousand. New life money." Maggie straightened, one hand clutching the bag tightly to her side as Ellie gawped at her.

They went inside, and once they were past the door, it looked like a cute diner that was filled with what looked like homemade patterned tablecloths, a bar with '50s style barstools, and the smell of fresh pie. Berries and cinnamon announced at least two flavors of pie, and somewhere a stereo system pumped out Appalachian music that might have been early 1900s or modern. A television mounted in the corner had a football game playing as part of the noon news. There was a timelessness to it that made Ellie think of Crenshaw.

"Sit anywhere you want," a curvy woman in a blue dress and quirky patterned apron called out. Aside from three customers—an older couple and a young man with a book—the only other person in sight was a cook. He was an older man who had made the unfortunate decision to comb the remaining straggling hairs over a shiny bald head.

Maggie picked a booth that was surprisingly not sticky. More importantly, it had a clear line of sight to the car. She was, seemingly, better at this whole life of crime thing than Ellie was.

"Where did you get that?" Ellie asked, glancing pointedly at the bag.

"My cousin is a hacker and an entrepreneur of somewhat dubious nature," Maggie whispered. Then louder she said, "It was good to see family."

When Ellie stared at her, Maggie whispered, "Act normal."

Ellie wasn't convinced Maggie's mimicry of normal was believable, but she did have a valid point. They'd escaped a magical world, bought a car from a stranger, and met with what sounded like a minor crime lord in the last day. Honestly, Ellie had no real compass for normal anymore.

"I wonder if the badgers were guilty of escaping," she asked as the waitress walked up.

"Badgers?" the waitress echoed.

"My friend had a strange dream," Maggie said too quickly, smiling broadly at the woman. "She fell asleep while I was at the wheel."

"Coffee?" The waitress smiled at Ellie, who noticed that the apron was covered in assorted fruit that all had speech bubbles saying things like, "I'm berry good!" and "Have a sweet day!"

"Tea," Maggie said.

Once they ordered, the waitress went off to get their omelets, breakfast potatoes, and pie. There was something to be said for all-day-breakfast spots, especially those that had fresh-baked pies.

Quietly, even though there was no one else in the diner, Maggie said, "I was thinking I could get something, drop it in his food, and once he's out—"

"Are you considering *drugging* your kid?" Ellie asked, mouth open in shock. "Do you hear yourself?"

"He's stronger than us." Maggie looked away. "Obviously, I don't want to drug him, but I can't abandon him. And I figured we needed a plan before we see your aunt."

The waitress came back with their tea. Although the tea was sweetened just this side of something that was fit only for hummingbirds or those wanting excess dentist bills, the overall atmosphere of the diner was calming.

"I'm not good at any of this," Ellie admitted. "I spent my life trying to avoid excitement and adventure. After Hestia vanished . . ."

"To there?" Maggie prompted.

Ellie nodded. "I was sure somehow that the only way to avoid going missing was to be the opposite of her. Be safe. Be boring. Be quiet."

Maggie said nothing for several moments. She glanced at Ellie before softly saying, "I gave up everything I wanted because my husband's opinion mattered more than mine. Craig was my one exception, my rebellion of sorts. I back-burnered my career. Hell, I wore my hair the way Leon wanted." She took a long drink of the cavity-in-a-cup tea. "I think being *there* made me believe that what I wanted would matter. That's how I ended up in bed with Sondre. I propositioned him."

Ellie was quiet, watching the waitress lift their plates of omelets and start toward them. The only sound was crooning mountain music.

"Maybe magic makes you feel free," Ellie offered once the waitress walked away.

"Maybe feeling free or confident makes you magical," Maggie rebutted.

Ellie chuckled. "Fair."

"I think there are parts of what they have that are good, but I'm not going to agree to being controlled again. Not by a man or a government." Maggie chewed a few bites of her food. "Alaska. Somewhere like that, where it's wilder and freer. That's where I'm going. We don't need to stay together, though. Maybe it's better if we don't. That way if they find one of us, they aren't going to find both of us."

Ellie looked away. Maybe it was selfish, but she wanted to have someone at her side if the Crenshaw witches came after them. Ellie wasn't sure she could defend herself. A memory of Prospero saying she'd spent "lifetimes" learning martial arts made Ellie feel both a familiar flicker of longing and a less familiar flicker of fear.

"Together," Ellie said. "Alaska is good."

As she looked up again, her gaze caught on the television. More specifically, it caught on a picture of Maggie.

"Mags . . ." Ellie hoped the waitress and the cook weren't looking in the same direction. "Drop cash on the table. We need to go. Now."

"Wh—?"

"Picture. Television. You." Ellie tried to keep calm, even as her magic pulsed against her body like a pressure was building. "We need to go."

Maggie turned and looked at the television, horror washing over her expression. As a man spoke, Craig at his side, Maggie's horror wavered into rage. The tea in her cup started to bubble, and Ellie realized her friend had become angry enough that she was literally boiling the contents of her cup.

"No magic!" Ellie grabbed Maggie's wrist. "Stop."

Maggie flinched away. "Fuck."

She scrambled out of the booth and ran toward the door, Ellie following close behind. A shimmer of something that Ellie already identified as magic built in the diner, and Ellie froze. "Go!"

There, standing like everything Ellie wanted and feared, was Prospero.

"Go!" Ellie yelled at Maggie again. She paused and stared at Prospero. "Don't come any closer. You lied. Craig's alive. You lied about everything, and I was stupid enough to fall for it." Ellie was shaking. "Seriously. Just let us go. Tell them you erased our minds. Tell them you killed us. You lie well enough to pull it off."

"Ellie." Prospero took a step closer. "I'm relieved to find you."

"No." Ellie raised a hand, and the floor lifted up like the asphalt serpents and the forest serpents once had. This time, though, Ellie had better control of it. It was no illusion. No accident. She stared at the woman she'd been falling in love with, and Ellie willed that black-tiled floor into a cage. She willed the silvered barstools into steel bars around those.

Doubly caged, Prospero stared at Ellie. "You're making a mistake."

"Let me go. Don't pursue us," Ellie half begged half demanded, and then she ran out the door and jumped into the waiting car.

With one last burst of magic, she shifted the car into a sleek Bugatti Chiron, reputedly the fastest sports car available according to a research paper she'd helped a library patron with last year. It looked like it was meant to carve the very air, an arrow-like form that would make speed easier than magic.

"Go." Ellie looked back. She couldn't see Prospero following them, and all she could hope was that a sliver of the woman's feelings had been real enough that she could let them escape.

46
Prospero

The retrieval unit was in North Carolina collecting the Lynch child, but Prospero had felt Ellie's magic somewhere else as surely as she felt her own heartbeat. "Keep him safe," she directed.

"You need to sleep. Nothing will wake you up until you hear my voice again." Prospero had implanted the thought as she spoke.

"And if you were to die?" Sondre had asked, arms filled with the now sleeping boy.

But she couldn't answer, not unless she wanted to wake the gangly teen. She'd rolled her eyes and vanished.

Only to be caged by Ellie Brandeau.

Prospero was at a genuine loss. Ellie's magic was no illusion; she literally transformed things, so the cage holding Prospero was as real as any jail cell—one without a door. More impressive, perhaps, was that Prospero's ability to return to Crenshaw was caged, too. Ellie had created a prison cell Prospero couldn't escape on her own.

And the people here—non-magical people—were staring at her like she was an exhibit. She'd heard of zoos, of course, from newer arrivals, but in her time the closest thing was a traveling sideshow. *Before* her time, there was the Great Exhibition in London, but in any case, she was neither a sideshow nor a rare animal.

Her glare swept the room. An older woman in the back made the sign of the cross, and the cook walked to the door.

Prospero whispered a muffled word to seal the door. It wouldn't do to have any of them out spreading tales of witches!

"I don't know what's happening, but I'm not—" The cook jerked on the door. Shoved it. Kicked at it.

"Ma'am?" the waitress said, gawping and blinking. She stood outside the cell, hands twisting her apron tightly. "How did you . . . how did this . . . ? Did that woman make a *jail* in our diner? How?"

"Magic," Prospero muttered.

The waitress began to laugh, sounding more hysterical than amused.

The cook pivoted, glaring at Prospero as if knowing she had stopped the door from opening. He stomped up to the tile and steel cage. "This is your fault somehow."

"Seriously, Lou?" The waitress gestured at the seemingly impervious prison that Prospero was inside. "How in the name of all that's holy would she do that to herself?"

The cook started pulling on the bars of Prospero's cage. "Where's the damn latch? Why are you here?"

"Magic," Prospero repeated. "Witch." She pointed at herself and then at the cage. "Magic."

The cook walked away and lifted the carafe of coffee. Without a word, he tossed the burning liquid on her. She cringed, swallowing a scream of pain.

The waitress was trying to dab Prospero clean through the cage. Another person, a rather wiry young man, handed her a cup of ice. "For pain," he said.

"Don't worry. You won't remember any of this," Prospero said, biting back the cruel words she wanted to spew.

Despite her circumstances, Prospero was still a witch of considerable strength. She erased the woman's mind, and attempted to concoct some sort of believable story. The only answers were still peculiar, though.

Prospero settled on: "There was a meteor. No one was hurt, but the building suffered damage. You've all been arguing on who to call for help."

She looked around at the remaining people, quickly adjusting their perception with the same lies.

A reasonable explanation for a mangled cage in the diner was outside even Prospero's wits at the moment. So was escape.

So she did a thing that she loathed to do: she called for a hob.

"Miss?" Clancy, one of the Crenshaw Castle hobs, popped into the cage. "You appear to be in a pickle, a jam, a—"

"Yes. I know." Prospero closed her eyes, concentrating very hard on not panicking. "We have escaped witches, and as we can't let them"—she gestured at the humans, who all needed mind correction—"know that you or I exist."

Clancy grinned. "Shall I remove you from your cage, Lady Prospero?"

"Indeed." She tried to look somber, proper, not at all panic-stricken, but hiding things from hobs was rather like lying to yourself. It might work, or appear to work, but not permanently, reliably, or even often.

The hob made a gesture that was like a flourish and a bow all at once, and Prospero found herself standing atop a table. She shot a glare at the hob. "That was unnecess—"

Clancy winked and vanished.

"I'm sorry I can't help with your meteor problem," Prospero said, gliding from mind to mind, making sure no one there would remember her, Ellie, Maggie, or Clancy. "The side effects appear to be headaches for the next day . . ." She pointed at the cook. "Except for you. You'll be impotent for the next decade."

Then Prospero swiped a pie. It wasn't exactly a bribe, but anything she could offer up to sweeten Walt's inevitable sour mood was a good idea.

Pie in hand, she returned home. That part of the magic, the hook in her belly that she could only resist by effort, was often one of the less appealing parts of being a witch. She'd ignored it often, but today she was grateful for it. She simply stopped resisting, and there she was—standing at the front step of her house.

"Bernice?" Prospero called out as she went inside.

Her hob appeared, wearing what appeared to be an entire feather duster as a hat. "You sound frazzled. Tea? Something stronger to go with your dessert?"

"I need the chief witch and headmaster to meet with me," Prospero said, still balancing the pie. As an afterthought, she added, "It's not my pie."

"Bribe pie." Bernice nodded. "I'll have a basket readied."

Prospero handed her the pie and slumped against the wall. There wasn't a good solution to be had. Ellie had to be brought back to Crenshaw—and Prospero had to explain why she'd failed at doing so already.

Bernice returned with a basket. It was a cheerful thing with a bright red bow on the handle. "Linens, forks, and plates under the pie." She held it out. "Walt says to come to Congress."

Prospero sighed and took the basket. She wasn't even sure what sort of pie it was. It was an impulse bribe.

"Trust your heart," Beatrice said as she patted Prospero's hand. "All is not lost!"

Few times in life had she felt so much like a failure. Prospero walked through Crenshaw, chin up, spine straight, eyes forward, and a basket of pie in hand.

The whereabouts of the retrieval team, the well-being of Mae, the location of Sondre. They were all a mystery to her, and though she was worried, her mind circled around the fact that she'd lost Ellie. She'd been bested by Ellie.

Her hope had been to talk to her, to avoid the solution Walt had recommended.

As she approached, she saw Sondre and Walter at the door for the Congress of Magic. Neither man looked particularly cheerful.

"Inside." Walt gestured her forward.

"No luck?" Sondre asked.

She shook her head. A part of her wanted to scream at him. Allies don't keep secrets, and there was no way that Sondre was oblivious to Maggie Lynch's machinations. She'd tried, truly, truly tried to reach out an olive branch, but just because they were in accord that Crenshaw was facing impossible options didn't mean they were friends.

Walt made a grumbling noise.

"I updated him on the capture of the Lynch boy," Sondre continued. "He says that we need to have Ellie here. If not, we'll keep dying."

"Says Cassandra," Prospero muttered.

"Now? *Now* you doubt her?" Walt raised two bushy brows in her direction.

No one spoke for a moment.

The trio walked into the main hall of the Congress building. It was the quietest, most secure location in Crenshaw. Sometimes, though, meeting here felt eerie. The desks where the heads of houses sat were all empty. No threats. No shouts. Instead, the hall was akin to a sepulcher; a deep silence seemed to weigh on them.

"Ellie . . . Miss Brandeau bent the tiles and metal of a restaurant around me in a cage," Prospero blurted out. "I had to summon a hob."

She shoved the basket of pie at Walt.

"I was expecting to be able to talk to them, reason with them, but—"

"Prospero?" Walt interrupted. "Can we dispense with formality? I am aware that you and Miss Brandeau are intimately involved."

Sondre started to laugh, but it died as Walt added, "And that you are intimate with the Lynch witch. I cannot prove that you aided their escape, Sondre, or you'd be badgered before sunrise. I might not have watchers in your room, but I know she was there before her escape. I sent out my own retrieval units—this one for information retrieval."

Sondre met Walt's eyes in silence.

"What I do know for certain," Walt continued, "is that both witches need to be brought home as soon as possible, by any means possible, and we need to concentrate on the plague. Witches simply ought not die at this rate. It isn't natural."

Prospero and Sondre exchanged a look as Walt opened the basket and pulled out the dessert and supplies. "Oh, a pie lifter! Your hobs really do take care of the details, don't they?"

When Prospero said nothing, Sondre tentatively spoke. "Walt, the witch *fabricates*. How do you propose we bring her back?"

"Or keep her here?" Prospero added.

Walt served them each a slice of some sort of red berry pie. "Modify her mind, Prospero. It's what I already said, and what you do and—"

"I can't."

"You suddenly have an objection," Sondre said incredulously.

"No . . . I *can't*. Her mind doesn't allow it. That's what Cass was hinting about the 'battery.' She knows I cannot erase Ellie's mind. I tried already." Prospero hated how foolish she sounded, how inept. Mind altering was her magic, the thing she could do that no one else could, and confessing she could not was mortifying. Her hands twisted, clenching the ends of her sleeves as if she could wring the stress out of her body.

"Eat your pie," Walt ordered. "What about the battery booster then? New witch that was trying to befriend the troublemakers? Take him with you. No one else has ever resisted. So if he aids your mindwork . . ."

Sondre glanced up from his pie. "It should work. Convince her she already chose to stay."

"Prospero." Walt pointed at her with his fork. "Give her a reason to stay near you. Make her your wife. The seeress said she was meant for you anyhow, so speed it up. That way she'll be with you daily. Easier to watch over. Easier to manage."

Prospero gaped at him.

"And the other one. It only seems fitting since Sondre is guilty—whether or not I can prove it." Walt ate another bite of pie. "He needs a wife anyhow. Maybe she can even cook."

Sondre's fork dropped. "Are you out of your mind?"

"Take her to wife? Or spend some time as a badger?" Walt didn't look up from his pie. "Maybe both of you will be more manageable with spouses to keep you busy, and it'll guarantee that they're under constant observation. No need for new housing either! They'd be secure, safe, and under watch."

"You can't just . . . take away their choices." Sondre stared at the chief witch. "It's barbaric."

"Break the law and there are consequences. We all know that. They—and both of you—broke the law." Walt finally looked up from the pie. "It's not like they're being married to strangers, and honestly, I can't spare the Brandeau witch when she's head of a house. I'm not sure I can spare either of you. So the way I see it, there's either two new happy couples or four inconvenient badgers. What's it going to be?"

"Ellie would choose being a badger over being with me," Prospero admitted, cheeks flaming. "She built a cage around me, Walt. A *cage*. And I didn't help her escape. Surely, you know—"

"I know a lot of things, including that you ignored my order to mind adjust her and ended up in a g'damned cage. Shall we discuss the *other* laws you broke?" Walt gave her a look, but he didn't outright mention her illegal trip to Ligonier.

"No, Chief Witch."

"Our people are dying. Those two are strong witches, and we all need to work together, so just do whatever it takes to get them here. Then erase their damn memory of the escape, and let's get to work. All of us. Together. Heads of houses, and you two, and your spouses. Am I clear?" Walt no longer sounded like an affable friend. This was the Chief Witch of Crenshaw speaking.

Prospero bowed her head. "Yes, Chief Witch."

"You're cold-blooded, Chief Witch." Sondre's voice held a thread of respect.

"When needs must." Walt gestured with his fork again. "Now eat the damn pie before you go fetch your brides."

47

Dan

When the chief witch, Sondre, and the scary witch all showed up at his door, he figured he was doomed. Maybe Prospero found out he was in the library or Sondre found out he was in the forest. He wished he could tell Axell goodbye before they sent him back or badgered him or something.

Dan dropped to his knees. "Please don't send me back."

The chief witch looked like he was ready to smack someone. He strode into the room. "You aren't a strong enough witch to stay without agreeing to be useful. Get up."

"I agree!" Dan stood, looking at his unwanted guests.

Sondre smiled at him, easing a little of Dan's worries. "Daniel tries very hard. He's had no doubts and—"

"Great. If Monahan does as he's told, he can stay permanently." The chief witch eyed him. "Understood? Help them with this, and do as you're told whenever I give you a job, and you are an asset. Refuse, and you are useless to Crenshaw. Clear?"

"No . . . ?" Dan looked between Sondre and the chief witch. "I mean, I understand the whole obedience thing. Classic villain sidekick . . . or minion, really. Maybe Renfield? Basically, be a lackey. That part makes sense, but—"

"Get it done." The chief witch left without another word.

Dan backed up until his knees hit his mattress. Mutely, he sat and stared up at Sondre. Whatever was going on had to be a big deal if Sondre was here with the chief witch.

"We need to go," Lady Prospero said, looking at Sondre instead of Dan. "Bring the amplifier."

Then she vanished.

"Where do we get an amplifier?" Dan asked Sondre.

But Sondre held out a hand. "You *are* the amplifier in this case. Just don't argue with her or ask questions. The less you know, the better it is."

Dan nodded, thinking yet again that he wasn't on the white hat side. If the chief witch and Lady Prospero—who was supposedly Sondre's nemesis—were also on Sondre's side, Dan wasn't sure there even *was* a white hat side, after all.

Doesn't someone need to be the good guy?

Oh shit! I hope that's not what I need to do!

He shoved that thought down, way down, like to his kneecaps down, and took Sondre's hand. Suddenly, everything felt woozy, like after too much mead and not enough sleep, so he scrunched his eyes closed to avoid throwing up.

When he opened them, he was in a field outside a nice house. There were no other houses in sight, and it felt like a giant crochet hook had caught his bottom rib. There was a tug there, and Dan was fairly sure that if he gave in, he'd vanish somewhere else.

"Crochet hook in my rib," he squeezed out.

"Ignore it. Sondre, hold on to him until I tell him to grab my shoulder." Prospero's words appeared before she did, like a creepy Wonderland cat, and weirder still, she now had a teen boy at her side.

"Craig?" Sondre asked.

"Do I know you?" He jerked away from Prospero. "I'm really sick of people trying to kidnap me. First the weird woman talking about my dead mom and now—"

"She's not dead," Sondre told him. He shot a look at Prospero. "Fix him."

Without a word, she stared at the teen, and he crumpled to the ground. When she looked back at Sondre, she said, "He had the sudden urge to nap longer."

"I'm really confused." Dan looked around at them. He understood that she'd magicked the boy to sleep. "Where are we?"

"Ellie's place." Prospero strode into the big white farmhouse. "Come on."

Sondre settled the boy with a remarkable degree of care. Perversely, it reminded Dan of how people arranged corpses for a wake. He looked away and then scurried after Prospero.

"It'll be okay," Sondre said quietly as he caught up and stood at Dan's side. "Trust me."

For a flicker of a moment, Dan wondered if Sondre was actually the good guy after all. Either that, or Prospero had erased his mind so often that he had no idea what was what anymore.

Then again, the three of them were about to break into Ellie Brandeau's house, and all Dan could think was that if *they* were the good guys now, that made Ellie the villain. That didn't sound like a great plan.

What if there are no villains?

What if there are no heroes?

Prospero didn't even knock. Maybe it was a witch thing—or bad manners. She opened the door, and they trailed behind her obediently.

They walked into a massive kitchen with a restaurant-level oven and counter space, only to find an angry old woman with a cane.

"Where's my Ellie?" The woman leaned on the edge of a desk with giant shelves above and beside it. She lifted her cane like she was brandishing a sword. Apparently, rudeness was hereditary.

"Why doesn't she . . . wait. *Hestia?*" Sondre's voice pitched higher in shock. "Ellie Brandeau is Hestia's kid. Is Walt—"

"No." The cane-wielding senior pointed her makeshift weapon at him. "I'm not her mother."

"Do you know me?" Sondre asked.

"Sure. You're the jackass that just barged in my house with this hussy and that scrawny fellow there." Hestia's nostrils flared like an angry bull. She glared at Prospero. "*You* I know somehow."

Foul temper is genetic, apparently.

Sondre turned to Prospero. "I have questions. *Citizens* who leave don't recognize us, and people whose family vanishes don't act like this."

Prospero rubbed her temples. "Hestia was resistant to erasure, like Ellie is."

Hestia started grabbing things from the shelf she leaned against. Several books and a large jar that looked like it belonged in a museum went flying. One book hit Prospero, and the jar would've hit Sondre if not for his quick reflexes.

"Oh for goodness' sake," Prospero grumbled. She put her hands on her hips; her face was pained as she concentrated on something they couldn't see. Then, she let out a forced laugh. "Ellie will be here any minute, Hestia. Are you getting senile? I'm here to pick you up to come stay with us. We eloped. Do you not remember? Or are you still mad?"

Sondre shoved Dan forward. "Shoulder now."

His hand gripped Prospero's shoulder as she continued repeating some version of the above sentences. This time, though, she added, "You're a witch, Hestia. Did you forget?"

Hestia stared at her, slack-jawed and blinking.

When Prospero shook him off, Dan slid into a chair that Sondre pulled out. Whatever was going on, Dan still wasn't sure, but he'd figured out that Prospero was changing people's reality—and he was adding a power boost to her magic to get it done.

Not the good guys. Not at all.

But if this was what it took to live in Crenshaw, this was what he *had* to do, right? He was at least 70 percent certain of that. One day.

One bad thing. It wasn't the worst thing, and the old lady seemed happy enough now.

His gaze strayed to the door to the yard where the teenager was sleeping.

It won't be one day, though.

Dan knew better. He wasn't stupid. It hit him, though, that this was how both heroes and villains were made: one action, one day. Little by little, they chose their path, and then suddenly, they were a little bit more of who they were becoming.

And Dan was fairly sure he wasn't becoming a hero.

48
Maggie

When they pulled up at the house, Maggie looked over at Ellie. "Do you feel that?"

"Magic." Ellie shuddered. "You can stay in the car. I can't abandon Hestia to them. Prospero has already poked around in her head once before."

Maggie wasn't about to abandon Ellie either. She opened her door and slid out. "Front door or back?"

"Back."

Neither woman closed the car doors. Logically, the witch inside already knew they were there, but hopefully, Maggie was overestimating Prospero. They crouched down, keeping to the edge of the house until they reached the back.

"Mags?" Ellie pointed at a pile of clothes on the ground.

No, not clothes.

"*Craig?*" She started forward, but Ellie caught her wrist.

"Look around first."

Maggie did, taking in trees, a little garden, and even an old-fashioned clothesline. "No one."

"I'm going in," Ellie whispered.

Maggie took off in a run to Craig. She wasn't sure if he'd remember her, likely he wouldn't. He might even hit her again, but she had to get him to safety. Her was her baby, her heart, and leaving him in a heap on the ground wasn't an option.

If he's alive . . .

Maggie dismissed the thought as soon as it came. He was. She could feel his heartbeat, like a second drum in her chest.

"Craig?" she whispered as she dropped to her knees at his side.

She shook him. Nothing happened.

Louder now. "Craig."

She shoved him, rolling him halfway over. No response.

Sondre's voice came from behind her: "He won't wake until Prospero wants him to."

Maggie looked up. "I'm not going back without him."

Sondre sighed, his hand dropping to her shoulder. "It's not your choice. You are a witch and—"

"I'll die before I leave him. I'll escape and—"

"You won't, Maggie." Sondre crouched down. "Prospero can alter your mind, make you forget. It's what she does."

Tears poured down Maggie's face. Then she grabbed her son's wrists and tugged so he was draped over her back. It wasn't perfect, but she wasn't about to just sit here and wait for them to steal her son. She started toward the car. "Tell Ellie I'm sorry."

Sondre pulled Craig away from her. "I can't let you go. Not this time. They know I helped you the first time."

"Give me my son." She pulled out the gun in her waistband. It wasn't her first choice, but magic or not, none of them were likely to survive a clip being emptied into them. Steadily, she aimed it at Sondre. "I like you. I really do, but no one separates me from my kid."

Sondre took a breath and lowered Craig to the ground gently. "The chief witch said we needed to do whatever it took to bring you back. What if what it took was bringing him, too?"

Maggie flicked the safety back on. "I'm listening."

"Prospero is going to change your memories," Sondre blurted out. "And I had a choice between being badgered and . . . marrying you."

Maggie felt like her heart had lodged in her lungs somehow. She managed to say, "Marriage to me is your *punishment*?"

"Not you. Marriage. Keeping a woman happy. Focusing on you, not my plans . . ." Sondre took her hand. "I like you well enough, Maggie Lynch."

"You're not awful either, man-witch."

"So either shoot me or agree to marry me," Sondre whispered, voice rough. "I can't take away your choice, not and . . . have you in my bed."

Maggie squeezed his hand. "It's not a real punishment to me. If you could guarantee my son was with me, I'd agree to marry you on my own."

Sondre looked at her, pondering things he didn't share. "I can suggest it, but we have orders."

"Fill me in later?" she asked. "Tell me what I forget. Promise."

"I'll do my best." Sondre stepped back. "I need you to come inside without a fight, without objecting to what I say or what she says. I know you want to help Ellie, but this is the only way to bring Craig to Crenshaw. And Maggie?" He waited until she looked at him. "He cannot leave the castle until we clear up the problem with the sickness. Neither of you can. If I'm going to be a . . . father"—he choked on the word—"he needs to obey me. Both of you do."

Maggie nodded. "Some things are outside my control, but you're welcome to try to make that happen." She gave him a wobbly smile. "I'll bite my tongue in the house today, and I'll try. That's the best I can offer."

Then with one last look at Craig, who was now sleeping on the grass again, Maggie slid her gun into her waistband and went toward the house.

49

Ellie

Ellie knew Prospero was here before she'd come inside—which to her mind meant all bets were off regarding the use of magic.

"Is there a wicked witch in the house?" she called as she walked through the kitchen, hoping and praying to whatever gods were real that Hestia was not home.

But hope and prayers were as useless as spitting on a fire.

"Are you two having a tiff?" Hestia asked, looking from the woman who sat nestled beside her to Ellie.

"Are we, dear? Is that why you weren't where you were supposed to be?" Prospero looked up, her face void of hostility. It was a lovely mask, pretending to care.

"I find liars objectionable," Ellie said mildly. "Come say hello to me, *dear*. No need to hide behind my aunt's skirts, is there?"

"Behave, girls," Aunt Hestia said. "We have a guest."

"Those are the cutest little soaps in your bathroom, Ms. Brandeau." Daniel came into the room, wiping his hands on his trousers. He stopped abruptly, blanching like he'd seen something awful. "Oh. You're here." He glanced at Prospero. "Ellie's here, too."

He walked up to Prospero and reached out like he was going to touch her shoulder.

"Give us a moment?" Prospero stood and walked toward Ellie. Quietly, she said, "Maggie's child will not wake without me. Hestia will suffer if I am injured. So, let's try to discuss the situation civilly."

"Threats are your version of civil?" Ellie scoffed. "Why am I not surprised?"

A flash of sorrow came over Prospero's face. "What did I do, Ellie? I thought we had . . . something good between us."

"You lied." Ellie folded her arms over her chest and walked away toward the kitchen.

Prospero followed. "I had no choice in the decision to not tell Ms. Lynch—"

"You could've refused to go along with it." Ellie spun to face her. The awkwardness of the next accusation warred with her temper, and her temper won. "Or told me that my room at the castle was not private. You . . . we . . . I'm not an exhibitionist. Were you just showing off for someone? Was anything you said true?"

Prospero looked abashed. "Honestly, Ellie, I couldn't think of anything when you touched me. I should've remembered that. I *should have*." She reached out. "You have to believe me, though. It was a mistake, not a deceit."

"Tell me that you really want me for me, that there are no political reasons, that it has nothing to do with . . ." Ellie's words faded as Prospero looked away.

"In time, I could love you. I know that to be true."

"But?"

"But there was a prophecy about you, and you are the first new head of house in—"

"I don't want any of that," Ellie yelled. "I wanted you and—"

"I'm here." Prospero caught Ellie's hand. "I'm yours. I'm here and yours, and I do want a chance. And I'm sorry if you were embarrassed that we were . . . indiscreet. That was not planned."

"You lied."

"Not by choice." Prospero kept hold of her hand, and in that moment it took everything Ellie had not to swoon into her. "I am bound by the Congress of Magic, Ellie. You are, too. All witches are."

"I'm not going back." Ellie pulled away. "I would rather be siphoned. I thought that you . . . that *we* were worth staying longer, trying, but I can't. You—your Congress—told Maggie her kid was dead. What other lies have you told?"

"You are coming back. It's not your choice. The chief witch decided—"

"What? Are you going to try to mind assault me again?" Ellie turned to go back to the living room. She paused then and looked over her shoulder. "You'd really do that? They sent you and Monahan here. He boosts magic and . . ." Her words trailed off as the pieces clicked together.

"Come home without fighting me, Ellie." Prospero's voice was remarkably close to begging. "I don't want to threaten Hestia. She was my friend. You know that."

"Ellie?" Maggie walked into the kitchen, Sondre behind her. "It's okay to go back if you want. They're letting me bring Craig and—"

"Oh?" Prospero stared at Sondre. "We are?"

"Chief Witch said, 'Any means necessary.' Maggie will come home as my wife if her son comes, too." Sondre draped an arm over Maggie's shoulders, and Ellie knew without asking this was a softer version of the plan they'd had in place.

Prospero pressed her lips together. "I still need to . . ."

"Erase my escape from memory?" Maggie said cheerily. "Fine. As long as I have my kid, I'll go along with whatever you need." She shot an apologetic look at Ellie. "This whole mess was my fault. You can stop fighting with them, Ellie. It's this, or I lose my son, so . . ." Maggie shrugged like everything they'd said and done was gone.

"So they lied, but you're fine going back to a poison-filled town—and you're fine taking your kid there?" Ellie shook her head and walked away from all three witches in the kitchen.

Hestia looked up. "Are you quarreling with her, lovey?"

When Ellie sighed, Hestia held out a hand. Ellie took it and let her aunt pull her in close. Ellie flopped on the sofa. Then she glared at Daniel. "Scat or else."

"I'm not your enemy," he said, but he still stood and fled to the kitchen to join the rest of the home invaders.

"Can you love someone you can't trust?" she whispered against her aunt's shoulder as Hestia pulled her in as if she were a small child with a scraped knee. "I want to trust her, but I don't know . . ."

"Is the thing you're fighting over a small thing? Your mother, bless her heart, used to get upset over ridiculous things. Toilet lids up or shoes left in a tumble outside the closet. Beds unmade and toothpaste uncapped. All the little stuff was really about your father's forgetfulness, though. He'd get absent-minded, but to her, it seemed like he expected her to tidy up after him. What *he* expected was that he'd get to it when he got to it."

"It's not little stuff."

"Ah, well . . ." Hestia craned her neck to look into Ellie's eyes. "Is the sex good enough to forgive whatever it was?"

Ellie closed her eyes even as she muffled a laugh against her aunt's shoulder. "You're incorrigible."

"True." Hestia patted her absently, swaying slightly even though they were seated. "Good sex and not sharing a house were how my best relationships worked. Can't stand a man in my bathroom or mucking up my kitchen. My space. My things."

"I've missed you," Ellie whispered.

"No one says you need to stay married," Hestia whispered back.

And that, of course, was part of the problem. It took no effort for Prospero to alter Hestia's mind. How was Ellie to trust someone like that?

"Ellie?" Prospero came and knelt in front of her. "There are no options here. What if Hestia came with us? Would that help?"

"Would she be safe?"

"We figure out how to make that happen, and then bring her to live where we are," Prospero countered. "I want to find a solution."

Ellie closed her eyes. "No. Just siphon me already. I'm not going back. Take Maggie if she agrees, but . . ." She took a breath, opened her eyes, and stared directly at Prospero. "You, Crenshaw, magic, none of it is what I want. I'm sure of it. I'd rather risk death."

"Worst breakup ever," Daniel muttered from somewhere in the room.

Prospero said, "I wish there was another option. I have orders, though." She glanced over her shoulder. "Daniel."

Behind her, Ellie felt Sondre's hands holding her still, preventing flight. Maggie started crying, and Hestia asked, "What's going on here?"

But then Hestia was asleep, and Prospero was holding Ellie's face in her hands, speaking softly.

Ellie felt her world shift. "You lying bitch," she managed to say.

And that was it. Everything shifted, and Ellie couldn't speak anymore. She pushed back, tried to hold on to reality, but Prospero's magic was too much to resist when Monahan was there feeding her boundless magic.

Remember, Ellie. Remember, a voice ordered.

The next moment, Ellie was in her wife's arms, and they were walking across the threshold of their home in Crenshaw.

"Hestia will stay at the castle while we get settled," Prospero said.

Ellie rested her head on Prospero's shoulder. "I'm the luckiest witch ever."

"Why don't you rest a bit?" Prospero suggested. "It's been an exciting day, and you'll have a lot of work to do on the rift this week. Plus more classes at the castle . . ."

Ellie sighed contentedly. "I can't believe we got permission to marry before I even finished at the college!"

Her new wife said nothing, simply gave her a small, tight smile, but Prospero was probably exhausted, too. *A whirlwind romance and wedding tended to do that, and fitting around classes at the college . . . ?*

"Why don't we *both* rest a while?" Ellie caught Prospero's hand and led her to their bedroom. "Come nap with me, wife."

Crenshaw had made Ellie's every dream come true.

Just like a fairy tale!

Acknowledgments

I sold my first book (*Wicked Lovely*) eighteen years ago, and writing this page still never gets easier.

Please note that the research on missing people is entirely my own, as are the details about Ligonier and Durham. I've spent years in both places, so the navigation is real. To my knowledge, no librarians working in Ligonier are actual witches, but honestly, aren't all librarians a little bit magical?

The most practical thanks go to Monique Patterson and Merrilee Heifetz, my editor and agent, who patiently worked around my nonlinear writing process. My brain doesn't think in a straight line, so when I decided to gut words at the last minutes to draft the *fifth* opening of the book they'd seen, neither of them flinched.

The Norwegian phrases in the book were checked by Åshild Stuen Jensen for accuracy—and conveyed back to me via my eldest child, Dr. Asia Alsgaard, who lives in Norway currently. Thank you both for making sure I am not misspeaking or misspelling.

The haircut on Axell is thanks to Danny, a dad at the park, who sports such a style.

Sondre was influenced by the biography of Chesty Puller by Colonel Jon Hoffman. I've never met Colonel Hoffman, but his book lingered with me twenty-some years after I read it. Though my character is in no way Chesty Puller, the idea of a good man—one who was a great Marine but restless in peace—stuck with me. Oedipus. Chesty. He's a type, and like the real Marines I've known and treasured, he's a type I love.

Thank you to my readers for almost two decades of support, as well as Kelley Armstrong, Jeaniene Frost, Chelsea Mueller, and Jaye Wells for talking sense to me when I decided to quit writing a few years ago.

And thank you to my wife, who suggested that there weren't enough fantasy books with women who love women for her to read. I might sometimes forget to make meals or misplace the car, but I wrote you a book, dear. (Disclaimer: Neither character is influenced by her! My beloved is neither a cagey Victorian witch nor a librarian.)

About the Author

Melissa Marr writes fiction for adults, teens, and children. Her books have been translated into twenty-eight languages and bestsellers in the United States (*The New York Times, Los Angeles Times, USA Today, The Wall Street Journal*), as well as overseas. *Remedial Magic* is the first of two books in a witchy lesbian fantasy-romance series. You can find her in a kayak or on a trail with her wife if she's not writing.

MelissaMarrBooks.com
Twitter: @melissa_marr
Instagram: @melissamarrwriting